NIGHT OF THE BLACKBIRD

HEATHER GRAHAM

NIGHT OF THE BLACKBIRD

ISBN 0-7394-2148-4

NIGHT OF THE BLACKBIRD

Copyright © 2001 by Heather Graham Pozzessere.

MIRA and the Star Colophon are trademarks used under license and registered
in Australia, New Zealand, Philippines, United States Patent and Trademark
Office and in other countries.

Printed in U.S.A.

First and foremost, with love for my mother
Violet J. Graham Sherman
of County Dublin
for being Irish,
for being a great mom.

In memory of Granny Browne and Aunt Amy
who taught me all about banshees and leprechauns—
at least, their versions of the tales.

For my cousin, Katie Browne DeVuono,
for being everything wonderful about the Irish.

For Victoria Graham Davant,
my sister, my best friend,
for all that we share from the past
and the present.

_____ Prologue _____

Belfast, Northern Ireland
Summer, 1977

"All right, my son, my fine lad!" his mum said, bursting into his square little room without even knocking. "Your da has made it home, and we are going to the movies!"

The mother was flushed and eager. Her work-worn face was transformed into beauty, for her smile was a young girl's smile, and brightness touched her eyes. He held his breath, barely able to believe. He wanted to go to the movies so badly. It was the new American film, making its debut downtown. At nine, he spent much of his time in the streets; few promises his parents made came to pass. Not their faults, just the way of the world, and there were many things that were the way of the world, or the way of his particular world, and that was just that, and he understood it. His father had his work, his mother had hers, and they had their time at the pub, as well, with their meetings and such. He was a tough kid, strong for his nine years, street smart and, sadly—as even he was aware—already wary and weary. But this...

It was a science fiction movie. Full of futuristic knights, space vehicles, great battles. The fight for right and, in the end—or so he figured—the victory of right over evil.

He threw down the comic book he was reading and stared at her with disbelief, then jumped up, throwing his arms around her. "The movies! Really? Wow!"

"Comb your hair now, boy. Get ready. I'll get your baby sister."

And soon they were walking down the street.

The street was something of a slum. Old brick walls were covered with graffiti. The houses were old, as well, small, drafty, and still required peat fires in winter. But it was a good neighborhood in which to live. There were plenty of dark, secret places in the crevices in the walls; there were gates to be jumped, places to hide.

Here and there, they passed a neighbor. Men tipped their hats. Women greeted them with cordial voices. The boy was so pleased, walking along with his folks. He held his sister's hand. She was just five, younger than he, with eyes still so bright and alive. She didn't know yet that the smiles that greeted them were usually grim smiles, that the people were as gray and strained as the sky that ever seemed dark, as the old buildings that always seemed somber and shadowed. She looked up at him, and her smile was real, beautiful, and though they fought at times, though he was a tough kid, a nine-year-old boy, and she just a little girl, he loved her fiercely. Her pleasure and awe in their outing touched him deeply.

"We're really going to see the movie?"

"We're really going to see the movie!" he assured her.

Their father turned around, grinning. "Aye, girl, and we're buying popcorn, as well!"

She laughed, and the sound of her laughter made them all smile; it even seemed to touch the ancient grimed walls and make them lighter.

They reached the movie theater. Some there were their friends, some were their enemies. They all wanted to see the movie, so some of the smiles were a bit grimmer, and now and then his parents exchanged stiff nods with others.

As he'd promised, their father bought popcorn. And sodas. Even candy.

He'd seldom felt closer to his parents. More like a boy. For a few hours he left his own dark reality for a far-off time and place. He laughed, he cheered, he gave his sister the last little kernel of popcorn. He explained what she didn't understand. He lifted her onto his lap. He watched his mother hesitate, then let her head fall on his father's shoulder. His father let his hand fall upon her knee.

They were halfway home when the gunmen suddenly appeared.

They had come from one of those dark and secretive places in the wall that the boy had learned so well himself.

The masked man in the front suddenly called his father by name.

"I am he, and proud of it, I am!" his father replied with strength and defiance, pushing his wife behind him. "But me family is with me—"

"Aye, ye'd hide behind skirts!" the second man said contemptuously.

The popping of gunfire, so suddenly and so close, was deafening.

The boy reached for his sister even as he watched his father fall. It had happened so fast, yet it was almost like slow motion in the movies. He could see the terrible end; he couldn't stop it.

The gunmen had come for his father. But a stray bullet hit his sister, as well. Somewhere in his mind, he knew that the gunmen hadn't intended it, nor could they afford to regret it. She was simply a casualty of this strange war.

He heard his mother shout his father's name. She didn't know as yet that her baby was gone, as well.

The lad held his sister, seeing the blood stain her dress. Her eyes were open. She didn't even feel pain; she didn't realize what was happening. She smiled, her bright eyes touching his as she whispered his name.

"I want to go home now," she said. Then she closed her eyes, and he knew she was dead.

He just held her, in the darkness of the street and the darkness of his life, and he listened to his mother's screams and, soon, the wailing of the police cars and the ambulances in the shadows of the night.

They had the services for his father and sister on a Saturday afternoon. They had waked them in the house in the old way, and family and friends had come and sat vigil by the coffins. They had drunk whiskey and ale, and his father had been hailed and put upon a pedestal, the loss of his baby sister made into a cause. There was so much press from around the world that many whispered that the sacrifice of the poor wee dear might well have been God's way in their great cause.

They hadn't seen her smile. They didn't know that she'd been just a child with hopes and dreams and a wealth of life within her smile and the brightness of her eyes.

At last it was time for the final service, the time when they would be buried—though nothing here, he knew, was ever really buried.

Father Gillian read the prayers, and a number of men gave impassioned speeches. His mother wailed, tore at her hair, beat her breast. Women helped her, held her, grieved with her. They cried and mourned and wailed, as well, sounding like a pack of banshees, howling to the heavens.

He stood alone. His tears had been shed.

The prayers and the services over, the pipers came forward, and the old Irish pipes wheezed and wailed.

They played "Danny Boy."

Soon after, he stepped forward with some of the other men, and they lifted the coffins. Thankfully, he was a tall lad, and he carried his sister's coffin with cousins much older than he. She had been such a little thing, it was amazing that the coffin could be so heavy. Almost as if they carried a girl who had lived a life.

They were laid into the ground. Earth and flowers were cast upon them. It was over.

The other mourners began to move away, Father Gillian with an arm around his mother. A great aunt came up to him. "Come, lad, your mother needs you."

He looked up for a moment, his eyes misting with tears. "She does not need me now," he said, and it was true— he had tried to be a comfort to her, but she had her hatred, and her passion, and she had a newfound cause.

He didn't mean to hurt anyone, so he added, "I need to be here now, please. Me mum has help now. Later, when she's alone, she'll need me."

"You're a good lad, keen and sharp, that you are," his aunt said, and she left him.

Alone, he stood by the graves. Silent tears streamed down his cheeks.

And he made a vow. A passionate vow, to his dead father, his poor wee sister. To his God—and to himself.

He would die, he swore, before he ever failed in that vow.

Darkness fell around his city.

And around his heart.

1

"What do you mean, you're not coming home for Saint Patrick's Day?"

Moira Kelly flinched.

Her mother's voice, usually soft, pleasant and well-modulated, was so shrill that Moira was certain her assistant had heard Katy Kelly in the next room—despite the fact that they were talking by phone, and that her mother was in Boston, several hundred miles away.

"Mum, it's not like I'm missing Christmas—"

"No, it's worse."

"Mum, I'm a working woman, not a little kid."

"Right. You're a first-generation American, forgetting all about tradition."

Moira inhaled deeply. "Mother, that's the point. We are living in America. Yes, I was born here. As disheartening and horrible as it may be, Saint Patrick's Day is not a national holiday."

"There you go. Mocking me."

Moira inhaled deeply again, counted, sighed. "I'm not mocking you."

"You work for yourself. You can work around any holiday you want."

"I don't actually just work for myself. I have a partner.

We have a whole production company. A schedule. Dead-lines. And my partner has a wife—''

''That Jewish girl he married.''

Moira hesitated again.

''No, Mum. Andy Garson, the New York reporter, the one who sometimes cohosts that mid-morning show, just married a Jewish girl. Josh's wife is Italian.'' She smiled slightly, staring at the receiver. ''And very Catholic. You'd like her. And their little eight-month-old twins. A few of the reasons we both really want to keep this company go-ing!''

Her mother only heard what she wanted to hear. ''If his wife is Catholic, she should understand.''

''I don't think the Italians consider Saint Patrick's Day a national holiday, either,'' Moira said.

''He's a Catholic saint!'' her mother said.

''Mother—''

''Moira, please. I'm not asking for myself.'' This time, her mother hesitated. ''Your father just had to have another procedure....''

Her heart skipped a beat. ''What do you mean?'' she asked sharply.

''They may have to do another surgery.''

''You didn't call me!''

''I'm calling you now.''

''But not about Dad!''

''He wouldn't let me call and tell you—he hasn't been feeling all that well and he didn't want to disturb you before the holiday. You've always come home before. We figured we'd tell you when you got here. He has to have a test on Monday—outpatient, and not life-threatening—and then...well, then they'll decide just what to do. But, darling, you know...he really would like you home, though he won't admit it. And Granny Jon is...well, she seems to be failing a bit.''

Granny Jon was ninety-something years in age and, at

best, maybe a good eighty-five pounds in weight. She was still the fiercest little creature Moira had ever met.

She would live forever, Moira was convinced.

But Moira was concerned about her father. He'd had open-heart surgery a few years earlier, a valve replacement, and since then, she'd worried about him. He never complained, always had a smile and was therefore, in her mind, dangerous—simply because he was too prone to being half-dead before he would agree to see a doctor. She knew that her mother worked very hard to keep him on a proper heart-healthy regime, but that couldn't solve everything.

And as to Saint Patrick's Day...

"Patrick is coming," her mother informed her.

Naturally, she thought.

Her brother, who had property in western Massachusetts, wouldn't dare miss his own saint's day. Few men would have such courage.

Still, it was easy for Patrick. He was in Boston often anyway.

In fact, she realized with a small touch of guilt, she had counted on her brother and her sister, Colleen, to make it all right that she wasn't there for the great family holiday that much of the country saw as an excuse to drink green beer or send out cute little leprechaun cards, though it meant far more to them.

"You want to see Patrick, don't you?"

"Of course, but I'm mostly worried about Dad."

"If your father and I were both to drop dead tomorrow—"

"My brother, sister and I would still see each other, Mum. Honestly, you're not going to drop dead tomorrow, but don't worry, we love each other, we'd see each other."

It was an old argument. Her mother said the same thing to her, she said the same thing back. Her mother said the same thing to her brother—who said the same thing back.

Her sister just sighed and rolled her eyes each time.

But Moira did love her family.

"Mum, I'll be home." She wasn't that far away, and it wasn't that she didn't get home frequently. This time, this Saint Patrick's Day, she hadn't thought much about it—just because she did get home so often. She had just been home for the Christmas holidays. Going home now hadn't seemed crucial, in part because of the filming schedule.

But it was crucial now.

"Did you hear me, Mum? I *will* be home for Saint Patrick's Day."

"Bless you, baby. I do need you."

"I'll call you back as soon as I get things straightened out. You make Dad behave, okay?"

"I will."

She started to set the receiver down, but then she heard her mother's voice. "Oh, sweetheart, I forgot to tell you—"

"Yes?" She brought the receiver back to her ear.

"You'll never guess who's coming."

"The great leprechaun?" She couldn't quite help herself.

"No!"

"Auntie Lizbeth?" She wasn't really an aunt, just an old neighbor from back home. She came to the States every few years. Moira liked her, though she seldom understood her—she simply smiled at the old woman a lot. She was even older than Granny Jon, had the thickest brogue known to man—and her wolfhound had chewed up her false teeth, since she hated them and was always leaving them on the table. To Moira, she had been almost totally incomprehensible even when she'd had her teeth, and now, well, it was almost impossible for Moira to make sense of her words. Still, Granny Jon and her folks seemed to do just fine understanding the old woman.

"No, silly. Not Auntie Lizbeth."

"I give up, Mum. Who?"

"Dan. Daniel O'Hara. Isn't that wonderful? You two were always such good friends. I know you wouldn't have wanted to miss him."

"Uh...no," she said, and her voice cracked only slightly.

"Goodbye, darling."

"Bye, Mum."

Danny was coming.

She didn't realize that she was still holding the receiver with a death grip until her hand began to hurt and the low buzzing sound from the phone began to sink in. Then a recorded operator's voice. If you'd like to make a call...

She hung up, stared at the phone, then shook her head in disgust. How long since she had seen Danny? Two years, maybe three? He'd been the love of her life—the love of her *young* life, she corrected herself. But he'd come and gone like the wind. She'd refused to see him the last time he had called to say he was in the States. He was about as dependable as good weather in a Boston winter. And still...

Her heart quivered with a little pang. It would be good to see Danny.

Now that she was really over him.

And she was seeing someone, so she really would be immune to his, "Ah, Moira, just a quick beer." Or, "Moira Kelly, you'd not take a stroll with me?" Or even, "You'd not like to make time stand still, hop in bed with me, girl, because you know, you do, that we were magic?"

No more, Daniel.

She had a hectic life; she would be busy, especially since she was about to ask everyone to reschedule everything for her.

She loved her business. She was still in awe of the fact that she and Josh had made a go of it, that they were a production company and that their show was a modest success. Ireland, the old country, remained a passion for her parents. America was hers. She'd been born here and she'd grown up here, and the diversity of her country was what she loved best. Since she'd first gone to college, she'd kept very busy. Forgetting what could never be. Or trying to.

Maybe, though, in the corner of her mind, she had always dreamed that Danny would come back. To stay.

With annoyance, she realized that the very thought made her wistful.

Okay, she cared for Danny, she always would. In a far, far corner of her mind! As far as a distant galaxy. She was a realist. She'd seen people through the years—not too seriously, because of her work. And she was seeing someone now, someone bright, compelling and with shared interests, someone who'd entered her life at the right time, in the right way....

So Danny was coming to Boston. Good for him. He would like...

For a moment, her mind went blank.

Michael! She was dating a man named Michael Mc-Lean. Of Irish descent, as well, but of normal Irish descent. They had a really great relationship. Michael loved a good movie and didn't whine about a bad one. He was an avid sports fan but liked a day at a museum just as well and was up for a Broadway show—or Off Broadway, for that matter.

He was nearly perfect. He worked hard for her company, too. He was always on the go, seeing people, checking on logistics and permits. In fact, he was off somewhere right now. She wasn't even sure where. Well, of course, she knew...she just couldn't think of it right now. Talking to her mother had that effect on her.

It didn't matter where he was. Michael always had his cell phone on him, and he always returned messages, whether they were personal or business related. It was part of his being so wonderful.

And still, just thinking about Danny...

Impatiently, she picked up a pencil and tapped it on her desk. She had other things to think about. Like business. She reached for the phone again and buzzed her partner, Josh.

It would be good to see Danny again.

She was startled by the wave of heat that seemed to wash through her with the thought. Like a longing to hop into bed this very second. She could close her eyes and see him. See him naked.

Stop it! she chastised herself.

"What's up?"

"What?"

"You called me," Josh said. "What's up?"

"Can we go somewhere for lunch?"

Mentally, she put clothes on Danny.

Then she sternly forced him to the far corner of her mind.

She realized that Josh had hesitated, and as if she were in front of him, she could see his shaggy brows tightening into a frown. Danny retreated to memory. Her partner was very real, always a part of her life, steady, and just a down-right, decent good guy. Josh Whalen was tall and lean, almost skinny. Good-looking. They had met in film school at NYU, almost had an affair, realized instead that they could remain friends for a lifetime but never lovers, and became partners instead.

Danny had been in her life then, coming and going. Josh would have been only an attempt to convince herself that she wouldn't have to wait forever for a man to love, but she'd realized that before she'd done anything they would both regret.

Once again, she firmly pushed Danny back where he belonged.

Josh was better than any man she had ever dated. They shared a vision—and a work ethic. They'd both slaved in numerous restaurants to raise the capital they had needed to get their small production company going; he had also worked in construction and dug ditches. They had both been willing to give a hundred percent.

"You don't want me just to come to your office?" Josh asked.

"No. I want to take you to a nice restaurant, buy you a few glasses of good wine...."

His groan interrupted her. "You want to change the schedule."

"I—"

"Make it a sports bar, and buy me a beer."

"Where?"

He named his favorite little hole-in-the-wall, just a few blocks from their offices in the Village. He had an interview with a potential new cameraman, she was supposed to have coffee with a potential guest, but they decided to meet right after their appointments.

As it happened, their potential guest missed her connection and called in to find out if Moira would be available in the afternoon. Relieved, Moira cheerfully agreed.

She went out walking. And walked and walked until it was nearly time to meet Josh.

Moira reached Sam's Sports Spectacular—a true hole-in-the-wall but a great neighborhood place—before her partner. She seldom drank anything at all during the day and was cautious even at night, but this afternoon, she ordered a draft. She was nursing it at the farthest table from the bar when Josh came in. He was a handsome, appealing guy in a tall, lanky, artistic way. He looked like a director or, she mused with a flash of humor, a refugee from some grunge band. His eyes were dark and beautiful, his hair reddish brown and very curly, and despite his wife's objection, he wore a full beard and mustache.

"Where's my beer?" he asked, sliding into a chair by the table.

"I wasn't sure what you wanted."

He stared at her as if she had lost her mind. "How many years have you known me?"

"Almost ten. Since we were eighteen. But—"

"What do I always drink?"

"Miller Lite. But—"

"There you have it."

"I'm a bit off today."

"You *are* a bit off." He raised his hand, and their waiter saw him. He gave his order, and the young man nodded in acknowledgment and started for the bar.

"Why are you off today?" Josh asked, leaning forward.

"My mother called."

He grimaced. "My mother calls almost every day. That's no excuse."

"You don't know my mother."

"I do." He grinned and feigned a slight accent. "She's a lovely lady, she is."

"Um. My dad's ill."

"Oh." Josh was quickly serious. "I'm sorry."

"I—" She hesitated. That wasn't really it. "I think he's going to be okay, although it appears he may need another surgery."

"So you want to go home for Saint Patrick's Day."

"I know we were supposed to be shooting at the theme parks in central Florida, and I know how hard you worked to straighten out all the paperwork and rights and—"

"Things have been postponed before."

"I truly appreciate your attitude," she told him softly, swallowing her draft, her eyes lowered.

"I never believed we'd be going to Florida in March."

She looked at him and flushed. "You think I have no spine?"

"I think your mother could take on the Terminator."

She flashed him a grateful smile. "I do have another idea. We can do a real ethnic Irish show and arrange with the Leisure Channel to do a live feed. It really might be a great idea. I think the viewers would love it." Josh mused over the idea. He lifted his hands. "You could be right. 'Fun, food, and fantasy—live from the home of the hostess herself.'"

"How do you feel about Boston in March?"

"Wretched, but then, it's not much worse than New York." He smiled at her suddenly. "Actually, I thought something like this might come up. I've had Michael checking into the permit situation in Boston as well as Orlando."

"You're kidding! He didn't say a word."

"He knows how to keep a confidence. I didn't want you to suspect I was second-guessing you."

"Great."

"Hey, kid, it's a show we should have done before this."

She grinned, suddenly feeling a tremendous sense of relief. "But you and Gina were looking forward to doing the whole Disney thing."

"We'll still do it. We'll just reschedule. And the kids won't mind—they didn't really understand what was going on anyway."

She smiled. He had a point. At eight months, the twins undoubtedly didn't care one way or the other whether they got to see Mickey Mouse or not.

"Do you want something to eat?" he asked her. "Or are you just going to drink your lunch?" He indicated her beer glass. It was empty, and she didn't even remember drinking the whole thing.

"I *am* Irish," she muttered.

He laughed, leaning forward again. "Hey! No ill will intended. I just wondered if you wanted food or not."

"Yes, yes, I guess I should eat."

"They make a nice salad here."

"Great. I think I'll have a hamburger."

"Ah, we're being a wild renegade today, eh?" He teased, motioning to their waiter.

"What? Are you trying to be just a wee bit condescending, so I don't have to be eternally grateful for making you change the entire schedule for the season?"

He laughed. "Maybe. Maybe it's just amusing to see you so afraid of going home."

"I am not afraid of going home! I go home all the time. Here comes the waiter. Just order me a hamburger—and another beer."

Josh did so diligently, but there was still a sparkle in his eyes.

"So what are you so afraid of?" he asked softly, once the waiter had taken their order and departed.

"I'm not afraid. I go home all the time."

"But this time you seem uneasy. Is it the fact that you think we should film at your home as an excuse to go there? The whole thing does fit nicely. There are a lot of Irish in the United States. And on Saint Patrick's Day—"

"Everyone is Irish. Yes, I know," she murmured. Her second beer arrived. She flashed the waiter a smile. He grinned and left. She took a sip of the brew immediately, then sat back, running her fingertip along the edge of the glass.

"So? It's perfect," Josh said.

"Perfect—and what a cast of characters we have."

"Your mother is charming. So is your father."

"Mmm. They are. Just..."

"Just what?"

"Well, they are...eccentric."

"Your parents? No."

"Stop teasing. You know Granny Jon. She had me convinced for years that I had to be really good or the banshees would get me on the way to the outhouse. I think that Colleen, Patrick and I were all out of high school before we suddenly realized the great flaw in her terror tactics—we didn't have an outhouse.''

"Your grandmother is adorable."

"Like a hedgehog," Moira agreed. "Then there's my father, who has yet to accept the fact that in the U.S., the Fighting Irish are a football team."

"Not true! I've watched college football games with him. Though he does root for Notre Dame, I'll give you that."

"My mother will give speeches on how the traditional dish is bacon and cabbage, not corned beef, and somewhere along the line, if you're not careful, Dad will get going on English imperialism against the rights of the Gaelic-speaking people of the world, and then he'll get going on the wonders of America. He'll forget that as a country we massacred hundreds of thousands of Indians and he'll start to list famous Americans of Irish descent, from the founding fathers to the Civil War—both sides, of course."

"Maybe he'll avoid talking about Irishmen who rode with Custer."

"Josh, I'm serious. You know my dad. Please, God, make sure no one brings up the question of Irish nationalism or the IRA."

"Okay, we'll keep him off politics."

She barely heard him as she rested an elbow on the table, leaning over, preoccupied. "Patrick will bring my little nieces and nephew, so Mum, Dad and Granny Jon will all be running around pretending there are stray leprechauns in the house. They'll have beer kegs everywhere, and everything will be green."

"It sounds great."

"We'll have all kinds of company—"

"The more the merrier."

She straightened and looked him in the eye. "Danny is coming," she told him.

"Oh, I see," he said softly.

He awoke very late and very slowly, and in luxurious comfort. The mattress he lay on was soft, the sheets cool and clean. The woman beside him still smelled sweetly of perfume, and of the scent of their lovemaking. She was young, but not too young. Her skin was tanned and sleek. Her hair was dark, and a wealth of it graced the hotel pillow. She'd had her price, but what the hell, so did he. They'd had fun together.

Coffee had brewed in a pot he'd set to go on a timer last night. Brewed and probably burned. He'd never imagined he would sleep so late.

He leaned against his pillow and the headboard.

America was good.

He had always enjoyed it.

There was so much here. Such an abundance. And such foolish people, who didn't begin to understand what they had. Aye, they had their problems; he wasn't at all blind to the world, nor did he lack compassion. But problems were different here. Spoiled rich kids, racial tensions, Republicans, Democrats...and, he had to say, though with all compassion, if they didn't have enough problems, they just made more for themselves. But it didn't change the fact that life was good.

The phone rang. He reached to the bedside table; picked it up.

"Hello?"

"Have you the order ready, sir?"

"I do. Shall I deliver, or do you want to come here?"

"It's probably better if you come here. We may have more business to discuss."

"That will be fine. When?"

He was given a time; then the phone clicked. He hung up.

The woman at his side stirred and moaned. She turned toward him; her eyes flickering open. She smiled. "Morning."

"Morning." He leaned over and kissed her. She was still a cute little thing. Dark-haired, dark-eyed, tanned. She reached for him beneath the sheets, her hand curling around his sex.

He arched a brow at her.

She laughed. "Freebie. I don't usually stay until morning—"

"I don't usually keep a who—a woman—till morning," he amended kindly.

Her fingers were talented, and he found himself quickly aroused. He noted, though, the light that was beginning to show around the edges of the curtains.

"What's the matter?" she asked him.

He smiled, crushed out his cigarette. "Nothing," he told her, drawing her head toward his, kissing her lips, then drawing her downward to continue a more liquid approach to her sensual assault on his body. He glanced at his watch. Plenty of time.

She was very good, and it had been a long time since he'd had such an opportunity to dally. He let her have her way, then returned the favor, and when he made love to her—if one could, even politely, call the act "making love" when it was with a woman who was a stranger and a whore at that—he did so with energy and pleasure, a courteous partner despite the fact that he swiftly climaxed. Even as he rolled to her side, he checked his watch again.

"Late," he muttered, then kissed her lips and headed for the shower. "Coffee's on. Cigarettes are by the bed."

He showered quickly, with an economy of motion learned over the years. He emerged well scrubbed, hair washed. He grabbed a towel from the rack and studiously worked at drying his hair while he opened the bathroom door and exited, head covered, body naked.

"Did you get your cof—" He began politely, but then paused, muscles tightening "What are you doing?" he asked sharply.

She was on her knees, his pants in her hands.

"I—" she began, dropping his pants, looking at him. She stumbled to her feet. Had she been about to rob him? He wondered what she had seen. He noted quickly that she had been through more than his pants. Drawers weren't quite closed; the dust ruffle around the bed was still up at the foot of it. What had she discovered that had caused the look of fear she wore?

Or was it merely what she was seeing in his eyes?

She stood, clad in her bra slip and stockings. He watched the workings of her mind. She was wishing she'd got dressed and got the hell out while he had showered.

But she hadn't.

Her eyes, glued to his, registered her fear. He didn't look away; he saw the room with his peripheral vision. She'd done a good job in the time she'd had. Thorough. She was just a working girl—and, it appeared, a thief.

Or was she?

"I was just looking around, just curious," she said, moistening her lips.

Whatever else she was, she was a damn poor liar.

"Ah, love," he said softly. "Hadn't you ever heard? Curiosity killed the cat."

"Ah, your good friend Daniel O'Hara," Josh teased. "Think of it. If it hadn't been for old Danny boy, you and I might be married now."

"And divorced—we'd have killed each other in a week," Moira reminded him.

"Maybe, maybe not. Let's see, you were intellectually in love with me, but you lusted after your old flame. I was the good, decent man who meant to do all the honorable things, but he was an unobtainable, intriguing and dashing young lover, and though never present, he took your heart as well as your—well, you know.''

"Josh, we would never have gotten married."

"Probably not," he agreed, a bit too cheerfully.

"Well, I don't appreciate the dramatics. He's an old family friend—"

"And the fact that he's built like a linebacker and looks like an Adonis has nothing to do with it?"

"You're being incredibly...shallow. As if I don't judge men by other standards. Besides, you're a very good-looking man yourself."

"Thanks. I'll take that. But I'm not sure I compare with your exotic foreign lover. And no, it's not just his looks that affect you. It's the accent, the voice, the tradition, the fact that he's an old family friend." He put on a Hollywood Irish accent. "Aye, me lass, your lover has a definite presence."

"He's not my lover!"

"How quickly you protest."

"I haven't even seen him in years."

"I can tell you when you saw him last. Summer, almost three years ago. And you wound up lying to your family, saying you were coming back to New York, but you stayed at the Copley with him in Boston. You thought he'd stay here, because you wanted him to. He wasn't ready, you got mad. And when he called again the following Christmas, you refused to see him."

"I never told you all that!"

"Well, I may not have made it as husband material, but I *am* your best friend. And there's something about him you can't quite shake."

"You're wrong."

"Am I?"

"Trust me, I *have* shaken him." She looked at her

watch. "How time flies when you're being tortured by your supposed best friend. I have to meet Mrs. Grisholm. She missed her connection this morning. She's the lady from that little mystery theater group in Maine where the audience joins in and they do the show together. They even cook and eat dinner together. You know. I told you all about her, and it sounds like a—"

"What's Michael going to say about the return of your old flame? Did you ever tell *him* about Daniel O'Hara?" Josh interrupted, amused.

"Dan is my past, Michael is none of your business."

Josh started laughing. Her cheeks flamed.

"Saint Patrick's Day could be lots of fun. Your sleeping arrangements may be none of my business, but we hired Michael as location manager before you two became involved, so I assume he'll be joining us in Boston."

"Yes, of course he'll be joining us in Boston."

Josh was still grinning.

"Oh, will you wipe that smirk off your face?"

"I'm sorry. As your one-time would-be lover, I find it amusing that you've spent half your adult life in celibacy and now you're going to have both of the great loves of your life home for the holiday."

"Josh..." she said warningly.

"Maybe that's not so bad. Mum and Dad can protect you."

She stood up. "I would thank you for being such a great business partner—"

"If I wasn't being such a prick." He was still laughing.

"I could tell your wife you're being a horse's ass."

"She knows all about my ancient crush on you. I think she'll find the situation just as much fun as I do."

"You're impossible, and I'm leaving."

"You're leaving because you're late, and you love me anyway," he called after her, since she was already heading for the door.

"I don't love you," she called, turning around. "Make sure you get the check, and leave a decent tip."

"You adore me!" he called after her.

At the door, she looked back. He was still wearing the same shit-eating grin. He arched a brow to her and started humming "Danny Boy."

2

It had been a damned long day. Michael McLean took his work to heart, and he accomplished what he set out to do, whether it took diplomacy and tact or a dead-set determination and a few strong-arm techniques.

When the phone rang, Michael jumped. He'd been lying there, half asleep, and though his work meant that he got calls at all hours, he hadn't been expecting the abrasive ring. He'd been traveling large expanses of the country—they had to be prepared for every contingency—and he was tired. For a moment the ringing was simply jarring, and he let it go on. Then he forced himself up, dragging his legs over the side of the bed, running his fingers through his hair. He started for his bedside phone, then realized that it was his cellular ringing. He rose, running his fingers through his hair, found his pants and dug out the phone.

He glanced at the caller ID. Moira.

"Hey, babe, what's up? You're all right, aren't you? It's late."

"I know, I'm sorry. I should have called earlier."

"You can call me any time, day or night. You know that."

"Thanks," she said, her voice soft.

There were lots of women in the world. He'd known his share. But the tenor of her voice slipped into him. There were others, yes. But none quite like her. He pictured her.

Moira was a beauty, with her true deep red hair and blue-green eyes. Tall, elegant, with a natural sophistication and the ability to dirty her hands and nails, laugh at any obstacle and get involved with the most absurd situations. When he'd answered the ad for an associate producer and locations manager for KW Productions, he'd known her from seeing her on the air, having studied what tapes he could find before applying for the job. She was good on tape. She was even better in person. He hadn't been ready for the excitement she could create or the emotion she could invoke. He wished she were there right now. Amazing what the sound of her voice could do to a man.

"I should have called you—*could* have called you—hours ago," she went on, then halted suddenly. "You haven't heard from Josh already, have you?"

"No."

He heard her sigh. "Yeah, he would make me do this one myself. And it's so late because I've been trying to get up the nerve to call you."

He was about to assure her that she never needed nerve to call him when she rushed on.

"I know how much work you've already done—"

"You are the boss, you know."

"Not really. Josh and I have always made decisions together, and since you've been with us, well, you've just been the perfect addition to the show.... Oh, Lord, Michael, I'm so sorry to be doing this, but...we're making a sudden switch in plans."

He'd been expecting this; still, he felt every muscle in his body tense. He knew what she was about to say.

"I know that you and Josh have made an incredible effort on the Orlando angle, that acquiring permits to tape has been a bitch...but we're switching locations for Saint Patrick's Day. I'm so sorry. I know—"

"Family pressure, eh?" he asked quietly.

"My father has to go in for tests next week. Nothing

serious, Mum assures me, but I'm willing to bet he's still working the pub himself until all hours of the night. Anyway, she made it sound as if I were punching the Easter Bunny or something, and I...I caved in.''

"Don't worry," he told her. "I've already looked into the Boston situation."

"What?"

"Josh and I both kind of expected this," he said.

She was silent.

"Moira, it's all right. Hey, I'm going to love meeting your family. I'll get to feel important, right? The man in your life, someone who means everything in the world to you, right?"

"You're incredible, you know that?"

"Well, of course, you'd have nothing less, right?" he said.

"You know what?"

"What?"

"You sound so good."

Her voice was almost like silk.

"I was just thinking the same about you."

"They're crazy, you know."

"Who?"

"My folks."

"Moira, you've hit the right guy here. My family is Irish, too. Okay, we don't own a pub and no one runs around whistling 'Danny Boy' all day, but I can deal with the leprechaun and banshee stories. Don't be so worried."

She was still silent. Then she said, "Mine do."

"What?"

"They run around whistling 'Danny Boy' all the time."

He laughed. "I've got nothing against the song. Hey, Josh and I had a wager going, you know."

"Who bet that I wouldn't cave in to family pressure?"

"Neither of us. The wager was on the date you'd finally do it."

"I can't wait to see you," she said. Once again, he pictured her. Not the woman on television. The one who should be here with him now. Softly scented, sleek and smooth, hair down and wild, naked as the day she was born. Maybe that was part of her allure. She could be so elegant and almost aloof in public, and so incredibly sensual and volatile in private.

"I don't think there are any planes at this time of night," he said regretfully. "Can't even hop a train. I could rent a car...if you're really needy."

"You're good. Very good."

"No, what I am is—"

"Never mind," she said, laughing again. "You know you can't rent a car in Florida and be here that quickly. And I have to—*have* to—tie up a few things here tomorrow and then head up right after. That will give us a week before the actual big day. Time so I can see my folks and so we can give the Leisure Channel a really good show."

"I can be there, if you want." He wondered if he should tell her that he wasn't in Florida. Maybe he'd better leave that one for Josh.

He was silent for a moment. Yes, there were other women in the world, he knew that well. The fingers of his free hand tensed and eased, tensed and eased. But none like her.

"Aye, me love, at ye olde pub!" he said, giving her his best Irish accent. "If you insist that we wait that long."

"You'd really drive all night...?"

"I would."

"I'd rather have you alive in the future than dead in such an effort," Moira said firmly. "Boston, night after next, Kelly's Pub, you'll meet the folks. I'll see you there?"

"All right," he told her. Then, though he had expected it, he found himself dreading the fact that they would all be in Boston together. He, Moira, her family, her past—

and the future. "I love you," he added, and he was surprised by the almost desperate ardor in his voice.

"I love you, too," she said, and he believed her.

A few moments later, they rang off.

Though it was late and he was still exhausted, Michael found himself rising and getting dressed. He glanced at the clock. Not that late; just after midnight.

He dressed and left the hotel room.

His destination was within easy walking distance. Boston was a good city in that respect. Narrow, winding streets in the old section and even in the newer areas. There was little distance here between the colonial and the modern. He liked Boston. Great seafood. A sense of history.

He walked quickly and came to the street he had checked out earlier that day. There, in the middle of the block, beneath a soft yellow streetlight, was the sign.

Kelly's Pub.

He stood there, staring at it.

And damning the days to come.

The doors were still open, though it looked quiet within. Weeknight. He thought about sauntering in, quietly ordering a draft, sitting in a corner, taking a look.

No.

At twelve-thirty, he turned and walked away.

Twelve forty-five.

From the shadows cast by the long buildings, another man watched Michael McLean leave the premises. He hadn't really seen his face, had never known the man previously, but even so, he was fully aware of who he was.

Dan O'Hara watched the man thoughtfully until he had disappeared. He had avoided the streetlight on the opposite side of the block and therefore had hardly been even a dark silhouette in the night.

He leaned against the old building. With the street clear, he lit a cigarette, slowly allowing the smoke to filter out of his lungs. Bad habit. He needed to quit, he thought idly. So that was Michael. He didn't have enough basis for any rational judgments, but by virtue of instinct, he disliked the guy. But then, Moira could be seeing a Nobel Peace Prize-winning certified saint and he would still dislike the guy.

He had to force himself to hold back any conclusions on Michael McLean. He couldn't even blame the guy for wanting a good look at the pub.

Kelly's. Dan loved the place himself.

How long had he been gone this time? Too long. Of course, last time he had come back, things had been different. No Moira.

How many times had he pushed her away? Doing the right thing, of course. At first she'd been too young. Then, even when they'd become lovers, he'd just known that he was wrong for her. Yet he hadn't realized that he still lived with the belief that she was his, that she would still be there. He truly wanted her to be happy, but he wasn't a man without an ego. Somewhere inside, he had believed that happiness for her would mean waiting for him.

Okay, so he was an ass.

An ass...yet he had done the right thing. She was a strong character, with a sense of the world, of right and wrong and everything that being an American meant. He hadn't been able to help it; he was Irish. An Irishman who loved America, but who felt...

Obligated.

Was he always going to feel obligated?

Hell, was he going to survive?

He thought angrily of how much he didn't like what was going on, and there seemed to be no help in the knowledge that it wasn't his fault. He'd never put any of this into motion, but there wasn't a damn thing he could do.

Moira was coming home. He'd talked to Katy Kelly on

the phone today, and she'd been in heaven, knowing that she would have her whole family home and in one place for the special holiday. She was also a little nervous. "She's been seeing a man, one her da and I have yet to meet," Katy had informed him, trying to keep her disapproval out of her voice.

"He's probably a great guy," Dan had told her. "She's grown up a smart woman, Katy, you know that. You should be proud."

"He's in television, too. Working for her and Josh." Katy had sighed. "Now Josh...there's a good man."

"A fine man." Danny could say so easily. He liked Moira's partner. And the fellow was married, was truly a friend and had never had an intimate relationship with Moira.

"Well, this new fellow is Irish."

"Oh? And what's his name."

"Michael. Michael McLean."

"Well, there you go. What more can you ask for?"

Katy sighed again. "Well, I suppose...for you two to have married, Danny."

"Ah, Katy. We were going different ways. Besides, I wasn't meant for marriage."

"I think you were."

She had gone on to insist that it wouldn't matter that Moira and her crew would be there—the back room of the pub was his, as it always was when he came to Boston. And yes, Moira knew that he was coming.

A strange sense of nostalgia stole over him. This place really was home to him, certainly as much as any other. His early years seemed a very long time ago. Living with his uncle, he had traveled a great deal. Brendan O'Toole, his mother's brother, who had married a cousin of Katy Kelly, had been a scholar and broker for antique manuscripts. He had given Dan his first love of literature. Of the written word and the power within it. He'd been a storyteller, another talent he had passed on to Dan. His house in Dublin had been home, but they'd been on the go constantly. Dan had seen many foreign countries, and he had spent a great deal of time in America. He did love the States.

And after any length of time away, he missed this old place.

It was time for him to be there. He could go on in. But he had said he was arriving in the morning. He would wait. No reason to tell the folks that he had been in Boston a bit before checking in with them.

Aye, he would wait.

As he stood there against the building, he saw another man striding down the street. He wore a huge overcoat and a low-brimmed hat. Nothing odd in that. Boston could be frigid this time of year.

But this man approached the pub oddly; then, as Dan had done himself, he paused, staring at the windows.

He stood there for a long time. Dan dropped his cigarette to the ground and remained still, watching the watcher.

The man was peering through the windows, trying to see who was in the pub.

Apparently he didn't see the person—or people—he was seeking, because after a long moment, he turned away and started down the street again, back in the direction from which he had come.

Nothing odd in that. A guy out to find friends at a pub, taking a look for them, realizing they weren't there, deciding to leave.

Nothing odd in that.

Except that the man in the huge coat and low-brimmed hat was Patrick Kelly, son of the owners of Kelly's Pub.

Dan lit another cigarette, feeling a new tension, as if rocks were forming in his gut.

He waited a while longer, then hiked up the collar of his coat and started off down the street, as well.

* * *

Moira seldom paused to window-shop; she was usually running somewhere, and besides, she had been in New York a long time. She still loved the beautiful displays that were put out for holidays, and she appreciated the fact that she could buy almost anything in the world in the city where she lived and worked. She loved clothes, but she also loved a day when she could take the time to try on outfits, go through a zillion pair of shoes, driving salesmen crazy.

But that morning, walking toward the new French restaurant in the Village where she was to meet the lady from Maine to discuss their taping schedule, she found herself stopping to stare at an incredible Saint Patrick's showcase. The stores usually had out all their Easter wares along with their Saint Patrick's Day items. This particular window had been done with real love. There were shamrocks everywhere, arranged artfully. A field of lovely porcelain fairies had been hung to fly above a rainbow with the traditional pot of gold at the end. Finely carved leprechauns with charming faces were set around the rainbow, as if they were busy at daily tasks. The leprechaun in the middle sat on a pedestal, facing a fairy on another pedestal. The fairy was exquisite, poised on one toe, with wings painted the colors of the rainbow. Pausing without realizing it, she stared at the fairy, charmed. She realized that it was a music box.

She glanced quickly at her watch and decided she had time to take a closer look. She went into the store, not surprised to discover that the shop owner was the cashier, that she still carried a bit of an Irish accent and that she was delighted with Moira's interest in the item.

"My mother would absolutely love that piece," Moira told her, and asked the price.

It was high, but the woman quickly explained. "The piece is one of a kind. The fairies and leprechauns, you see. The porcelain fairies are limited, but the carved pieces are hand-crafted by two brothers in Dublin. Each is individual, and signed. I believe they'll be very popular in the future, but it's not the fact that they may be highly collectible one day that makes them so dear. It's the time taken for the work that goes into each one.''

"I hate to ask you to take it out of the window.''

"Oh, no, dear, I love the darling little things. Please, it's my pleasure, even if you don't buy. You seem to truly appreciate the art of it.''

Moira assured her that she did, indeed. And when the woman took the piece from the window and put it before her, she found that it was even more beautiful than she had thought. The carving of the face was exquisite. The fairy created a feeling that was totally ethereal. She was simply magical. *All that is good and enchanting about the Irish people,* Moira thought.

"I'll take her,'' Moira said.

"Don't you wish to hear her play?'' the woman asked, twisting the key at the bottom of the small pedestal.

"Sure, thank you. What song does she play?''

The woman laughed softly. She allowed her accent to deepen as she jokingly said, "Why, besure and begorrah, dear. She plays 'Danny Boy.' You know, 'Londonderry Air.' ''

The little fairy began to spin, to fly on her pedestal. The music tinkled out, charming, beautiful, sweet, the haunting melody familiar and yet light, different.

"Danny Boy.'' Of course. What else? There were so many beautiful old Irish tunes, but naturally this box would play "Danny Boy.''

"Is something wrong?'' the woman asked.

"No, she's lovely, thank you so much. I'll definitely buy her for my mum.''

"I'll wrap her very carefully for you.''

"Thanks so much.''

As Moira waited, she realized that she would be spending the next week listening to "Danny Boy." Might as well get used to it now.

"Are you sure there's nothing wrong, dear?"

"Not at all. In fact, I'd like both of those little stuffed leprechauns, please. They'll make cute little gifts for my nieces. Then I need something for a boy."

"I have a small, hand-held video game just in. Banshees against fairies, with the leprechauns being the chance factor, some of them good, some of them bad."

"Sounds perfect," Moira said. "Thank you so much."

Tomorrow she was going home. And suddenly, here in this shop, anticipation mingled with her dread.

Kelly's Pub was already in full nightly swing when Dan O'Hara emerged from the back room of the tavern, the guest quarters, where he had been staying. The pub band, Blackbird, was already playing a mixture of old and new Irish music with a bit of American pop thrown in here and there. He knew all the members from way back.

It was the first time he had come into the pub during opening hours, and he was ready for the greeting he knew he would receive.

"And there he is!" Eamon Kelly called from behind the bar. "The best and brightest of you lot of reprobates, Mr. Daniel O'Hara."

"Hey, Danny, how are you?" asked old Seamus.

"Danny boy, you're back in town!" Liam McConnahy said.

The lineup at the bar was made up of Eamon's longtime friends, some old country, some born and bred in the USA. He recognized Sal Costanza, an old school chum who had grown up in the Italian sector along the North Shore. Eamon Kelly had created his own little Gaelic empire here, but he was a good-hearted, friendly fellow, with a keen interest in everyone around him and—usually—a nose for a decent character in any man. But now Dan didn't like what was happening here. He would have done anything in his power to keep Kelly's Pub and the Kellys themselves out of what was happening. But things had been set in motion; he had no choice. Whatever was going down had been given the code name Blackbird, and that could only refer to Kelly's Pub.

Hell, a Kelly could be involved.

"Back in town," Dan said easily, embracing both old Seamus and Liam, then shaking hands with the others as each man spoke a quick greeting.

"So," Seamus said, his thick, snow-white brows rising over cloudy blue eyes, "have you been hanging around back in the old country or gallivantin' around the States?"

"A bit of both," Dan said.

"You've been in Ireland recently?" Liam asked. He had the same cap of white hair as Seamus, except that his was thinning now.

"That I have," Dan said.

"The Republic—or the North?" Seamus asked, a slight frown denoting his worry.

"A bit of both," Dan said. "Eamon, how about a round for my old friends at the bar? It's good to see them again. Sal, how's it going in the pasta business in Little Italy? I've been hankering for a taste of your mum's lasagna. No one makes it as good as she does."

Sal answered, and Dan kept smiling, nodding in reply to the thanks he received for the round of drinks. But as he engaged in the banter at the bar, he looked around the room. Though the band was in action at one end, the scene remained fairly quiet. An attractive young couple, with either his or her parents, were having dinner at a center table. A group just off from work—probably from the IBM offices or the bank around the corner—huddled around a couple of tables near the band, winding down from their nine-to-five workday. Patrick Kelly was in. Eamon's son, tall, with a head full of dark hair touched by a reddish sheen. He was a good-looking fellow, on stage now with the band, playing along with the violinist. He saw Daniel and gave him a wave and a grin, beckoning to him. Daniel nodded and smiled in return, motioning that he would join them all soon. Patrick nudged Jeff Dolan, lead guitarist and group leader, and Jeff, too, nodded Dan's way.

Still scanning the room, Dan saw a lone man in a business suit seated at a far corner table, a darkened table. A stranger. Dan had the feeling the man was surveying the occupants of the pub, just as he was doing himself.

"What are you drinking yourself?" Eamon asked him.

"What's he drinking?" Seamus said indignantly. "Give him a whiskey and a Guinness!"

"Now, Seamus, I'm in the grand old USA," Dan protested. "A Bud Lite on draft, if you will, Eamon. It may prove to be a long night—back with a party of Boston's black sheep!"

"How's the place look, Danny?" Liam asked. "You miss it when you're away?"

"Why, the pub looks just fine, and old friends look even better," Dan replied. He lifted the stein Eamon had brought him. "Slainte! To old times, old friends."

"And to the old country!" Eamon declared.

"Aye, to the old country," Dan said softly.

The sky was overcast when Moira's shuttle from New York to Boston made its initial descent for landing. Even so, she stared out the window for a bird's-eye view of the city where she had grown up, and which she still loved so much. Coming home. She was excited; she loved her family dearly. They were all entirely crazy, of course. She was convinced of that. But she loved them and was happy at the prospect of seeing them.

But then…then there was this whole Danny thing.

The plane landed. She was slow to take off her seat belt

and slow to deplane. No one was picking her up; she had made the last-minute decision to take an earlier shuttle than the rest of the cast and crew, who would be taking the last flight. When the people in the seats behind her had filed out, she grabbed her overnight bag and walked out, thanking the flight attendant and the pilots, who were waiting for her exit to leave themselves.

Outside Logan, she hailed a taxi. Once seated, she realized that the driver, a young man of twenty-something with a lean face and amber eyes, was staring at her by way of the rearview mirror.

"You're Moira Kelly!" he said, flushing as she caught his eye.

"Yes."

"In my cab! Fancy that. You just travel on a regular plane and get in a regular taxi?"

"Seems to be the best way to get around," she told him, smiling.

"You mean you don't have a private jet and a limo waiting?" the man demanded.

She laughed. "I don't have a private jet at all, though sometimes we do hire private cars."

"And no one recognizes you—and hounds you?"

"I'm afraid that all of America doesn't tune in to the Leisure Channel. And even those who do don't necessarily watch our show."

"Well, they should."

"Thank you. Very much."

"What are you doing in Boston?"

"I'm from here."

"Wow. Right. And you're Irish, right? Are you home to see family, or are you going to film stuff here?"

"Both."

"Wow. Well, great. Hey, it's a privilege. If you need more transportation while you're here, call me. I've got the cleanest cab in the city. I grew up here, too. I know the place backward and forward. No charge, even. Honest."

"I'd never take advantage that way of anyone making a living," Moira said. "But give me your card, and I promise when we need transportation we'll call you." In fact, he did seem to be a good driver. Boston's traffic was as crazy as ever. There was always construction; the freeway was as often as not a stop-and-go place. Once they were out of the tunnel and off the highway, the streets were narrow and one-way. And then there were the traffic circles…. The old character and ultra-thin roadways were part of the charm of the city—and the bane of it, as well.

The young man kept his right hand solidly on the steering wheel and slipped her a card with his left hand.

"Hey, I'm Irish, too."

"Your name is Tom Gambetti."

He grinned at her in the rearview mirror. "My mum is Irish, Dad is Italian. Hey, this is Boston. There are lots of us living on pasta and potatoes! Both your folks are Irish?"

"Oh, Lord, yes!" Moira laughed.

"Right off the old potato boat, eh?"

"Something like that," she said, then leaned forward, pointing. "There it is—Kelly's Pub."

The street was narrow. Though both corners held large new office buildings, the rest of the block still had a lot of old character. The building that housed the pub was two stories, with a basement and an attic. It dated from Colonial days, as did many of its nudged-in neighbors. An old iron tethering pole remained in front, from the days when the country's forefathers had come to knock back a pint or two. Kelly's Pub was lettered on an attractive board above the door, and there were soft friendly lights issuing from lamps on either side. When the weather was warm, tables spilled onto the narrow enclosed patio in front. There were two windows in the front, as well; they were closed now, in deference to the winter, but within the pub, the lace-edged curtains were drawn back so that passersby could see the welcoming coziness to be found inside.

"Want your suitcase right in the pub?" Tom asked.

"No, thanks, just on the sidewalk. I'm going upstairs first."

"I'll be happy to take it up for you," he suggested.

She shook her head. "No, thanks. I appreciate it, but—"

"But a homecoming is best alone," he said.

She paid him as he set her bag down. "Thanks. And I will call you if we need transportation."

"You may not have to call me. It looks like a great pub."

"It is," she murmured, listening to the laughter and music coming from within. "It's everything a pub is supposed to be. *Céad mile fáilte.*"

"What does that mean?"

She looked at him, smiling wryly. "A hundred thousand welcomes."

"Nice. Well, good luck. I'll be seeing you."

"Thanks."

He got in his car and drove away, it seemed regretfully. Nice kid, she thought. Then she hefted her suitcase and started up the outside stairs that led to the family living quarters above the thriving business.

Her mother was a model of domesticity. The porch beside the front door of the home area was set with white wicker café tables, and the canvas overhang was clean as a whistle, even in the dying days of winter. Moira set her case down by the door and knocked, her fingers colder than she had realized inside her gloves. Knocking was easier than trying to find her key.

The door opened. Her mother was there, taking one look at her face and giving her the kind of smile that would have made a trek halfway around the world worthwhile.

"Moira Kathleen!" And then, though Katy Kelly was thin as a reed and two inches shorter than Moira's five feet eight, she enveloped her daughter in a fierce hug with the strength of a grizzly.

"Moira Kathleen, you're home!" Katy said, stepping back at last, hands on her hips as she surveyed her daughter.

"Mum, of course I'm home. You knew I was coming."

"Seems so long, Moira," Katy said, shaking her head. "And you look like a million."

Moira laughed. "Thanks, Mum. Good genes," she said affectionately. Her mother was a beautiful woman. Katy didn't dye the tendrils of silver threading through her auburn hair. God was granting her age, in her words. A head full of silver wasn't going to matter. Katy was trim from moving a thousand miles an hour every day of her life. Her eyes were the green of her old County Cork, and her face had a classical beauty.

"Ah, sweetie, I miss you so!" Katy said, kissing her. "It's been so long."

"Mum, we're just heading into Saint Patrick's Day. I spent Christmas here. And we all did First Night in the city together, remember?"

"Aye, and maybe it's not so long, but your brother, Patrick, you know, manages to get back at least once a month, he does."

"Ah, yes, my brother. Saint Patrick," Moira murmured.

"Now would you be mocking the likes of your brother?" The question came from behind Katy. Moira looked past her mother to see her grandmother standing there, Granny Jon. On a good day, Granny Jon might be considered an even five feet. At ninety something—no one, including Granny Jon, was quite sure what year she'd been born—she was still as straight as a ramrod and spry as a young girl. Her keen sense of humor sparkled in hazel eyes as she playfully accosted Moira.

"And there—the heart of Eire herself!" Moira laughed, stepping forward to hug her grandmother. As she hugged Granny Jon, she felt the old woman shake a little. Spry and straight she might be, but her grandmother was still a tiny mass of delicate bones, and Moira adored her. She'd given Moira leprechauns and legends, wonderful tales about the banshees being tricked or bribed to go away, and then, when she'd been older, true tales of the fight for freedom for the Irish through long years of mayhem throughout history. She was keen and wise and had seen the battlefield of her city torn to shreds, yet had somehow maintained a love for all the humanity around her, a glorious sense of humor, and a sound judgment regarding both politics and people.

"Why, Moira, you haven't aged a day," Granny Jon teased. "Katy, have a heart now. The girl is out there doing us proud. And she is living in New York, while Patrick has stayed in the state of Massachusetts."

"Um. As if western Mass weren't nearly as far away as New York City," Katy said.

"But it hasn't the traffic," Granny Jon said.

"Then there's my evil younger sister," Moira teased, rolling her eyes.

Katy inclined her head with a wry smile for the two of them. "Well, then, Colleen has gone as far as the west of the entire country now, hasn't she? And she'd never even consider not being here for Saint Patrick's Day."

Moira sighed. "Mum, I'm here, and I'm even bringing in the non-Irish for you to convert," Moira told her.

"Ah, now, 'tis enough," Katy said. "We'll give you a quick cup of tea. Granny Jon was just brewing—"

"And it will be strong enough to pick itself up and walk itself right across the table, eh?" Moira said, teasing her grandmother and putting on her accent.

"We'll have none of that," Granny Jon said. "And I

do make a good pot of tea, a real pot of tea, nothing wishy-washy about it. And what have we here?''

The main entry to the living quarters was a foyer, with the kitchen—a very large room with added warmth in winter from the oven—and a hallway leading to the bedrooms, library and office straight ahead. Moira hadn't heard a thing, but when she looked beyond Granny Jon, she saw three little heads bobbing into sight.

Patrick and his wife, Siobhan, had nearly repeated her parents' pattern of procreation; their son Brian was nine and daughters Molly and Shannon were six and four respectively.

"Hey, guys!" Moira called delightedly, hunching down on the balls of her feet and putting her arms out for the kids. They came running to her with whoops and hollers, kissing her, hugging her.

"Auntie Mo," Brian said. As a baby, he'd never quite gotten her name right. She'd been Auntie Mo to the kids ever since. "Is it true we're going to be on the telly?"

"On the *telly?* Oh, dear, you've been hanging around the Irish too long, me lad!" she teased. "Yes, of course, if you wish, you'll be on the telly."

"Cool!" Molly told her.

"Cool!" Shannon repeated, wide-eyed.

"Oh, yes, all the kids at the preschool will be talking!" Moira said, ruffling her nieces' hair. Brian was almost a Mini-Me of her brother, with his hazel eyes and deep auburn hair. The girls had acquired their mother's soft true-blond hair and huge blue eyes. Leave it to Patrick. They were wonderful children, well-behaved without being timid, full of personality and love. Chalk that all up to Siobhan, Moira thought. Her sister-in-law was a doll. Patrick…well, as Granny Jon had once said, he could fall into a mire of cow dung and come up smelling like roses. She adored her brother, of course. She just wished he didn't manage to go his own way all the time and still wind up appearing to be the perfect child on every occasion. He should have been a politician. Maybe he would be one day. He'd gotten his law degree and now practiced in a tiny town in western Massachusetts, where he also owned land, kept horses and a few farm animals and still maintained a home that always seemed as beautifully kept as something out of *Architectural Digest*. Business frequently brought him to Boston, where, naturally, he always stopped in to see his parents.

Her brother had married well, she decided. She knew Siobhan, née O'Malley, had taken a chance with Patrick after his wild days in high school, but apparently the chance had paid off. They both seemed happy and still, after ten years of marriage, deeply in love.

"Cool, cool, cool, Auntie Mo!" Shannon repeated.

"Cool. I like that. Good American slang term," Moira said seriously.

Her mother let out a tsking sound. "Now, Moira, if you can't hold on to a few traditions..."

"Mum! I adore tradition," she said.

"And you, you little leprechauns!" Katy chastised the children. "It's nearly nine. You're supposed to be asleep now. You've gotten to see Auntie Mo, now back in bed."

"Ah, Nana K!" Brian protested.

"I'll not have your mother telling me I can't handle her poppets in my old age," Katy said. "'Tis back in bed with you. Off now."

"Wait! I'll take full responsibility! One more hug each," Moira said. The girls giggled; Brian was more serious. She kissed their cheeks, hugged them tightly one more time.

"Auntie Mo has to go down and see your father—and Granda," Katy said. "Besides, she'll be here for the week, like the lot o' you. And she's promised to get you on the telly, so you'll be needing your sleep."

Brian nodded seriously.

"We don't want bags under your eyes," Moira teased, then winked. Brian's lips twitched in a smile, and he gave his grandmother a rueful glance. "And," she added, "I have presents for all three of you. So if you go back to bed right now, you'll get them first thing when I see you in the morning," she promised.

"Presents?" Molly said happily.

"One apiece!" Moira said, laughing. "Now, like Granny Katy has told you, back off to bed! And sound asleep. Or the Auntie Mo fairy—just like Santa and the tooth fairy—will know that you've been awake, and no present beside the teacup in the morning!"

Her mother gazed at her and rolled her eyes. Moira grimaced, then laughed.

"Night, Auntie Mo," Brian said. "Come on, girls." He led them toward the bedrooms.

Molly tugged on his hand and stopped him. "Granny Jon," she said seriously. "There aren't really any banshees around tonight, are there?"

"Not a one," Granny Jon said.

"No monsters at all!" Brian said firmly.

"Not in this house! I'll see to it. I'm as mean as any old banshee," Granny Jon said, her eyes alight.

The kids called good-night again and went traipsing off down the hall. Moira rose and stared at her grandmother sternly. "Now, have you been telling tales again?"

"Not on your life! They spent the day watching 'Darby O'Gill and the Little People.' I'm entirely innocent," her grandmother protested with a laugh. "And you, young lady, you'd best get downstairs to the pub. Your father will be heartbroken if he hears you've been here all this time and haven't been to give him a hug."

"Patrick, Siobhan and Colleen are down there?" Moira asked.

"Siobhan's off to see her folks, but your brother and

sister are both downstairs," Katy said. "Get along with you."

"Wait, wait, let her have a sip of her tea before they ply her with alcohol," Granny Jon protested, bringing a cup to Moira. Moira thanked her with a quick smile. No one made tea like Granny Jon. Not cold, not scalding. A touch of sugar. Never like syrup, and never bitter.

"It's delicious, Granny Jon," Moira said.

"Then swallow it down and be gone with you," her mother said.

She gulped the tea—grateful that it wasn't scalding.

"I'll put your bag in your room—give me your coat, Moira Kathleen," Katy said. "Take the inside stairs down. You know your father will be behind the bar."

"I'll be rescuing the teacup," Granny Jon said dryly.

Moira slid obediently out of her coat and handed it to her mother. "I'll take my bag, Mum. It's heavy."

"Away with you, I can handle a mite of luggage."

"All right, all right, I'm going. 'So happy you're here, now get out,'" she teased her mother.

"'Tis just your father, girl," Katy protested.

"How is he?" she asked anxiously.

Her mother's smile was the best answer she could have received. "His tests came out well, but he was told that he must come in without fail for a checkup every six months."

"He's working too hard," Moira murmured.

"Well, now, that was my thought, but the doctors say that work is good for a man, and sitting around and getting no exercise is not. So he got all the permission he needed to keep right on running his pub, though the Lord knows, he has able help."

"I'm going down right now to see him."

Her mother nodded, pleased.

Moira gave both her mother and grandmother another kiss, then started through the foyer to the left; there was a little sitting room there, and a spiral staircase that led down to a door at the foot of the stairs that opened to the office and storage space behind the polished oak expanse of the bar, where she would find the rest of her family—and all the mixed emotions that coming home entailed.

3

As soon as she opened the door, Moira could hear the chatter in the bar and the sounds of the band. She groaned inwardly. Blackbird was doing a speeded up number from the Brendan Behan play *The Hostage.*

"Great," she muttered aloud. "They're all toasting the Republic already."

She slipped in, walked through the office and the swinging doors, and saw her father's back. Eamon Kelly was a tall, broad-shouldered man with graying hair that had once been close to a true, luxurious black. Though he was pouring a draft, she sneaked up behind him, winding her arms around his waist. "Hey, Dad," she said softly.

"Moira Kathleen!" he cried, spilling a bit of draft as he set the glass down, spun around and picked her up by the waist. He lifted her high, and she kissed his cheek, quickly protesting his hold, worried about his heart.

"Dad, put me down!" She laughed.

He shook his head, beautiful blue eyes on her. "Now when the day comes that I cannot lift my girl, that will be a sad day indeed!"

"Put me down," she said again, still laughing, "because I feel as if everyone in the pub is looking at me!"

"And why not? Me daughter has come home!"

"You've got another daughter in her—"

"And I've already made quite a spectacle of Colleen, I have. Now it's your turn!"

She managed to regain her footing, then hugged him fiercely again.

"You know the boys at the bar, eh, daughter? Seamus and Liam, Sal Costanza, the Italian here, Sandy O'Connor down there, his wife, Sue—"

"Hello!" Moira called to them all.

"Well, now, I'd be taking a hug and a kiss," Seamus told her.

"And you'd not leave me out!" Liam protested.

"One more for Dad, then I'll come around the bar," she said, holding her father closely to her once again. "Are you supposed to be working this hard?" she asked him softly.

"Ah, now, pouring a draft isn't hard work," he told her. Then he pulled back and frowned. "And you, did you fly in alone?"

She smiled. "Dad, I live and work in New York City. I travel all over the country."

"But there's usually someone with you."

Puzzled, Moira shook her head. "I took a cab to the airport, got on a plane, then took a cab here."

"Boston's not the safest city in the world these days," Liam said. Moira noted that he and Seamus had a newspaper spread out between them at the bar.

"I don't think it's ever been crime free," Moira said lightly. "No major metropolis goes without crime. That's why you raised intelligent, streetwise children, Dad."

"He's thinking about the girl," Liam told her.

Moira frowned. "What girl?"

"A prostitute found in the river," Seamus said.

"Dead," Liam added sadly.

"Strangled," Seamus finished with sorrowful drama.

She looked at her father, finding the situation sad, as well, but wondering why this news should suddenly make him worried about her. "Dad, I promise you, I haven't taken up the world's oldest profession as a sideline."

He shrugged. "Now, Moira—"

"He's afraid there might be a serial killer in the city," Liam said, shaking his head. "Apparently the woman plied her trade around the hotel and attracted men of means. Therefore, you see, any lovely lass might be a target. But we're not here to get you down, Moira, girl. There are fine things happening as well. Let's look to the good news! We're getting one of the most important politicians in Northern Ireland for our very own Saint Patrick's Day parade. Mr. Jacob Brolin is coming here, right to Boston, can you imagine?"

"Oh?" Moira murmured, afraid to say more. Josh, who hailed from the deep South, had told her about a round table he had attended where men still sat together, engaging in deep and sometimes passionate discussions regarding the American Civil War. Josh was an American history buff. At Kelly's, too, often they relived battles—and the fighting that had eventually led to the Irish Free State and the Republic of Ireland. They drank to the Easter Rebellion solemnly, bemoaning the fate of the freedom fighters executed after the surrender. They argued the strategies of the leaders, they spoke for and against the hero Michael Collins and ripped apart Eamon De Valera, the American-born first president of the Irish Republic. Of course, it always came back to the same thing: if only, from the very beginning, the island had been recognized as one nation—an Irish nation—they would never have had The Troubles that followed. She personally felt rather sorry for Michael Collins. He'd risked his life time and again, devoted himself wholeheartedly to the cause, managed the first true liberation of any of his people, and, in the end, been killed by a faction of his own people for not managing to take the entire island at once.

"Aye, a fine man, this Jacob Brolin," her father said, brightening. "Why, the flyers are out at the front entry, daughter. We're privileged, we are. You ought to know this already.''

She tried to keep quiet, but she couldn't. She shook her head. ''Dad, you'll all have to excuse me if I think that violence against anyone is horrible and if I don't know every move made in a foreign country regarding the hoped-for union of an island nation. You all can dream of a united Ireland, but I'm sorry if I think that bombing innocent people is beyond despicable. I have friends who are English who have no desire to hurt anyone Irish—''

''Why, Moira Kathleen Kelly! I have good Englishmen in here all the time,'' her father said indignantly. ''Englishmen, Scotsmen, Australians, Cornishmen, Welsh and a good helping of our close friends the Canadians, not to mention Mexicans, French, Spanish—''

''And excuse me, but have you forgotten your truly closest friends in Boston? The Italians, naturally. To the Italians! Salute!'' Sal said, smiling, meeting Moira's gaze and winking in his attempt to defuse the argument.

''God, yes, the Italians! Salute!'' Moira said.

''To the Italians!''

The men at the bar were always happy to toast to anyone and everyone.

It did nothing, however, to change the gist of the conversation.

''Moira, you would admire this man Jacob Brolin,'' Seamus said earnestly. ''He's a pacifist, working for the rights of every last man in Northern Ireland. He's arranged social events where all attend; he's worked hard for the downtrodden and poor and he's loved by Orangemen and Catholics alike. There's seldom been so fine and fair a man to reach a position of power.''

Moira let out a long breath, feeling a bit foolish. All she'd wanted was to get everyone off the subject. Instead, she'd nearly created a passionate argument herself.

"Well, then, I'm thrilled that this man is coming to our country, to our city—"

"You'll want him on your program," Seamus said.

"Aye, and then maybe we'll all get to meet him," Liam agreed.

"Well, we'll see," Moira murmured. "We planned on asking Mum to make a traditional Irish meal, tell leprechaun stories, things like that."

"Aye, but you'll want the parade on your show," her father insisted.

"Moira?"

She had seldom been so relieved to hear her name called. She spun around, delighted to see her younger sister, Colleen, coming to her, threading her way through the crowd.

They'd fought like cats and dogs as children, but now Colleen was incredibly dear to her. Her sister was beautiful, Moira's height, with red hair a far softer shade than Moira's deep auburn. She had Granny Jon's hazel eyes and a face of sheer light and beauty. She had been living in Los Angeles for the last two years, to their parents' great dismay. But she had been hired as the lead model for a burgeoning new cosmetics line, and though they were disconsolate that she spent so much time so far away, they were also as proud as it was possible to be. Her face was appearing in magazines across the country.

Colleen hugged her. "When did you get in?"

"Thirty minutes ago. You?"

"Earlier this afternoon. Have you seen Patrick yet?"

"No, but he's down here, right?"

"With the band. Along with Danny."

Moira jerked her head around. She'd heard the band playing since she'd come in, but Jeff Dolan had been doing the singing—she'd heard Jeff play and sing at least a third of her life, and she knew the sound of his voice like the back of her hand. Now she saw that her brother was indeed up with the group, playing bass guitar.

And Danny was there, as well, sitting in for the drummer this time. As if he had known the exact moment she would look his way, he suddenly stared across the room, meeting her eyes.

He smiled slowly. Just a slight curl of his lips. He didn't miss a beat on the drums. *Ah, yes, Moira, love, I'm here.* Was that part of his appeal? The slow grin that could slip into a soul, amber eyes that seemed always to be a bit mocking, and a bit rueful, as well? She tried to stare at him analytically. He was a tall man, which seemed oddly apparent even as he sat behind the drums. His hair, a sandy shade that still carried a hint of red, was perpetually unruly, an annoyance to him when it fell low on his brow, but somehow rakish and sensual to the female gender.

His shoulders, she assured herself, were not as broad as Michael's. Michael was quintessentially tall, dark and handsome. And more. He was decent. Kind, entertaining, courteous and concerned with the well-being of those around him. When she'd first met Michael, right after the Christmas holidays, she'd thought he was definitely appealing, sexy. Then she'd thought he was intelligent, bright and witty. Then she'd started becoming emotionally involved with him. But with Danny...

He had just been there. A whirlwind in her life, coming and going, visiting her folks with his uncle when he'd been young, coming on his own once he'd turned eighteen. He was Patrick's age, three years older than she was, and he'd been someone she'd adored when she'd been ten and he'd been thirteen, the first time he had arrived. He'd come back when she was fourteen, fifteen, sixteen and then eighteen, and it had been that year when she'd realized there was nothing in the world that she wanted as badly as she wanted Dan O'Hara. Maybe he'd resisted at first. He'd just graduated from college with a degree in journalism. He had a passion to write; to change the world, and she was still wet behind the ears, not to mention the fact that she was also the child of his good American friends. So she'd set out to have what she wanted. She was enthralled, in awe, and being with him changed none of that. Neither did it change Danny. He'd told her that he was bad for her, that she was young, that she needed to see the world, know the world. And still, year after year, she had waited, going to school, loving the learning, looking, always looking, hoping for someone who could make her forget Danny was in the world somewhere. Danny, with his passion and, always, a level of energy about him that was electric. She knew that he cared for her; perhaps in his way he loved her. Just not as much as he loved the rest of the world—or at least his precious Ireland. As she'd gotten older, she'd begun to understand him in a way. She was an American, and she loved being an American. And she had her own dreams and aspirations. They weren't meant to be together, but that had never stopped her from wanting him.

But now she had found someone. Michael. She inhaled deeply, forced a casual smile. *So you're here, Danny. Good for you, nice to see you. Now, if you'll excuse me, I have a great life that I'm living....*

She meant to turn away, but Danny's smile deepened as the number ended, and in the midst of the applause, she saw him lean over to whisper to Jeff Dolan and her brother.

"Oh, no," Colleen breathed. "They've seen us together."

"So what?" Moira whispered.

"I said I wouldn't sing until you showed up."

"Colleen!" Moira protested.

"Hey, folks, we've got a special performance for you this evening," Jeff announced over the mike. "The prodigal daughters have returned for Saint Patrick's Day. We're going to get them both up here for a special number in honor of all the Irish in America—and remember, on Saint Patrick's Day, all Americans are a wee bit Irish!''

"Daughters, go on now," Eamon said proudly.

"Come on up, Kelly girls," Jeff said, encouraging them determinedly. "Ladies and gentlemen, a real treat. The Kelly girls. No one can do a rendition of 'Danny Boy' with quite such melodious Irish beauty."

"What do we do?" Colleen whispered. "I can't believe they're doing this to us. I haven't even heard the song in ages."

"Um. Not since the last time we were here," Moira said dryly. "I guess we go up there. We can't hurt Dad."

Danny had instigated this. She knew it. She walked toward Jeff, trying to ignore Danny with casual negligence as she took the mike. "Irish-American melodious beauty," she said, smiling at Jeff and apologizing to the patrons in the pub. "No guarantees, but we'll do our best."

The first strains of the violin brought a sigh from the crowd. Moira reflected briefly that, with this particular audience, she and Colleen could have sung like two crows and sentiment alone would have evoked wild applause. But she did love the song, and she and Colleen had done it together since the Saint Pat's program at church when they had been in grammar school. Her sister's voice harmonized perfectly with hers. They might not have produced the most melodious Irish beauty ever, but they did the song proud. She loved the music. There was a magic to it, to being home, to singing with Colleen...and even in knowing that Daniel O'Hara was playing a soft beat on the drums behind her.

Naturally the crowd went wild when they ended the tune. Of course, here, it was singing to a group of proud relatives. Moira smiled along with Colleen, thanking those who called out compliments. She felt an arm around her, and before she could completely stiffen, she realized it was her brother.

"Patrick, hey." She hugged him.

"What about me?" Jeff protested.

Jeff Dolan looked like a latter day hippie. She gave him a hug and a kiss. Jeff had put himself through the wringer. On drugs, off drugs, politically wild—protesting everything from toxic waste to government spending. He'd survived. Cleaned up. He was still an activist, but one with temperance and vision. At least, she hoped so. She gave him a warm hug, along with the three other regulars, Sean, Peter and the odd man out, Ira, an Israeli.

"Did you notice me back here?" Danny asked her. "Or am I supposed to line up?"

"Danny," she murmured, trying to sound as if missing him was an oversight. She kissed his cheek perfunctorily. "How could anyone ever forget you?"

He grinned, catching her after the kiss, hugging her tightly and planting a kiss firmly on her lips. She escaped his touch as quickly as possible. It was far too easy to underestimate Danny. The quick strength with which he held her belied the lean appearance his height afforded him. Energy always seemed to radiate from Danny. In a flash of time, she felt as if her flesh burned.

"Good to see you, Danny," she murmured.

"Something light, fellows," Jeff instructed the band members.

"'Rosie O'Grady,'" Ira suggested.

Stepping from the stage, Moira looked across the room to the bar—and froze. Josh and Michael were in the pub, standing behind the taps near her father.

They had arrived far earlier than she had anticipated.

Josh had a camera running. Michael was still applauding, meeting her eyes, a sparkle in his. She wasn't sure why, but she felt as if she had been caught off guard. She was irritated with Josh, filming her unaware, and yet warmed by Michael's presence and his never faltering support. She also wondered if Danny, pounding out a new beat, was aware that Josh had arrived with another man. She was sure that he had noticed; Danny always seemed to be aware of what was happening around him. And certainly, since Danny had apparently been there a while, he had spoken with her parents and knew there was a man in her life.

She wasn't given to effusive public demonstrations, but she smiled at Michael and hurried across the room, leaning past a bar stool to give him a welcoming, openmouthed kiss. Very emotional, she thought. And perfectly natural, despite the sound of her father clearing his throat. She hadn't seen Michael in a while. He'd been traveling, making connections, when she'd made the decision to come here for Saint Patrick's Day.

"Beautiful, babe," he said softly.

"Thanks."

"Very nice," Josh agreed.

She gritted her teeth, wondering why she was so irritated with Josh for taping the performance and wondering just how much of it he had captured on camera. Why was she angry? This was the centerpiece of their planned coverage: an Irish pub in America. She was a performer; she was on a show almost every day of her life, vulnerable to criticism and ridicule. Part of the game. But this...

This was her personal life. Danny had kissed her on stage.

An old friend, that was all.

And she herself had opened this can of worms.

She lowered her head, counting for a minute.

Her smile was still forced when she looked at Josh. "Josh, you know my dad. And, Dad, I guess Josh has introduced you to Michael.... I didn't know they'd be arriving so early."

"I did all the introductions," Josh said.

"Great. When did you arrive?" she asked him.

He arched a brow, knowing her well, and noting the

tone of her voice when no one else did. "In time to tape the whole thing," Josh told her.

"You know your partner," Eamon said, making an attempt to speak lightly. She grimaced inwardly, aware that her father was a bit put out that she had greeted a man he had just met with such public affection.

"It was terrific," Josh said, determined to show her that he was amused by her restrained annoyance. "A real demonstration of the diversity of Americana. You'll like it—trust me."

"How did you two manage to get here so early?" she queried.

Michael slipped an arm around her, grinning. He had a terrific smile. Dimples. A square face that still offered a fine bone structure and a strong chin. He was tall, well-built, as gorgeous as usual in a handsome business suit. She loved the aftershave he used. Everything about him was perfect—perfect for her. She knew her own mind and who she should be with.

As long as Michael was there. As long as he stood beside her.

"Josh gave me a call at the hotel and said you'd left already, so he managed to get us on an earlier flight, as well," Michael said. "I met him at the airport, then we came straight here."

"Wonderful," she murmured

"I can tell you're thrilled," Josh teased.

"I like to know when I'm on camera," she said.

"Well, there, then, that's the beauty of it, eh?" Liam chimed in. Her father's cronies never seemed to think that there might be a conversation in which they weren't included. "You're doing a real live Saint Paddy's Day show, me darling, and what's better than a picture of you and your sister singing 'Danny Boy' at home? It was lovely, girl, lovely."

"Thank you, Liam."

"Your nose isn't a-shinin' or anything, Moira Kathleen," Seamus added.

"Thanks, guys, thanks so much," she said softly, and her words were genuine. The men were all sincerity, her true supporters. "Dad, I think I'll take Michael up to meet Mum—"

"Aye, daughter, don't be a' leaving me now! The place is getting busy. Come back here and give your old man a hand."

"Colleen—"

"Now, do you see your sister? She's escaped somehow."

"I'll take Michael up to meet your mother and Granny Jon," Josh volunteered cheerfully.

She tried to skewer him with her eyes.

Michael looked at her with a rueful smile and a shrug, his countenance assuring her that he totally understood her situation. "I'll be fine with Josh."

"Be prepared for strong tea," she warned him, walking around the bar to join her father.

He caught her hands and whispered softly, "Save those kisses for later. Maybe at the hotel—after pub hours? Totally discreetly, of course," he teased, his eyes rolling. "I don't want your father hating me before he gets to know me."

"Just make sure he knows your family is Irish. He'll love you," she whispered.

"Come on, Michael," Josh said. "I'll show you the back way."

As Josh brushed by Moira, she caught his arm and hissed at him. "Just you wait! See if I ever baby-sit again."

"Turning coward on me now, are you, Moira Kathleen?" he teased. "Sorry, kid, face this den of lions yourself. Or is it only one lion that frightens you?"

With that, he was gone, leading Michael behind the office and storeroom to show him the stairs.

"Bastard," she muttered.

"You don't mean me, do you, Moira Kathleen?"

She spun around. She should have known that Dan O'Hara had joined her behind the bar. He wore his distinctive brand of aftershave. She should have felt him there, next to her, helping himself to a beer from the tap.

"Does it fit?" she inquired sweetly.

He didn't respond, just drank deeply and looked her up and down. "Maybe it does," he said at last, with a casual shrug. "You're looking quite the sophisticated lady. Lovely, as usual."

"Thank you so much."

"Work is good?"

"Wonderful. And you? Stirring up strife and rebellion, as usual?"

"Ah, now, my weapon, if I have one, is the pen, you know. Or the computer, these days."

"Whatever."

"You never understood me, love."

"I think I understood enough."

He leaned against the bar next to her. Too close. "You need to spend time with me, Moira."

"Can't, this trip. Sorry, I'm in love."

"Ah, yes, with perfect Michael."

"He's quite wonderful, really."

"As good as me?"

She was surprised to find herself moving closer to him, eyes slightly narrowed. "Better. So damned good, in fact, that it was only my father's presence that kept me from full-fledged sex on the bar."

To her annoyance, he started to laugh.

"I'm so glad I always amuse you."

He shook his head, sobering. "Sorry. It's just

that...well, if he were that good, you wouldn't have felt the need to tell me.''

She straightened, staring at him with all the cool dignity with which she could cloak herself. "No, no, it's different this time. Sure there were those years when I just hopped from man to man, affair to affair, my heart bleeding for you, but things change. Now I'm in love.''

"Sure you are. And like hell you hopped from man to man. You want a dossier on a man before you go to dinner with him.''

She turned, clearing away empty glasses. "Things change, your ego doesn't. Did you really think you were the only man who ever made me happy and fulfilled?''

She was surprised at the seriousness with which he spoke. "I didn't think I could ever make you happy, and that's why I never stayed,'' he said. His tone changed instantly, so that she thought she might have imagined the strange passion in his first comment. "Now, as to the fulfilled part...come see me. I understand the love of your life travels all the time, as well. On your business, of course, but still... I'll be just down here, right in ye olde guest quarters, for the next few days. Come see me when you admit to yourself that it's exactly what you want to do.''

He tipped an imaginary hat to her and started around the bar.

"That will be a freezing day in hell, Danny boy,'' she called softly after him.

She couldn't see his face as he left her, but she thought she saw his shoulders shaking slightly.

He was laughing.

He stopped, suddenly and came back to her, leaning against the bar. "A freezing day in hell before you admit it—or before you do it?'' he asked.

She didn't respond fast enough.

"I feel a chill coming on,'' he said softly, and once

again turned to thread his way through the crowd and head for the stage.

This time, he didn't turn back.

She was tempted to throw a glass.

Is it only one lion that frightens you?

Josh's words came back to haunt her. She wasn't frightened, she was furious. And she was furious because... Because she was afraid of lions. Or at least... One lion.

Yet, turning to look at that lion, she realized he wasn't looking at her. Danny was playing the drums again, apparently enjoying his time with the band. His interest seemed to be totally on the task at hand.

Yet when he looked up, she got the sense that he was watching the room. Not casually. It was as if he was looking for something, or someone, in particular.

Moira looked around. The room had gotten busy. Couples, nine-to-fivers easing down after work, the old crowd at the bar, a few loners at tables. One man alone, in a casual suit, sitting at a table in the far corner. Business traveler, probably.

Everyone seemed as ordinary as ever.

So just who was Danny looking for?

Josh's word flitted through her mind again.

Lions.

That was it. Danny was watching the room like a lion. Lying in the sun. Tail twitching. Calculating. Watching...

As if he could spring into action at any moment. She couldn't help but wonder, just what prey was Danny watching?

Strangely, she felt a sense of fear. As if something near and dear to her was somehow being threatened.

She turned to a man at the bar who had asked her for something, determined then to shake her feelings. It was Danny doing this to her, damn him.

Just Danny.

4

Surprisingly, it turned into a very nice night.

Michael and Josh returned to the bar after having tea with her mother and grandmother. Josh was happy; he had spoken to his wife, who was coming up with the babies the next day. Michael had looked in on her nieces and nephew as they slept and insisted on telling her just how adorable they were, as if she didn't know that already. That always sat well with her. Love me, love my dog, she realized. She didn't have a dog, but the same thought applied. She might be a bit wary of her family, but she did take tremendous pride in them, and she couldn't help but be pleased that Michael seemed to be fitting in so well.

He really was wonderful. He got behind the bar for a while. He chatted with her dad's friends as if he had known them all his life. He had a conversation with Patrick regarding a group of Americans that was forming to support Irish orphans and provide scholarships for those, Protestant and Catholic, who were of college age and had lost their parents through natural causes or violent events.

He was amazing.

She smiled at him across the bar at one point, hoping that he could sense what she was thinking.

At last it came time for Kelly's Pub to close. The band stopped, and the last of the customers, the old-timers, departed. She was wiping down the bar when she felt Danny behind her. This time she knew he was there before he spoke. "You've not introduced me to the new love of your life, Moira," he murmured.

"Oh, really? Imagine that—and when I've seen so much of you, too."

"I've been playing hard, all for the good of the cause," he said softly.

"Don't even use the word 'cause' near me, Daniel O'Hara," she said, voice lowered.

"Moira, it's just an innocent word," he said, amused.

Michael was walking toward her, a bulwark against this thorn in her side.

"Here he comes. So you get to meet him," she said softly. "There you are, Michael," she said in a normal tone, dropping her bar rag and walking toward Michael to slip an arm around him. He hugged her back. She gave him an adoring gaze, then pretended to realize that, oh, yes, Danny, an old friend, was standing there. "Dan O'Hara, Michael McLean. Michael's working with us as an associate producer and locations manager," Moira said.

Michael, smiling, stretched out his right hand to shake Danny's. His left arm remained around Moira's shoulder. "I hope I'm a lot more than that," he said ruefully. "Dan O'Hara, it's nice to meet you. I understand you're an old family friend."

"Oh, much more than that," Danny said lightly. "A pleasure to meet you, too, Michael McLean. If I can be of any assistance while you're in the city, please don't hesitate."

"An Irishman who knows Boston so well?" Michael said.

"My home away from home," Danny said.

"He's a citizen of the world," Moira's father announced, joining them and throwing an arm around Danny. "We're about to close up the place, Moira Kathleen. And if you've such a busy workload tomorrow, perhaps your friends should get on to their hotel rooms."

"Moira, are you coming back with us for a while? Check out what we've done with the scheduling?" Michael asked. His voice was all innocence; after all, her father was standing there.

Moira was determined, under Danny's watchful eye, to say yes and to say it with enthusiasm. But before she could open her mouth, her father was speaking.

"Ah, daughter, not tonight. Please, don't be going out on the streets tonight."

"Dad, I'm not going far. Just over to the Copley."

"It's late."

"Dad..."

"They've just found that poor girl's body."

"Dad, I'm as disturbed as you are about the murder, but I'm not going out soliciting—"

"Moira Kathleen! It's the hour. And what makes you think the innocent are less likely than the sinners to be harmed?"

"She may not have been a sinner. She might have just been trying to get by," Moira told her father, then wondered why she was arguing the point.

"Moira, perhaps your dad is right. It's very late, and it's your first night home," Michael said. His eyes spoke his regret, but it made her happy that once again he was trying to make everything work with her family. That kind of attitude meant that they were in it for the long haul.

"All right, it is late," Moira said. "I'll see you in the morning," she told Michael. She stood on tiptoe to give him a kiss good-night. He smelled good, she thought. The texture of his jacket was nice against her hands. *I really do care about this man,* she thought. *He's handsome, sexy and so much more. Solid, decent, confident, exciting.*

"Girl, he's leaving for the night, not the millennium," her father said with a soft sigh.

She laughed, letting go of Michael. She gave Josh a kiss

on the cheek. "You two be careful going back to the hotel."

"We'll be fine," Josh assured her.

They both bade her father and Danny good-night, and she walked them to the door of the pub, catching Michael's scarf to stop him after the men had donned their coats and kissing him one last time.

"Well, it's about all done," her father said when the door had closed. "You go to bed, Moira Kathleen, and Dan and I will finish up here."

"No, Dad, I'm home tonight. You go up to bed and get some rest. I think you're supposed to be resting far more than you are."

"If a man stops working, he stops moving, and it's all over after that," Eamon said, shaking his head.

"Dad, I'm here, safe and sound in the house, and it won't hurt you to go to bed this one night," she insisted. She made a mental note to have a long talk with her mother. Kelly's was open every day of the week. Eamon employed good people, but he had a tendency to make his business a very personal affair, and she was sure he let his work put too much strain on him.

"Well, then, fine. Tonight you and Danny can pick up the slack for the old man," he told her, winking.

He pulled her to him, giving her a strong, fierce hug once again and kissing the top of her head. "Love you, girl, that I do," he said, a husky timbre to his voice.

"You, too, Dad. Now get up to bed. You've got a full house tonight."

"Aye, but I've a sainted mother, who puts up with everything and manages a house like the best of construction foremen. Aye, she's a rough taskmaster, that one," he said. "Good night, Moira, and, Danny, see that she gets up to bed soon herself."

"That I will, Eamon," Danny assured him.

As her father headed for the inner stairway, Moira

walked to the bar. There were only a few glasses still sitting out and the beautiful old bar to be wiped down. The place had been a tavern in colonial days, and the bar was several hundred years old. She had always loved it and loved the sense of history she felt when wiping it down.

Danny checked the door to the street, making sure it was locked, then walked to where she was cleaning. He leaned against the bar, his eyes sparkling as he looked at her.

"I believe you're supposed to be working with me," she told him, not looking up from her task.

He shrugged. "You shouldn't be dating him, you know."

Moira didn't stop wiping the polished wood of the bar. She forced Danny to move an elbow.

"You're listening to me, love, and we both know it," he said, leaning against the wood once again. "You shouldn't be dating him."

"Oh?" she said, staring at him, surprised to find that the amusement had left his eyes. "And why not? Because you've decided to grace us with a visit?"

"No, not because of me at all."

"Why, then?"

"He has beady eyes."

"Beady eyes?"

"Dangerous eyes."

"Dangerous eyes? Well, how lovely. How wonderfully exciting—and sexy. I hadn't realized just how much Michael has to offer."

"You should have married Josh. Now there's a good fellow, and safe."

Moira took up scrubbing the perfectly clean bar once again. "Now that will be great for Josh's ego—you calling him safe."

"What? A man doesn't want to be dependable and safe?"

Moira sighed deeply. "I don't know, Danny, you'd have to answer that one. Have you ever been dependable—or safe?"

"As dependable as a rock."

"A rock that skips all over the place."

He shrugged. "I love the United States. I was born in Ireland. That creates a divided heart, you know."

"I read somewhere the other day that there are far more Irish in America than there are in Ireland."

"Are you asking me to move here permanently?" he queried.

"I'm merely informing you that since you seemed beguiled into coming to the States time and time again, you might want to consider immigration."

"If I did, would you put a cease and desist on the fellow with the beady eyes?"

"No. And please, get going, grab those glasses and get them washed. I want to go up to bed."

"Ah, now, was that an invitation? In your father's house? Moira Kelly!"

"That was definitely not an invitation. What are you doing here now, anyway? Shouldn't you be at home celebrating Saint Patrick's Day?"

"I'm visiting old friends," he said.

"Don't you have any friends in Ireland who need to be visited?"

"All over the island. I wanted to be here."

"Why? Will you be preaching to the Americans again? Do you have a new book out? All about the imperialism of the English and how the entire world should just stop whatever else it's doing and force the unification of Ireland?"

He arched a brow. "That's a rather biased way of seeing the situation—and me."

"Oh, I agree, but isn't it *your* way of seeing it?"

"No, not at all. I think you've mixed up a bit of personal

resentment with logical judgment. I was never a fire starter.
I never claimed to have all the answers, and I don't begin
to claim to have them now. You're American, right? You
do insist that everyone knows that all the time.''

"I *am* an American. I was born here.''

"Okay, so you're first generation. The 'English' in
Northern Ireland have been there a much longer time. Centuries, for some families. The difficulties are easy to see.
For so many centuries, the Irish people were reduced to
second-class citizens in their own country. The English,
the Protestants, had the power and the money, and vicious
hatreds have been inbred into the people. But what to do
now...well, that's a very difficult question. In my mind,
there has to be a reconciliation between the people there
themselves, and only then can you ever have a united Ireland.''

She stopped and stared at him. "You think that one
morning all the people in Northern Ireland are going to
wake up and say, 'Hey, this whole thing has been ridiculous, let's just get on with each other'?''

"Things have been much better in the last ten years or
so,'' he told her.

"Danny, I watched you speak once, after your first book
was published, and your talk was about ancient history and
all the wars the Irish have fought.''

"I was young then, but you never heard me suggest that
there was an easy solution, or that anyone should take up
arms against anyone else. Yes, I was a student of Irish
history, from the Tuath de Danaan to the Easter Rebellion
and beyond, and in the middle of trying to decipher how
such a mess between people came about, I discovered I
loved both writing and speaking. I hope I'm not quite the
total ham I was as a very young man, but I still love to
lecture. Especially to Irish Americans. But never about taking up arms. You should know that about me.''

"Danny, you know what? I don't know you, or anything

about you, anymore. I probably *never* knew you. But I *am* an American. And I deplore violence no matter what.''

"You haven't been listening to me. What do you think I'm about? Carrying an Uzi in the street?"

"I just told you, I don't know. And I don't care. I'm American to the bone, and we have enough of our own problems in this country. I'm going to bed. Good night. Finish up the glasses, since you told my father you were going to help.''

She headed for the winding stairs to the house.

"Moira.''

"What?'' She stopped. At first she didn't turn around, but held still, her shoulders stiff. At last she turned to face him. "What?'' she repeated.

"You do know me. Deep inside, you do know me.''

"Great. Good night.''

"I'm still your friend. Whether you know it or not. And here's a friendly warning. Watch out for men with beady eyes.''

"Michael has beautiful eyes.''

"Beautiful? If you say so. Rather hard for me to tell. So okay, beautiful, if you insist, but still beady.''

She sighed with impatience. "Good night, Danny.''

"Good night, Moira.''

As she started up the stairs, she could hear the clink of glasses. She hurried to her home above the pub and quickly locked the door at the top of the stairs.

The house was very quiet. Down the hallway, all the bedroom doors were closed. Her parents had taken Patrick's old room and given him and Siobhan the master bedroom, with the little nursery off it for the kids, Brian happily taking possession of the air mattress. She had offered to sleep with Colleen, so the children could have her room and her parents could stay in theirs, or to take a room at the Copley with the rest of her crew, but her parents had wanted no part of that. They were too happy just to have their family together. Their children, their grandchildren and Siobhan, whom they loved like a daughter.

She hadn't seen her sister-in-law yet, she thought. Unusual. Siobhan had gone to visit her folks, but it was odd that she hadn't taken the children or come into the pub when she returned.

Moira passed the master bedroom as she headed for her room. She had nearly reached her door when she was startled to hear the sound of voices. Muffled, low, angry voices. One masculine, one feminine. Obviously her brother and sister-in-law.

"Oh, Christ, Siobhan, get off it!"

Then Siobhan's voice, so low that Moira couldn't catch the words.

"I'm not involved in anything."

Siobhan again, still too soft to hear.

"No, it's not going to lead to anything else. It's a cause for children, for God's sake!"

Siobhan must have spoken, though Moira didn't even hear her voice.

"Baby, baby, please, believe me, believe in me...."

His voice trailed off. A few seconds later, she heard her parents' old bed squeak.

Standing alone in the hallway, she flushed so hotly that she felt her face flame. Great. First she'd been standing there eavesdropping on her brother and sister-in-law, and now she was listening to them have sex.

"At least someone is getting some."

She jumped and almost screamed at the sound of her sister's soft whisper.

"Colleen," she managed to say.

Colleen covered a giggle, dragging her down the hall.

"I didn't even hear your door open," Moira said.

"I wasn't in my room. I was on the phone."

"The phone?"

"It's only eleven in California."

"Business at eleven?" Moira asked.

Colleen waved a hand in the air.

"A guy. A new guy, nothing deep or heavy or anything like that. I mean, I wouldn't crawl all over him in Dad's own pub in front of Dad the way you did with your Michael tonight."

"Do you crawl all over him when Dad isn't around?"

Colleen laughed. "What have you become suddenly? The moral conscience of the family?" she said teasingly.

"I didn't mean to be eavesdropping. I just...I heard voices on the way to my room."

"Voices, yeah, right."

"Seriously, Colleen, they were arguing. And I really didn't mean to listen."

"But since you did, you're about to ask me if I know if anything is wrong between them."

"Well?"

"Not that I know about. But I just came in today, too. Speaking of which, should we make tea? No, no, way too late, and you're here working, right? We'll have to talk tomorrow. I'm dying to hear. He's good-looking—your Michael, that is. Tall, broad-shouldered. Big feet. And you know what they say about men with big feet."

"That's an old wives' tale."

"I'm sorry to hear that."

"Damn it, Colleen, what about asking me how the show is going, what's coming up next—"

"I watch television, and the show is doing just fine. And if I had anything good to tell you, I'd give you all the juicy details."

"More so than I'd need to know," Moira agreed.

"I was wondering, with Danny here and all..."

"Danny has nothing to do with anything."

"Oh, you liar."

"He's an old friend."

"Come on, big sister, your nose will grow," Colleen

warned her. "The heat waves used to bounce off you two. And tonight...it was like one of those static electricity things. Wow, come to think of it, I don't envy you. Tall, dark and handsome on the one side, wild wicked past with the bad boy of Eire on the other."

"Colleen, be quiet, will you? Mum and Dad never knew—"

"They're Catholic, Moira, not stupid. And not even a deaf, dumb and blind female would be immune to Mr. Daniel O'Hara. I think he's as tall, or maybe taller, than your new love. Hmm. Taut muscles, great buns. Wow, choices, choices, kid."

"Danny is ancient history, Colleen."

"Sure he is," Colleen said skeptically.

"You just said that Michael—"

"Yeah, he's pretty damn perfect. Great voice. But then again, Danny's got that wee touch of an accent...."

Moira groaned. "This coming home thing isn't easy. I expect to be tortured by my parents, but you're worse than they are."

"I'm your sister, the only one you've got, and you're supposed to thank Mum and Dad daily for giving you a sister," Colleen informed her.

"I get that speech, too. But enough about me. What about this guy in California? What's his name? Is he tall? Big feet? You can check out that anatomy equation for yourself."

"His name is Chad Storm, and yes, he's tall."

"Chad Storm?" Moira rolled her eyes. "Is he an actor? Couldn't he have made up a better name?"

"He's a graphic arts designer, and he didn't make up the name, it's the one he was born with," Colleen said indignantly.

"Shush! We're going to wake up the house."

"All right, all right, we don't want our cherubic little rug rats waking up. Patrick and Siobhan will kill us. I

mean...well, they'd really kill us! I'm going to bed, and
I'll let you get your beauty rest. But tomorrow I want
details. Down and dirty, graphic and—"

"Go to bed, Colleen."

"You're going to confess all, you know."

"Good night, Colleen."

"Yeah, yeah, good night." They exchanged a warm,
brief hug and started down the long corridor to their doors,
opposite one another at the end of the hallway.

As they passed the master bedroom, they could still hear
the bed creaking. They looked at one another, burst into
laughter and quickly slipped into their own rooms.

Daniel thoughtfully dried the last of the glasses and
glanced at the nineteenth-century clock at the rear of the
bar.

Nearly two. He'd taken his time picking up the place,
feeling distracted and wounded. Tense night. Naturally.
Here he was, closing in on Saint Patrick's Day.

He'd scoured a number of the pubs in the city, learning
what he could, watching, always watching.

Just as he was probably being watched himself.

He would keep watching, too. He'd seen the man who
had sat by himself at the rear table before. The man wasn't
all that good at what he did. A man came into a pub and
interacted if he wanted to go unnoticed. Still, Daniel was
convinced that the man he was looking for was going to
be someone he had never seen before. Someone who
shouldn't know him, either.

Unless, of course, it turned out to be Patrick.

"You're slowing down, boy," he told himself, setting
the last glass on the wooden ledge behind the bar. Maybe
he hadn't taken so long. The pub had stayed open late that
night.

Kelly's didn't always keep the doors open until one,
though sometimes, on a Saturday night, the pub was

known to be open until two. It all depended on the clientele. On what was happening. The kitchen closed at ten, but if a hungry soul wandered in after that hour, someone could usually be found to scrounge up some food. Kelly's never changed. From the time Daniel had been little more than a kid, he'd been coming here. Eamon was a good man. A hard worker and a lover of mankind. No harm should ever come to Eamon or anyone in his family.

The phone began to ring. Danny picked it up. "Kelly's," he said automatically. Then his fingers tensed around the receiver.

"Kelly's," he repeated. He hesitated, then added, "Where Blackbird plays."

"Blackbird?" a deep-throated, husky voice inquired. Male or female?

"Yes, Blackbird," he said firmly.

"I—" the caller began, then, "wrong number," the voice uttered harshly. And that was it.

The line went dead. Not the wrong number, he wanted to shout.

Then he heard a slight clicking sound.

The phone had been answered by someone upstairs, as well. Had the caller paused because two people had answered? He hit star sixty-nine on the phone. The number came up as unavailable.

With a sudden fury, he hurled the rag he'd been using across the bar. He shook his head and, gritting his teeth, opted for a shot of whiskey before bed. He swallowed it in a gulp. Damn, but it burned.

He walked through the office and storeroom to the stairs leading to the home above. At the top, he checked the door. Locked.

In the bar, he suddenly bolted out the front and ran to the side, taking the stairs two at the time. The outside door to the residence was also firmly locked, although anyone with a real intent to get in and a talent for breaking and entering could jimmy the bolts.

He went down the stairs, into the pub, to his allotted room. He took a hot shower, then slid beneath the sheets and comforter. He flicked on the telly. CNN. The world was in bad shape. Violence flaring in the Middle East. In Eastern Europe, a terrible train wreck, the fault of an antiquated switching system. The weather taking a gruesome toll in South America.

Then the news reporter, who had just given a grim tale regarding flooding in Venezuela, put a smile on her face and began talking about Saint Patrick's Day. She showed a cheery scene in Dublin, crowds in New York, then a brief interview with the Belfast politician, hailed worldwide, who was en route to Boston to help celebrate with the Boston Irish.

The news continued. Dan stared at the picture on the screen but didn't hear much more.

It was a very long time before he slept.

5

The house seemed quiet when Moira left her bedroom the following morning. She saw that Colleen was just ahead of her, walking down the hall to the kitchen.

She followed her sister. "Good morning," she murmured, as they entered the kitchen together. Her mother had evidently been up already; coffee had been brewed in the automatic coffeemaker, and a pot of tea sat on the big kitchen table, as well. Her brother was up, sitting at the table, sipping coffee, reading the newspaper.

"Top o' the morning to you," Colleen returned, eyes rolling as she turned them on Patrick. "And you, brother, dear. You're looking well-rested for a man who spent half the night playing—"

"With the band." Moira interrupted in horror, amazed that Colleen would make any reference to the fact that they'd been outside his door the previous night. She slid into her old chair at the table and cast Colleen a warning glare.

"Playing with the band," Colleen repeated. "That's exactly what I was saying," she continued, glaring at Moira, eyes wide with innocence and mock indignation.

Moira felt like hell. She hadn't fallen asleep until three or four. And then, perhaps out of force of habit, she'd found herself wide awake and unable to pound her pillow into any semblance of comfort when she'd realized she didn't have to be awake so early this morning. She did have things to do, of course. Michael and Josh had done their work well. Permits to tape the parade and the goings-on in various areas of the city had been procured. But she needed a plan of action, and she needed to pretend that she had been on it from the moment she had hung up after talking to her mother and making the decision to come to Boston.

Patrick looked at them both, slightly puzzled. "I feel just fine, thanks. Colleen, you look all right, but Moira...hmm. Trust me, you don't look as bad as you sound. Wouldn't do, would it? Can't have bags beneath your eyes that stretch to your chin when you're on camera, now, can you?"

"Great. How come Colleen looks all right but I merely look better than you think I feel?" Moira asked him.

Patrick grinned. "You've had this shell-shocked look since you arrived," he told Moira.

"Has she?" Pouring coffee, Colleen turned to study Moira.

"If you're going to turn that cup-filling ritual into a day long event, perhaps you could let me go first," Moira said.

"Give her the coffee—she needs it," Patrick said.

Moira glared at her brother. "How come you're saying that?"

"I heard you tossing around all night."

"Me!" Moira protested. She stared at Colleen, and suddenly she couldn't help it; she burst into laughter, and Colleen followed suit.

"What's the inside joke?" Patrick asked, eyes narrowing as he looked from one of them to the other.

"Well, we were trying to be discreet..." Colleen began.

"But honest to God, surely, that old bed frame hasn't created such a noise since...well, probably since Colleen was conceived," Moira said.

Patrick's heritage was instantly visible as his cheeks flamed a brilliant shade of red.

"You two are full of it," Patrick managed to sputter. "How rude. I mean, this is our parents' house...."

"Hey, we're not chastising you," Colleen said, retrieving the coffeepot from Moira.

"No, we're simply happy—"

"For you both, of course," Colleen interrupted.

"That after all your years of marriage," Moira continued.

"And at your ripe old age," Colleen added.

"You can still get it up, that's all," Moira finished.

Patrick set his cup down, shaking his head, eyes lowered. Then he stared at them both across the table. "Well, all that from the woman who nearly attacked a stranger in the bar last night."

"Michael's not a stranger," Moira protested.

"Hey, we've never met him before."

"I know him very well."

"Apparently so. What, you met him after the Christmas holidays? That doesn't exactly make you eligible for a diamond anniversary band."

"Cute," she told Patrick.

"Well, she probably only did it because of Danny," Colleen said, yawning.

Moira glared at her sister. "Hey, whose side are you on here?"

Colleen instantly looked sheepish. "Sorry."

"You're not supposed to be taking sides against me to begin with," Patrick protested.

"Ah, now, are the girls beating up on you again, Patrick?" their mother asked, sweeping into the kitchen from the hallway. "Shame on you, the both of you. Now, don't I spend half my life reminding you that—"

"That we're all the greatest gifts you ever gave to any one of us," the three of them said in unison, creating an outbreak of laughter around the table.

Katy shook her head. "One day you'll know the truth

of it. When the world is against you, when friends have failed you, you always have your family.''

''Oh, Mum,'' Moira said, rising and walking to her brother to give his shoulders a hug—and his arm a pinch. ''I adore my big brother. Honestly.''

''And me, too, of course,'' Colleen said.

''And you, Patrick?'' Katy demanded of him firmly.

''And me?'' Patrick asked, grinning at Moira. ''Why, my sisters are the light of my life. Though there is that other person. My wife. Oh, and my kids, bless the little demons. My life is just one big radiant ray of light.''

''Enough of that,'' Katy said with a grin. ''Moira, move back a bit. Patrick, scooch in your chair. The children are awake—they'll be out for breakfast any minute now. Let me get the eggs going. Girls, would you give me a hand?''

''Girls?'' Colleen asked.

''Aye?'' Katy asked, puzzled.

Moira slipped an arm around her mother. ''Mum, what she's saying is that you're being sexist. Patrick can help out just as well.''

''After all, you're cooking for his children.''

''Well, now, Patrick can't help out,'' Katy said.

''And why is that?'' Colleen asked.

''Because he's the most useless human being in a kitchen I've ever seen. Granny Jon says that he's the only person she's ever met who's incapable of boiling a pot of water.''

''He only pretends he can't cook,'' Moira said.

''To get out of the work,'' Colleen explained.

''Now, the lot of you!'' Katy said indignantly.

''Just kidding, Mum,'' Moira said. ''I'll get the bacon.''

''The bottom batch, please. The lean stuff at the top from McDonnell's is for the bacon and cabbage we're having tonight.''

''Bacon and cabbage,'' Moira murmured.

''And colcannon,'' Katy said. ''And some broccoli and

spinach, because they're good for your father's heart. Moira Kathleen, I need the oatmeal, as well. Your dad has taken to getting it down plain every morning, for his cholesterol.''

Moira brought out the requested items from the refrigerator, then got the oatmeal from the cabinet. She looked at her mother. "That's it. We'll cook. For the show, we'll let you take over, and we'll videotape your preparation of the Saint Patrick's Day meal.''

"We're not having bacon and cabbage for Saint Patrick's Day, we'll be having a roast,'' Katy said.

"Mum,'' Moira groaned. "I don't care what we're really having on Saint Patrick's Day. Bacon and cabbage is a traditional Irish meal. It will be a terrific segment for the show.''

"Oh, now, daughter, I'm not good on camera,'' Katy protested.

"Can we put Patrick in an apron?'' Colleen asked hopefully.

"Not on your life,'' Patrick protested.

"Oh, yeah, great. Let him be traditionally Irish by drinking beer and playing with the band,'' Colleen teased.

"You know, it's just one of those things,'' Patrick said. "I can wear a suit well, which is good for an attorney. I look pretty good in hats. Aprons...I just don't seem to have the right build.''

"We won't film you in an apron,'' Moira said. "Since you can't cook, you can do the dishes when we're done.''

"I've got an appointment this morning,'' Patrick protested.

"I bet he just thought it up,'' Colleen said.

"Do you really have an appointment?'' Katy asked him.

Before he could answer, there was a tap on the inner door. Moira felt an inexplicable wave of tension instantly tighten her muscles.

Her mother and sister had turned toward the sound. Only Patrick was looking at her.

"So, it is Danny," he said softly.

"Don't be ridiculous," she murmured. "Should I get it?" she asked her mother.

"No, it's just Danny, at this hour," Katy said. "Come in, Dan!" she called.

"I locked it last night when I came up," Moira said.

"Danny has a key, of course," her mother replied impatiently.

She heard the key twisting in the lock even as her mother spoke.

She wondered why it bothered her so much that he had a key. To her home. No, not *her* home, her *parents'* home.

And he had always been welcome here.

He walked in, freshly showered and scrubbed, as evidenced by the dampness that remained in his combed hair and gleamed on newly shaven cheeks. He was wearing jeans and a gold knit sweater beneath a casual leather jacket. She had to admit that he looked good. A bit of age had given his natural ease a slightly weathered and dignified look. He wasn't as handsome a man as Michael, she thought, almost analytically, and only partially defensively. Michael had classic good looks. Pitch dark hair, striking blue eyes and a clean-cut face. Daniel was craggier. His chin a bit squarer, cheeks leaner, features more jagged. He had good eyes, though. A strange shade of hazel that made them amber at times, almost gold at others. He saw her studying him but only smiled, addressing her mother.

"I could smell Katy Kelly's coffee way down in my room," he told her, slipping his arms around her waist affectionately and kissing her cheek.

"There's a coffeepot behind the bar," Moira said rather sharply. Patrick looked at her. She widened her eyes. "How else would we make Irish coffee?"

"I think we're all aware that there's a coffeepot behind the bar," her brother said.

"I was merely suggesting—" She began.

"Ah, but my coffee would never be as good as Katy's," Danny interrupted.

"And you'd not be wanting to have it alone," Katy said firmly. "You've been up here every morning, and now the girls are here, as well. Naturally you want to spend time together." Katy said the last casually, but sincerely.

"Of course we want to spend time with him. He's like another older brother. A nice one," Colleen teased.

Patrick groaned audibly.

"Just like a brother," Moira said sweetly.

Danny had poured coffee and taken a seat next to Patrick. "Sibling torture this morning, eh?"

"Tell me, would you wear an apron so that your sister could humiliate you on national television?" Patrick asked.

"It's just a cable show," Moira murmured.

"A highly rated cable show," Patrick said. "Well?"

For a moment, as Danny stared at her, Moira thought that his face had hardened strangely with anger. "I don't have a sister," he said.

"But you're just like a nicer older brother," Patrick reminded him.

"Oh, right. Well, what does the apron look like?" Danny asked, and the casual conviviality was back in his voice.

"I'm sure Mum has one with a leprechaun on it somewhere," Colleen said.

"No one has to wear an apron!" Moira protested.

"Right. We'll cook neatly," Danny said.

"I didn't say anyone but Mum needed to be in the show," Moira reminded them.

"That's right. The long-suffering siblings get to wash dishes offstage," Patrick said.

"Hey," Colleen protested, "I've got the kind of face they say can launch a thousand ships."

"Naturally you're invited to cook with us on camera," Moira told her sister.

"Thanks. I'll have to check with my agent."

"Colleen Mary!" Katy said indignantly.

"Just kidding, Mum."

"That *is* a face that could launch a thousand ships—*sis,*" Danny told Colleen. "Congratulations. I'm seeing it more and more every day now."

"Really, Danny?" Colleen asked, her voice a little anxious. For a moment Moira reflected that her sister was really just a nice kid. She was doing exceptionally well, yet she was still amazed that people really thought her looks worthy of attention. She had managed to develop enough confidence to go forward and retain enough humility to remain grounded.

"Really. And I've heard from Patrick and your folks that there's a budding romance in the west?"

"Just budding," Katy said firmly. "So my daughter tells me."

"Absolutely just budding," Colleen said, laughing. "Mum, I'd never get serious without bringing the poor guy home first and making sure he had the stamina for a real relationship."

Patrick looked at his sister without the twitch of a smile. "Um, stamina?"

"He's a nice guy?" Danny asked. "Nothing else would do for my, uh, baby sister."

"The nicest. Hey, you come to California now and then. Maybe you'll be out there soon. I'd love for you to meet him."

"Dan can size him up for you just like that," Patrick told her.

"Colleen has a good head on her shoulders. I'm sure he's a fine fellow," Danny said. "Now, as to Moira..."

"Moira and her Michael," Katy said.

"He's great, Mum, and you know it," Moira said.

"He does seem decent," Patrick acknowledged.

"He's a hunk," Colleen said decisively.

"Beady eyes," Danny said, shaking his head.

"Oh, God, that again," Moira said irritably.

"Well, I think his eyes are fine," Katy said thoughtfully, taking the comment entirely literally.

"Look again—they're beady," Danny said, staring at Moira.

"Fine, I'll take another really good look at the man, Danny," Katy said, setting strips of bacon into a huge frying pan with incredible precision, getting more bacon into the pan than Moira would have thought possible. "But really, he's courteous, and very handsome. And he does adore Moira."

"Yes, I guess he does," Danny said grudgingly.

"A vote of approval at last?" Moira inquired.

"I'm withholding final judgment."

"And he's been so effusive with his comments regarding you," Moira said.

"Really?" Danny asked.

"Actually, no. He hasn't mentioned you at all."

"Well, I'm just an old family friend. Not a real member of the family who he needs to impress."

"But you'll definitely be on top of the guest list for the wedding," Moira said over the rim of her coffee cup.

Her mother gasped. "Moira Kathleen!"

"No, no, no, Mum," she said quickly, with a sigh. She had to watch this sparring with Danny in front of her parents. "We're not planning anything—yet."

"I truly wish you every happiness," Danny said. His eyes were steady on hers; his voice was sincere.

For some reason, that made her more irritated.

Maybe she didn't want him to be happy for her. Yup,

that was it. Completely. She wanted him to be sorry he'd blown everything himself.

"Thanks." She forced herself to speak casually. "Excuse me for a minute, please. I've got to make a phone call and get going on the day. Mum, would you really mind if I taped the preparation of tonight's meal? If it will really make you uncomfortable..."

"No, no, it's all right. I mean, I just don't want to appear...foolish. You'll be with me all the time, right?"

"Of course. And we'll have Colleen and Siobhan and even the kids, if they'd like. It will be fun. Honestly, Mum."

"Maybe."

"No maybe about it," Colleen assured her.

Katy nodded again. Moira started to her room to make a call, just as the kids came scampering out of the master bedroom.

"Auntie Mo!" Brian said.

"Morning, handsome," she told her nephew.

Molly was right behind him. "Auntie Mo, Auntie Mo! Presents!" she said, hurling herself into Moira's arms.

"Molly," Shannon said as she came up behind her sister, very mature at six, "we don't ask for presents."

"It's all right," Moira assured them both quickly. "You can ask your aunt but not other people," she reminded Molly. "But I'm your aunt, and I've promised you a present, so it's okay. I've got to make a call, and then I'll bring the presents out."

"Thanks, Auntie Mo," Brian said.

"Where's your mum? I haven't seen her yet."

"On her way out," Shannon said. "She told me she didn't sleep much last night, and that when you get older, it's harder to wash away the wrinkles."

Moira laughed. "Tell your mum that she doesn't have anything that so much as resembles a wrinkle." She smiled suddenly and couldn't help adding, "Tell her I'm sorry she didn't sleep well."

She slipped past Brian and the girls and went into her room, where she dialed the Copley and asked for Michael. No answer. She asked for Josh's room, and he quickly picked up, telling her they'd just talked to the four-man crew Michael had hired and that they would all be ready to go in about half an hour.

"So what are we doing? I mean, we've flown by the seat of the pants before, but..."

"We're going to tape right here today. Traditional Irish cooking. Come on over whenever you're all ready. Oh! I couldn't reach Michael."

"I talked to him earlier. I'll give his cell a buzz and tell him to be at your place."

Moira hung up, then gathered the presents before starting down the hall to the kitchen. When she got there, she saw that her sister-in-law had preceded her and was talking to her mother at the sink. She turned as Moira came in, smiled broadly and hurried over to her.

Siobhan was a beautiful woman, with long blond hair and deep blue eyes. She looked wonderful, but she also looked tired, really tired. Her slender features were leaner than ever. She was pale, and there was a hint of mauve beneath her eyes, despite her practiced application of makeup.

"Moira, hey!"

"Siobhan, you look terrific," she said, hugging her sister-in-law tightly and wondering if she sounded as if she was lying.

"Thanks, but I feel like hell this morning," Siobhan said with a laugh. "So we're doing a typical, natural, completely unaffected and spontaneous cooking section for your program, hmm?"

"Completely spontaneous," Moira agreed with a laugh. "Even though you'll have to open the door five times so we can get all the right angles on tape, trust me, you'll be completely spontaneous.''

"I was joking. You want me in it, too?''

"Sure, it will be fun. We'll whip up some scones first, so the kids can sit in the dining room and eat them, and then the four of us will do all the stuff in the kitchen. A family thing.''

"A family thing? What about the guys?''

"We'll film them lounging around on the couch, drinking beer, scratching and watching a football game.''

Siobhan laughed. Eamon Kelly, hearing the conversation, instantly protested. "Daughter, how can you say such a thing?''

"Eamon, don't complain,'' Danny said lazily from the kitchen table, where he was playing a game of war with Molly, who was slapping her little hand on the cards on the table with a happy giggle. "Sitting on the couch, drinking beer, watching a game—scratching an itch now and then—sounds like a fine way to spend the day,'' he said.

"Dad, everyone knows that you work like a horse,'' Moira said, ignoring Danny. "You sit on the couch and take it easy.''

"I'll be down seeing to the pub, girl, you know that,'' Eamon told her.

"I'll open for you, Eamon,'' Danny said. "That way you can watch your daughter at work.''

"I really do have an appointment at one,'' Patrick said regretfully.

"Patrick, I thought this was a family vacation,'' Siobhan protested.

"Honey, it's an hour's meeting with an important client,'' Patrick said.

"Auntie Mo!'' Molly suddenly wailed. "Presents!''

"Molly!'' Siobhan was the one to chastise her that time.

"Hey, I promised her a present ten minutes ago. That's

an eternity when you're only four,'' Moira said. ''Molly, catch!''

She tossed one of the wrapped plush leprechauns to Molly, who missed. Danny retrieved the gift from the floor for her, while Moira turned to pass out the gifts for Brian and Shannon. When she was done, she walked over with the music box and set it next to her mother.

Katy looked at her with a question in her eyes.

''It screamed your name,'' Moira explained.

''Moira, it's neither Christmas nor my birthday—''

''Mum, chill,'' Colleen said lightly. ''Just open the gift, let us ooh and aah, and say thank-you to Moira.''

Katy grinned sheepishly, then opened the present almost as quickly as the children. Molly squealed happily over her stuffed toy, and Patrick let out an affirming, ''Oh, wow, cool.''

But Moira was busy watching her mother as she unwrapped the delicate little fairy and her eyes widened with delight.

''Moira, she's breathtaking.''

''She's a music box.''

''What does she play?''

Moira picked up the figure to wind it.

'''Danny Boy,''' Danny said softly before the music began.

Moira turned to stare at him as the rest of the room watched the little fairy dance. He was watching her strangely, she thought. The light in the room reflected off his eyes, making them appear golden and yet oddly shielded.

''How did you know?'' she asked him.

''Lucky guess,'' he said with a shrug. ''Hey—bacon's starting to snap.''

''Mary, Jesus, and Joseph,'' Katy gasped, seeing her pan smoking.

''I've got it, Mum. Go put her on the mantel or wherever

you'd like her,'' Moira said, quickly flipping the breakfast bacon.

"I'll grab the eggs," Colleen said.

"Danny, Patrick, you get the juice," Moira suggested.

"Juice?" Molly said.

"Hey, where's Granny Jon?" Patrick asked.

"I'll see if she's up," Danny volunteered, leaving the kitchen.

Katy left the room with her little treasure but was back quickly. With an efficiency that only appeared to be confusion, breakfast arrived on the table. Danny came in escorting Granny Jon, who was apologizing for oversleeping.

"Everything is under control, Mum," Katy assured her.

"Tea?" Granny Jon asked.

"Strong enough to walk itself across the table," Moira said in unison with not only her brother and sister, but her parents, as well.

Everyone laughed at that except for Granny Jon, who gave them all an indignant sniff as they grouped around the kitchen table. It was big, but there were eleven of them, and they were tightly packed. For a few minutes the conversation centered entirely around such comments as, "Can you pass the salt, please?" and, "Who has the juice?" and, "Oh, no, Molly, that glass is way too full."

As Moira was rescuing the glass from her niece, the doorbell rang. "I'll get it," she said, jumping up. "Must be my crew."

She poured some of the juice from Molly's plastic cup into her glass, set it down, then headed for the door. When she opened it, she saw that Michael had arrived. There was a nip in the air, and she shivered as she felt the chill. Michael didn't seem to notice it. He looked like an ad for Armani, in a long wool coat and black scarf.

"Morning," he said. His voice was nicely husky.

"Good morning. Come in, it's freezing out there."

"The cold is okay, but last night was awfully lonely," he told her.

"I'm sorry," she murmured. "My dad, you know...."

"I've got it perfectly," he said softly. "It's still just a shade, well, you know, lonely." He was looking over her shoulder. She saw that Danny had followed her to the door.

"Michael, good to see you. You must be a man accustomed to the cold, standing around on the porch like that. What's your pleasure, coffee or tea?"

"Coffee," Michael said, moving in as Moira shut the door. He slipped out of his coat, allowing Moira to hang it on the eighteenth-century hall tree, and removed his gloves, meeting Danny's eyes. "Coffee, please. I think I've had six cups this morning, and it still doesn't seem like enough."

"Right you are. One coffee coming up."

Danny turned to get Michael coffee, his attitude as courteous and casually friendly as could be.

"Don't trust him," Moira whispered to Michael.

"Oh?"

She shook her head, leading him into the kitchen.

"Morning, Michael. Bacon and eggs—or oatmeal?" Eamon asked, rising to shake Michael's hand in greeting.

"Nothing, thanks, I grabbed a bite early."

"Michael, you haven't met my sister-in-law, Siobhan, yet," Moira said, introducing the two.

"Hello, Siobhan. A pleasure."

"Very nice to meet you," Siobhan replied, studying him with an open smile.

"Was that bacon and eggs you decided on?" Katy asked.

"I think he said he ate, Mum," Moira said.

"They're only happy, and they'll only love you, if you eat, you know," Danny warned Michael.

"Then bacon and eggs it is," Michael said.

"Now, Dan O'Hara, that's not at all true," Katy protested. "Though surely everything here will be better than at your hotel."

"Oh, I'm positive of that," Michael said. "But, Katy, all this food... And you're just going to clean up and start cooking again so we can film?"

"I'm cooking again because we're planning on having dinner," Katy said. "And I've lots of help."

"Except for me," Patrick said. "Appointment," he explained. "And I want to go by and check on the boat." Besides his wife and children, his one real love in life was his boat. He kept it berthed at the docks in Boston because he loved going out on the open sea, except that it was something he seldom did in winter when the seas were too rough. It was a nice toy, forty-five feet, sleek as a devil, with sleeping facilities for eight people.

Patrick glanced at his watch. "If fact, I've got to get moving. Moira, I'll try to be back in plenty of time to do my part, sitting on the couch, scratching, drinking beer— and doing the dishes, as well. Sweetheart..." He paused by Siobhan's chair to give her cheek a kiss.

She didn't offer him anything more.

"Okay, munchkins," he said to the kids, delivering only slightly distracted kisses to the three of them. "Behave now, okay?"

"The kids are always fine," Eamon said. Moira was curious at his tone. She wondered if her father wasn't a little bit disturbed by her brother's exit.

"Bye, then," Patrick said, taking his coat from the hall tree. Maybe he felt all eyes on him. He turned at the door. "Honest, I'll drink a lot of beer and do a lot of scratching," he said. Moira offered her brother a slightly pained smile. His eyes fell on his wife.

But Siobhan wasn't watching him. Her eyes were purposely lowered as she buttered toast for Molly.

Patrick departed, and Danny cleared his throat. "Well, now, can't let Patrick be the only bad child. I'm off for

some cigarettes. Nasty habit, I know. I'll keep it outside.
Katy, do you need anything while I'm out? Something
traditionally Irish you might be missing for your meal?''

"Now, Danny, you know that between the pub and the
house, we don't often run out of what we need," Katy
said.

"Actually, I think we're a bit low on butter," Colleen
murmured. "The real thing, no margarine."

"Colleen, we can't be making a guest go to the store,"
Katy said.

"Sure we can," Colleen said quickly. "He's not a
guest, he's a big brother, remember?"

"Katy, how much butter?" Danny asked, starting for
the stairs that led out through the pub.

"Better make it two pounds. We've a full house," Katy
said.

"Right," Danny said. "I'll be back soon. I don't want
to miss the fun."

"You told my father you'd open up the pub," Moira
reminded him.

"And so I did. I guess I, like Patrick, will have to do
my share of scratching and guzzling a bit later."

With that he left, but something about his departure
seemed odd to Moira.

Only Michael was still eating. Siobhan rose, picking up
plates from the table. "I'll wash," she said.

"Fine, I'll dry," Colleen added.

"Then I'll get the rest," Moira said, quickly busying
herself with plates and condiments.

"Now, let Michael finish his meal before you go steal-
ing his plate," Eamon told her.

"Right, Dad." As she took her grandmother's plate, she
saw that Granny Jon was looking curiously at the floor.
But she looked at Moira quickly, as if her attention had
never been anywhere else. "The kids drop something?"
Moira asked, ducking.

But the kids hadn't dropped anything.

Granny Jon had been staring at the brand-new pack of cigarettes that lay on the floor beneath the chair where Danny had been sitting.

Patrick hurried down the street, tightening his wool scarf around his neck and hiking up his collar. Having spent the majority of his life in Massachusetts, he was accustomed to weather that could be brutal far into the spring. Stopping at a traffic light, he stomped his feet and spoke aloud to himself. "No wonder the fucking Pilgrims all died," he muttered. He looked up. At least, for the moment, there was no snow. Just a blue sky with puffs of white clouds, fast-moving.

The light changed. He suddenly looked back, struck by an eerie feeling of being followed.

No one on the streets except a kid on a scooter. *Wait till the ice forms toward night, kid, you'll be sorry,* he thought. It was a Saturday morning, still fairly early. Bostonians took some time to get going on Saturdays. Still, it seemed as odd to him that the street was empty as if it had been full.

Why had he thought someone was following him? Nerves? Guilty conscience? Maybe it was just the weather.

He moved quickly, then glanced back again. No one there.

Still, that feeling. Unnerving. As if he heard silent footfalls echoing in his mind.

Someone's breath, whispering at the back of his neck.

Right. And maybe he was being followed by leprechauns, little people in green, trailing along behind him.

And maybe he'd just been home too long, listened to too many stories as his parents and grandmother entertained the kids.

Tales about fairies, mischievous leprechauns...

And then, of course, there were banshees, black shadow

creatures tracking a man, wailing in the night, foretelling his death.

He looked back once again and hesitated, eyes scanning the street.

There were no fairies, no leprechauns or banshees. Both the good and the evil in the world came from men.

He started forward with determination. He had made up his mind, set his course.

He was going to do what he thought was right.

6

Moira was delighted to see that her mother was a natural in front of the camera. After a few minutes of being a little bit nervous about the camera, the lights and the overhead mike, held on a pole above her head by a total stranger, she was just fine. Katy Kelly loved to cook. She warmed to her subject, instructing her daughters and talking about being a little girl in Dublin, how times had changed drastically in a way, and then again, not at all. Somehow, in the midst of cooking, instructing Colleen to keep an eye on the cabbage, Moira to watch the meat and Siobhan to make sure that the mixture of chopped cabbage and onions was properly sauteed for the colcannon, she also got going on the temperament of the Irish people. Too many people thought of Ireland as a divided island, she said, but what they forgot was that over the years everyone had become Irish. Northern Ireland might technically be part of Great Britain, but Eire was a great place whose spirit entered the souls of those who loved her. The Vikings had come and invaded and created terrible havoc, but then many had settled and stayed. The English had begun coming to conquer in the eleven hundreds, but from those ancient invaders had come some of the most well-known Irish surnames of today. Being Irish was more than being born on the island, more than heritage. It was a spirit of warmth, of storytelling, of a special magic, and it was in so many Americans today.

Moira, meeting Josh's eyes at one point, signaled her pleasure with her mother's natural dialogue, as well as her amazement. Josh gave her a thumbs-up and a big smile. It was going to be a good show. Her family was charming. It was all going to work.

Eamon Kelly was beaming with pride at his wife. Watching them both, Moira realized that she was lucky in many ways. So many of her friends had parents who were divorced, had never known what it was like to grow up in a household with both a mother and a father. And her parents weren't together just for the children or any other practical reason. After all these years of marriage, they still loved one another.

Michael and Josh were getting along wonderfully with her family, and the crew was great, too. She watched some of the tape as they reran it, and it was excellent. Katy was pleased, blushing at the congratulations bestowed on her by both her family and the crew. She was like an old pro when Josh asked that she repeat steps over and over again so the cameraman could focus with more detail on exactly how to prepare the meal.

The kids had been taped sitting at the table, but then, not long ago, they had disappeared. While Josh was busy talking about how to edit the segment, Moira wandered into the family room. Granny Jon, who was scheduled to have her moment in the sun discussing, naturally, the elements of a really good cup of tea, was busy with needlework as she waited. She told Moira that the kids were in the pub; they had grown restless, and Danny had returned to entertain them.

"I didn't see him come back," Moira murmured.

"He was careful not to disturb the work, but he told your father he'd open the pub, and so he did, taking the kids down to help set up," Granny Jon said.

"I'll walk down and see how things are going," Moira said.

When she got downstairs, she realized how late it had gotten. The lunch crowd had come and gone. Danny was behind the bar, while Chrissie Dingle, Larry Donovan and a new young waitress, Marty, whom Moira had never met before, worked the floor. Joey Sullivan and Harry Darcy were cooking in the kitchen. Brian, Shannon and Molly were at a table in the corner. When Moira approached them, she discovered that Danny had brought them Irish coloring books. Molly's leprechauns were bright purple instead of green. Moira rather liked them.

"I don't really color like this often, you know," Brian told his aunt gravely. "Uncle Dan asked me to keep an eye on the girls, so I'm watching them."

"And a fine job you're doing," Moira said, and winced. There she went, sounding like her mother or Granny Jon again.

"We had ice cream for lunch," Shannon told her.

"Brrr," Moira said. "Great coloring. You're being little angels. Patrick doesn't deserve you."

Brian frowned at her seeming criticism of his beloved father.

Moira quickly hugged him. "Your daddy is my brother, you know. I love him with all my heart, but you know how you tease the girls sometimes? I like to tease Patrick that way."

Brian smiled, happy again.

"I'll be back," Moira promised.

She walked to the bar, ready to bite the bullet and thank Danny for helping her dad out while they'd been filming. But when she reached the bar, Chrissie was at the taps. Thirty and attractive, Chrissie was also efficient, with a no-nonsense manner.

"Where's Danny?"

"He just walked over to see to the kids," Chrissie said.

When Moira turned around, she saw that not only had Danny gone to sit at the table with the kids, but Michael had come down, as well. They were both there, each with a pint of beer.

"We're going to include your dad in this thing, too, Moira," Michael told her, rising. "He's going to tell us about the Irish beers he has on tap and the Irish whiskies he carries."

"Great idea," she said. "We'll stay entirely away from the political."

"What are you so afraid of, Moira?" Danny inquired, watching her.

There was something about his voice. She should have walked away quickly.

"I'm not afraid of anything, Danny."

"Then why are you so determined to be 'politically correct'?"

"Because I do a friendly little travel show, that's why," she said angrily.

"And we're making sure all the Irish look good," Michael added lightly.

"All the Irish. Well, you know, that's just great," Danny said, his tone equally light. "Let's just pretend that everything is always perfect. That the Irish haven't been trod upon since the time Henry the Second came to power and forced the Irish chieftains to submit to him. And that Henry the Eighth didn't come to power, want a divorce, create his own church, fight the Irish of the established church who couldn't see changing their religion because he wanted a new wife, beat them to a pulp and confiscate the lands of all those who opposed him. And let's just forget about William of Orange and the Battle of the Boyne and the subjugation of the people who had supported the rightful king."

"Dan, those things happened hundreds of years ago," Michael reminded him.

"And the Easter Rebellion, where the leaders of the hoped-for Irish Republic were shot dead, executed *after* they had surrendered.'' Dan was speaking as if he hadn't even heard Michael's words.

Moira was about to speak when Michael answered Danny sharply. ''And let's not forget those leaders who willfully and cold-bloodedly assassinated English public servants in Ireland. And let's not forget the bombs that went off and killed dozens of innocent people, including children.''

Moira realized that though Molly and Shannon were still coloring, ignoring the tones taken on by the adults at their sides, Brian was staring at them.

''Is there still a war in Ireland?'' he asked.

''No,'' Moira said.

''Yes,'' Michael answered angrily, staring at Danny. ''Some people insist on fighting one.''

Danny shrugged suddenly, a slow smile curving his lips. Moira realized that he had intentionally provoked Michael. Trying to break the tension, she said, ''I think we should go shopping, maybe take the kids down to Quincy Market. Have pasta for lunch in Little Italy. Or find a Chinese restaurant.''

''The kids just ate,'' Danny told her placidly.

''They're kids. They'll be hungry again,'' Moira said sharply.

Danny shrugged.

Michael sighed, rising. ''I've got to get back to Josh. We're going to bring your father down now, while there's a lull after the lunch crowd.'' He curled his fingers around Moira's. ''Later? We'll do something later?''

''Absolutely,'' she told him.

He rose and walked by her, close, slipping an arm around her, kissing her cheek. ''Sorry,'' he whispered softly.

''Not your fault,'' she told him, purposely letting Danny hear her. Michael frowned, then squeezed her hand and walked by.

"What the hell is the matter with you?" Moira asked Danny angrily as she dragged him away to where the children couldn't overhear.

His eyes narrowed on her speculatively and seemed to gleam with a golden, predatory light. He shrugged. "Just trying to suss out the lay of the land."

"Why? Leave him alone."

"He's Irish, isn't he? That's what your mother told me."

Moira waved a hand impatiently. "Emigration has been going on for hundreds of years. Some people get to the States and become Americans. He's Irish—he's just not *Irish,* the way some people insist on being."

"Moira, I'm sorry, but I *am* Irish."

"Fine. But this is America."

"So it is."

"Auntie Mo," Brian called suddenly, "are you going to marry Michael?"

"No," Danny assured him.

"Yes, I think I just might," Moira said.

"Your auntie Mo is willing to go to great lengths to aggravate me," Danny said.

"To aggravate you?" Moira said incredulously. "Gee, he's smart, good-looking, charming and willing to tolerate a lot of abuse for my sake. What on earth could be wrong with my marrying such a man?"

To her surprise, Danny replied softly, "I don't know. That's the problem. I just don't know." She realized that he wasn't looking at her. The television set over the bar was on. He rose, and said, distracted, "Excuse me." Standing before the television, he slid his hand into his pocket and watched the set. Curiously, Moira walked over and joined him.

"Turn it up, please, will you, Chrissie?" he asked the woman behind the bar, who obliged him with a quick smile.

There was a tall, broad-shouldered, white-haired man standing on the steps of New York's Plaza Hotel, answering questions put to him by news crews on his way into the hotel.

"Mr. Brolin, how does it feel to be in America?" a tall, dark-haired reporter asked.

"Great," the man replied. "It always feels wonderful to be in America." He had a deep, rich speaking voice and a light brogue, enough of an accent to mark him as Irish. He was clearly comfortable with the mikes thrust in front of his face.

"Have you come here for diplomatic reasons, sir?" a woman queried, getting her question in next.

"Well, now, as part of the U.K., Northern Ireland has a fine relationship with America. As part of the Irish people, we in Northern Ireland want you Americans to come see us when you're visiting the Republic in the south. Some of the greatest places of legend, for Northerner and Republican alike, are in the north. Armagh, Tara, landscapes so beautiful they take your breath away. They belong to all of us, and to the Irish in America, as well."

"Mr. Brolin, do you have a campaign to see the island of Ireland reunited again?"

"My first campaign is to see people united again," Brolin said.

"Can such a thing ever happen?"

"We're into the twenty-first century now. I believe we see more clearly, that we can get to the root of our problems. Not to say that decades of bitterness can be wiped away overnight. But in the past ten years, we've made some giant leaps. We are working together in the North. Come now, you all know that we want your American tourist dollars. That's a goal that can get all the people working together right there."

He started to turn away. For a split second, it was possible to see the exhaustion on the man's face.

"Mr. Brolin, Mr. Brolin, one more question, please," a tiny woman, who had just maneuvered her mike near the politician, called. Brolin hesitated, and she went on. "We've thousands of good Irish Americans right here in New York. What made you choose Boston for your appearance on Saint Patrick's Day?"

Brolin smiled slowly, eyes alight. "New York is as fine a city as a man can find, with many a good Irish American, indeed. I didn't choose Boston, though it, too, is a fine American city. They invited me. Invite me to New York next year. I'll be delighted to come."

With that, he waved a hand in the air and started up the steps of the hotel. Moira noted the police in attendance, protecting him.

"He's charming," she murmured. "So even and moderate. I wonder why on earth he has such a large police escort?"

Danny looked at her strangely. "Because some people don't want to be moderate," he told her. "Ah, look, here comes your father. I guess you're back on. Time to give Eamon a chance to promote the brews of Eire—and Boston, of course." He turned away, walking to the street door at the front of the pub. He lifted his coat from a hook and left without so much as a glance back.

She could hear her father, Michael, Josh and some of the others coming down to the pub but, curious, she followed Danny, sliding past one of the tables by the window and looking out. He'd been in such a hurry to leave, but he hadn't gone anywhere. He was just standing in front of the pub, lighting a cigarette. He turned, almost as if he knew she was there, and she shrank from the window. Danny looked at the Kelly's Pub sign for several long moments. Then he crushed out his cigarette and started down the street.

"Moody bastard," Moira murmured to herself, then turned to the others.

They went to work. Lights and sound levels were set. Eamon stood at his taps, while Moira settled onto a bar stool in front of him. Eamon gave a great recitation, explaining the differences between lagers and ales and stouts. Customers began to filter in, making it all work perfectly. Chrissie, shy at first, got into the act. Seamus and Liam arrived and talked about the heart of the pub, how it was a place like home, a haven where you came to be with friends. "A beer...a beer you buy anywhere," Liam told the camera. "But a place where a man belongs, with friends to argue and agree, where the bartender always knows what you're drinking, now that's not so easy to come by."

Moira was stunned to find herself having fun as she began to move around the room to speak with customers. She put the kids on camera again, coloring at their table. Jeff Dolan had come in to set up early for the night, and she caught him teasing the kids while they laughed and crawled all over him. Jeff was the one to tell the video camera, "A pub is far more than a bar. A pub offers family fare, meals for the kids, good warm food, as well as ale. Well, now, I grant you, until recent times there existed many a pub in Ireland where the men had their place, and the women, well, they had their place, as well, but not on the same side with the men. I'd be willing to bet such a place or two still exists in the old country. But nowadays, I know I can come here alone—when I'm not working, of course—and I know I can come with kids, relatives, more. There's a dartboard in the back, and I was teaching my nephew just last week how to play. We always have the games on—I'm a big Patriots fan myself. The point is, you can get a good beer, but also a whole lot more. The true Irish pub is the heart of the neighborhood. Kelly's has a lot of heart, even here in America, and that's a fact."

Josh, who'd been following Moira with the camera,

switched off the tape. Moira smiled with delight and kissed Jeff on the cheek. "That was wonderful."

He blushed. "I'm glad. Thank God you didn't warn me. I'd have been awful."

"I'm glad we didn't warn you either," Josh told him. "This is going to be one of the best pieces we've done. Moira, I'm going over to talk with Michael and the sound guy. I want to make sure we're good with what we've got." She nodded, and Josh walked away.

Jeff seemed really pleased. "Seems to me you've got enough tape for a ten-hour show," he told her.

She shook her head. "We'll be editing everything we've got, taking out pauses, the amazing long spaces you get once you look over the video. Cutting and slicing shots...you'll see."

"You mean you're still going to be taping in here?" he queried.

"Sure, why not? Hey, I didn't know Josh was going to come in last night and tape while Colleen and I were on-stage, but it might be good stuff. I haven't looked it over yet. That's how you get a lot that's really good for a show like this. Spontaneous pieces, you know."

"I don't think it's such a good idea," Jeff said.

"Why not?"

He hesitated, gazing toward the equipment he'd been setting up.

"What happens," he asked her, "when you get some-one on tape who doesn't want to be seen on camera?"

"Jeff, we do what the big guys like Disney do. We put up signs warning people that there are cameras going."

"And you think everyone reads signs?"

"We ask for releases from anyone we feature," she told him, then frowned. "Jeff, I'm not sure what you're so worried about. So far, I've come across an incredible group of hams. They all want to be on camera."

"Yes, but..."

She shook her head, smiling. "Jeff, you're not into any... I mean, there are no drugs being passed around in my dad's place, right?"

"Moira, I've been clean as a whistle for over five years. Ask your dad—I barely have a beer or two now and then."

"I wasn't accusing you, Jeff...."

"I'm just a little worried about you, Moira, all right? Be careful what you get on camera. I don't think your own brother is going to want everything going on in here videotaped."

"My brother!" Despite her surprised tone, she'd had her own uneasy suspicions regarding her brother's activities since overhearing his conversation with Siobhan.

"Yeah, yeah, you know, he's an attorney. Has to be careful."

"Jeff, this is a friendly little travel show!"

"Right. I know. Just watch what you're filming. For me, okay? This place is important to me. I admit to being a wild child. Well, hell, you were there, you know. I was on drugs, off drugs. I went through a spell of being a tough guy on the streets and I tried to raise money to send arms overseas. I spent a night or two in jail. Your dad kept faith in me when my own folks were ready to call it quits. You be careful. Just be careful."

He didn't wait for an answer, just ran his fingers through his unruly dark hair and turned to the band equipment.

She wanted to quiz him further, but she couldn't because Michael came up behind her, slipping his arms around her waist. His aftershave smelled good. The texture of his cheek against hers as he leaned down was pleasant and alluring. She felt warmed and was glad for the moment.

"Want to slip away somewhere?" he asked huskily.

"I do."

"I mean, really away. We don't want to find out that Josh has decided to film Saint Patrick's Day mating rituals or anything like that."

She laughed aloud, turning to face him. "He wouldn't dare."

"Let's sneak away to the hotel."

"Let's."

Moira started across the pub to tell her father she was leaving. It wasn't busy at the moment. Chrissie was tending to the three women at the bar, and Eamon was poring over a newspaper.

Moira was surprised to feel a little bit like a guilty kid as she approached her dad. She wasn't sure what she was going to say. She was well over twenty-one, of course, but she knew she was going to make up a story about needing something or going to scout locales or some such thing. What woman, no matter how old, would ever want to admit to her father that she was getting a little bit desperate to get away from her family for just a few minutes of... quality time with the new man in her life?

"Dad..." she began.

"They haven't found a thing," Eamon said, looking up.

"Pardon?"

"On that poor girl, murdered the other day. The police have been questioning half the city, and they haven't found out anything. She was at a bar the night she died, a high-priced place. I guess she was what they call an escort these days, a high-priced girl herself. Everyone remembers her sitting at the bar by herself. No one remembers who she left with. They haven't been able to connect her murder with any others in the city."

"Dad, unfortunately, it often takes months, even years, for the police to crack down on a killer," Moira said. "And sometimes, as you know, people get away with murder."

"I don't like it," Eamon said.

"Of course not, Dad, it's tragic."

Michael was behind Moira. "Eamon, I can tell you're afraid for your daughters, and I'm making no judgments, but it's true that a call girl takes her chances. Your daughters would never be in such a position.''

"It just bothers me, in the bones," her father said.

"I'll be safe in the city. I'm always with Michael or Josh, Dad," Moira said. There was her opening. "And as to that—"

Just then Colleen came in from the office behind the bar and straight up behind her father. "Hey, it's time for dinner," Colleen said.

"Dinner?" Moira repeated blankly.

"Dinner. Remember that stuff we cooked all day for your program? Well, Mum has it in her head that we're all going to gather around and eat it. You know. Dinner.''

"Now?" Moira said.

"Six o'clock seems like a pretty good time for dinner to me," someone said from behind Moira.

She turned. Danny was back. Golden eyes on her speculatively. He seemed to know she'd been about to leave. With Michael. And he obviously found her situation amusing.

Colleen leaned over the bar to whisper to her, "Don't you dare walk out on dinner after all the effort Mum went to get it right for your show!"

"She'd kill me, huh?"

"*I'd* kill you," Colleen assured her.

She was going to have to explain to Michael. No, she wasn't. She felt his hands at her waist. "Dinner sounds great," he said softly.

She turned into his arms, meeting his eyes. "You're really too good," she told him.

He shook his head. "You're worth any wait, Moira."

She touched his cheek. Then, aware that she was still being watched by Danny, she took Michael's hand and said softly, "Let's go on up."

Upstairs, the delicious scent of her mother's Irish bacon and cabbage dinner filled the air. The kids were already in their chairs, and Siobhan was helping them butter their Irish soda bread. It was a wonderful scene; Moira immediately thought she should be filming again.

"No cameras when we sit down to dinner," her mother announced firmly, as if she had read her mind.

"No cameras," she quickly agreed.

No cameras.

She suddenly remembered how worried Jeff had been about her continuing to tape in the pub.

Why?

What was he afraid she would catch on camera?

America was an amazing place. From his hotel room high above New York City, Jacob Brolin looked at the hive of activity below him. His windows overlooked both the street below and the park, and he could see people moving. They were faceless figures from his distance, some obviously taking in the sights, others walking as if they were in a rush to return home from whatever they'd been doing. Tourists stopped and haggled with the carriage drivers on the street. He'd been gratified earlier to see that the horses all seemed to be in fine shape. No scrawny, ill-fed nags pulled the people along the streets and through the park. Many of the horses wore blankets in the chill of mid-March, and some were festooned with flowers. One, almost directly below him, seemed to be wearing a hat. Many of the drivers were Irish; they had watched and cheered when he had checked into the hotel. Aye, he was glad to see how well-kept the horses were. It was strange, he thought, or maybe not so strange. Many a man like himself had witnessed terrible violence against human beings yet found himself torn by the plight of an animal. But the horses were kept in fine shape, and that was good.

"Mr. Brolin?"

He turned from the window. Peter O'Malley, one of his aides, had tapped on the door connecting the parlor with the bedroom. O'Malley was one big son of a bitch. Six-four if he was an inch. Close to three hundred pounds of hard muscle. He wore a suit, and wore it well. Brolin thought few people would realize that a wee bit of the man's bulk was the bulletproof vest he wore beneath his jacket.

"Peter?"

"The call has come."

"Thank you. I'll take it in here."

He picked up the phone and identified himself. The caller spoke in Gaelic. He listened gravely, then spoke with soft determination.

"I'll not cancel. I'll be there tomorrow afternoon."

After a brief exchange, he hung up the phone and walked to the window. This time, however, he closed his eyes.

1973. He had taken a different road. It had seemed the only choice. He'd been running with Jenna McCleary, and things had gone badly awry. The battle had taken to the street. Bullets had been flying as they ran.

"We have to split," Jenna had said.

He'd nodded. Split, disappear right into the midst of it. Where to hide but in plain sight? So he had agreed.

He'd gone into the first pub and ordered an ale. He wasn't sure what path Jenna had taken; all he knew was that, later that night, she'd been picked up.

He'd heard about it. About the way she'd been questioned. How the official in charge had sent her back with soldiers who had just lost a chum. Shot down in the street when they'd been running. Maybe Jenna had pulled the trigger that particular round. Maybe he had. Jenna had paid. She had been young, beautiful and taught vengeance since she'd been a wee babe.

She hadn't been beautiful when they'd finished with her. There had been a plan, of course; they'd never simply deserted their own. But by the time they stopped the convoy transporting her from holding cell to prison, something had been dead within her already. When the bomb had exploded in front of the car and they'd gone to release her, she hadn't run. She had just stood there, knowing that the bullets would fly again.

He had watched her fall. Watched the motion as the bullet had struck, watched her jerk, spin and hit the earth. And he had seen her face clearly for a moment. Seen the hopelessness, seen the death in her eyes before they had glazed over. He had stood in the street, and it was surely a miracle that he hadn't been struck. And in those moments, he had suddenly known that they had all killed her. They had all of them, every one of them, killed her as surely as if they had shot her down themselves.

There was a tap on the door again. O'Malley had returned.

"Mr. Brolin?"

"We'll be on the one o'clock shuttle, right after the television appearance, just as planned, Peter."

"Sir, perhaps, with what we know, and with what we don't know—"

"Just as planned, Peter."

O'Malley inclined his head and left, quietly closing the door.

Brolin looked at the street.

Aye, it was good to see that the horses were in such fine shape.

7

Dinner was pleasant. Moira sat beside Michael, and Danny was down the table between Brian and Molly. After the conversation they'd had in front of the kids that afternoon, Moira was a little worried about what Danny might be saying to them. She made a point of rising throughout the meal for more drinks or anything else that might be needed, just to walk by Danny's end of the table and see what he was saying. She needn't have worried. He was doing nothing more than telling them about Saint Patrick. As always, Danny was a good storyteller.

"Patrick's life, you know, is shrouded in mystery," Danny explained. "He was the son of a man named Calpurnius, who was most probably a wealthy Roman living in Britain. Now the Romans had gone just about everywhere, you know, but they didn't do much more than skirt the edges of Ireland. The island was very wild at the time, and the people were fierce, and they lived in tribes. They were good-looking, of course, even back then, but they believed very much in magic, and in the wind and the sky and the power of the earth. They were fine seamen, too. So Patrick was a boy growing up in Britain—Wales, many people believe. And he was out late at night when he shouldn't have been—which is a lesson to the three of you to stay close to your parents and family when you're out. Patrick wound up being captured by pagan Irish sea raiders and taken across the Irish Sea to be sold as a slave. To a nasty fellow, so they say. Patrick became a shepherd, and he tended his sheep well, but he knew he must escape. It was very dangerous for him, because slaves attempting to escape could be executed at the will of their masters. But Patrick was a brave fellow, and he meant to go. In time, he convinced rivals of his master to help him escape across the sea again, and he came back home. His parents were very happy to see him, of course, but Patrick believed that God had come to him and told him that he must go back and help the Irish people. Patrick knew he had a special calling. His father wanted him to go to be a business-man—''

''Like Daddy,'' Shannon said.

''Like Daddy. Being a businessman is certainly a fine enough thing to do in life,'' Danny assured her. ''But Patrick knew that he couldn't do what his parents wanted. So he convinced them at last that he must go on to become a man of the Church. Years later, he returned to Ireland to preach a message of peace to the pagans, who were still practicing their strange beliefs. He might have been caught by the mean master he had escaped and put to death, but he came back anyway. Some say God helped him by letting the pagans see certain miracles. Others say that Patrick's wit and mind were miraculous in themselves, and that his power was in his words and his way with people.''

''Either way, gifts from God,'' Granny Jon added.

Danny smiled across the table at her. ''True enough. So here's our good Patrick among these people. He walked all over Ireland, North and South, because they were just one back then, with many kings ruling different areas and sometimes an Ard-Ri, or High King, sitting at Tara. When Patrick came, so legend has it, there was a High King at Tara, and he was a powerful man with deep belief in his pagan priest. The pagan priest wanted to trick Patrick into a fire, where Patrick would burn to death and leave the pagan priest as the most powerful one. But the Ard-Ri wanted the truth, and he forced both his own priest and Patrick to walk through the flames. Patrick proved that his faith in God was the greatest magic in the world, for he passed easily through fire, and the pagan priest who wanted to hurt Patrick was the one who perished in the flames. Ah, but that didn't end the trials Patrick had to go through. He had trouble with other churchmen, jealous of his success in Ireland. But in the end, Patrick plugged away, sure of his love of Ireland and the Irish people, and sure of his faith in God, and he passed through all his trials, changed Ireland forever, and guess what?''

"What?" Brian demanded.

"He went on to live to a ripe old age, still in his beloved Ireland, and so we celebrate a special day for him every year, even here in America."

"Saint Patrick's Day is a public holiday in Ireland, Moira, you know," Katy said.

She smiled. "Yes, Mum. In Ireland."

"Did he really pass through fire?" Brian asked Danny very seriously.

"Well, now, I wasn't there. Is that truth, or legend?" Danny said. "It's all a matter of belief."

"Did Saint Patrick bring the leprechauns to Ireland?" Molly asked.

"No, you see, the wee people were always there, living in the magic of the mind," Danny told her, and winked.

Moira left a bottle of soda in front of the group at the end of the table and moved back to her seat.

Michael leaned close to speak softly to her. "He's quite a fine storyteller."

"Oh, yes, he has lots of stories."

"You're not so fond of your old family friend?" Michael asked curiously.

She hesitated. She'd never mentioned Danny to Michael before this had all come up. No reason to. They hadn't torn apart their pasts. She hadn't given him a questionnaire about his previous relationships or talked about her own. Now she felt guilty.

And still totally disinclined to tell the truth.

"He can be very charming, and very irritating," she said simply. She looked at Danny. "Like a brother," she said, loudly enough for Danny to hear.

A slight smile curved his lips. He went on to tell Molly about a special girl leprechaun called Taloola. Moira had heard a lot of Irish fairy tales in her day, but she had never heard that one. She decided Danny must have been making up the story as he went along, creating it especially for the kids.

That was fine. Just as long as he didn't launch into a speech about the oppression faced by their people over the years.

Moira looked across the table to discover that her grandmother was watching her with a grave expression. She arched a brow. "Pass the colcannon, please, Moira, will you?" Granny Jon said.

Moira obediently passed the food over, wondering why her grandmother had been watching her so strangely.

After dinner, she, Colleen and Siobhan made her mother go sit in the den with Granny Jon. They served them tea there, making a big deal of putting them into the most comfortable chairs, pulling up footrests and making them do nothing but rest. Granny Jon seemed bemused, her mother restless. Once the tea was served, the younger women forced the older women to stay put and went in to clean up the dining room and kitchen. It seemed strangely empty with just the three of them.

"Where are the kids?" Moira asked. "They don't have the poor little things back down in the pub again, do they?"

"Patrick is putting them to bed."

"Good," Moira said to her sister-in-law.

"Yeah, well, usually he's a good father."

Rinsing a dish, then setting in into the dishwasher, Moira wondered whether to say something further or to keep her mouth shut.

"Has he been really busy lately?" she asked.

"Yeah," Siobhan said, handing Moira a plate. She looked as if she was about to say something, hesitated, then shrugged. "I really don't know what this new deal is. He met these people involved with a charitable association in Northern Ireland. They raise American money for Irish kids who've been orphaned, to help them pay for an education."

"It sounds like a decent cause," Colleen said.

"Yes, it does, doesn't it?" Siobhan said.

"I'm lost, then," Moira murmured. "What's the problem."

Siobhan shook her head. "He's been in Boston an awful lot lately. Times when he hasn't even stopped by to see your folks."

"Well," Moira murmured, surprised to realize she was coming to her brother's defense, "if he's just coming in for some quick business, he may not stop to see them because he thinks he'd never get back home if he did."

"Yeah, sure," Siobhan said.

Siobhan's words might have meant that she agreed with Moira or that she didn't believe a word Moira had said. All that was clear was that she didn't want to talk about it anymore. And all that Moira knew was that something about her brother's behavior was troubling.

"Hey," Colleen said, breaking in on the awkward moment, "I've got to tell you, Siobhan, every time I see them, I'm prouder than ever of being an aunt to those little munchkins of yours."

"Beyond a doubt," Moira agreed wholeheartedly. "They're adorable and well behaved, even though they're still so young."

"Thanks," Siobhan said, smiling. "They are kind of

worth everything, aren't they? You're going to make a terrific parent yourself one day, you know. Whoops, sorry, both of you are going to make terrific parents. I was merely addressing Moira because she's older,'' Siobhan explained to Colleen.

"Thank you for pointing that out," Moira said.

"Well, you are closing in on the big three-oh," Siobhan said.

"That's right, Moira, no matter how old I get, you'll be older."

"You're both so kind," Moira said.

Siobhan laughed. "So is this Michael thing serious?"

"He's definitely great to look at," Colleen said.

"Looks aren't everything," Siobhan reminded her.

"But when you're not speaking to one another, at least the scenery's nice," Colleen said.

"He's not the temperamental type, is he?" Siobhan asked.

"Not at all," Moira said.

"He's practically perfect in every way," Colleen remarked.

"I'd say he's doing exceptionally well," Siobhan noted. "I mean, this isn't an easy household to crash, and he's holding his own quite nicely."

"Yes, he is."

"So *is* it serious?" Siobhan persisted.

"Could be."

"You would have great-looking children," Colleen murmured.

"Just because you're now the face on a zillion magazine covers, you shouldn't obsess about looks," Moira chastised.

"Okay, what a dog you're dating."

Moira sighed, Siobhan laughed, and the cleanup went on, the next line of inquiry focused on Colleen's love life. Moira kept from questioning Siobhan further, because her sister-in-law obviously didn't want to answer questions, but when they finished and Siobhan excused herself to see to the kids, Moira still felt uneasy.

After Siobhan walked down the hall and left them, Colleen asked Moira, "You don't think Patrick could be cheating on her, do you?"

"I can't imagine it," Moira said. "If he is, he's a fool."

"Think we ought to tell him so?"

"I...I think we need to stay out of it, unless one of them decides to talk to us," Moira said.

"I guess you're right, except that..."

"You don't think that..." Moira began.

"What?"

"Patrick wouldn't be involved in...anything illegal, would he?"

"He's an attorney! What are you talking about?"

"I know. Never mind. I don't know what I'm talking about myself."

"I'm going to head down to the pub and see if Dad needs any help," Colleen said. She set the dish towel she'd been using on the counter. "He loves it when we're down there, you know."

"I know. I'll just check on Mum and Granny Jon, then be right down," Moira said.

They went their separate ways. When Moira slipped into the den, she found that her mother had gone to bed and Granny Jon was watching the news. She smiled at Moira, nodding toward the sofa next to the big upholstered chair where she was sitting.

"All cleaned up, eh?"

"Yep, all done. I came to see if I can get you anything else."

"You know, Moira, thank the good Lord, I'm still mobile."

"I thank Him all the time," Moira said earnestly. "You're very precious to us."

Granny Jon nodded, smiling. "Thank you. It's truly good to have you children home. It's good to be able to take care of yourself, but it's also very nice to have loved ones who want to do things for you."

"We're lucky, too."

"Oh?"

Moira waved a hand in the air. "I have so many friends whose parents are divorced and don't really have a home to go back to. Every time they have an important occasion in their lives, they have to figure out how to manage the logistics. I know I'm lucky."

Granny Jon nodded gravely. "Good. Half the time in life, people don't appreciate what they have." She paused. "Don't be too hard on them for remembering the old country, though, Moira."

"I...I don't mean to be."

Granny Jon was silent for a minute, then she said, "I am very old, you know."

"Age is relative," Moira said.

"Yes, but there is a lot I remember, you see. I was a child in Dublin at the time of the Easter Rebellion, you know. I saw the streets in flames. I had friends—little children—who were killed in the crossfire."

"I'm so sorry," Moira said. "You've never talked about it."

Granny Jon shrugged. "Dublin is a wonderful city now. And the Irish are a wonderful people. I'm just saying this because...well, sometimes when people are born into violence, scars remain. Sometimes the old-timers can't help talking about what was—and about what they hope for in the future."

"Granny Jon, I just can't believe that bombs and bullets—"

"Bombs and bullets are wrong. The murder of innocents is wrong. I'll never say otherwise. I just want you to understand how people feel at times."

"I do understand. Honestly, Granny Jon, I know the history of Ireland. It was impossible to grow up with you and Mum and Dad and not know it."

"Your father wanted to come here, you know. To America. Not that he didn't realize that every country had its injustices to fight. But we had family in the North."

"I understand."

"I'm not sure if you really do. In the last few years, there have been giant steps taken toward real peace, the ceasefire in 1997, the Good Friday Agreement in 1998. President Clinton spent time in Northern Ireland, working things out. But you know as well as I do that there remain those who wish to die and don't mind sacrificing the lives of others for their beliefs. You've just got to remember, Moira, that we are Irish and proud of it, and that you're Irish, too."

Moira stood, then kneeled down by her grandmother, putting her arms around her. "I'm so sorry if I led you to believe that I was ever anything but completely proud of all of you," she said softly.

Granny Jon pulled away, smiling at her, smoothing her hair. "I don't say there aren't problems in Ireland. But you know, though it may well be the greatest country in the world, there are problems in America, as well."

"I always knew you were wonderful," Moira told her, "but I don't think I ever knew before just how incredibly savvy you were."

Granny Jon grinned. "Sometimes...well, there are times when I'm afraid, too. But get on down to the pub now, girl. Go sing 'Danny Boy' for your dad."

"We sang it last night."

"Sing it again—it makes him happy."

"You don't need anything..."

"If I did, I'd ask."

Moira smiled and started out of the room.

"Moira?"

She paused in the doorway. "Yes?"

"Remember, the country we're from is beautiful. The Irish in years past kept the art of books alive. In the Dark Ages, Irish monks worked endlessly to keep the written word going. Some of the finest craftsmen in the world were Irish. There's a spirit there, as well, in the wind, the sea, the crags and cairns. Legends and stories, art and drama. Remember it all, Moira."

"I do, Granny, I do. Honestly."

Granny Jon nodded. "Go on with you, then. Go have fun being with your family. The taping you did today was lovely."

"Thanks. Hey, would you let me tape you telling the kids a story tomorrow?"

"If you're sure you want an old woman on your show."

"I want an incredibly bright and wonderful woman on my show."

Granny Jon smiled her pleasure. "Go on now."

"You sure? You're not watching the television or reading or anything. I hate to leave you alone."

"I'm thinking, girl. Reflecting. At my age, it's an interesting occupation."

Moira nodded and left her, ready to head down to the pub.

Dan saw the man in the navy sweater at the corner table the minute he came down and stepped behind the bar with Michael McLean.

McLean was evidently wary of him, but the guy was doing everything he could to fit in. He was obviously very much in love with Moira and willing to prove it. Not that he was behaving like a sycophant in any way. He was steady, determined and willing, unafraid to speak his mind and capable of doing so with diplomacy. Actually, Dan reflected, under other circumstances, he might have liked the guy.

They'd come together behind the bar to allow Eamon Kelly time to sit with his old cronies for a while, and solve the future of the free world. Working the bar was easy enough—most orders were for drafts. The pub was busy, but there was still time to watch the floor and talk to the regulars. The band was playing, and the television was on with the sound turned down. It seemed a typical enough night. Something going on everywhere.

The guy in the corner was alone. At a two-seater table, he nursed a single beer. He'd been at it for a while. A nondescript fellow, brown hair cut short, Ivy League look. He might have been an accountant, a banker, a lawyer or a businessman of any variety. White-collar type, though, beyond a doubt.

"They're at it again," Michael said, then added a quick, "sorry."

Dan arched a brow at him.

Michael McLean shrugged. "I forgot how important it is to all of you—every event in the history of Ireland."

Dan nodded, tuning in to the old men's conversation. It was a familiar one.

"Well, I ask you again," Seamus said. "Are you an American?"

"Don't be daft, man," Eamon Kelly replied, shaking his head. "Yes, I'm an American. I applied for my citizenship the day I'd been in the country long enough. I'd had a son by then, and Moira was on her way. Katy and I had talked about it long and hard. We'd decided that we were bringing the children up in Boston, and that was that."

"But you're still an Irishman."

Eamon groaned. "I was born an Irishman."

"So what if America went to war with Ireland?" Seamus demanded.

"America will never go to war with Ireland."

"But what if it did?"

"Seamus, I'm telling you again, you're daft, man."

"You're missing the point."

"I'm not missing the point. You're saying that an Irishman is always an Irishman, above and beyond anything else. The American Irish and the Northern Irish both."

"But you do think the island should be united."

"*You* think the island should be united."

"Aye, but I don't know how it's to come about."

"That's why a man like Jacob Brolin is so important. He knows The Troubles backward and forward. He knows that the religious divide is an economic divide, that laws in the past have created half the problems, that the healing has to come from the people. And if you can unite the people, you can eventually unite Ireland."

"What about those who like their financial ties with England?"

"Why are we arguing about this, Seamus? We both feel the same way," Eamon said, irritated. The two men looked as if they were about to exchange blows. Dan knew that they often looked this way.

Seamus shook his head, looking sorrowful. "There's trouble brewing."

"In my pub?" Eamon said scornfully.

Seamus suddenly lowered his voice. "Do you remember that soldier in seventy-one?"

"I'm a Dubliner, Seamus."

"But you remember, because you knew him. Family ties, Eamon, and they run deep. The poor kid was a twenty-year-old British soldier. The IRA kidnapped him after a street brawl in Belfast. He lived in Paddy McNally's house for two weeks, and everyone who met the fellow liked the chap. But the British refused to free a few of the IRA men who had been picked up, so they took that poor kid out and shot him dead, despite the fact that they had all but adopted the lad."

"And the world condemned the IRA faction that did the

deed as terrorists," Eamon said angrily. "Seamus, what are you going on about? I'm telling you, I can't solve the problem and I know it. I'm an American, running a pub in Boston. Praying for peace everywhere, like the whole damned rest of the world. The governments of North and South both know that the time of war and revolution is over, that in the small world we live in now, negotiation is the way to go. Jesus, Seamus, how you're going on. We've both seen it. Kids taught to throw rocks from the time they're walking, rocks that turn into bullets when they're old enough to tote a gun. We've learned to fight with words—"

"Oh, aye. And every time there's an agreement signed, there's sure to be a bomb going off somewhere."

"Excuse me, Seamus, but I was over in Belfast not more than a year and a half ago, and I'm telling you, the Northern Irish want tourist dollars the same as the rest of the world. They're on the road to change."

"*Most* of the Northern Irish," Seamus muttered.

"Seamus, just what are you trying to say to me?"

Seamus suddenly looked straight at Dan. "I'm saying that the North still has terrorists."

"And what would you have me do?"

Seamus shook his head suddenly, looking into his beer. "Whispering," he muttered. "Gaelic. I've been hearing it, here in the pub. There's something going on—I've yet to put my finger on it, but I've heard...Gaelic."

"I can still speak the old language myself, Seamus, so what in the Lord's name does that have to do with anything?"

Seamus looked up and caught Dan watching him.

He lifted his beer. "It's a fine old language."

Colleen was at the service end of the bar with a tray, ready to place an order. "Hey, one of you guys want to make a blackbird?"

"I thought Blackbird was the band?" Michael said, setting a Guinness in front of a balding man near the end of the bar.

"The blackbird is an old house specialty," Seamus told him. "Coffee, two parts Irish cream and one part Irish whiskey. A dollop of whipped cream on top. Haven't had an order for one in a long time."

"I know the drink," Dan said. "I'll get it."

"Who asked for it?"

"Some guy over there," Colleen said, pointing vaguely to the back of the room.

"I'll make it and take it to him," Dan said.

"Just make it for me, I'll take it to him," Colleen said, rolling her eyes slightly. "We don't want Dad thinking he's got to get behind the bar again himself, not when he and Seamus are having such a good time."

Dan made the drink. Though the bar became more crowded and people were standing behind the stools calling out orders, he watched as Colleen delivered it.

As he had suspected, it went to the man in the navy sweater at the table in the corner.

The pub was a zoo. Well, it was Saturday night preceding the week when Saint Patrick's Day would fall. As she entered the bar area, Moira was glad that she had come down. Her father was a good businessman; he had planned for the crowd. But it was very busy.

She was surprised to see Michael behind the bar with Danny. He looked a little frazzled, but he was gamely pouring beer and mixing drinks. She slipped up behind him.

"You all right?"

"Fine, I think. Working hard at it, anyway." He dropped his voice, whispering, "Trying to earn points, you know. Think I can make it into the family circle?"

She laughed, delighted that he was trying so hard. "You have the right background. Good last name. I think you'll make it just fine. You're doing an exceptional job. But I had thought you might want to slip away tonight.''

"Moira, if you'd suggested that earlier, we might have had a chance.''

He was watching her with a rueful grin, and she knew he was right. She could never leave when the place was roaring along full tilt, as it was now, and every hand was needed. She slipped her arms around him. "You're incredible.''

"Don't press so tightly. I'm suffering the agony of the damned as it is.''

"I can slip out later, you know.'' She sighed. "Much later, of course.''

"Now that's an enticing possibility.''

"You know I mean it, Michael. You're really wonderful.''

"In more ways than one, if you recall.''

"Vaguely,'' she teased. "I'd love to have my memory refreshed.''

"We'll see,'' Michael said, his lips curved in a smile. "Will you really sneak out of Dad's house?''

"Hey!'' Chrissie called. "Is anybody back there actually working?''

"Sorry, Chrissie,'' Moira said quickly. She strode to the service area.

"I need a Gibson, extra onions, two Guinness drafts, a Murphy's, two white wines and a burgundy.''

"Got it,'' Moira said.

"Know what? You're better at this than I am, but I *can* write down orders,'' Michael said. He cast a glance along the bar. "I'll leave you with good old Danny boy there and work the floor with the others.''

She nodded. It was true; she could make the drinks a lot faster than he could.

Moira took over the service area and was surprised when she heard Danny whispering in her ear a few minutes later.

"He's racking up some points tonight, eh?"

She turned halfway around while still keeping her attention on the drinks she was pouring.

"What are you talking about?"

"Tall, dark and handsome. Old beady eyes. He's worming his way in."

"He's helping out. And even if he *is* doing it all to make my father like him, I appreciate the effort."

"Beady eyes, Moira."

"Danny, I hear someone calling you."

"Am I too close? Is that it? Is the memory of what's really good shooting through your bloodstream? Is your pulse pounding? Let me answer for you. You're feeling the heat. You're watching my hands on the taps and remembering just how good they felt on your flesh."

"Oh, yeah, heat, Danny. I'm under a friggin' blowtorch." She leaned closer to him. "Know what I'm really thinking?"

"That I'm to die for?"

"I'm thinking you're delusional," she told him.

He grinned. "Maybe, love. Maybe I'm the one with the memories, recalling just how good it feels to have my hands on you. We were good together, eh?"

"That was then, this is now," she said simply. "Chrissie!" she shouted over the heads of the customers packing the bar. "Was that martini up or on the rocks?"

"Rocks!" Chrissie called.

"I do love you, Moira Kelly," Danny said softly.

His whisper seemed to touch the back of her neck. Like the stroke of a finger. Suddenly she was filled with memories. She found herself staring at his hands on the taps. A hot flush rushed over her, and she found herself thinking she was a terrible person. But it was true. He *was* good in bed.

So was Michael. She had been in love with Danny once. Maybe half her lifetime. She'd waited for years for something else. Something real. Michael. She wasn't a fool. She was mature enough to have learned that what felt good wasn't always right.

And still...

Danny's eyes. The curl of his lips, his humor. The way he could laugh with her or at himself. The way he could slip an arm around her, hold her, give warmth and a sense of understanding at just the right moment. And then suddenly turn sensual, purely sexual in a way that left her gasping....

"Seamus needs another draft," she said, to distract herself from her dangerous thoughts.

"Seamus has had too many."

"Patrick is back. I see him over there. He'll walk old Seamus home—he's just a few blocks away. Give him another draft. He's having fun with Dad."

"I think *you* should have a beer."

"Maybe I will."

"Maybe I can get you to have enough of them."

"Enough of them for what? For you to get me back in bed? Are you bored to tears or something this trip, Danny? Have I become a challenge because Michael is here? Because I really care for someone else after all these years?"

"Because I really love you."

"Danny, you don't know the meaning of the word."

"I've always known it, Moira."

"Moira, do we have Fosters?" Colleen called.

"Only on tap."

"That's fine. I need one Fosters, two Buds and a Coors in the bottle with lemon instead of lime."

"Danny, get me the Coors," she said. He was too close. She had always liked his aftershave. The scent was subtle, and...

And it filled her with memories.

Maybe she *would* have that beer. No, maybe she would have a straight shot of whiskey and slap herself in the face.

As she made the drinks for Chrissie, Moira heard the phone ringing. "I'll get it," she told Danny as he set the Coors on the serving tray.

"I've got it," he told her.

She heard him answer the phone with the single word Kelly's.

"Moira, I need two more Buds!" Colleen called. "In the bottle."

As Moira walked to the cooler, she heard Danny talking. His voice had dropped very low.

She tried to make out the words but couldn't hear him.

Then she realized that she *was* hearing him; she simply wasn't understanding him. He was speaking in Gaelic.

His voice was very low, but tense.

He caught her watching him and grinned, shrugging. But it wasn't Danny's usual grin. A moment later, he hung up.

"Who was that?" she asked.

"Oh, just some old-timer. Wanted to know if it was a real Irish pub. I thought I'd convince him that it was."

She didn't speak Gaelic. Oh, she knew a few words here and there, but she had never really learned the language. She had taken both French and Spanish in school. Far more useful in the United States.

She decided to lie. "You know, I've been taking some Gaelic, Danny," she told him.

She wondered why he hadn't decided to be an actor. She was certain that he tensed, but he wasn't going to allow her to see whatever it was that really bothered him. Or else he was calling her bluff.

"It's about time, Moira Kelly," he said. "It's calming down in here. I'm going to leave the bar to you," he told her, walking toward the exit.

But he paused and came back and took her suddenly by the shoulders, no hint of amusement in his eyes as they met hers.

"If that's the truth, Moira, don't go letting anyone know, do you hear me?"

"Danny—"

"Listen to me for once in your life, Moira. Don't let anyone know that you understand a single word."

"Danny, what—"

"I mean it, Moira."

His fingers were hurting her, they bit into her shoulders so deeply. There was something so serious about his face that she felt a strange whisper of fear seep into her.

"Danny—"

"Please, Moira, for the love of God."

She suddenly realized she had really never known this man.

She found herself nodding. "All right. Damn it, Danny, stop it, you're hurting me."

"Sorry." His hold eased. "Moira, you've got to be careful."

"Of what?"

"People who are too passionate."

"And what the hell does that mean? You, Michael, old Seamus there?"

"Anyone and everyone. Do you understand me?"

"No, I don't."

"Moira, leave it alone. Just leave it alone."

She suddenly realized that Michael was watching her from the floor. She wanted to get Danny away from her.

"Leave 'it' alone? What 'it'? Leave *me* alone." She tried to back away.

"Moira—"

"I don't really speak or understand Gaelic, Danny. I know nothing more than good morning, good night, please, thank you and Erin go bragh."

"Then don't pretend you do."

He turned and left the bar area. She stared at him as he

went out on the floor. Chrissie asked her for something, and she responded mechanically.

Michael came up to the service area. "Are you all right?" he asked.

"Of course."

"That looked like a very intense moment."

"Disagreement over drink recipes," she lied.

"You look...frazzled."

"It's a really busy night."

"I know. I'm worn out, too."

"I'll make this all up to you."

"I'll hold you to that."

"What's your room number?"

He smiled and gave it to her, then added, "Oh, I need three draft beers."

"What kind?"

"Buds. And I need another one of those bird things."

"A blackbird?"

"Yeah, that's it."

She laughed and made the drinks. She watched him as he delivered the beers, then took the blackbird to the man at the corner table who had been sitting alone for several hours, listening to the band, nursing his drink.

Michael wasn't as bad at this as he seemed to think he was. He had talked with the threesome who'd ordered the beers, and he paused long enough to exchange words with the fellow in the navy sweater. Someone called her name at the bar, and she gave her attention to the taps.

When she looked up, she saw Danny walking across the room. She realized that he was approaching the man in the corner. The man in the navy sweater, the one who had ordered the blackbird.

A few moments later, Danny got his coat from the hook by the bar and left the pub.

Not five minutes went by before the man in the navy sweater did the same.

She wondered if the man was known to anyone in the pub. She decided to ask her brother if he knew the fellow. But looking around, she realized that she didn't see Patrick anywhere.

Nor, for that matter, did Michael seem to be anywhere on the floor, either. In fact, in a few minutes' time, it seemed that the bar had half emptied; people who had been there throughout the evening had all seemed to vanish into thin air.

"Damn them all," she murmured to herself. She couldn't even see her father anywhere.

A feeling of deep unease settled over her. It was Danny again, damn it. His ridiculous temper after she had lied to him about the Gaelic.

Tomorrow, she decided, she would have it out with him.

"Moira, one more Guinness for me old bones," Seamus said to her. He was sitting alone. She finally saw her father, who had gone to speak with Jeff by the bandstand.

She poured the drink and brought it to Seamus, then set it down with a disapproving frown. "That's the last, now, Seamus."

He nodded. "As you wish, Moira." She started to walk away. "Moira Kelly," he called, stopping her. She turned back.

"Moira, be a good girl, eh? See how quiet it's become? Ominous," Seamus muttered. "Watch the streets of Boston these days."

"Seamus, what are you on about?"

"That girl was found dead."

She sighed, then walked to him, leaned across the bar and kissed the top of his head. "I promise not to go out soliciting, Seamus. I especially promise not to solicit using the Gaelic language. How's that?"

"Stay close to home," he told her seriously.

"Seamus..."

"There are always troubles," he said softly.

They'd all gone daft, she thought.

She poured herself the shot of whiskey she'd been debating about ever since her conversation with Danny and downed it in one neat swallow.

It was so hot—it indeed burned like a blowtorch.

Coming home was never easy, she decided.

"Watch out for strangers," Seamus said. "Don't go talking to any."

"Seamus, this is a public establishment. We serve strangers all the time."

"And friends, even," Seamus said sorrowfully. "Sometimes friends...can be stranger than...strangers."

"Seamus, you are definitely cut off."

"I am not drunk, Moira Kelly," he said defensively.

"Then you're talking like a madman."

Seamus leaned forward, very close. "There are whispers, Moira."

"About what, Seamus?"

He sat back, shaking his head and looking around uneasily. As if he had said too much. "You take care, girl," he said again. Then he stood up, leaving his drink half finished. "Night, lass."

"Seamus, wait, I'll get someone to walk you home."

"Walk me home? Moira, I'm sober, I swear it, and I've been walking meself home from this pub more years than you've been alive."

"Seamus, you're not drunk, but you *have* had a few. I wouldn't let you drive tonight, and I'm not so sure you should be walking."

He lifted a hand in farewell.

"Seamus!"

But Seamus was already across the room on his way toward the door. She couldn't help but be worried about him. "Chrissie!" she called. "Can you take the bar, please?"

She didn't wait for an answer but slipped out and hurried after old Seamus. He had made it to the door already. Moira didn't have a coat handy, but she followed him anyway.

Once outside, she was amazed to see that he had already disappeared. The streets were deserted and cold. Very cold. The chill bit into her.

The night was dark, clouds covering the moon. Beyond the spill of lights from the pub, the street was cast in shadows.

"Seamus?" she called anxiously.

She started down the street, knowing the path Seamus would take to reach his home. Down the block, she turned to the left, stepping into the shadows.

The cold wrapped around her.

As she walked, she cursed herself for the idiocy of leaving without a coat. Then she cursed herself for running out in the darkness at this hour of the night. The sidewalks were slick with a thin sheen of ice. And yet...

It was more than just the dark, icy grip of the Boston winter night that held her, she realized. The chill was inside and out. She had walked these neighborhood streets for most of her life, and the family knew their neighbors. She knew the cold, and she even knew the shadows. She had never felt this kind of unease before, never felt as if the chill were inside her, something that would never go away.

She turned the corner to the left. Ahead, the eaves of an old building cast a spill of total Stygian blackness over the sidewalk. Moira moved against the building, instinctively afraid, seeking the protection of darkness.

She was almost upon the two figures before she realized they were there. And she couldn't help but hear the exchange of low murmurs. Whispers, the words just barely audible in the stillness of the night.

"So it's definite. Let the blackbird fly."

"Which piece?"

"You'll receive it."

There was a sudden silence; it seemed to stretch forever, but it was probably no more than the beat of a second. She had stopped walking without realizing it.

Blackbird...

It was as if a giant blackbird had suddenly erupted from the shadow, wings sweeping over the street, brushing her. It was as if the wind picked her up, spinning her around. She found herself moving, catapulted forward. Her feet found no grip on the ice. She went sliding, desperately trying to catch her balance, terrified of the dark presence that suddenly menaced her from behind, darkness rising with a stealthy force. Something struck her hard. She found herself falling to the ground, the shadows rising all around her, the stars glimmering in a sky that had been nothing but cloud and darkness before.

8

When she tried to get up, Moira slid again. She was staring at the sky when a face appeared in the cloud-covered night.

"Moira Kelly! What on earth are you doing out here like this?"

Danny. He reached down, catching her hands. He didn't pull her straight up but hunkered at her side first, studying her eyes. "Whoa, now. Did you hurt yourself?"

"I don't think so."

"You're all right? Nasty spill on the ice? Where's your coat, girl? It's freezing out here."

"I'm well aware that it's freezing, thank you."

"What are you doing out here?"

"It's freezing, Danny. Stop asking questions and help me up."

"Good shoes for the ice," he observed. "You're sure you're not really hurt? So what was it? Lovers' quarrel? Were you racing after that beady-eyed Michael?"

"No," she said indignantly. "Michael and I don't quarrel, and I don't think anything is really hurt. I was—"

She broke off suddenly as he helped her up. *Pushed.* She'd been about to say that she'd been pushed. Instinct kept her from speaking the truth. There was no one out here except Danny. The man who'd been warning her not to let people think that she spoke or understood Gaelic.

Had he pushed her from the shadows, then turned around to help her?

"You were what?" he asked her, eyeing her closely.

"Nothing, I was…I was concerned about Seamus. He'd been drinking quite a bit. I came out after him, and I fell."

As she spoke, Danny took his coat off, draping it around her. The warmth felt awfully good. She also realized, as she began to thaw a bit, that she was sore from head to toe. "What are *you* doing out here?" she asked him.

"Saying good-night to a few old chums."

"Where is my brother? Were you with him?"

"Haven't seen Patrick in a bit," he told her. He arched a brow. "Are we all supposed to report in to you these days?"

"I couldn't find anyone to walk Seamus home, that's all," she lied. She wondered why she didn't tell Danny the truth. That she'd come outside, overheard two men talking about a flying blackbird and been pushed to the ground.

The reason was obvious. She was alone on the street with Danny. As much as she hated to think it, he might have been the one who had pushed her.

"Let's get in," she said. "It's freezing out here."

He nodded, taking her arm as they turned toward the pub.

"Did you see someone out here?" he asked.

"No."

"Why are you lying to me?"

"I'm not." She wasn't. She hadn't actually seen anyone. Just shadows. Figures in the dark.

She was looking straight ahead, but she could tell that he was watching her suspiciously.

"Fine, then."

A statement that he didn't believe her. She was suddenly very anxious to get into the pub.

Danny obliged, moving quickly. She nearly went sliding

again. He caught her instantly, keeping her from going down. As they neared the door, she increased her speed.

She felt herself slide on the ice the moment she hit it. This time, not even Danny's hold could keep her from falling. He tried so hard, though, that even as she flailed in what seemed like slow motion, he lost his footing, as well. He managed to get beneath her as they went down. She wound up sprawled on top of him, staring into his amber eyes. For a moment they just lay there, winded, staring at one another. Then Danny smoothed a stray hair from her forehead.

"Hey, this isn't bad," he told her.

She immediately struggled to rise, slipped, then slammed hard against him once again. The breath was knocked out of him, but he laughed.

"Quit laughing!"

"Hey, I'm the injured party here. Throw your flesh and bones down to be chivalrous, and what do you get? A knee in the groin."

"I did not jab my knee into your groin."

"Not on purpose. I don't think."

She let out a sound of total aggravation, rolling off him. Danny was already up, offering her a hand. She took it. Looking at the door to the pub, she saw that Colleen was standing there, laughing, as well. "If you children are through playing in the snow, it's much warmer inside."

Danny's coat was lying on the ice. She bent to retrieve it, but he had already picked up the garment. "Inside, yes. I guess that would be good. Although, I was rather enjoying myself," he said with a grin.

Moira went through the door. Danny entered behind her, his arm around Colleen. "And what were you doing, venturing out in the ice and snow?"

"It's not snowing."

"Figure of speech."

"I was wondering how the entire pub suddenly seemed

to disappear,'' Colleen said lightly. "Even the band has quit for the night, and Jeff took off somewhere. Oh, Moira?''

"Yes?''

"Michael was in a moment ago, looking for you. He said to tell you he was heading back to the hotel.''

"Thanks.''

She'd practically promised to slip out to join him at the hotel, and she knew she should keep that promise. Except that she was tired and sore, and afraid that she would give away the fact that people at her father's pub were all behaving very strangely. Especially her brother.

And Danny.

Moira saw that Chrissie was behind the bar, picking up glasses, breaking down. Moira took a tray from the bar and went on the floor, where she started clearing tables. Behind her, Colleen and Danny did the same.

"Moira Kathleen!'' her father suddenly exclaimed.

She nearly dropped her tray full of glasses. "What?''

"What happened to you?''

"Nothing. Why?''

"You're bleeding, girl!''

She looked down to discover that her stockings had torn and a thin trickle of blood was seeping from her knee down her shinbone.

"Just a meeting with the sidewalk, Dad. I tripped outside,'' she said. "Danny helped me up.''

"You need to take care of that right away.''

"I'll go upstairs,'' Moira said.

"There's a first-aid kit right in the office,'' Eamon said.

"I can just go up—''

"Not on your life,'' Danny said. "You might need stitches. We'll have to take a look at that.''

He was by her side in a moment, golden mischief in his eyes.

"Danny, I skinned my knee.''

"Ah, but you're *the* Moira Kelly. Can't have scraped knees showing on camera. Let's take care of it right away."

He ushered her around the bar toward the back.

"First-aid kit is in the—" Eamon began.

"Top drawer," Danny finished.

A minute later, Moira found herself seated at the desk, with Danny on his knees before her, digging in the drawer.

"What are you doing?" she asked him.

"Taking every lecherous opportunity I can to get closer."

She started to rise, but he already had her shoe off. She gave up.

"Let's get those stockings off, as well," he said.

"They aren't stockings. They're panty hose."

"All the better."

"Danny..."

"You've got to be careful, Moira. You can't go running out of the pub after people."

There was no lightness to his tone. Nor was there a teasing look in his eyes. He was suddenly dead serious.

"Okay, Danny, I won't go running out of the pub after people anymore," she said. She lowered her head, speaking softly. "If you had been around, I could have asked you to go after Seamus."

"That's right. But Seamus is a grown man."

"Seamus was acting very strange tonight."

"Oh? What did he say?"

"I don't remember," she lied. "He was just speaking...strangely."

"Was he afraid?"

"Should he have been?"

"I'm just trying to figure out why you went running after him. Moira, take off the panty hose. I'll close my eyes. Promise. Not that..."

"Danny, I'll just go up and take care of my own injuries."

"You're that afraid of me touching your leg?"

"I'm not at all afraid of you touching my leg. So apparently what I'm supposed to do now is prove it by slipping out of my panty hose?"

"Well, yeah," he said, offering a rueful grin.

She was suddenly tempted to reach out and touch his hair. Always a bit unruly and unkempt, it fit him. Like the half smile he so frequently wore.

"You're trying to ruin my life," she told him.

"Never."

"I have a great job and a wonderful relationship."

"He has beady eyes."

"He's a bona fide decent man."

"I disagree. Besides, is that what you want to settle for? Decent?"

"You told me I should have married Josh."

"I didn't mean it."

She rose suddenly and stepped behind the desk to shimmy out of her panty hose. Then she sat in the chair. His fingers were gentle as he studied the gash on her knee. "And you didn't even feel this?"

"I felt like an icicle from head to toe, how was I going to feel anything else? And what is that you're about to put on me? Don't you dare—"

"Peroxide. It won't hurt."

It didn't. The peroxide bubbled and nothing more. He wiped at the wound with a square of cotton. She watched his hands and his lowered head. Great hands. Danny always had great hands. Long fingers, clipped nails.

Strong hands. He had always been able to open the most stubborn jar known to man.

"And what's that?" she demanded cautiously.

"Neosporin. It won't hurt you, and since when do you act like such a big baby?"

"Since I'm so tired and aggravated. What were you doing outside?"

"I told you, I was saying goodbye to some friends. My turn—what were you really doing out there?"

"Running after Seamus. Danny, damn it, what's going on around here?"

"Nothing, most certainly nothing." He placed a Band-Aid on her knee. "Not if I have any say in it," he murmured.

She caught his chin, lifting his eyes to hers. "What are you going on about?"

"Nothing, Moira. All I'm saying is that I'd die before I'd let anything happen to anyone in your family."

"Why should anything happen to anyone in my family?"

He let out an aggravated sigh. "I was just speaking hypothetically, Moira, all right?"

She stood abruptly. He wasn't going to say anything more to her. "I'm going up to bed. Thanks for the first aid."

"Hey!"

She started and looked toward the doorway to the bar. Patrick was standing there, staring at her and Danny, who remained on the floor as she stood.

"It's getting to her head, eh, the television thing? She's got you on your knees before her," Patrick observed.

"He was giving me first aid," Moira said.

"I've heard she likes her men on their knees," Danny quipped in return.

"Careful there, I'm her older brother, remember?"

"And where have you been?" she demanded.

Patrick arched a brow. "The guy from that charity thing was here tonight. I was just walking down the street with him, pointing out how close his hotel was to the pub. Why? You know, I have a wife now, to give me a third degree. What's the matter?"

"I wanted somebody to walk Seamus home."

"He lives a few blocks away."

"He'd had a few too many," she said.

"I was gone, you were gone—even her precious Michael was nowhere to be found," Danny said. "And then, poor lass, trying to be an escort herself, she went sliding right across the ice."

"Where was precious Michael?" Patrick asked.

"Precious Michael—" she began, then sighed with aggravation. "Michael doesn't work here."

"Neither do I."

"It's our pub."

"Right. I'll try not to let you down next time. Good thing you didn't skin your ass, huh, Moira?" Patrick said.

"Cute, big brother, real cute."

"That could have been interesting," Danny murmured.

"Go to hell, both of you," she said sweetly.

She turned and went upstairs.

She could feel Danny watching her as she went.

It was late night. Very late.

Or early morning, depending on one's point of view.

At that time of night—or morning—he went by a different name. He had identification to match many names.

The art of subterfuge, of course, was always to hide in plain sight. The eyes didn't always believe what they saw because the mind went by what it was told. Glasses could change a man, a change of hairstyle or color, facial hair, no facial hair. For the most part, people went along their day-by-day routines noting very little.

He had always felt sorry for the kids he knew as faces on milk cartons. Few people, pouring a drop into their coffee or drowning their cereal, ever looked twice at those little faces. And that was how they were in life, too.

It worked well for him.

He should have been keeping a low profile. They were

in the waiting period now. Nothing to do but wait and see how events progressed.

Wait...

Days were easy enough. Nights were hard.

Restlessly, he walked the streets. He picked a different bar for a nightcap. A place in a not-so-great section of town where the hours went by unnoticed and the drinks were watered but cheap. He'd really had no plans other than a drink, but there was something about the girl at the end of the bar. She had long hair, thick, with a reddish tinge.

Dye.

No matter. The bar was dark and dingy.

Her skirt was very short; her stockings had a snag. Her boots, displayed nicely by legs wound around her bar stool, were stilettos. *Sweet love, you should just wear a sign around your neck that says prostitute,* he thought with some amusement. But there was a forlorn quality about her face. From a distance, she was even pretty. A little girl lost, gone the wrong way. And now here she was in this life, no way out....

She looked up and noticed him watching her. He offered a smile. "Hi."

She smiled back, perking up, surveying the cut of his clothing. He had dressed down for tonight. Still, for this place, he was well attired.

"Can I buy you a drink?" he asked.

Her smile broadened, and she slid off her stool, hurrying to take the one next to his. "Lovely," she said. He frowned, noting an accent in the one word. "I'm Cary. How do you do, and thank you very much. And you are...?"

"Richard. Richard Jordan," he lied.

"English?" she said with a frown, trying to place his accent. "I should really know, I suppose."

"Australian," he said. "But I've been around."

"It's a glorious accent, really."

"And yours."

She made a face. "I can't seem to leave County Cork behind."

"And do you want to?"

"Oh, yes. Things back home are so fucked up."

"It's a beautiful place."

"Not if you had me mum and da," she told him. "Him going off all the time, fighting a silly war, cheatin' on her. Her taken' in boarders. That's what she called her men. When I told her that no matter what I did, I'd call a spade a spade, she hit me and threw me out of the house. I don't give a damn about the old country, except that..." She paused, looking at him ruefully. "Sorry, this isn't what you expected. I'm a little tired. There are masses of Americans in town who think they're Irish. So many assholes!"

"Ah, I see," he murmured.

"Cold?" she asked him.

"Eh?"

"You have gloves on—inside."

"Um. It's a bit chilly."

"I can warm you up, you know," she told him. Then shrugged. "I told you, I call a spade a spade myself. I was about all in. Too many assholes. But you're...different. I mean, I'm not offering a freebie or anything, I am a working girl. But with you...I'd throw in a few extras at no charge."

There was that look about her. Innocence turned to dime trash. Optimism ground down by weariness. She had attracted him, angered him and aroused him. She was trash. Gutter trash.

But he was restless. In a mood to roll in the dirt.

"Fine. Get your coat while I pay for the drinks."

* * *

On Sunday morning, the first and foremost event in the Kelly household was church. Moira, on the phone with Michael, told him he certainly wasn't obliged to go.

"I wouldn't miss it," he assured her. "I'm very carefully working my way into your father's heart, you know."

"Well, I admit, an appearance at Mass always sets well with him."

"What happened to you last night?" he asked her. "Did the Sunday thing kick in after midnight?"

"What happened to me? Where did you go? You left without saying goodbye."

She heard a soft sigh. "I'm embarrassed to tell you."

"Tell me anyway."

"I forgot to collect a check. The people walked out. My indignation kicked in, and I went out after them."

"People walked out on a check? At my dad's place?"

"I must be a very bad waiter."

"No, you're a wonderful waiter, I'm sure. Most of the people who come in are regulars, but it is a public establishment. You simply lucked out and got the bad eggs."

"Ah, there you go. Loyal to the core. No wonder I love you."

"I love you, too."

"Anyway, I never found the people, so I slipped back in and paid the check myself so I wouldn't have to tell anyone. Then I looked for you, to say goodbye, but you weren't around, so I went back to the hotel. I waited up, though."

"I'm sorry. Things happened, and I..."

"This family bit isn't easy, is it?"

"Michael, truly..."

"Hey, I understand. Saint Patrick's Day will come. And go. I'll meet you at the church."

"You can come here—"

"You've got enough people there to keep track of. I'll go with Josh and his wife and the twins. We'll meet you there."

* * *

There was definitely confusion, getting out of the Kelly household. In a thousand years, Moira knew, she would never be the kind of mother Katy Kelly managed to be. Despite the confusion, breakfast had to be served early enough to make sure all food would be consumed an hour before communion. Siobhan got the girls into the tub, sending Patrick to pound on Moira's bathroom door, telling her that he had to take a shower, too.

"Hey, I just got in here!" she shouted at her brother.

"Just wash all body parts once—soaking is only necessary for laundry."

"Oh, yeah? Like you know anything about laundry."

"Moira, how dirty can you be?"

"Go shout at Colleen to get out of her bathroom."

"I think she fell asleep in there. And aren't you supposed to be helping Mum or something?"

"You can help Mum, too, you chauvinist."

"I'm not a chauvinist. I give credit where credit is due. You're a wiz with toast, Moira Kelly, that you are."

"Go use Mum's and Dad's bathroom."

"Brian is in there. He's a big lad now, you know. He doesn't hop into the tub with the girls."

"Then next time you can drag your butt out of bed faster than your kids, Patrick."

"You could have been done by now, little sister, if you weren't so intent on fighting with me."

"Quit tormenting me. Go downstairs and kick Danny out of the guest bathroom."

"How rude. You want me to torment a guest?"

"Danny's no guest."

"Besides, he's a guy, and he probably took a normal shower."

Her brother disappeared, much to her delight. When she emerged, she discovered that Siobhan had finished with her shower and the kids' bath; the girls were outfitted beautifully in velvet dresses. They were at the table, helping their grandmother by smothering toast with enough butter for a dozen batches of cookies. "Whoa there, let me give you a hand," Moira suggested, sitting with the girls.

"Thanks," Siobhan said softly. She was in the process of flipping bacon. When her sister-in-law turned, Moira saw that she seemed even paler than she had the day before. Circles rimmed her beautiful eyes.

"Just a bit, that's all we need," Moira told Shannon.

"I have it right, Auntie Mo," Shannon said gravely. "It's Molly. She likes to eat butter just plain, you know."

"Well, Molly, today we're going to have a little toast with our butter," Moira said. Her niece giggled and looked at her adoringly. She patted the little head of angel soft hair. "Today we're going to be really good, Ok? I have a special treat in store for you later. Your mum looks a little tired, so be really, really good for me, okay?"

Molly nodded gravely. "Toast with the butter."

"Right." Moira walked to Siobhan at the stove. "Are you all right?"

"Of course," Siobhan said, too quickly.

"You need a break. You and Patrick need to get out without the kids."

"Patrick is always out without the kids. Our kids, at any rate," she murmured. She quickly flashed a glance Moira's way. "You know, he's busy."

"So are you."

"A different busy, I guess. He's the breadwinner and all that. I'm not being disloyal. I love your brother."

"So do I, but that doesn't mean he might not need a good kick in the butt. I needed him last night, and he was nowhere to be found."

"Oh, really?" Siobhan murmured, staring at the bacon she flipped. "What was wrong?"

"I thought Seamus needed someone to walk him home. Naturally I couldn't find any of the guys."

"Men!" Colleen announced, sweeping into the kitchen and making the announcement as if she'd been in on the entire conversation. "That's the way it goes." She looked around to see if her mother was anywhere in the vicinity. "They're like leeches when they want something, especially sex. Need them, and only the good Lord knows where they've gotten to."

"Now, darlin', that's not true a'tall," Danny said, making an appearance from the den. He had apparently been upstairs for some time, Moira thought, and wondered why that made her uneasy. "I'm here, right here. And I can cook. Siobhan Kelly, you take a seat. I'll finish this up."

"Where's Mum?" Moira asked as Danny ushered Siobhan into a chair.

"Finally taking a shower," Danny said. "Colleen, me fine beauty, take a seat."

"Thanks, I'll sit and watch you, too—closely," Moira said.

"Ach, there she goes, the star in motion. Moira, take care of the bacon there while I whip up the eggs."

She had a fork in her hands before she knew it, and Danny got busy with the eggs. Colleen didn't sit; she started bringing out juice, coffee and tea.

Moira flipped the bacon onto a plate covered with paper towels to absorb the grease, watching Danny. He could cook, and he was efficient. He looked damned good in the jacket and trousers he had donned for church, and he was freshly shaven, his scent far too appealing.

"Where's lover boy?" he asked.

"Meeting us at church."

"Ah, he's a good Catholic boy, is he? Or is he just making more Brownie points with your father?"

"Naturally he's a good Catholic boy," she said sweetly. "And of course you know, if we're married, being the daughter I am, we'll be married in the family church in Boston, so it's good that he gets to attend a mass there now.''

"*If,*" Danny said.

"What?"

"You didn't say when, you said if. There must be some doubt in your mind."

"Not a lick," she told him sweetly.

"Oh, thank the Lord. It's all under control," Katy said, sweeping in from the hallway. "Danny, you are a doll."

"Danny? Siobhan was doing it all," Moira said.

"No, actually, Danny was in here before. He just had to make a phone call," Siobhan said.

"A phone call? In the middle of making bacon? How important it must have been," Moira muttered.

"All my phone calls are important," Danny informed her. "Eggs are on, and the oatmeal for Eamon is just about right. Katy Kelly, you have a seat. I'll serve."

Eamon came out from the long hallway, wishing everyone a good morning. Molly ran over to him with a piece of toast. "Granda! I made it just for you."

"Oh, Molly dear, Granda can't have that toast. He'll be in the hospital with a coronary for sure," Katy protested.

"Katy, I'll not really eat it," Eamon assured his wife. "Molly Kelly, you bring me that toast. It will be extra special delicious."

Patrick arrived from downstairs, Granny Jon walked in, and the family sat. Eamon said grace, but before the amen he paused and looked around the table. "Thank you, Lord, for letting me have me family all here. Thank you for this squabbling tribe of ruffians who still do their old dad proud by coming home for Saint Patrick's Day, and thank you, too, for old friends who are like kin, and giving us Danny here for this happy occasion, as well."

"Amen to that, and let's eat," Patrick said.

"Patrick, your father was praying," Katy moaned.

"Aye, and bless the Irish, and let's eat!" Patrick said.

"I wasn't quite finished," Eamon said sternly. "I was about to bless the Lord for gracing me with a daughter-in-law like Siobhan, beautiful inside and out, a lady who has given me three of the greatest gifts a man could ever hope for, Brian, Shannon and Molly, who helps to make the world's most incredible toast."

"Here, here," Moira said, staring at her brother. "To Siobhan—and the kids, of course."

Molly giggled. Granny Jon glanced at the old silver watch pendant she always wore. "To Siobhan. And Patrick's right—let's eat. We'll be closing in on communion if we're not careful."

"The very last toast," Danny announced, lifting his coffee cup. "To Eamon Kelly, his lovely wife Kathleen, and to the bacon and toast."

"Ah, there we go. Now, let's wolf this down and get going," Patrick said.

"Busy day?" Siobhan asked him sweetly.

He looked at his wife. "Church," he replied, just as sweetly.

"Mass waits for no man," Danny murmured.

Michael, Josh and his family were already at the church. Since it was her family's church, Moira greeted Michael instantly and affectionately but discreetly, despite the fact that she had sat in the back of the family car between Siobhan and Danny on the way to Mass and had been dying to throw herself at Michael the moment she stepped into the cathedral. She was able to be more openly enthusiastic with Gina, Josh's wife, hugging her friend and admiring the twins, who seemed to grow by leaps and bounds every week. She instantly picked up one of the twins to hold during the service. The babies were angelic little boys who already looked like Josh. She held Gregory, the older of the two, who lay in her arms sweetly sleeping.

She sat during the sermon, giving more attention to the warm bundle in her arms than to the priest, until she heard him talking about Saint Patrick's Day and announcing the arrival of Jacob Brolin in the city of Boston and asking his congregation to pray for Brolin and the message of peace he brought not only to Northern Ireland, but to all men in Ireland, all men of Irish descent and all men throughout the world. His sermon was stirring, one that reminded his congregation that more than the arms procured for violence in other places came from American financing, that American businesses and tourists helped bring prosperity and the hope of peace. It was a good sermon, earning a round of applause at the end, despite the final words being, "Let us pray."

The applause woke Gregory, who immediately began to cry. Moira tried to soothe him, only to find the infant being plucked from her arms by Danny, who lifted the boy high in his arms, whispered a few words and immediately—to Moira's annoyance—elicited a coo of soft baby laughter.

"I'll take him back," she whispered.

"You'll only get him crying again."

"I will not."

"You're edgy, and he knows it."

"I'm not edgy."

"You reek of hostility. You're even angry that I can manage an infant."

"I am not."

"You're arguing, Moira, during the most holy passages of the Eucharist."

"Damn it, keep the baby."

"Moira Kathleen Kelly! We're in church."

"Darn it, then. Keep the baby. What are you doing next to me, anyway?"

"I slipped past Colleen when I saw that you were in distress."

"I'm not in distress."

"There's your good Michael, on his knees next to you, love. Don't you just feel the urge to kneel down beside him? He's praying. What do you think he's praying for? Peace among the Irish, or for you to make good on a promise and show up in his hotel room in the middle of the night? Or even...for something more sinister?"

"Danny..."

"I know what I'm praying for."

"Peace in the world?"

"Oh, that, too, of course."

"I'm going to hit you in a minute, even if we are in church."

"Your whispers are growing awfully loud."

"*My* whispers?"

"You're supposed to be on your knees, Moira. Bonding with your love. I truly wish I could hear your Michael's prayers."

"You should be on your knees."

"I'm holding a baby, in case you haven't noticed."

Moira ignored him, kneeling beside Michael, taking his hand. He squeezed hers in return. When Moira rose for the Lord's Prayer, she managed to take the baby from Danny, and, after kissing or shaking hands with her family and everyone nearby, she changed her position to Danny's other side.

Outside the church, the Kelly children dutifully greeted all their parents' old friends, and Moira introduced Michael around.

Danny had enough friends of his own.

Standing with Michael, waiting for her folks to finish the after Mass coffee, Moira felt the warmth of their close-knit little community within the large city. She closed her eyes for a minute. She loved New York, but she also loved Boston. She even loved the Irish eccentricities of her family and friends. Everyone was so enthused about the arrival of Jacob Brolin. They spoke about him as if they were speaking about the Second Coming.

"He's from Belfast, isn't he?" Michael said.

"What?"

"Your old friend. Danny. He's from Belfast."

"He was born there, yes. I don't know that much about when he was really young. He was brought up by an uncle who traveled a great deal. He was here a lot, and he also spent some time growing up in Dublin, I think."

"I've heard he was a wild man in his youth. IRA?"

"Was Danny actually in the IRA? I don't think so," Moira said, noticing that the man in question was approaching them.

"Well, Michael, how did you survive family day at church?" Danny asked cheerfully.

"It's rather charming," Michael said.

"Yup. Everyone praying for Jacob Brolin."

"He must be quite a man. Moira, you should call him, ask about an interview for the show."

"You're the locations manager, right?" Danny said. "You haven't tried to reach him yourself?"

Michael shrugged, ignoring the suggestion of rebuke in the question.

"I'm not Moira Kelly. I think that kind of request would be better coming from her. I just handle places, she handles people. Having him on tape. That would be a coup for the show. Right, Moira?"

She was listening to Michael but noting that Seamus was in a group not far from them. "Excuse me, will you? There's Seamus. I have a bone to pick with him."

"We'll say hi, as well," Danny said, following her as she started in Seamus's direction.

The group around Seamus was saying goodbye. Seamus didn't seem to notice. He was too busy staring at the three of them as they approached.

"Seamus, there you are," Moira said. "Why did you run out on me like that last night?"

Seamus wasn't looking at her. He was watching the two men.

"Seamus?"

He suddenly snapped his attention to her. "Ah, Moira, I merely took myself on home."

"You were behaving so strangely."

"I'm Irish, eh? We all talk fairy tales. I'll be seeing you later, Moira Kelly, at the pub. Drinking me ale and nothing more. Ta, now."

He turned and left.

"What on earth is up with him?" Moira murmured, more to herself than to Danny or Michael.

"He's Irish, like he says. You can't go worrying about every one of your father's friends. The old coot is eccentric. Let it go, Moira," Michael said.

She felt Danny's hand on her arm and heard his soft whisper. "For once, lover boy is right. Let it go, Moira. Let it go."

9

"Beady eyes, eh?" Moira whispered to Danny.

He seemed impossible to shake.

They had decided to take their filming to the streets of Boston that afternoon. Moira still wanted a segment on her grandmother telling the old tales, but after a meeting with Jeff and Michael, they had decided that they also needed more general scenes in the Boston area, so she'd decided to combine the two. Michael had already arranged a permit for Quincy Market and the Faneuil Hall area, so they had brought the cast and crew to the historic area where shops designed to meet contemporary tastes now abounded.

Her mother, always concerned that things work out, had arranged for friends to bring their children. Moira had her grandmother seated on a bench, surrounded by a flock of children.

It was an old adage, but true—it was never easy filming animals and children. She hadn't asked for any animals, but the children were all going crazy over every pooch being walked through the area by a pup-loving Bostonian.

Michael was doing the best anyone could expect on critter control, herding children to where they were supposed to be, assuring dog owners that they could be in a crowd shot as long as they were willing to sign releases. As the last minute camera angles were set up, Michael took control of the children, assuring them that since there were a few monsters in Irish lore, they would be entertained. After getting the last child seated, he left, placing a gentle hand on Molly's head as he went. Moira hadn't been about to keep her nieces and nephew out of this group, and she'd been glad of it, because Patrick and Siobhan had come to watch the taping, and their offspring, together.

"Okay, so he's good with kids and canines," Danny admitted, drawing her line of thought away from her family. "Just remember, Hansel and Gretel thought the witch in the woods was a kind old lady until they were nearly stuffed in the oven."

"Wise, Danny, wise. I'll remember that."

"Your grandmother is holding her own," he pointed out.

It was true. Granny Jon had her crowd spellbound. "The banshee, you see, is a death ghost. She howls and cries in the night when she comes for the souls of those about to depart this world. In America you have hundreds of monsters—so many from the cinema, right? Well, when I was a little girl in Ireland, we had the banshees. We knew the terrible wail they could make and knew when to be afraid. And the older folk used to warn us to behave, because if we didn't, do you know what could happen?"

The kids were all watching her expectantly.

"What?" whispered one young boy, perhaps eight or nine years old.

"The banshees would get you on your way in or out of the outhouse."

"What's an outhouse?" a little girl asked.

"Ah, well, there I go, showing just how old an old woman I am," Granny Jon said. "Way back when I was a girl in Dublin, we didn't have a bathroom right in our house. No charming little place with tile and scented soaps and the like. Our loos—" She paused and looked at the kids and laughed. "Sorry, our toilets were in a little house behind the main house. And sometimes, at night, when it was very, very dark, and maybe a storm was coming, and you slipped outside at night, you could hear the wind howling in the trees. The branches would sway and cast huge shadows, and in those shadows, you could see the sad, dark form of the banshee as she swept down into the night.''

''Did she ever get you?'' a little boy asked anxiously.

''Well, now, no, of course not, or I'd not be here to tell the tale.''

The kids burst into laughter.

''Please tell me they had the tape running for that,'' Moira murmured.

''You've got it,'' Danny said, pointing to the cameraman.

''There's another tale involving children,'' Granny Jon went on. ''There was a great king, and his name was Lir. He had four children, and he loved them dearly. He lost his lovely wife and later remarried. But his love for his children remained the greatest love in his life. His new wife had magical powers, and she was very jealous of the children. She took them to the lake and cast a spell upon them, turning them into swans for nine hundred years. She wasn't really a terrible witch, and she felt guilty immediately, so she gave the swans the gift of song. They could sing like nightingales. The swans became honored all over Ireland. That was in the ancient days, and during those nine hundred years, a man named Saint Patrick brought Christianity to Ireland. The nine hundred years ended, and the children turned into people again, but their years of being swans had weakened them, and they were frail. They were baptized, however, before they passed on, and became children of God. Their father was bereft and ordered that, in their honor, no swan should be killed in Ireland, and to this day there is a law protecting swans in all Ireland.''

''Their father was still alive?'' a towheaded girl asked, amazed. ''He was even older than my daddy!''

"Oh, yes, he was very, very old," Granny Jon said, and winked. "That's why we have stories, though, myths and legends and tales. And in most legends, a little bit is true, a little bit is exaggerated, and some of the story is a downright lie. But Irish stories are like all others, tales we tell to explain what goes on in life, or perhaps stories that are just for fun."

"Like leprechauns?" a boy asked.

"Oh, no," Granny Jon said. "Leprechauns are real. Well, so legend has it."

The taping went wonderfully. Stray children wandered over to join the crowd. Patrick and Siobhan watched delightedly, arm and arm, as they observed their own brood piping up with pieces of information they already knew, becoming stars to the kids around them.

When filming was finished, the Boston crew broke quickly, making arrangements with Michael and Josh for the following day. Granny Jon was tired, eager to go home. Danny immediately volunteered to take her and suggested the kids might want to go, too, telling Patrick and Siobhan not to worry, if Mum was worn out, he would do the babysitting. Siobhan gratefully accepted the offer.

Josh suggested that they have supper somewhere in the area.

"Little Italy has some of the best food in the world," Patrick said.

"Not as good as Kelly's Pub, surely," Michael said.

"Sal's family has a place down here, and it's excellent," Moira said. "And Italian will be a wonderful change."

"I won't tell Mum you said that," Patrick told her.

"Mum loves Italian food," Moira said. "But we won't stay late, anyway. This may be Sunday, but that never stopped an Irishman from going to a pub. And we're getting closer and closer to Saint Patrick's Day. I don't want to leave Dad in the lurch."

"Colleen is home," Patrick reminded her.

"Yes, but he may need more help."

"That's true," Patrick said. "We should stick around and help, as much as possible."

"Yes," Siobhan murmured. "You have so many friends and associates coming in these days, after all."

There was an underlying bitterness to her tone, Moira thought, but she was the only one who seemed to hear it.

"We won't be long," Josh said. "But Italian food sounds great right now."

"Josh, you sure as hell don't have to work at the pub," Patrick said. "Why are you worried about time?"

"I can't leave Gina at the hotel all night with the kids alone."

"Call her and tell her come down," Moira suggested.

"No, she'll have eaten and she'll be getting the twins to sleep. I'll grab something with you, then head on back. It shouldn't take too much time."

"No, it's early for the real dinner crowd. We can walk over. Little Italy is right across the road," Siobhan said.

As they walked, Patrick commented that they never quit with the roadwork in Boston. Siobhan pointed out that they were in the very heart of a city that was trying to accommodate a growing population, so the work was necessary.

"It's a crazy city," Patrick said.

"I love Boston," Moira protested. "It has something for everyone—the old, with buildings dating from the birth of the nation, and the new."

"It has the ethnic—the Irish and the Italians," Siobhan added.

"And everyone else now. A growing Asian population, Hispanic, European, everyone," Moira protested.

"Let's not forget Boston baked beans," Patrick said dryly.

"And if the kids were here, they'd tell you that Boston

baked beans make the snobby people fart, and then they can't be so snobby anymore," Siobhan said.

"There you go, a city with everything, culture—and wicked good farting," Patrick said.

He slipped an arm around his wife. As they walked, Moira found that she and Michael were at the rear of the crowd, almost alone. They passed a restaurant where an outside sign advertised Live Maine Lobster, 2 for $19.95.

"Does that mean we'd have to eat them while they were still alive?" Michael queried lightly.

"A grim thought, those claws snapping at you as you munched down," she responded.

"This is nice," Michael said.

"What?"

"Me, you. A distance from the rest of your world. The absence of your old buddy boy, Dan O'Hara."

"Michael, he's a longtime family friend. There's not much I can do about that."

"I'm delighted that he skipped dinner."

"So am I."

His arm around her shoulder, he squeezed her tightly to him. "You know, he was right about one thing."

"What's that?"

"I should have contacted Jacob Brolin's people."

"I'm sure he's being bombarded by the networks and the major cable stations."

"But you have an edge. You're a beautiful woman, and you're Irish."

"I'm an American—and thanks for the compliment."

"First generation, and the compliment is due. I think you definitely have an edge. Maybe...maybe I was afraid to say much more at the time. I feel this macho power struggle thing with your Mr. O'Hara, and I didn't want to admit that I might fall short in any way. But in all honesty, I think you might want to try to make contact yourself.

You are an Irish American, a woman, and your father does run one of the most prestigious Irish pubs in the city.''

''Hmm.''

''What?''

''I don't know. I never thought of the pub as being prestigious. Warm, fun, a great place. My dad is an excellent host. He creates a really great atmosphere. But we're not like a gourmet restaurant or anything.''

''I'm willing to bet that if old Jacob Brolin has heard anything about Boston, he'll have heard about Kelly's Pub.''

''There are tons of pubs here.''

''But your father's is down-home authentic.''

''All right, I'll call Brolin. Or call his people—that may be as close as I can get.''

''Good for you. I'm convinced you're the best man— sorry, woman—for breaking the ice.''

''Maybe you're right.'' She pointed to a shop along their way. ''You can buy the best cannoli in the world in that store. Sal's aunt owns it. The older generation sits outside, arguing in Italian and playing checkers—when the weather is decent, of course. The Old—''

''—North Church is right down there,'' Michael finished for her. ''Hey, I'm your locations manager. I scout things out.''

She laughed, hugging him.

''C'mon, quick kiss. Your brother isn't looking.''

''My brother knows all about you.''

''You talk about that with your brother?''

''Well, no, but I'm sure he knows the extent of our relationship.''

They paused in the street, where he pressed the lightest kiss against her lips. She felt the bulk of his shoulders in her arms, the strength in his height as he cradled her to him. She buried her face against his chest. Yes, she was in love with him.

"You know," he murmured.

"What?"

"Watch out for him."

"Who?"

"Your friend. Danny."

She drew back. "Watch out for him. Why?"

He shook his head. "Last night, when I was trying to hunt down the group that stiffed me on the bill, he was outside. In the shadows. Looking very suspicious. The guy *is* from Belfast. He could be a loose cannon. I don't know—maybe I'm just jealous of his position in the bosom of your family. But...for me, be careful. Something about him makes me uneasy. I know he's a good friend and all, and this is just a feeling, but keep your distance a little, huh? Just to humor me?"

He was staring at her, deep blue eyes incredibly serious.

"Hey, are you two coming?" Patrick called.

Moira realized that they were standing in front of Paul Revere's house. The sun was completely gone; the last of the tourists were leaving.

The restaurant was right around the corner.

"Sure," Moira called.

Michael thought that she was agreeing with him, as well, and he smiled. Taking her hand, he hurried toward Patrick, who was waiting impatiently at the corner as if, after all these years, Moira just might forget where Sal's family's restaurant was situated.

"Kids, Granny Jon, I've got one quick stop to make, if you'll allow me. I want to pick up some of those cannoli Katy likes so much," Dan told his passengers. He was driving Eamon Kelly's minivan. The kids were wearing their seat belts; they were well-trained. Even little Molly immediately buckled up the minute she got into a car.

Granny Jon, next to him, nodded. "Pick up a few of

those Italian cookies, too, please, Danny. The ones with vanilla, not anise."

"Got ya. Kids?"

"Chocolate!" Shannon said. And with a sigh way older than her years, she added, "You can just buy a stick of butter for Molly."

"Butter cookies," Brian said.

"Chocolate-covered butter cookies." Molly giggled. "Candy."

"No candy. It's an Italian bakery, silly girl," Dan teased.

The first parking space he could squeeze into was about a block from the restaurant. Perfect. He left the car running, the heat on.

"No driving," he warned Brian.

Brian grinned.

"I'll hurry," Dan said.

"We're just fine here. I'll keep the kids amused," Granny Jon said.

Dan nodded, closed the driver's door and started down the street at a brisk walk. He knew the exact shop he wanted and slipped in quickly. He smiled at the dark-haired girl behind the counter. Elena. He'd bought pastries here before.

"A box of cannoli, some sugar cookies…biscotti with vanilla, not anise, and…have you got anything with chocolate?"

"Frosted butter cookies?" Elena suggested.

"Perfect. I'll be making a phone call."

The phone was right inside the doorway. He dropped coins into the slot and dialed the number he needed. A soft female voice answered with a simple hello.

"Liz, it's Dan."

"Where are you?"

"Public phone. Have you got anything for me?"

"Well, I've checked out your man."

"And?"

"Born in Ohio, actually, Irish-American parents. Good schools, good jobs. Film major, degree from UCLA. He's worked as a production assistant, cameraman, sound tech—anything and everything behind the camera. Never acted. He won some film school prizes for production and direction. Left California, worked in Florida, Vancouver and, last year, made the move to New York."

Idly staring out the window, Dan tensed. Patrick and Siobhan Kelly were ambling past the shop. Josh was walking alone, catching up with the two of them. Dan stepped back against the support beam that would allow him to look out but keep passersby from noticing him.

"So he came to New York—and took his first job with Moira Kelly's show?"

"That's what I've got here. And you know I know how to trace people."

"You're sure? There's nothing on him at all? No political activities, no protests against cruelty to animals, nothing? No protests against American military action?"

"Dan, the guy doesn't have his own Web page. I haven't managed to get any warm, fuzzy photos of him with his old teddy bear. But from everything I can find, the guy is clean. I can tell you he has no arrest record, no known political affiliations—his voter's registration even has him as an independent. He's never even been late paying a parking ticket, as far as I can make out."

"He seems suspicious to me anyway. And there's word on the street about something going down."

"Well, if there's anything dirty about him, it's well-hidden, that much I can tell you."

Frustrated, Dan kept looking out the window. The object of his inquiry was walking by, an arm tightly wrapped around Moira's shoulder. *Slime bucket.* Moira was smiling at him, laughing. Oh, yeah, the guy was picture-perfect. Dan narrowed his eyes. Tall, in damned good shape, probably lifted weights, kickboxed and had a black belt in karate.

All the better to be...

Fucking picture-perfect.

And, on paper at least, he was as pure as the driven snow.

"Keep looking," Dan said. The pair had stopped outside the Revere house. They didn't seem to notice the tourists streaming by them.

Together, they were definitely picture-perfect. Moira, absolutely stunning, red-tinged hair streaming down her back as she lifted her classically beautiful face to his ever so tender kiss. McLean, tall, seeming to tower over her in masculine protection, though Moira was tall herself.

"Dan, you there?"

"Keep looking," Dan insisted.

"For what?" Liz asked.

"I don't know. But something isn't right."

"You're obsessed, Dan O'Hara."

"It's my job to be wary."

"It's your job to do a hell of a lot more than that," Liz reminded him.

"Has he ever been to Ireland?"

"Yes—his first semester of college."

"Hmm. There. There's something."

"Oh, yeah, there's something. Something done by countless college kids with money. He toured Ireland, England, Scotland and the Continent. Spent most of his time in Florence and Rome. Dan, I've checked him out with a fine-tooth comb."

"Keep looking," Dan insisted. There they went, down the street, Moira still in his arms.

"Dan—"

"Keep looking."

"Just in case you're interested," Liz said dryly, "Patrick Kelly has gotten pretty deeply involved with a group called Americans for Children.''

"It's a legitimate charity, right?''

"It's new, but it appears so. Still, some of the founders are old IRA guys, émigrés to the States. May be Patrick Kelly has his eye on your movements.''

"Right.''

"Then there's Jeff Dolan.''

"Dolan has a rap sheet that would put the toughest inner-city kid to shame,'' Dan said impatiently. "But he's burned out.''

"He could still be keeping his eyes on you. He could be the one.''

"Lizzie, like I said, I'm wary. By nature. *I'm* watching him, and I'm sure he's keeping tabs on me, as well. Have you talked to The Man?''

"Of course. I'm in constant communication.''

"And we're still on? For sure?''

"Yes.''

"Damn.''

"What's the matter? You're supposed to be good.''

"Oh, Lizzie,'' he teased back. "You don't know just how good. It's what's at stake that chills my blood.''

"Keep your eyes open. He can't be swayed. And he'll contact you in his own way, in his own time.''

"Yeah. And you keep checking on Michael McLean.''

"Don't you go letting your heart—or your dick—get in your way,'' Liz said bluntly.

"You know me, Lizzie,'' he said lightly. "I never let anything get in my way. Never.''

He hung up the phone. Elena had finished his order. He paid her, hurried out of the shop and down to the car.

Dinner was going beautifully—and then Danny arrived.

"Hey, where are my kids?'' Siobhan asked, seeing him come in the door. He was not to be missed. The restaurant was small and intimate, as were many of the restaurants in Boston, especially in Little Italy, and he was a big man.

Danny strode over, shedding his wool coat as he did so and hanging it on the rack. Moira hadn't thought to worry that she was at the edge of the semicircular booth, Michael beside her, Siobhan beside him, Patrick next and Josh in the chair drawn up to the free edge of the table.

Bad choice, she realized, as Danny slid in beside her. "The kids? Oh, I dropped them in traffic, naturally."

"Seriously..." Siobhan began.

Patrick let out an impatient snort. "Seriously, he dropped them in traffic."

"Seriously," Danny said, smiling at Siobhan, "your mother was delighted to have some time alone with them. What's good, huh? Everything, right? Hey, I see that Sal is working his own restaurant for a change."

"We're having the house special," Patrick said. "A pasta sampler with ziti, lasagna, spaghetti, and an antipasto."

"I'm not sure what it all is, but it's great," Siobhan added, looking at the large platter filled with Italian delicacies in the middle of the table.

Sal had reached the table, taking Danny's hand, shaking it. "Hey, it's my Italian amico," he said. "Benvenuto."

"Grazie, Salvatore," Danny said. "Hey, this looks wonderful. What is everything?"

"I don't want to tell you, not in front of Siobhan."

"Ah, now, Siobhan managed to eat haggis when Katy made it for that Scottish convention a few years back," Danny said, smiling at Siobhan. He made a face. "Sheep's stomach or bladder or some such filled with entrails. Thank the Lord the Scots came up with it or we Irish would be to blame again."

"Well, there's nothing more evil than octopus on that tray," Sal said, "so I guess the Italians are off the hook for the moment, too."

"I don't know, Sal. You all fool around with squid ink an awful lot," Danny said warily.

"It makes good pasta," Sal said. "Excuse me, I'll add another order of the special special for the table."

Sal left, and Danny helped himself to wine from the bottle already at the table. "So, what did I miss?"

"Earth-shattering events," Moira said sharply.

"A lovely time," Siobhan said. "We've been getting to know Michael. He does great imitations. You know, Michael, you should be in front of the camera. You're not just gorgeous, you're talented."

"Are you now?" Danny said, looking past Moira to Michael.

"He can do your accent to perfection," Siobhan said, and Moira wanted to kick her for the innocent remark. Michael had been great, surprising even her with his mastery of a Boston accent, a Bronx intonation, a deep South drawl and, a moment ago, Danny's light brogue.

"I was a film major," Michael said with a shrug. "I never wanted to be in front of the camera, but...thanks," he told Siobhan. "We had to take speech and dialect classes to get through school."

"I'd love to hear you do me," Danny told Michael.

"Can't do it when I'm put on the spot," Michael said.

"Just do a quick Granny Jon, then," Siobhan urged.

Moira moved closer to Michael, distancing herself from Danny. Michael sighed. "Now I'll mess it all up," he said. "All right. 'I'd like me tea strong enough to pick itself up and walk itself right across the table,'" he mimicked, his brogue heavy, but missing here and there, as it had not been before. "See why I can't be in front of the camera?" he asked Siobhan. "I fold under pressure."

"No, no," Danny said. "That was excellent. Why, I would have believed you were from the Old Country meself."

Michael smiled along with the others, but Moira didn't think he was particularly amused.

"Look, here comes dinner," Patrick said, breaking the tension.

Sal assisted the waiter, serving them all quickly. "Delicious," Danny said, digging in. "And safe—no black pasta on the plate, Siobhan."

"Black pasta?"

"Flavored with squid ink," Sal told her, winking. "It's safe, entirely safe. Unless you've gone vegetarian?"

"No, I'm afraid I still chow down on cows."

"Cows have those big brown eyes," Patrick teased her. "So much better to eat them than some creepy-looking squid."

Siobhan smiled at him and looked at Sal. "Whatever it is, it's wonderful. My husband hasn't left the table once to say a quick hello to a business associate. I think I may just turn in the Irish flag and become Italian, Sal."

Sal took her hand. "Cara mia, you may become Italian anytime."

"Sal, let go of my wife and behave, before your own very Italian wife comes out of the kitchen and hits you with a frying pan."

Sal grinned. "Okay, maybe I'll become a Mormon. How about you, Danny?"

"I'm afraid for some of us, Sal, there's just no way out of being Irish," Danny said. "But thank the Lord, even in Ireland, we have lots of Italian restaurants." He looked at Michael, smiling. "Good imitation there, Mikey. Damn good. You're better than you think."

"Oh, I know what I'm good at," Michael told him.

"And you're damn good at whatever it is, right?" Danny asked.

"Damn good," Michael repeated evenly.

"So am I," Danny told him. "So am I."

Moira felt strangely as if she were the buffer between two boxers spoiling for a confrontation.

And oddly, she didn't feel as if she was the prize in the competition.

Josh turned the conversation to his pleasure at the way the filming had gone that day, approving when Moira told him that she was going to try to get an interview with Jacob Brolin. "Danny actually pushed it a bit, and Michael told me later how right he was," Moira said, hoping to create an atmosphere of peace.

"Well, we can try," Josh said. "And we're fine with the crew. I've booked them through the eighteenth. That way we can cover anything we might to have for a post-show. We do that sometimes, follow-ups on places or events we've covered," he told the others, then glanced at his watch. "I've got to go. My hopes for a few in-room dirty movies and a night of wild passion dwindle with each passing moment. The twins are a handful. These days it's a late night for Gina when she makes nine o'clock."

"But the twins are worth it, right?" Moira said.

"Yes. And I'm going to remind you of that when you finally decide to procreate. Only I'm going to wish triplets on you. Night, all."

Josh departed. Sal came by, offering coffee. Danny declined, saying he thought he should get back to the bar.

"You said Katy was fine with the kids," Siobhan reminded him.

"But I'm worried about Eamon with the pub. Chrissie called in sick tonight—seems she ate a bad taco for lunch or something," Danny said.

"Then I should get back, too," Moira said.

"Stay, spend your time with Michael and Siobhan and Patrick. A double date with your brother and his wife, eh?" Danny said. "I've still got your father's car, and you all are in Patrick's." He shook his pocket to jingle the keys and left them.

"We should be there," Moira said to Patrick.

"We'll only be a few minutes longer. I would love to have my coffee in peace before we return to the Irish zoo," Patrick said.

"A cappuccino would be heavenly," Siobhan agreed.

"Espresso for me," Michael told Moira, smiling.

She nodded. "Espresso, sure."

The first person she noticed when she walked into the pub that night was the stranger. The man who had been there before, ordering the blackbird.

She wanted to walk straight to him, but the bar was three deep, so she hurried around to help her father, dropping her purse in one of the empty wells.

"Ah, Moira, how was your dinner?" her father called cheerfully.

"Good, Dad. I should have been back here sooner, though."

"Thank you, daughter, but we do survive when you and your brother and sister are off living your own lives—as you should be," he added quickly.

She took the time to give him a quick kiss on the cheek before she started taking orders and filling glasses. She saw that Seamus was at the bar with Liam. As soon as she had a moment to breathe, she walked toward Seamus's stool. "Are you all right?" she asked him.

"Couldn't be better, Moira Kathleen," he assured her. "Now, don't you go staring at me beer mug. I've had one real beer and one of those nonalcoholic things."

"Good for you, Seamus."

"I'll just spend the evening keeping track of meself, Moira. One and one. Slowly, of course. Don't want you worrying about me. Danny said you took a nasty spill chasing after me."

"I'm fine. Danny shouldn't have said anything."

"Well, he's a good lad. Worried about us both."

She forced a smile for Seamus, then noted that her father was doing just fine at the bar. When Colleen came up with an order for a blackbird, Moira told her sister she would make the drink and deliver it herself. "It's the guy in the corner, right?"

"Yeah, how did you know?"

"Same guy who ordered one the other night."

Moira didn't bother with a tray, since she only had the one drink. She made her way through the tables until she reached the man. Tonight he was in a dark brown sweater. He appeared to be of medium build, perhaps thirty or thirty-five, with brown eyes and neatly trimmed dark hair.

"Hello, welcome to Kelly's. You've been here a few nights now."

"Great band," he told her. He didn't smile, just watched her gravely.

"We hadn't had an order for a blackbird in a while."

"Heard about it from a friend," he said casually. "You're Moira Kelly?"

"Yes."

"I've seen your show." He didn't mention whether he had liked it or not. She was surprised when he said, "Can you sit a minute?"

Moira looked around. Danny was behind the bar with her father, and Colleen was out on the floor. The crowd had thinned out enough that Patrick and Michael had taken seats at the end of the bar and were talking to each other.

"I suppose," she murmured, taking a seat opposite him in the booth against the wall.

"Interesting place you have here," the man said.

He smiled, but there was something insincere in it, Moira thought.

"Lots of people," he went on.

"It's a pub," Moira said flatly.

"Very Irish."

"It's an Irish pub."

"Have you ever had any trouble here?"

"Trouble?" Moira said. "Um, let me see. Once a man got ornery when my father said he'd had too much and refused to serve him. We called the cops, and he was escorted out."

"Hasn't your band man, Jeff Dolan, been arrested a few times?"

"He was a wild kid. He's straightened out."

"Don't always count on people being what they seem."

"Excuse me, what's your name?"

"Kyle. Kyle Browne," the man said, smiling and offering his hand across the table. Moira shook it briefly.

"You know, Americans finance half the trouble that goes on around the world."

"In Northern Ireland, you mean."

Kyle Browne shrugged. "Your father is a very political man."

"He is not!"

"Then there's your brother."

"He's an attorney, and he doesn't even live in Boston."

"You don't know all your clientele."

"Are you insinuating," she asked, keeping a check on her anger, "that my father's place is some kind of harbor for the IRA and their sympathizers?"

"I'm not insinuating anything. What about your family friend? The writer. Just how well do you know him? Think he's up to something?"

"Are you a cop?" Moira asked bluntly.

"Let's just say I'm a friend, keeping an eye on things."

"Fine. You keep an eye on things. Let me tell you about my father. He's one of the nicest men you'll ever meet. He came to America because my family was mixed. Good Irish Catholics with a few Orangemen thrown in. You know—marriage, in-laws, things like that. My dad didn't like the kind of conflict that could arouse back home. He never believed in any man killing another over his belief

in God. Of course, in this day and age, the religious thing
has really become political and economic. Sure, a united
Ireland would be great. But my father doesn't believe that
thousands of people born in Ireland, whose families have
been in Ireland for hundreds of years, should all be lined
up and shot. My dad holds nothing against the English for
something a brutal king did hundreds of years ago, and he
understands how the Protestants in Northern Ireland are
afraid of what will happen if they're not part of the United
Kingdom. He's an American citizen, a Catholic and a man
of the Republic, but he's a moderate who hopes that time
and negotiation and good and honest men will bring peace.
Does that answer your questions about the pub?''

She stood angrily and started to walk away, then returned to the table, still angry. ''See the couple at the end
of the bar? They're English, and they moved into the
neighborhood about two years ago. They love to come
here, and they're more than welcome. Danny, my good
friend, was born in Belfast. As was Peter Lacey, the tall
skinny guy talking to my dad right now. He's a Protestant.
Well, he was. He married a stunning young Jewish woman
and converted. He's welcome here, too. Sal who just came
in, well, Sal is half Italian. We love his food, he loves our
beer. And you, God knows where you're from or what
religion you practice, or if you practice any at all. Hell,
my father even lets atheists drink in here. He puts up decorations for Kwanza, for God's sake. So you're welcome
in here just like everyone else. You can come in and drink
any time you want, or eat—we serve good food. You can
sit there and watch and listen all you like. But take it from
me, if you're looking for a conspiracy going on here,
you're crazy.''

She started away again. He caught her hand, smiling.

''Hey, sorry,'' he said softly.

''Yeah. Great.''

''No, I mean it, I'm really sorry to have upset you.

You're a beautiful woman, and it's a fine place. I'd hate to see bad things happen here.''

"They won't.''

"How about the old codger at the bar?''

"Seamus?'' she said incredulously. "He's harmless. Completely. Don't you want to accuse my sister of something, as well? Or my mother, perhaps?''

"I'm not making accusations. I'm watching.''

"Fine. It's a public establishment, as I've said.''

"The drink is terrific.''

"Good. It's on the house.''

She freed her hand and walked away, and was startled to realize that she was rattled. She walked behind the bar. The Englishman, Roald Miller, lifted his glass. "Finally, a good bartender. Hey, Moira, how come you had to go off and become successful? We really miss you around here.''

"Thanks, Roald. What was in that glass you're lifting to me?''

"Sarah and I are having Fosters.''

She set the beers down and was startled to hear Danny behind her a moment later. "You really gave that fellow a piece of your mind.''

She flushed. "You heard me?''

"Most of it. I was trying to appear far away and busy.''

"The nerve! Insinuating that my father—''

Danny interrupted her with a sigh. "He doesn't have to be insinuating anything about your father. There are lots of people in this pub.''

She spun on him and whispered softly, "What is going on, Danny?''

He shook his head. "I don't know. I wish I did. But now that you've given that bloke the what for, I suggest you stay away from him.''

"I think he's a cop.''

"Maybe. Maybe not. But don't go dating him, eh?''

"You know that—"

"You're in love. Right. With old beady eyes. You should stay away from him, too."

"If I were to listen to the guy in the corner, I'd definitely be staying away from you."

"But you have to go on instinct, don't you, Moira? And you know I'd never hurt you."

"If you only knew. You've hurt me time and time again."

"I'm sorry for that. It was never my intention. Honest to God, I'm trying to make up for it now."

"And I'm sorry, but you're too late."

"Am I? Am I really, Moira?"

She looked down the bar, where Michael was still talking to Patrick. The two had gotten into a conversation with Liam and Seamus.

Michael looked up as if he had sensed her needing him. He smiled and lifted his glass. I'm doing my best to be part of it all, he seemed to be saying.

She smiled in return and looked at Danny.

"Yes, you're really too late," she said softly, and turned away.

As she did so, she caught the eye of the man in the corner. Kyle Browne. He was frowning, as if...

Warning her.

About what, or...

Who?

10

Moira wasn't sure why, but she was still worried about Seamus, despite the fact that he had been drinking more moderately that night. Her brother was next to her behind the bar when the place finally wound down for the night. Liam had long gone, as had most everyone else, but Seamus was still there.

"Patrick?"

"Yeah?"

"Do me a favor."

"What?"

"Walk Seamus home."

"Why? He only lives a couple of blocks from here."

"Please? Just humor me."

"Oh, sure, let me just run out into the bitter cold in the middle of the night to humor you."

"I'll ask someone else."

"No, Moira, damn, I'll do it. I was teasing you. Remember what teasing is? But why are you worried about the old coot?"

"I don't know." She walked past her brother to the end of the bar, facing Seamus. "Patrick is going to walk you home tonight."

"Now, Moira, I switched between the real stuff and the unleaded all night."

"And how many did you have in all?"

"Just a few."

"About ten, I believe." Colleen piped up from the floor. She was gathering bottles and glasses from the tables.

"Ten? It's amazing you have kidneys left, Seamus," Moira said.

"Irish kidneys. The best to be had," Seamus said.

"I'm proud of you for switching. Next time, just not quite so many altogether. I wouldn't have served you so many."

"Ah, but that's the trick, lass. You get the real stuff from a different bartender each time."

"Shame on you, Seamus," she said firmly.

"Now, I don't drive, Moira."

"You'd be cut off after the first one if you did."

"All right, girl. I'm going home."

"With Patrick."

"Sorry, Patrick," Seamus said sheepishly.

"No bother," Patrick said cheerfully, grimacing over his head at Moira. "Come on, then."

Kyle Browne had departed at about one. It was nearly two now.

Saint Patrick's Day made for a long week.

"Get Dad to go on up," Patrick told Moira in a soft whisper as he followed Seamus.

"Right," she said, but Colleen was already chastising their father, urging him up the steps.

"I guess I should get out, too, let the family close up," Michael said quietly to Moira. She looked at him, saw the gentle concern in his eyes.

"One of these nights I *will* get over there."

"I'll be waiting."

"My dad is gone. Kiss me goodbye?" she said, walking him to the door.

He curled his arms around her, then lifted her chin with his thumb and forefinger. He kissed her lips lightly, but she clung to him, demanding more. She turned it into a long, wet, openmouthed kiss, the kind that would have stirred her had she any energy left in her body whatsoever.

Michael withdrew when her sister cleared her throat and asked, "Shall we all leave the room?"

Michael's eyes were on her, intense, curious. "Was that a kiss?" he whispered. "Or a performance?"

She felt a shiver snake through her. "A kiss," she said firmly. "And maybe a performance. I'm just establishing a few things. Is...that all right?"

"Oh, yeah."

He touched her lips briefly with his. "It's after two. We'll all be as tired as you look in the morning."

"Thanks," she murmured.

He grinned. "Good night. I'm out of here."

Cold wind swept in as he departed. She closed and locked the door and turned. Colleen and Danny were staring at her.

Danny applauded, clapping his hands slowly.

"You could have gone with him. I can clean up with Danny," Colleen said.

"I—great. You two clean up. I'm going to get some sleep."

She started around the bar and through to the office, then remembered her purse in the well. She came back in, but couldn't find it where she had thrown it.

"Hey, Colleen, did you move my purse?"

"Nope. Haven't seen it."

"Did you leave it at the restaurant?" Danny asked.

"No, I'm certain. I came in, the place was wild, I walked behind the bar and threw my purse in the well."

"Maybe Dad picked it up. Or Patrick," Colleen suggested.

"Maybe," Moira said, frowning and haphazardly moving bottles around to see if she had stuck it somewhere else. "Damn, I can't find it."

"It's got to be there somewhere," Danny said. "I didn't see any customers hop the bar to make off with it."

"Moira, calm down. That's Dad's best aged whiskey you're pushing around there. What's in your purse that—"

"Just my identification, my credentials, everything!" Moira said.

"I was about to ask what was in it that you needed before the morning," Colleen said. "I'm sure someone merely moved it."

Moira sighed. "Yeah, I guess you're right."

Danny caught her by the shoulders. "Hey, go up to bed. You really do look worn out. Go up and get some sleep."

"You're right."

"And don't be going back out at night."

She looked at him warily.

"Really. Please," he said softly.

"I wasn't going back out tonight."

"Good."

"That's not going to keep me from sleeping with him, Danny."

"I don't think I need to be in on this conversation," Colleen said, humming, trying to make a racket as she picked up the tables.

"Maybe you're not really so sure you want to," Danny said, his hand on her arm. "Maybe that's why you gave that Academy Award-winning performance at the door."

"And maybe I'm just really, really tired."

"There is no such thing as really, really, tired, not if you're really, really certain and if you've been with your family this much time."

"How do you know where I've been all this time?" she demanded.

"Trust me. I know."

"Great. You're spying on me? Watching me?"

"Circumstances, Moira, nothing more."

Colleen started singing "The Irish Washwoman." Loudly.

"Look, just for now, don't be on the streets at night alone, okay? A sensible woman wouldn't go wandering out alone in the wee hours of the morning anyway. Right?"

"I carry Mace."

"In the purse you can't find. And Mace is no defense against a gun."

"Why would someone use a gun against me?"

He sighed with impatience. "Moira, Boston is a big city. Remember the dead prostitute? And God knows how many murders there are here a year. That's the way of the world. Please, don't go out alone late at night."

"I'm not going anywhere, Danny, except to bed."

He released her at last. Tawny eyes met hers. She wished she didn't like his face so much. An interesting face. She wished fervently that Danny had been called to Timbuktu to give a speech that particular Saint Patrick's Day.

"Night. Night, Colleen," she called, and turned her back, going upstairs.

"Hey, Patrick?" Seamus said sheepishly as they walked down the street.

"Yeah, Seamus?"

"You don't have to do this. I don't know what got your sister going, but you know I'm a man who can hold me ale."

"Seamus, it never hurts to have company on the walk home. Besides," he said with a shrug and a smile, "it gives me another chance to slip away."

"To slip away to do what, at this hour of the night?" Seamus asked.

"Well, I really have had business here. I haven't been

around as much as I should have been these past few days.
I'd like to head downtown. And stare at my boat."

"In the middle of the night?"

"Sounds weird, huh?"

"Sounds like an excuse for something else," Seamus
told him.

"Oh, yeah?" Patrick said, stopping and staring at Seamus.

"But then," Seamus said quickly, "that's what you
were doing. Something else. Everyone knows a man can
stay in a pub till all hours, not even drinking, just talking.
Talking. There's the crux," he suddenly muttered. "I
shouldn't have talked so much. Or maybe I should have
talked some more."

"What are you going on about, Seamus?"

"Nothing, nothing." Seamus looked sideways at his escort. Patrick Kelly was a tall man, lean, but solid. He had
a fine face. All of Eamon Kelly's children had fine faces,
probably thanks to Katy Kelly. Hard to tell, though; he
and Eamon had aged and wrinkled and grizzled together,
but Eamon Kelly had been a fine-looking man in his prime.

"Are you all right?" Patrick asked.

"Oh, I'm fine. I'm a big fellow. Did you know I used
to box?"

"I'm sure you were a hard hitter."

"Aye, that I was. And only a wee bit of me ale has
gone to me belly."

"You're still a heartthrob, Seamus, I'm sure."

"I'm tired and worried, that's what I am," Seamus muttered.

"Worried? About what?"

Seamus shook his head, wondering if he should pour his
heart out or muzzle his lips. "Those orphans you've been
looking into, Patrick. What's the deal with that? You need
money? I can donate a bit. I'm not a charity case, you
know. In the old days, we needed sponsors and jobs to get

into the United States. Me uncle sponsored me, and I worked hard in the fishing business for over twenty years. I made some good investments, too.''

''Seamus, I've just gotten involved, but as soon as I know a little more myself, you'll be the first man I hit up, how's that?''

Seamus thought Patrick was looking at him a bit strangely. ''Sure, sure,'' he said quickly. ''Well, now, there's me house, just along the street. Old man Kowalski lives on the first floor. Polish fellow. Nice enough. Has his kids in all the time, always lots of people around. You don't have to see me in, Patrick.''

There was sweat on his upper lip, Seamus realized.

''You don't want help walking up the stairs?'' Patrick asked doubtfully.

''No, no. The day I can't make it up one flight of stairs...well, I'll move to a ground floor somewhere, that's what I'll do.''

He slipped his key into the lock, opened the door and waved to Patrick, who waved back, then turned to go.

Seamus went up the steps two at a time. ''There,'' he told himself. ''I'm spry as a young rooster still, when need be.''

At the top of the stairs, he realized that he hadn't locked the lower door. He'd been so eager to rid himself of his escort and find the safety of solitude. Now he worried and started down the stairs.

As he did, the downstairs door opened. He heard the creaking. He squinted, looking out. The streetlights outside made his visitor no more than a dark image, a silhouette. A man in a hat and a coat. That was all he knew.

''Seamus, Seamus, Seamus. Shame on you, Seamus,'' a voice said. Deep, rich, throaty, menacing, with the soft cadence of the Old Country.

He knew instinctively that, indeed, he knew too much. Had said too much.

He turned, his heart thundering. His door was not so far away. And he *was* spry, spry as a young rooster.

He missed the first step he tried to take. He wavered briefly, then fell.

He hit his head. Hard. Every bone in his old body ached.

"Sorry, me old man. Sorry," that Irish-inflected voice said. Seamus was vaguely aware of footfalls landing lightly on the stairs, coming toward him. "Indeed, sorry, old man. But I can't take the chance of you giving me away. Nothing, you see, must stand in my way."

Seamus wanted to scream. He'd lied. Old Kowalski was deaf as a stone, and he'd never had a wife, much less children. Seamus wanted to scream anyway.

He couldn't. He felt the powerful grip that seized him. Then he was falling. Flying first, then falling, falling, falling.

When he landed that time, there was an instant of agony.

The sound of something snapping.

Then no pain. No pain at all.

On her way through the house to her bedroom, Moira noticed a small box sitting at the edge of the kitchen table. Inspecting it, she saw that it was a videotape. Frowning to see the title in the dim light, she saw that it had been recorded by someone off TV. Her brother's handwriting on the cover announced his title for whatever he had taped: The Results of the Troubles in Ireland. She started to put the tape down, then hesitated. They had shared things all their lives, and Patrick had left the tape out where anyone could see it. She took it to her room.

Was she prying? Too bad. She wanted to know what Patrick was up to.

She slid the tape into the VCR in her room and watched for a minute, but the tape seemed to be little more than a travelogue. Yawning, she went into the bathroom, listening as she washed her face and brushed her teeth. She heard music with a voice-over talking about traditional Irish music and dance.

Nothing too evil so far.

Letting it run, she hopped quickly in and out of the shower. Wrapped in a towel, she walked from the bathroom to the bedroom, where she slipped into a T-shirt with a yawning, frazzled cat on the front, saying, ''Got coffee?'' The Irish music and dance were finished; the narrator had gone on to talk about The Troubles, the thirty years of violence that had gripped Northern Ireland at the end of the twentieth century. Then-President Clinton was on the screen saying, ''I don't think reversal is an option.'' She rewound the tape. The narrator spoke about Clinton's visit, his meetings with Irish Prime Minister Bertie Ahern, Gerry Adams and Martin McGuinness of the Sinn Fein. It went on to discuss his journey to Dundalk, a town just south of the Northern Ireland border long known as a recruiting station for the Real IRA, a left-wing faction, that had claimed responsibility for the 1998 car bombing that killed twenty-nine people in the town of Omagh and threatened the fragile Good Friday Agreement, providing for a joint Catholic-Protestant government and approved in April of 1998. Clinton's face appeared on the screen again as he pointed out how past violence had destroyed the lives not just of those killed, but of those left behind. The important issue of tourism and American business dollars was brought up. Another speaker appeared on the screen, pleading for reason and the value of every human life to both the Unionists, mainly Protestants who worked for continued unification with Great Britain, and the Nationalists, mainly Catholics longing for a united Ireland. The tape went on with shots of Clinton visiting David Trimble, Protestant first minister in the new Northern Ireland government, and Seamus Mallon, the senior Catholic in the government. The tape moved on to interviews with children, orphaned or left with one struggling surviving parent due to the violence. They all talked about the future, about turning Ireland around, making her as prosperous and welcoming as her age-old adage promising hospitality. One attractive teenager, raised by nuns after the deaths of her parents, walked the photographer around the county of Armagh and Tara, the beautiful site made royal by the ancient kings. Northern Ireland, often shunned by tourists because of The Troubles, offered wonderful archeological locations, striking Norman fortifications, haunted castles, magical vistas and more. The girl was charming and sincere, ending her speech with a longing for the kind of education that would allow her generation to offer the world an Ireland at peace. She ended with the words, "There are more Irish in the Unites States now than there are in Ireland. This is still your home. Please help us, and the land that remains in your heart."

The sound track ended, and a loud buzzing filled the room. Moira quickly hopped up and hit the reverse button, rewinding the tape. As she did so, she thought she heard a strange thumping sound. She stopped the tape, listening. She heard nothing, but remained certain that she had heard a noise coming from the pub below.

"Danny," she murmured aloud. It had to be Danny. But what was he up to?

She exited her room, closing the door quietly behind her. She didn't bother with slippers or a robe, just tiptoed along the hall, listening. She thought she heard movement downstairs again. Was he going for a beer? It was nearly half past three in the morning.

Maybe her brother had returned, and he and Danny were talking.

Whatever was going on, she wanted the truth.

She opened the door at the top of the spiral stairway, closing it behind her very quietly. She waited there a moment, listening. Voices. Droning voices. People talking? Or a television or radio left on?

Silently and slowly, she moved down the winding stairway, inwardly damning the fact that a night-light was on in the office, while the bar beyond lay in darkness. Still, she moved downward, step by step, trying to discern just what she was hearing and from where the sound was coming. She came to the ground floor and held very still. She couldn't make out the words being said. It had to be a radio or television. After a minute, she stepped forward carefully, realizing only then that the floor was very cold, the wooden boards covering concrete, and her feet were freezing. Goose bumps were breaking out on her arms, as well.

She left the office area, creeping behind the bar. The noise, she thought, was coming from the rear of the bar. Probably from Danny's room. The bar was empty. At least Danny and her brother weren't sitting around conspiring together.

She started very carefully through the tables in the darkened room toward the guest room door. She wasn't going to knock or anything like that. She just wanted to assure herself that she was hearing the droning of a television.

Halfway to the rear of the pub, she realized that she was feeling a cold draft. She paused, looking around. It was so dark, both inside and outside, that she couldn't make out the door. She should have been able to; there were streetlights just outside. But they didn't seem to be bright enough that night. Finally her eyes grew accustomed to the darkness, and she could see the door. It appeared to be closed, but it might be ajar. It had to be ajar. Cold air was coming in. A deep, bone-chilling cold. How the heck could the door be open? Patrick would never be so careless as to forget to lock up when he came in.

Hugging her arms around herself, she started weaving her way through the tables and around the bar. When she reached the end of the bar, still staring at the front door, she suddenly felt an entirely new sensation, as if a ghost were whispering at the nape of her neck, warning her to stop, to turn back. She did so, coming to a dead halt and turning.

The door to Danny's room seemed to be ajar, a faint ray of light spilling from it. That door had not been open before. She was certain. She would have noticed the light. It suddenly seemed imperative that she reach the front door, make sure it was closed and locked.

She turned back. The darkness seemed to thicken before her, as if a cloud had converged on the room. Groping blindly, she slid her feet forward. There was something in her path. She tripped, stumbling. She reached out, trying to find something to break her fall. Cloth...a body? Something...someone...blocking the light.

But there was nothing for her to grip. She flailed helplessly, then went down, her feet entangled in something. She crashed to the floor, hands ahead of her to break her fall.

She hit the ground face forward, her forehead connecting with the green linoleum behind the bar. Pain suddenly shot through her head. Odd, it seemed to come from the back of her skull rather than the front. Sharp...then fading. The room became blacker than ever.

She closed her eyes.

"Moira, now what the hell are you up to?"

She blinked, then realized that she must have passed out, if only for a few minutes. There was a light on behind the bar, and she was being held in a man's arms. Danny's. She was still on the floor, but he had lifted her up and was studying her face.

"Danny," she breathed. She stared at him, not sure whether to fling herself against him or find the strength to leap away in terror.

"Who else were you expecting down here?"

"Were you out?" she asked.

His eyes narrowed. "For a bit. Why? What are you doing down here? Judging by the way you're dressed, I don't imagine you trekked down the stairs to seduce me."

"Danny, damn it, did you just conk me on the head?"

"Are you daft?"

"Who was in your room?"

"No one I know about." He seemed tense. "Why?"

"There were sounds. Voices."

"From my room?"

"Yes."

"The television?"

She hesitated, staring into his eyes. In the murky light, they seemed a pure gold. His features were in shadow, which seemed to emphasize the lean planes and rugged angles of his bone structure. She had been so frightened. Here, in her family business. In a room where she had spent half her life, in a place where she had never been afraid before.

She'd heard voices, seen shadows, touched...something. She'd sensed the danger, felt it at her nape, known it in her bones....

And it might well have been him.

But the fear was ebbing from her, just as the darkness had ebbed from the area around the bar.

"Moira, what's up? You said you heard voices."

She sighed, sitting up, rubbing the back of her head. There didn't seem to be a bump there.

"It might have been a television," she admitted. "I thought the front door was open...then it seemed your door was open. It was cold, and I thought Patrick had come back and forgotten to lock up properly...." Her voice trailed off.

"You weren't on your way out to lover boy's hotel room, eh?" he teased.

"Shoeless and in a T-shirt?" she retorted.

"Ah. You save the bare feet and T-shirts for me. How sweet."

She frowned. "I really hit my head. I think I blacked out."

He leaned toward her. "You hit your forehead. Poor baby. Hang on."

He rose, walking behind the bar, finding a clean towel and filling it with ice. As he came back to her, she tried to rise. "No, no, you might be dizzy, don't try to stand. Hey, were you drinking tonight?"

"No!" she said indignantly. "Two glasses of wine at dinner. Danny, I could have sworn there was someone in front of me when I fell. Were—were you there all along?"

"No, I wasn't, and the front door was locked when I came in." He hunkered down by her, pressing the ice to her temple. She shivered.

"That floor is probably cold. Grab the ice."

She did so automatically. She was cold, and the ice, though it felt good against her head, sent rivers of frost racing through her.

She realized he had given her the command so he could scoop her up. "Danny," she murmured, still holding the ice but slipping her free arm around his neck so she wouldn't fall.

"You're like an ice cube yourself," he said huskily. He strode with her in his arms toward the back, making his way through the tables much more fluidly than she had. Of course, he had light to guide him.

He juggled her weight so he could open the door to his room, which was also closed, though not locked.

"Hey!" she protested.

"I'm not going to attack you or anything. Just warm you up," he assured her.

He paused in the doorway with her in his arms. He smelled good. The underlying scent of the aftershave she had always known and loved so much.

She realized that he was studying his room—his guest suite, as her father called it. Not really a suite. Her father had always imagined that in the old days, the room might have been a secret little harbor where the American Founding Fathers had met to ponder the question of separation from the mother country. Sam Adams might have written some of his stirring rhetoric here. Now it held a queen-size bed, two dressers, a mahogany entertainment center and a modern bath.

The doors to the entertainment center were open. The television was on. CNN. Headlines on the hour.

"Nothing seems out of place," he murmured.

"I guess I heard the television," she replied.

He remained still, looking around. He didn't seem to notice her weight. She had forgotten that although Danny appeared slim, he was built like rock. A lean machine, pure, supple muscle. He turned, still not seeming to notice that he was carrying her.

"Danny, you can put me down."

"Yeah. Let's get you under a blanket."

Still holding her with seemingly little effort in one arm, he stripped the throw and comforter from the bed, then placed her against the pillows and immediately covered her up.

"Danny—"

"Are you any warmer?"

"A little. I've got to go upstairs. I must have been imagining things."

"Let me take a look around out there. Keep that ice on your forehead."

He left her in the bed. She stared at the television. The volume was low, but she could hear every word clearly. She wondered why the sound had been so strange and garbled before. Because she had been listening through a closed door?

Danny seemed to be gone awhile. She turned from the

television to see that he had returned and was standing in the doorway to the bedroom with something in his hands. Her black knit purse.

"My purse." She rose from the pillows. "Where was it?"

"By the end of the bar. It's what you must have tripped over."

She frowned as he brought it to her. "Danny, I know damn well I didn't set it there. And if it was there, why didn't you and Colleen see it when you were cleaning up?"

He shrugged. "Maybe it was wedged beneath the bar."

He slipped out of his coat, hanging it on the hook by the door, then pulled his sweater over his head and took a seat by her on the bed. "Check it out," he told her. "See if anything seems to be missing."

"You think someone stole my purse and put it back?" she queried.

He shook his head, eyes on the purse, his slow, rueful smile slipping into place. "I think someone moved it from the well, meant to give it to you, walked around with it, set it down by the bar and forgot it. But since it seems to have mysteriously moved of its own volition, perhaps you should check it out. Besides, I want to see if you've got a bump on your forehead." He reached out, taking the ice-laden towel from her hand and her head, studying her seriously.

"No bump. Not even a bruise."

"Good," she murmured.

"Headache?"

"Not really."

"Want an aspirin?"

"For my imagined injury?"

"I never suggested you had an imagined injury." He rose, disappearing into the bathroom, returning with two aspirin and a paper cup of water.

She took the pills from him. "I really don't feel bad," she murmured. "I should. I'm sure I blacked out."

He wasn't listening to her. He was watching the television. The reporter was explaining the route the parade would follow on Saint Patrick's Day.

Then suddenly he was looking at her. He reached out, smoothing a tangle from her hair.

He was close. Warm. His fingertips were like magic. "You know, you're really beautiful."

"You're not supposed to be attacking me," she murmured.

"I'm not attacking you. I'm trying to smooth out your hair."

"How romantic."

"I'm not supposed to be romantic, since I'm not allowed to attack you, remember? Of course, the devastating negligee is a real turn-on. Are you sure you didn't come down here with the express thought of attacking *me?*"

"Attacking *you?*"

"Seducing me?"

"Danny..."

"You know, the lovely heroine in distress, fallen on the floor. The strong, silent hero sweeping her up and all that?"

"When the hell were you ever the silent type?"

"You have a point there."

His fingers were still moving through her hair. And somewhere along the way he'd stretched out beside her. When she closed her eyes, she breathed him. She seemed overwhelmed by a sea of physical memory. Sight, touch, the sound of his voice, the huskiness, the slight touch of a brogue. She could even remember the taste of his lips on hers, his flesh beneath the pressure of her whisper soft kisses, and more. How long had it been? How in God's name could she feel so natural, lying here with him, wanting to reach out and touch and taste and breathe and more again?

"You know, even dressed that way, you're absolutely beautiful," he said softly.

"That's a stock line."

"I mean it."

"You're prejudiced. Being an old family friend and all."

"Longtime friend, not old. You're not going to marry him."

"Michael?"

"You have to ask?"

"Maybe I am."

He shook his head. "You're here with me. You never risked the night to run out and be with him."

"Honestly, Danny, if I don't marry him, I'm a fool. He's doing everything in his power to get close to my family. He knows what's important to me. And he cares. He isn't trying to save the world, or destroy it, whichever you're after. I've never been sure. He's an American." Danny's fingers were still moving through her hair. He seemed to have settled more comfortably beside her, radiating a startling heat. "Grounded," she continued, wishing it didn't seem quite so hard to keep her focus on what she was saying. He was smiling at her, apparently listening. His face was close. His scent and warmth seemed to seep into her, sweep through her. Irish magic. "Good-looking," she managed. "Damned good-looking. Dependable. Reliable."

He curled a tendril of her hair in his fingers, amused. "Dependable. Reliable. What words to describe a passionate relationship."

"You should listen to a few of my friends who have been divorced. They'd go for dependable over exciting any day."

He shook his head. "Some of your friends probably do

need reliable and dependable. But *you* need reliable, dependable—and exciting.''

"Michael is—'' she began.

His lips touched hers, very gentle. Then he moved his face a fraction of an inch away. "Touch of friendship, not an attack," he swore, his whisper brushing her cheek. "Michael is...?''

"Um...exciting and dependable...''

This time his lips touched hers with a greater force. His kiss parted her lips, brought a wealth of wet, sweeping heat. She was wrapped in his arms, tangled in her T-shirt and the comforter, and the kiss went on and on, wet, ragged, his plunging tongue seeming to reach inside to her womb, caressing every erotic zone in her body. She didn't protest. The amazing thing was that she didn't protest. Every ethic, every tenet of right and wrong, seemed to slip away. Her fingertips moved against his face, threaded into his hair. His lips broke from hers. "That's an actual kiss," he murmured.

"What? Um...no more so than what I shared with...''

"Michael," he supplied.

Somehow he was over her. She felt the T-shirt tangled around her waist.

"Michael," she agreed.

"No, no. With Michael, it was a performance. With me, it was a kiss. Allow me. I'll show you the difference again.''

"You're not supposed to be attacking me," she reminded him.

"This isn't an attack," he whispered. "You're free to go, you know.''

"With you draped over me?''

"Well, I don't actually want to make it easy for you to leave.''

She could have pushed him away, but it was easier to convince herself that he was blocking her exit. She lay perfectly still, staring into his eyes. When he kissed her again, she brought her hands between them but still made no move to push him away. As they rolled to the side, mouths still fused together, she found her fingers curling around the buttons of his shirt. She touched his bare flesh. So familiar. The mat of tawny hair that teased her fingertips, the taut muscle beneath. A second later he was halfway up, struggling out of his shirt. Then his hands were on her and her shirt was on the floor. When he wrapped her in his arms again, she was instantly aware of the length of him. Wired muscle, tension, heat. She loved his chest, the feel of her lips against his throat and collarbone, the cradling way he cupped the back of her head. He used one foot against the other to shove off his boots, and she felt his foot move along her calf. The stroke of his hand was on her thighs, fingering the delicate panties she wore. His mouth closed over her breast, and he worked his body down the length of her. He knew how to do things with his tongue that defied silk and mesh. If there had ever been a time to protest, this was it. She spoke his name, but it was nothing more than a whisper. Her hips were moving, arching to his erotic, liquid manipulation. Lava seemed to burn deep inside her, then erupt and flow like a cascade. She nearly screamed aloud at the force of her climax, bit her lip, shuddered in his hold and allowed the volatile climax to sweep through her.

She was barely aware of his movement, his jeans joining the rest of their clothes on the floor, the force of his body between her thighs when he settled over her and into her. Her fingers laced together against his back; her legs locked around his hips. She had forgotten this; she had never forgotten this. Danny made love like he lived, passionately, vehemently, with electric force. He filled her with his physical presence, aroused her anew where she had been shaken and sated, pulsing slowly, giving, taking away, then finding a beat that raced like thunder, building a need within her that was a sweet agony until she bit lightly against his shoulder, feeling her climax seize hold of her again, euphoric pleasure like a blanket of honey streaming through her system. Danny eased to her side, flesh bathed in a fine sheen of perspiration. He had a way of holding a woman after sex that kept the warmth glowing. Fingers in her hair, smoothing dampened strands. Sated, catching her breath, she felt the wave of thoughts bombarding her mind, thoughts that the previous moments had not allowed. She was an evil human being. If there had been any chance of this happening, she should have been honest with Michael. But there *shouldn't* have been a chance of this happening. She was an adult, she was mature, she was...not as much in love as she had tried to convince herself she was. But what she had done was still wrong. Really wrong.

"I have to go," she murmured.

"That's all you have to say?"

"I have to go *now.*"

He drew his arms away. Shadows hid his amber eyes.

"What did you expect?" she whispered.

"Oh, I don't know. Something like, 'What was I thinking, even pretending to be so totally in love with another man, when here's Danny, and together we're just so damned good.'"

"Obviously you're good," she murmured with a trace of bitterness. "I'm here."

"Well, you know me. I don't just want to be good. I want to be the best there is."

She didn't tell him that he'd certainly managed that. "And I should have spent my life waiting for those moments when you chose to be in the country?"

"You're right," he said. "I'm being unfair."

She had said she needed to go, yet she was still lying beside him, loath to leave. Her knuckles brushed over his abdomen.

"Now you're being an evil woman," he informed. "That's truly unfair if you're intending on leaving."

His abdomen gave new meaning to the term "six-pack." "You're in incredible shape," she told him. "Curious, for a writer and lecturer."

"The better to seduce you during those moments when I'm in the same country."

"You're being flippant. I'm talking about real life."

"You shouldn't marry Michael."

"Apparently," she murmured, "Michael shouldn't marry me."

"You're on a misdirected guilt trip."

"Oh, right. He's in a hotel room where I keep saying I'll appear, but I shouldn't feel guilty for being in your bed instead."

"He's not right for you."

"Because he happens to be here when you are?"

He shook his head, staring at her intently. "Because he has beady eyes."

"Oh, God, Danny, stop with that." She almost managed to rise at that point, but their legs were still tangled together. "Danny, I really should leave," she said softly.

He shook his head stubbornly. "For what? So you can race upstairs, feed on your guilt and decide to make it up to the guy by running over there and throwing yourself into his arms? Either confessing—or not confessing—and trying to make it up with another performance?"

"No!" she protested angrily. "I would never do anything like that. It isn't me, and you know it."

"That's right. You're far too Catholic. You'd need a long hot shower, cleanse away the sin and all that."

"Damn it, Danny, if we'd had any time at all together in the last several weeks—"

"Aha," he murmured.

"Aha, what?"

"That's not love," he told her. "I mean, to come to me

just because you haven't had time with him...I'm sorry, but you're not in love with him.''

''There's love and then there's sex,'' she said primly.

''Yeah, and it's a hell of a lot nicer when they go together.''

''Oh, yeah? Well, in all those years, it never actually occurred to me that you'd come back one day and declare that you actually loved me. To total distraction, above all else, et cetera, et cetera,'' she murmured dryly.

''I never said that love should rule your every moment, or that it should make you behave insanely, or take precedence over everything else, like responsibilities, living, et cetera, et cetera.''

''I never know what you're actually saying, Danny. Or what you mean. Maybe that's half our problem.''

''There you go. You're admitting we have a problem, which means we're an us.''

''Danny, *you* are the problem.''

''I'm going to be a lot more of a problem if you keep tickling my ribs that way.''

She clenched her fingers into a fist.

''I didn't really mean you should stop.''

''Danny, I shouldn't be here. I shouldn't have been here. I certainly shouldn't stay.''

''But the sin has occurred already,'' he said, shifting his weight so that he pinned her to the mattress. ''And, you know, I really do love you.''

''Danny, I believe that you care about me.''

He groaned softly, lowering his head. His hair brushed against her breasts. She wondered how such a simple thing could feel so terribly erotic. ''The sin has already been committed,'' he repeated softly.

''I think it's worse when you sin twice. Especially when you should have known better the first time.''

''That's the point. You did know better the first time. And since you've already sinned, at least in your own mind, you should go with it. All the way. Everything in life should be done with passion, commitment, all the way.'' His eyes rose to hers for a moment, glowing amber.

"Danny,'' she murmured, "if I stay now, for a while, you can't go thinking that...''

"That?''

"It means...''

"Don't worry, I won't go thinking anything. It's simply easier, more convenient, to go for the guy in the house rather than the one outside it. Nothing personal. You need sex, just sex, hey, I'm happy to oblige.'' He spoke sarcastically, but with an underlying note of bitterness that somehow dulled the anger she had felt at his words.

"No, Danny, I...''

She felt the pressure of his lips against her throat, her collarbone.

"That was rude. Uncalled for. I should...hit you,'' she whispered.

"Never opt for violence,'' he murmured against her breast. "And you can't hit me, I mean, that would mean that one of us was taking this...personally.''

His hand sculpted the length of her body. Fingers caressed her flesh. Zeroed in. Moved with practice and subtle precision. He was her every breath, close, hot. Breathing Danny was too easy, too natural, as familiar and electric as life....

"Damn you, Danny,'' she murmured.

"My name...how personal and intimate,'' he said. "It's only courteous to respond in kind.''

His caress traveled the length of her.

Very personally, very intimately.

"Danny...'' It came out like a long moan when she said his name again.

"I've always believed in actions rather than words.''

11

Hours later, before the crack of dawn, Moira rose to leave.

She rescued her T-shirt from the pile of clothing by the bed. Danny had been sleeping. Or so she had thought, until she turned to see that he was wide awake, watching her. If he'd been sleeping, he'd awakened at her first slight movement.

She thought he meant to protest her leaving again, though surely he knew it was nearly morning and the household would be stirring soon.

He rose on one elbow, watching her. "Tell me again. Exactly why did you come down here last night?" he asked.

"What?"

"What were you doing down here last night? You asked me if I'd been out, said you thought there might have been someone in my room. And you thought that someone was in the bar area—you suggested I might have knocked you on the head. Why were you down here in the first place? Dressed the way you were, you weren't on your way out to the hotel to meet Michael."

"I heard a noise."

"A noise? You heard this noise in your room?"

"Yes."

"And you thought it came from down here?"

"Yes."

"What kind of a noise?"

"I don't know. A thumping noise. As if…as if someone were moving things around or dropped something. I don't know. I just heard a noise."

"You're certain?"

"I don't seem to be certain about anything these days," she told him.

He rolled out of the bed, strolling to her naked, taking her by the shoulders. "All the way, Moira, remember, all the way. Go with your instincts. Passion, commitment. Get rid of old beady eyes, today."

"Don't you dare say a word to him or try to make up my mind for me about right and wrong and my future."

"I don't need to make up your mind for you. I know you. You did that last night. As for old beady eyes, my love, I intend to let you wrestle with your demons all by yourself."

"Maybe my mind isn't made up. Maybe you're not as good as you think." She lifted her chin, meeting his eyes.

"Moira, whatever you're thinking, be careful. When you hear noises in the night, you shouldn't go prowling around."

"This is my family home and my family's business," she reminded him. "I grew up here, learning to clear tables from the time I was a little girl. Why should I have to be afraid to walk around my dad's place, even in the middle of the night?"

He watched her, weighing the question for a minute.

"Because there's evil in the world, that's why. When you're a child, your parents teach you to watch out for strangers. Think of Son of Sam, the Boston Strangler, the Zodiac Killer, Jack the Ripper."

"Right. But none of them has keys to my dad's pub."

"Yes, but your brother is here these days, I'm here, your associates are here. Doors may be left open."

"Danny, why don't you just tell me the truth?"

"About what?"

"About whatever is going on."

"I'm not privy to anything that might be going on."

She watched him for another moment. Her eyes slid down the length of him, far more analytically than in the previous hours. Danny was really toned. He could have stepped right out of the pages of a brochure on martial arts. Again she wondered how a lecturer and writer stayed in such excellent shape.

"All right, Danny," she murmured. She turned, starting for the door.

"Moira."

"What?"

"You know, *you* are keeping things from *me*."

"Oh?"

"Like what really happened out on the ice the night before last."

"I slid."

"Trust is a two-way street, Moira."

"So it is."

"And?"

"I don't see any cars coming toward me, Danny. No one to meet halfway."

She turned again. He caught her arm. "Moira, listen to me. If you hear something, anything strange at all, it's important that you let me know."

"I'll keep that in mind." She looked at his hand where he held her arm. The slightest unease swept over her. "I have to go upstairs, Danny."

He let her go. She walked out, closed the door to his room quietly behind her, then made her way through the bar and up the winding stairs. When she slipped into the house, she carefully locked the door. In her room, she took the videotape from her machine and put it on the table where she had found it. It was still very early. She showered and dressed, then sat in her room, staring at the phone and hesitating. She went to the living room and found Sunday's newspaper. There was an article about Jacob Brolin, talking about his expected arrival in the city and mentioning the hotel where he would be staying.

She walked to the kitchen, where her mother, in a terry bathrobe, had just risen to start breakfast. "Mum," she said, walking behind her and slipping her arms around her waist.

"Moira, darlin', 'tis so early."

"Yep."

"What's on your agenda for today?"

"Well, I'll definitely be helping Dad in the pub tonight."

Katy turned around and cupped Moira's face between her hands. "You children are not responsible for the pub."

"But it's fun, and I like helping Dad. And we're getting a great show, really."

"Then I'm glad. Since I did rather manipulate you into coming home."

"Dad seems to be in great health," she commented with a smile.

Katy shrugged. "He did have to have a battery of tests." She sighed. "I was worried because he works so much. But the doctor told me that work was good for him, just like an ale or a stout a day would do him no harm. Too many men retire and sit around becoming couch potatoes, and that's what kills them, the doctor said."

"You know who works too hard, don't you?"

"Who?" Katy asked.

"You."

"Oh, no, Moira, dear."

"Cooking, cooking, cooking."

"When it's just your dad and me, there's oatmeal in the morning. And I don't fix his breakfast because he's a tyrant, I fix his breakfast because I love to, and I like being a wife and mum. I'm happy as a lark that my girls have gone off and done well, but for me, well, I like my lot in life just fine.''

"I know you do, Mum. But today..." Moira paused, feeling a bit guilty. Her mother was vindicating her desire to be a housewife, confessing to manipulation, and she was manipulating things herself.

"Mum, I still say there's no job in the world harder than yours. The coffee is going, and that's the thing we all need first. Now, I want you out of your bathrobe. I'm taking you out to breakfast this morning.''

"Moira! The children are here, your sister, brother—''

"I don't mean any insult, but Granny Jon can cook, and Danny will come up, and Siobhan and Colleen are here— not to mention the fact that it would be good for Patrick to try cooking for a change. I've an urge to get away with just my mother, to have you all to myself.''

"But, Moira—''

"Please.''

"I'll just tell your father.''

"We can leave a note.''

"Moira, I have to change out of me robe anyway.''

"You've got a point. But hurry, please.''

Katy did as she was asked, flushing like a schoolgirl. Moira wasn't sure whether to feel guilt or pleasure that her scheme seemed to have made her mother so happy.

Jacob Brolin was staying close to the New England Aquarium, just outside Little Italy. Moira told a little white lie, assuring Katy that she'd heard of the hotel's restaurant and that they were known to prepare very special eggs Benedict, which she'd been harboring a craving for the last few days.

"You know, Moira Kathleen," Katy said as they sat, "I can cook eggs Benedict. You only needed to say you wanted some.''

"Oh, I know, Mum. Like I said, I wanted to get you out."

Moira looked around the dining room, wondering if Brolin and his party would come down to breakfast. This was really a wild shot. He would probably order room service.

She realized suddenly that her mother had put down her menu and was studying her, sliding her reading glasses down her nose and watching her suspiciously.

"Moira Kathleen."

"What, Mum?"

"There are no eggs Benedict on this menu."

"You're kidding!"

"You're not a good enough actress for your mother, girl."

"No, Mum, I thought that—"

"Don't add insult to injury, daughter. What are we doing here?"

She leaned forward. "All right, Mum. I thought that we might run into Jacob Brolin here."

Katy put down her menu. "Why didn't you just try calling him?"

"I'm not with one of the networks, or even a major cable channel, Mum," Moira said. "And...I kind of wanted to do this on my own, too."

Katy nodded. "All right. Why didn't you just ask me to help you scope out the situation?"

"I really haven't had any time with you alone, Mum," Moira said earnestly, giving her entire attention to her mother.

Their waiter arrived, wishing them both a good morning and asking if they needed more time.

"Not at all," Katy said. "A strawberry waffle, coffee and orange juice. Moira?"

"The egg scramble with cheese and ham, coffee and

juice, please,'' Moira said. When the waiter left, Moira leaned toward her mother. ''Mum, I...honestly, I needed to be with you.'' That was surprisingly true. She hadn't wanted to be alone with her confusion regarding last night. And she hadn't wanted to be in the house if Michael and Josh had arrived early with ideas for the day's filming or eager to hear what she wanted to do next. They had lots of tape. Plenty for an hour's show, even if they decided not to do a live segment on Saint Patrick's Day. Which, of course, the Leisure Channel was expecting.

''Are you all right, Moira?'' her mother asked.

She squeezed her mother's hand across the table. ''A little confused, Mum, that's all.''

''Danny?''

''Am I that obvious?''

''No, you're practically rude to him.''

''Mum, you like Michael, right?''

''He's trying very hard. And he's handsome indeed. Probably more so than Danny, though I am prejudiced toward the Irish lad. You say he's dependable and he works hard, and he likes the theater and music and a ball game.''

''Yes. He's willing to try anything. He's polite and courteous, and in the same business I am.'' Moira fell silent as their waiter arrived with juice and coffee. When he had gone, Katy leaned toward her.

''You make it sound as if you're dating off a computer matchmaking program.''

''But I'm not, Mum. I've enjoyed him. Enjoyed being with him, I mean. I like the theater and all, too. He's a great companion.''

''So is a Great Dane.''

''No, he's nice, he's fun...I've really enjoyed being with him,'' she repeated without conviction.

''And...'' Katy said, then hesitated, shaking her head. ''You're hedging, daughter. All right, this isn't something you want to discuss with your mother, so I'll go first. Your father is a great companion, but I can tell you quite frankly that I...that I also find him quite exciting.''

''What?'' Moira said, startled.

''Well, I wasn't born yesterday. And I like to think I raised children with morals, but being compatible sexually is not a bad thing.''

''Whoa, Mum,'' Moira said, laughing, then shutting up as their food arrived.

''This isn't a bad place. They're fast and efficient,'' Katy said.

''I'm so glad you like it, at least.''

''Thus far,'' Katy said, cutting into her waffle. ''If we're talking, let's talk. Don't go being all horrified that I like your father. We're not that decrepit yet. Honestly, child, where do you think you and your siblings came from? I do realize that children don't like to think of their parents in such a light—''

''No, I certainly know where we came from, it's just that...''

''I don't want you sharing more than necessary with me, no details, daughter. I'm just trying to really understand your dilemma.''

''I'm attracted to them both,'' Moira said. She leaned forward, speaking more softly. ''Does that make me bad, Mum?''

''My dear child, I adore your father, and we've had a good marriage. No, we don't burn with passion the way we did when we were kids, but we're comfortable together, and we do still have our moments. No life is a mass of excitement hour after hour, there's always the mundane. But we do have our moments, and we cherish them still. And that's what's kept us together sometimes when we've disagreed and been at one another's throats. It's human nature, girl. You may be attracted to more than one man.

It's when you make a commitment that it must be real. And there's your man.''

''What?''

''There's your man. Brolin. He just walked in with what looks like a group of four prizefighters. Don't spin around too obviously.''

Despite her mother's words, Moira spun around instantly.

''I said not to be so obvious,'' Katy protested.

''Sorry.'' Moira picked up her juice and sipped it, trying to appear casual. ''Mum, I should do this, right?''

''You've had a TV show some time now. How have you approached those other celebrities?''

''Until recently, Josh called. Lately it's been Michael's job. And usually we focus on little bits and pieces of Americana, with far more average—though wonderful—people.''

''You're not afraid?''

''I'm just not sure how to approach him.''

Katy set down her glasses and napkin and rose. ''Excuse me, then.''

''Mum,'' Moira began. But her mother was already walking to the table. Moira noticed that, as harmless as her mother appeared, the men with Brolin immediately rose.

Moira rose instantly to follow her mother, ready to fiercely protect her should the need arise.

''Excuse me,'' Katy said very politely. ''Jacob, it's Kathleen Kelly. Do you remember me?''

Brolin rose with a huge smile. He was a big man. Not just tall, but big. Iron gray hair, deep blue eyes. A face filled with character. Wrinkled like a bloodhound's, yet somehow still very pleasant.

''Kathleen!'' he said, and, stepping past his bodyguards, he took her mother's hands.

"Then you do remember me?"

"Of course, how could I forget?"

Moira stood stone still a few feet behind her mother.

"I knew you were here, of course. I'd meant to stop by Kelly's—after Saint Patrick's Day."

"Really?"

"Of course. I'd heard you'd married Eamon Kelly and moved to the States. Kelly's is known in the homeland, Katy. My, you haven't changed a bit."

"Ah, well, that's kind, but it's been over thirty years."

"I still say you haven't changed a bit."

"Jacob, come now. We both look a great deal more... tired," Katy said, and laughed. Moira stood dumbfounded. Was her mother flirting? No, not really, but...

"Katy, did you come here to find me?" Brolin asked.

She shook her head. "I was just having breakfast with my daughter. I'd love you to meet her. In fact, she's been meaning to call you."

"Oh?" Brolin looked past Katy and saw Moira standing there. He smiled broadly for Moira. "Why, she's just like you, Katy." He strode past his bodyguards, taking Moira's hands and giving her a kiss on both cheeks. "Now, lass, why were you going to call me?"

"I, uh, I'd love to have a few words with you on tape for an American travel show, Mr. Brolin," she said. "We're trying to show the magic of Saint Patrick's Day in America. Actually, a lot of it is focused on the old saying that everyone is Irish on Saint Patrick's Day." She paused, wondering if she was babbling. She had been taken by such surprise. Did her father know Brolin, too? If he did, wouldn't he have mentioned it when Seamus and Liam had been talking about the man with such awe?

Brolin looked to one of the big men at his side. "We can fit something in somewhere, can't we? We will. Call the hotel room tomorrow and we'll set you up. Will you and your mum join us?''

"I'm afraid we can't, we have to get back," Katy said. "But indeed, Jacob, we'd be more than thrilled to have you as our guest when your obligations are finished here."

"How are things at Kelly's Pub?" Brolin asked.

"Busy. You know a pub on Saint Patrick's Day," Katy said.

He nodded. Moira was surprised to realize that he was studying her. "Well, now, that's fine. And yes, I'd love to visit you and Eamon and your family."

"Then we'll be seeing you, Jacob." She smiled at his guards. "Please excuse the interruption."

Jacob Brolin kissed Katy's cheek, and Katy took Moira's arm. "Time to leave, I think," she murmured, starting out of the dining room.

"Don't forget to call, Moira," Brolin called.

Moira stopped to turn back. "Thank you."

"Come along now," her mother said. "In all these years, you've surely learned how to make a proper exit."

"I didn't finish breakfast."

"I'll make you eggs Benedict. This is our exit."

"Mum! Our exit is going to be rather embarrassing if I don't pay the check!"

"Oh. Oh, of course," Katy said, then stood by the table as Moira summoned the waiter and left the money.

Out on the street, Moira looked at her mother. "I—I had no idea you knew him."

"I don't really know him. We met, many years ago."

"Was he...was he...?"

"Was he what?"

"I don't know. Like a great love in your life long ago or something?"

Katy shook her head impatiently. "You're mocking me, daughter."

"No, Mum—"

"The younger generation always thinks they're the first to discover sex and passion, but it's been going on for centuries, Moira." She started down the street toward the subway station.

"Mum, I was about to tell you that I was impressed—"

"Well, don't be."

"Mum, he's a very important man."

"He's a man like any other. He just knows both sides of the problem."

"But how did you meet him? I thought we were from Dublin? And you've never been involved in politics."

Katy looked at her with sheer exasperation. "You're from Boston, you live in New York, and you've traveled all over. And you know something about the American Civil War. Fathers fought sons, brothers were against one another, families were divided."

"Yes, but they were fighting for a cause, for something that had more to do with what they believed than where they were born—"

"Trust me, the fellow fighting for his plantation, his income, cared where he was born, and believe me on this—every man has a cause. Life is what it is. Catholics have married Protestants. People move. People living in the tiniest town in Limerick might be politically active, while a man living in Belfast might wear blinders and walk to and from work daily, not really caring who's in power, just so long as he can take his vacation in Spain. Moira, do you know why we came to the States?"

"Dad wanted a pub in America. The economy wasn't great at home, and he'd read about America all his life. It was a dream and a new beginning."

"All that's true. But we married, and moved, after a cousin on my father's side was killed. She should have known what she was in for—she was active in a violent group. She inflicted her share of violence and received it in return. That's what your father couldn't bear. A life in which children were taught to hate. She was a kid when she was killed, Moira. Twenty-one. I wanted revenge, but your father had the kind of courage to say no and walk away. And he's lived with that kind of courage every day of his life, teaching you all that a man's color, race or religion doesn't matter, just the mettle of the man. Brolin, too, learned that kind of commitment. He wasn't always lily white, but he learned his lessons the hard way. I've watched his career from afar. He's one of the few people in power to realize that hate can be taught, that it's passed on from generation to generation. He knows that even if you can't erase decades—or centuries—of bloodshed, oppression and, on both sides, cold-blooded murder, you can work hard to create a new world where men and women talk instead of shoot.''

Moira stood openmouthed, staring at her mother, stunned.

Katy went up the subway stairs and started down the street. Moira followed her. ''Mum, where are you going?''

''Walking. I—I want to go see your brother's boat.''

Moira followed her. ''Mum?''

''What?'' Katy snapped.

''Um, if you really want to see Patrick's boat, we have to cross the street and go that way,'' Moira said.

Katy spun and stared at her, smiled, then laughed out loud. ''Sorry,'' she murmured.

Moira walked up and hugged her mother. ''I always loved you for breakfast every morning, for harping at us to get out of bed for school, for being there with tea and whiskey when we had colds. I loved you for down pillows and fluffy comforters, and for being the world's greatest mum. And I never doubted that you were smart, but I never knew how very wise you were, and just how incredibly wonderful. Forgive me for not seeing all that you were.''

Katy pulled away from her, patting her cheek. ''There are tough choices in life, daughter, always, for everyone.''

''Tell me more about Brolin,'' Moira said. ''How did you meet him?''

Her mother hesitated, then said, ''My cousin died. She had been living in Northern Ireland, and I met him at the funeral. It's not a time I like to remember. Come on, let's get going. I want to see that boat. It's March now, we'll be able to get out in it soon enough. Sometimes I wish we'd moved to Florida. I do love the water. And Patrick has been out checking that boat over so many times this year. He's getting restless, I think. He does love the ocean. And I'm glad. It keeps him coming in to Boston.''

They had reached the dock leading to Patrick's boat. One thing she'd always known about her mother: she could outmove a power walker. Moira was almost breathless.

''The gate is locked,'' Katy said with dismay.

''I doubt it. The people around here are fairly casual.'' Moira pushed the gate open. ''See...it should be locked, but it never is.''

They walked down the dock. A sharp wind blew in. March was always an unpredictable month.

''Ah, there she is,'' Katy murmured.

The boat was called *Siobhan*. She was beautiful and sleek, freshly painted, with sails and a motor. Patrick had only had her pulled out of dry dock a few weeks back, anticipating the coming of good weather.

Moira saw that, beneath the tarp Patrick had over the helm, there were a number of boxes. ''I guess he's been out here, stocking her up,'' Moira murmured.

''Well, of course he's been out here. It's where he said he was going. Why did you say that?''

"Oh, I don't know. I think Siobhan has been worried about him a few times. He's getting involved with that group supporting orphans. At least, that's what he's been saying."

Katy spun on her. "If that's what he's been saying, that's what is. When you love someone, you trust him."

"Of course," Moira murmured.

"You're talking about your brother, Moira."

"Hey, don't worry, I love my brother. I just hate to see any trouble between him and Siobhan."

"They'll weather this. They're lucky. They were young when they met. But they really love each other. Sometimes, it isn't easy to trust someone. But when you make it through, well, then you know your heart has been in the right place."

"Mum, don't worry. I always defend Patrick. I haven't wanted to deck him in almost ten years now."

Her mother smiled but stared at her very seriously. "Let your brother manage his affairs. You've got to worry about your own situation now, don't you? What do you feel, Moira? Thinking isn't a bad thing, but what you feel is usually much more important."

Moira hesitated, staring at her mother. "Mum, I don't know what I feel. Do I spend my life waiting for an exciting, combustible, perhaps even dangerous wild card, or trust in someone who's right here, with all the right virtues? There's a lot to be said for compatibility. If I had any sense, I'd certainly go for dependable, just as..."

"Just as I did?" Katy suggested, then she shook her head, smiling. "You've got it all wrong. Your father was the wild card, the one with the real beliefs, the dreams, the one taking me away from everything I had known and loved. He said that we were going to get to America or be damned. Choices are never easy. And never clear-cut. To this day, I admire other men, but I love your father. He was my gamble, and I played against the odds. I played by instinct, and I played by heart." She turned and started walking along the dock. "Let's get on home now, eh? Your business associates have probably been calling all morning."

Katy started off again at her usual brisk pace. Moira followed.

Strange morning indeed. She'd gotten what she'd set out for.

And a great deal more.

12

Moira was surprised to see how late it had gotten when they returned to the house. Colleen was finishing cleaning in the kitchen, but a squeal from the family room assured them that the house was not empty.

Katy Kelly arched a brow to Colleen.

"Gina is in there with Granny Jon, Siobhan and all the kids," Colleen explained. "Molly and Shannon are fascinated. They think Siobhan should have twins so they can play with babies all the time."

"Oh, dear, all Siobhan needs is twins!" Katy said, heading into the family room.

"Where's everyone else?" Moira asked.

"Dad's already downstairs setting up. He says that Mondays are usually slow, but since it's almost Saint Patrick's Day..." She shrugged.

"Patrick?"

"Who knows? He's off."

"Danny? Josh? I'm assuming Josh was here, if he's left Gina for the day."

"Yes, Josh is downstairs with Dad, helping out. And Michael and Danny are out—together."

"What?" Moira said incredulously. She felt a chill on the inside as a sheen of sweat broke out on the outside. "Danny and Michael left here together?"

Colleen glanced at her sharply. "You took off this morning without leaving any hint of your filming schedule.

Josh reminded Michael that you'd been going to do a musical overlay or something, showing the doors of some of Boston's finest pubs. Those not quite as fine as Kelly's, of course, but worthy of note. Danny mentioned that he knew every pub in the city, from the most elite to the down and dirty. Anyway, they went out together—in Dad's car, as a matter of fact—to scout out pub doors. What's the matter? You look as white as a ghost.''

Moira shook her head. "Nothing," she said, a bit too quickly. "Nothing at all. I just can't see the two of them getting along."

Colleen narrowed her eyes, setting down the dish towel she'd been using and walking over to Moira. "You never told Michael that once upon a time you had a fling with the old family friend, huh?"

"Colleen..."

"You didn't, did you?"

"It didn't matter. We both know there have been other people in our lives," Moira said. "We never felt it necessary to give names, dates and license numbers."

Colleen laughed softly. "Well, no, not if he dated some girl in L.A. or Ohio. But you brought him home when Danny was staying here."

"I didn't think that it mattered. I really didn't."

"But now they're out together and you never told him and... Oh!" Colleen exclaimed, staring at her very closely.

"Oh, what?"

"That's where you were last night."

"What?"

"You were with Danny."

"Colleen, will you shut up!"

"As long as you don't lie to me."

"How do you know I wasn't in my room?"

"I couldn't sleep, so I went to find out if you wanted to make tea or talk or something. Oh, my God."

"Colleen, stop, please."

"I thought you were really in love with Michael. Then again, I didn't think you'd ever really be out of love with Danny. You can be so stubborn.... Of course, Danny does come and go, and Michael really is one wicked hunk, but... You have to make up your own mind, of course. Though if it were me...well, to be honest, sex is so important in a relationship—"

Moira could hear footsteps coming from the family room. She clapped her hand over her sister's mouth. "Please..."

Colleen tugged free of Moira's hold. She looked toward the family room. "Whoever it was turned back. Do guys talk, do you think? Oh, Lord, Moira, do you think they're out together talking about you? What do men say, do you think?" She broke off, wincing. "Lord, what am I saying? Sorry, you must be really miserable. I know you. You'd never just... I mean, there had to be a reason. I love you, and this must be so difficult. Don't worry, they're not going to come to blows. If I know Danny, he won't say a word to Michael. Honestly. It's going to be all right. I'll make tea. According to Granny Jon, that solves everything. Maybe you need some whiskey in yours. That can be arranged."

"No," Moira said. "I'm going down to the pub. Cover for me with Mum and Granny Jon and Gina, please?"

"Sure, sure, I'll say you needed to talk to Josh." Her sister sensed her misery, caught her by the shoulders and gave her a kiss on the cheek. "Honest to God, it will be all right."

"It's not all right. Michael is really good and decent and trusts me—"

"And maybe now, if you decide he's the right man, it will be without hesitation. Moira, you didn't turn into the town slut." Colleen stared at Moira, shaking her head. "Hey, kid, no one's going to do anything worse to you than you're doing to yourself.'' She sighed. ''You met Michael right after the Christmas holidays, right?''

Moira nodded.

''And knowing you, you saw him a zillion times before anything happened.''

''No, we went out about twelve times in January, then at the beginning of February—''

''Okay, I'm not really that detail oriented, at least not right this minute,'' Colleen said. ''And when is the last time you really went out in the last...however many years it was since you last hooked up with Danny?''

Moira shook her head.

''No one?'' Colleen gasped.

''I went out.''

''But you went that long without...without sleeping with anyone? Boy, and I just thought that you were really discreet. Moira, don't go beating yourself up over this. Trust me, by the standards these days, you're practically a nun. Please, don't be so upset.''

''I'm not upset, I'm confused. I really do love Michael. And I guess that I've always loved Danny. But I should have...refrained.''

''He didn't exactly drag you down into the cellar, huh? Were you drinking?''

''No. But I really need a drink now.''

''Yeah, maybe you do. Hey, big sis, I'm here, okay?'' Colleen hugged her tightly once again. ''Any time, any circumstances. I'm here.''

''Thanks. I'm going downstairs for that whiskey.''

Moira kissed her sister quickly on the cheek and escaped. As she closed the door to the spiral stairway, she could hear Gina asking for her and Colleen making an excuse.

Her father and Josh were at one end of the bar. Her father was calling out names, while Josh went through open liquor boxes on the floor, trying to supply the right bottles for the empty spaces in the wells.

"Hey, there," Josh called.

"Welcome, daughter."

"Hey, Dad. Josh. Hey, Josh, how long have—have the guys been gone? Are we going to tape the pubs today?"

"They were going to call the crew from the road," Josh said. "They really don't need either of us for this. Of course, it isn't Dan's job at all, but he seemed to want to help. And he does know the pubs of Boston."

"Oh, yes, that he does," Moira muttered, striding behind the bar to the Irish whiskey. She poured herself a shot while both her father and Josh stared at her. She smiled sheepishly at her father. "Bad night. I didn't get any sleep."

"I was afraid you were going to tell me that a couple of hours alone with your mother had made you crazy," Eamon said.

"Dad!"

"You were the one running for the whiskey, girl, not me."

"Mum and I had—" She paused, remembering the way Jacob Brolin had instantly remembered her mother after thirty years. "Mum and I had a lovely time out together."

"Good. Your mother is a wonderful woman, and you should appreciate that."

"I do. I told you, no sleep," she said.

"Gina and the twins okay?" Josh asked.

"Yep. The other kids are entertaining them," she said. She swallowed her whiskey in a single gulp. It burned like a son of a gun. Just what she needed. Almost like a slap in the face. Guilt was now, beyond a doubt, settling down hard on her.

She heard a noise from the rear of the bar and looked back. Maybe they were wrong. Maybe Danny was in his room.

But it wasn't Danny. It was Jeff Dolan. He was setting up the instruments and doing sound checks.

"Hey, Jeff," she said. "Need any help?"

She left the bar area quickly, aware that her father and Josh were studying her way too closely—and they both knew her too well.

"Sure, Moira," Jeff said, "though I'm almost done here. I was going to get something to eat, walk around awhile, before we had to get started tonight. It's going to be a long one, for a Monday. Well, for me. We don't usually play on Mondays, you know. Plug in that amp for me, please?"

"Sure." She did as bidden.

Jeff gave her a long sideways glance, brown eyes curious. "You all right?"

"Of course."

"I saw you talking to that guy the other night."

"That guy?"

"Drinking the blackbird, sitting in the corner." He grinned. "In fact, I heard you. I would have come up and applauded but...is he a cop?"

"He gave that impression."

"Yeah? Well, you told him. I'm surprised the guy didn't come right up to the stage and frisk me."

"I thought your record was as white as snow these days?"

"I'm whiter than snow," Jeff said, reaching down to straighten a few wires. "But there's no way to clean up your record."

"Jeff," she said very softly, "is something going on here?"

"No," he replied, too quickly.

"You're lying."

"No, I'm not. Really. Hey, why aren't you working?"

"The guys are off taping pub doors."

"Ah."

"Jeff—"

"You want to get a sandwich with me?" he asked.

"We can go upstairs and I can dig something up for you. Of course, the kitchen staff should be here by now, too."

"No, do you want to go out and get something with me?" he persisted.

"I—sure. Of course," she said. He was going to talk to her. But not here. "I'll just go up for my purse."

"Your dad pays us decently. I can buy you a pop and a sandwich."

"Okay, great."

They walked toward the bar. "Dad, Josh, I'll be right back. Jeff wants to get a grinder."

Eamon, looking up from his stock list, frowned. "Jeff, you're always welcome to any food in the place."

"Thanks, Eamon. I had a hankering for one of those grinders at Zeno's, down the street."

"And I'm really in a mood for a gourmet coffee," Moira added. "I promise, we'll be right back."

"Take your time," Eamon said. "Josh here is proving to be an excellent pub keeper."

"Keeping at it, just in case the film thing ever fizzles," Josh told her. But Josh knew her well, and he was watching her suspiciously.

As they started out the door, she heard her father swear as he slammed his head against the bottom of the bar, trying to rise quickly. "Moira!"

"What is it, Dad?"

"You stay with Jeff."

She looked at him, surprised. "Dad, it's broad daylight."

"They just had it on the news. They've found another dead girl."

"He's telling the truth," Josh said, handing her father a bottle of tequila.

"Another prostitute?" she asked.

"An Irish girl," her father said.

"Dad, I'm American, not Irish. And Jeff is going to pimp for me so I can become a prostitute, okay?"

"Moira Kathleen!"

"Dad, I'm sorry. It's horrible, really horrible. But please, you don't have to worry. I won't go off with any strange men. I'll stick to Jeff like glue."

"If I'd known, I'd not have been so fast to let your mother and you off alone this morning," Eamon said.

"Dad, I swear, I'll be careful."

"Did you want a sandwich, Josh?" her father asked. "Maybe you should be going with them."

"Eamon, I ate too much breakfast a very short while ago," Josh said. "And I'm helping you here, right? I worry about your wayward daughter, too, but I have to admit, she usually uses good sense. Well, sometimes."

"Eamon, I'll guard her with my life, I swear it," Jeff said patiently.

Eamon nodded. "Well, on with you, then. But come back quickly."

"Sure thing, Eamon," Jeff said.

They walked outside. "It really is terrible," Moira murmured.

"The dead girls?"

She nodded. "I didn't see the news, though. Did you?"

He nodded. "Your father had it on before you came down. Thank God I don't know anyone in the business now."

"Now?"

He shrugged. "In my wild days, I knew several working girls. Hey, you know I did some pretty bad shit when we were kids. Drugs. Hell, they got me for vandalism, and armed robbery, though I wasn't the one with the gun. I shaped up with your dad's help. I have a beer now and then. No drugs. No guns. Okay, a little nicotine..." He pulled a pack of cigarettes from his jacket and lit one as they headed down the street. "That's why your cop the other night made me nervous."

"You're nervous about more than that, aren't you?"

Jeff waved his cigarette in the air. "Rumors, Moira. Nothing more than rumors."

"And what are the rumors?"

He shrugged and inhaled deeply before answering her. "Jacob Brolin."

"What about him?" She tensed, praying suddenly that this had nothing to do with her mother.

"Well, he's a bigwig. And a moderate. And you have a huge population tired of bloodshed and violence in Northern Ireland. But you've had decades now, too, of a group—an ever-changing group, of course—who still believe that only violence has the power to change anything. And you have to remember, the Republic of Ireland was won through violence."

"Jeff, please, I don't know what you're talking about."

"Moira, don't be a dunce. Assassination."

She stopped dead still on the sidewalk. "Assassination?"

"Moira, there could be a dozen lunatics in the street ready to do something violent, either because they're psychotic assholes or because they don't believe in moderation and negotiation."

"So what does that have to do with us? If it's that obvious, surely Brolin knows it. He walks around with—" She broke off and started over. "Surely he walks around with a bodyguard. And he probably has a police escort, too."

"Of course, of course. And I'm not in on anything, I swear it. There was just some talk about blackbird being some kind of a code word. And Kelly's being a place where people might meet and find one another."

She gasped, staring at him in horror. "That's terrible! And it can't be true. We need to tell the police."

"Apparently, they already know. Hence your guy ordering the blackbird the other night."

She let out a long breath. "Rumor. Where did you hear this rumor, Jeff?"

"Oh, Moira—"

"I need to know."

"There's the sandwich shop."

"Jeff, I need to know."

He sighed deeply. "Seamus. Seamus said he'd heard people whispering one night. It was dark...after hours. He didn't know what was going on, and he was afraid. He talked about it in the pub, thinking he was safer surrounded by friends. I told him to keep his old mouth shut."

"Jeff, you should go to the police with what you know."

"What do I know? That Seamus—who's half-deaf—heard whispers? Blackbird is the name of the band. And a drink. And the police are aware there could be crackpots in the city. What could I possibly tell them that they don't already know? I'd get myself arrested on some trumped-up conspiracy charge, and that would be that."

"Jeff—"

"Your father's right, Moira," he said, stopping at the door to the sandwich shop. "Don't trust any strangers. And be damned careful, even in the pub. If you want to know more, you're going to have to ask old Seamus. Now, there's a fellow who *could* go to the police—but he won't. Yeah, Seamus is one straight arrow. He came to the States, worked his ass off and became a model citizen. But I sincerely doubt that he'll talk to you, and I can guarantee he won't go to the police."

"Why not?"

"Because it's dangerous to let anyone know that you know too much," he told her.

"But if—"

"Trust me, the radicals, the moderates and even the just-don't-really-cares have excellent intelligence systems. The police are here already. We're usually filled with our regulars, the lunch crowd and the cocktail crowd. The dinner crowd, and those who come in for the music. And most of them look familiar to me after all this time. But I've been watching the people in the bar lately. Lots of strangers."

"There are always strangers in the pub."

"Yes, but trust me. There are more than usual. I bet even Brolin's people are here already. Jesus, Moira, trust me on this. Keep out of it—completely."

"It's my father's pub."

"Nothing is going to happen in your father's pub. And there's nothing that any of us could tell Brolin's people that they don't already know."

"If everyone is so smart, how come so many people have been killed through the years?"

"Because there are too many people who see their side as a just and true cause, and they're willing to die for it. You need to keep your mouth shut, and Seamus needs to keep his mouth shut. Ignorance isn't just bliss, Moira, it's life. Okay, they're beginning to stare at me from inside for keeping this door open so long. We've got to go in. And I'll never say a word about any of this to you in front of anyone else. Now, what kind of sandwich you want?"

When she returned to Kelly's with Jeff, her father was gone. Chrissie had come in and was working the bar. Patrick and Josh were sitting at one of the front tables, drinking coffee and talking to a blond man of about forty-five, nicely dressed, long legs casually stretched out from his seat at the table.

The stranger saw Moira as she entered. He stood, bringing both Patrick and Josh to their feet.

"Moira, I don't think you've met Andrew McGahey as yet. He works with the Irish Children's Charities group. Andrew, my sister Moira. And you have met Jeff Dolan, right?" Patrick asked.

"Moira, how do you do?" McGahey said. His accent wasn't Irish. It was New York City, if anything. He went on to shake Jeff's hand. "Of course I've met Jeff. I've heard the Blackbirds many a time now. Wonderful group."

"Thanks," Jeff said.

"Coffee, you two?" Patrick asked.

Moira lifted her cup. She hadn't forgotten to stop for the gourmet coffee she had told her father she was craving.

"I'm fine," Jeff said.

"Moira, did you have any more plans for the day?" Josh asked.

"What?"

"Plans. For taping. The guys are off with the crew. They called in, and they're doing fine with the pub door segment. Was there anything else you wanted to do today?"

She'd forgotten about her own show. Forgotten that she'd detoured Josh and company from a delightful vacation to come home to film Saint Patrick's Day.

"Uh, no, not today. But," she said hastily, "I think I can get an interview with Brolin. I have to call his people back in a bit for a time and a place, but I think it will work out."

"You got Brolin," Josh said appreciatively.

"I think," she murmured.

"You didn't tell me that," Jeff said.

"Or me," Patrick said.

"Well, it just happened. This morning," Moira murmured uncomfortably. She didn't mention her mother's role, not because she didn't want to give credit where it was due, but because she didn't know if Katy wanted people knowing that she had been, at the least, acquainted with Brolin in Ireland.

"Great," Josh said. "If we're done for the day, though—or if I'm done, at least—I'm going to take Gina sight-seeing."

"Hey, thanks for the help down here," Patrick told him.

"Not at all," Josh said, waving goodbye.

"Where's Dad?" Moira asked.

"I'm not sure," Patrick said, frowning. "He got a call, asked us to man things and took off like a shot." Her brother looked unhappy. "I asked him what was wrong, and I was going to follow along, he was so damned white. But he told me he needed me here."

"That's strange. You're sure he was all right?"

"No, he wasn't all right. But I couldn't knock him down and insist he tell me what was going on. He will, in his own good time. And by the way, Andrew came by today specifically to meet you."

"Oh?" She looked at the blond man.

He smiled. A mature charmer, tall and good-looking, with a single dimple. He had an air of casual sophistication.

"I'm hoping you can help us along with your show, somewhere along the line."

"Ah," she murmured. "How?"

"Airtime."

She nodded. "Of course. Did you mean...now? For this show?"

He shook his head. "Oh, no, we're just putting the whole thing together now. Your brother has been doing our legal work. I'm hoping to get Jeff and his group to do a special CD for me, with the proceeds going to my cause. Once we get it going, we'll be hitting the news stations, papers and all, but with your show...well, it would be nice to touch the heart of America's travelers. They usually have money."

"What exactly is your charity doing?" she inquired.

"Moira, you're sounding like an inquisitor," Patrick murmured.

"I need to know," she told her brother. She didn't know what was goading her on, but she was being rude. "I want to make sure you're trying to teach kids about art and literature, language and mathematics, computer science. I mean, you're not conducting a school for the manufacture and use of weapons, are you?"

"Moira," Patrick said angrily.

"It's all right," Andrew said, smiling. He folded his hands on the table, looking at Moira earnestly. "There was a lot of violence in the seventies and early eighties, even into the nineties. Did you know that half the population of Ireland is under fifty years old? Bad times caused a lot of emigration. And a lot of orphans, or kids growing up in single-parent homes. A lot of poverty. Ireland is coming along financially now, both in the North and in the Republic. But we still have a generation coming into the working world that has grown up with little assistance. Young adults with little education and few skills. We're hoping to change that."

"Well, then, when you get your charity up and rolling, I'll be happy to see what I can do," Moira murmured. Patrick was still staring at her as if he wanted to kick her leg under the table. Even Jeff was watching her with a slightly rueful expression. Was she becoming ridiculously paranoid? Every politician in the world took a chance, trying to change things, even trying to make a better world. There was always someone out there with the capacity for violence.

"Thanks," Andrew said. "Hey, I can show you one really special kid." He took out his wallet. She almost jumped back, wondering for a moment if he was reaching for a gun.

He flipped open his billfold, showing her the picture of a young woman of about eighteen, with long dark hair.

"Jill Miller. Both folks killed. She was blinded in the explosion that took their lives. A car bomb. Anyway, she's a wonderful natural musician. She plays the guitar like an angel. She's got the talent, and she wants to come to the States, to go to Julliard."

Moira nodded. "Well, I hope she makes it," she said softly.

"She will," Andrew assured her. "The world is filled with trouble. Eastern Europe, Africa, and naturally we need to learn to help ourselves right here in the States, too. God knows, AIDS is an epidemic killing us all. But I think that this is a good cause. In my mind, there's never been anything to outdo the value of a good education."

"Yes, of course," Moira murmured.

"And it's not a bad thing for those of us who have done so well in the States to give back," Patrick said.

"You're an American," she reminded her brother.

"I'm American, as well, born and bred in New York, as I'm sure you can tell," Andrew said. "But I'm first generation, just like you. My parents talked so long about doing something like this that I've finally realized they were right. Anyway, thanks for listening. And I'll appreciate your help, whatever you're willing to give."

"Like I said, I'm very willing to see what you're doing."

"And I'll want to show you—really show you. When the time is right." He smiled at Moira, then turned to her brother. "Hey, Patrick, I think it's closing in on cocktail hour. I'd like to try one of those specialties of the house. A blackbird."

Moira thought he was staring straight at her as he said the words.

A blackbird. Sure. They hadn't made any in years, but what the heck, it was becoming popular now.

"One blackbird, coming right up. You sit, Patrick. I'll make him his drink. I think I'm becoming an expert."

As she rose, the pub door opened. Moira turned toward it.

Her father was standing there, his face gray, beyond ashen.

"Dad!" she cried with alarm, rushing to him.

He didn't protest, but he didn't seem to notice that she had his arm.

"Dad? Dad, are you all right?" she asked. "What is it?"

Patrick was standing, as were Andrew and Josh, everyone looking at Eamon.

"I need a chair," he muttered.

Patrick was instantly at his other side. They walked their father to a chair at a table. Andrew moved back instantly, allowing Eamon to sink into the chair.

"Do you need your pills?" Moira asked anxiously. "Is it your heart?"

"My heart is fine, girl."

"I'll get Mum."

"No, not yet." He waved a hand dismissively in the air.

"I'll get a whiskey," Patrick said.

"That I need."

"Dad, please, what is it?" Moira asked anxiously.

Patrick set a shot glass of whiskey on the table before his father. Eamon picked it up, put it to his lips, cast his head back and swallowed the shot whole.

He set the glass down, staring at it.

Then he looked at the foursome surrounding him.

"Seamus is dead," he said softly.

13

Long moments of disbelief followed Eamon's announcement.

"Dead!" Moira exclaimed.

Seamus, dead? No. Seamus, so good a friend, a man who had been in their lives like a family member, dead. She didn't speak words of denial. She knew by her father's face that it was true. Tears stung her eyes at the loss. What had happened to him? Had they not paid enough attention to his health? Had he been ailing? What?

Then a niggling of fear and suspicion swept through her sorrow. She looked at her brother accusingly. "Patrick, I told you to walk him home last night."

"I did walk him home, straight to his door," Patrick said, staring at his father. "He was fine. He was certainly not drunk, and he...he was fine."

"How? What happened?" Jeff asked.

Eamon shook his head, staring at Moira. "Don't go blamin' your brother, now, Moira. I'm sure he did as he said. Seamus died trying to help another, so it appears. It was the strangest thing. His neighbor, the old fellow downstairs, must have been having a heart attack and known it. He was found right outside his door, dead as well. The best the police could piece it all together, Mr. Kowalski must have called out for help, trying to get Seamus to come down. Seamus...Seamus apparently fell down the stairs in his hurry." Eamon was quiet for a moment. "He broke his neck. They say it must have been instant. He didn't suffer. That's all the good they could tell me. He didn't suffer.'' He buried his head in his hands for a moment. ''They were just lying there, the two of them. If the UPS man hadn't needed a signature for a delivery, they might have lain there...well, until one of us went to find out why he wasn't in the pub tonight.''

''A UPS man found them?'' Patrick asked, his voice strange.

Eamon nodded. ''He saw them through the glass door and called the police. The police arrived and called the medical examiner's office. Apparently they died in the wee hours of the morning. When the police...when they'd investigated and taken the bodies away, they called me. Seamus was an organized man, neat with paperwork. He'd left my name and number right in his wallet and by his phone upstairs. I'm Seamus's executor. He had no family. We were his family. The pub was his real home. Here in America.''

''Kowalski had relatives,'' Patrick said dully.

Eamon looked at his son. ''No, not really. Like Seamus, he never married. That's what the police said. There's a grandnephew in Colorado somewhere.''

''Strange,'' Patrick murmured. ''Maybe Seamus was more addled than I thought. He told me that Kowalski had kids and that there were people in and out all the time.''

''No,'' Eamon said, frowning slightly. ''Not according to the police. I was there awhile with them, answering what questions I could about Seamus.''

''You told them that Seamus was here last night, right?'' Jeff Dolan asked.

''Well, of course. I hadn't known, though, that you walked him home last night, Patrick. I'm glad to hear it. He had friends with him to the end.''

''I left him at his front door—on the street,'' Patrick said. ''I think he was a little put out. He didn't think he really needed an escort, he'd been watching his drinking. I asked him to let me walk him to his door, but he kept insisting he was fine.''

Eamon put a hand on his son's shoulder. ''And he probably was fine, then. The officers investigating the accident seemed certain they'd pieced it together right. Kowalski had come out to his doorway, right in the midst of his heart attack. Seamus must have been up the steps already when he was called back. You were with him, Patrick, just remember that. He loved you kids, our family.'' He sighed, looking around. ''He loved this place. He spent his last night here. We were his family, and he'll have us through the last respects, as well. His funeral will be what he wanted. I don't know what will be happening with Kowalski. The nephew will be coming for his body. There's to be an autopsy on both men—there always is when there's a situation like this—but we should be able to wake Seamus by Wednesday night and have his funeral on Thursday morning. Saint Patrick's Day. That would have pleased him. He had a great faith in God, and he loved Saint Patrick's Day.''

They all sat there in silence, watching Eamon, not knowing what to say. Moira was afraid to look at her brother. She wasn't sure what she would see. Her eyes kept filling. She remembered the times she had given Seamus a hard time. Arguing with him that they were Americans. Insisting that he get over it and quit reliving the Easter Rebellion. She could see him on the bar stool, telling her that he could well handle another Guinness. She remembered when they had all been younger, when he seldom came to the pub without some kind of special chocolate in his pockets for the kids.

And still, somehow, no matter what her father said, something about his death wasn't right. She was hurt and angry...and suspicious.

She felt ill. Absolutely ill.

"Well," Eamon said, "I'm going to have to go up and tell your mother and grandmother. Colleen and Siobhan. And the kids." He looked at Moira as if he'd been reading her mind. "And the kids," he added. "He loved it when the kids were here. He said he could stuff his jacket with candy again and see little eyes light up. He should have had his own family. He would have been a fine father." He shook his head. Then he looked around the pub. There was a single man on a bar stool and one couple at the back having a late lunch or early dinner. "And things go on," Eamon said. "The place will be jumping tonight. Without Seamus. Still, it would be the old Irish way. Death is a passage, and the fullness of a man's life is to be celebrated at its end."

"Dad," Moira said, "you go up and see Mum and Granny Jon, and we'll manage down here."

"Ah, now, daughter…"

"She's right, Dad," Patrick said. "Spend the evening getting some rest. With Mum. You can talk about celebrating a man's life all you want, but I know how you're feeling. You lost one of your best friends. Tomorrow you'll be making his funeral arrangements."

"Flannery's," Eamon said, nodding. "Flannery's. That's where he wanted to be waked. Actually, in the old days, we might have waked him right in the bar and lifted a pint or two over the coffin. Now that, Seamus would have liked. But Flannery's. That was his choice. His coffin was chosen, his plot bought. He didn't leave me much to do for him but be there."

"I'll take you on up, Dad," Patrick said.

"I can make it," Eamon said.

"Dad, let me go up with you," Patrick insisted.

Before any of them could move, the pub door opened again. A wild gust of wind blew in, and Michael and Danny were there, silhouetted in the dying afternoon light. "Evening, folks," Danny said. "I've been teaching Michael here a few good Irish drinking songs. He's got them down pat. Ready, Michael? Here we go...come on, Michael, join in.''

Danny began to sing, Michael joining him and doing the Irish accent quite well right along with Danny, who purposely deepened his brogue.

''The dear old lady, God bless her! She jumped into the drawer of her dresser. For the north wind blew and sailed, and the black-heart banshee wailed, oh, that dear old lady, God bless her, a-lying in the drawer of her dresser!''

They finished the ditty together. Michael seemed very proud and pleased.

The group in the pub stared at them both.

Danny frowned, stepping in the doorway, bringing Michael along with him, his arm around the other man's shoulders. ''We're not really wasted, you know. We stopped in a few pubs along the way,'' Danny said, ''but honest, Moira, I didn't bring your Michael home drunk.''

Michael was frowning, as well, as he stared at Moira. ''We did a great job, I think. You and Josh will have to see the tape, of course. And we did stop in a few pubs, but...'' He trailed off as he realized she was clearly upset. ''Are we late? Did we miss something?''

Danny was suddenly dead sober and serious. ''What's wrong? What's happened?'' he asked.

''Seamus is dead,'' Moira said.

''My God,'' Danny breathed. ''What happened?''

''Seamus?'' Michael murmured.

''My dad's friend, seventh stool down, you met him,'' Patrick said briefly.

Danny walked straight over to Eamon, kneeling at his side. ''Eamon, I'm so sorry. Are you all right?''

''Aye, son, I'm good, thank you. He'd lived himself a full life, a good life. Could have been longer...but he was, at the least, up in his years. Doesn't seem to matter how old a body is, though. When he's gone, he's missed. There's just an emptiness, you know?''

"Aye, Eamon." Danny was frowning. "Did his body give out? I didn't know his exact age, but he seemed a fine and healthy man."

"I'll explain," Moira said, rising. "Patrick was taking Dad upstairs. My mother and grandmother and the others have to be told."

"Come on, Dad," Patrick said softly.

Eamon stood. Moira felt the tears stinging her eyes again as she watched her father. He suddenly seemed old. The loss hit her again. She gripped the back of her chair. "Dad, you go on up. You and Mum need each other tonight."

Eamon touched her cheek, then allowed Patrick to lead him to the rear. He stopped suddenly, looking back. "Danny?"

"Aye, Eamon?"

"You'll host the place tonight for me, eh? There will be the usual customers coming in, and you know the right way. We'll do his wake and his funeral proud, but there must be words for his friends tonight."

"I'll see to it, Eamon. I swear," Danny promised.

Patrick and Eamon disappeared through the door behind the bar. Danny stared at Moira.

He might have visited a few pubs, but he was stone cold sober now. "What happened?" he demanded.

Moira watched him closely. "According to the police, the man who lived on the first floor—"

"Kowalski?" Danny interjected.

"Yes. Apparently he started having a heart attack. Maybe he had just heard Seamus come in. He called to him. Seamus tripped on the stairs in his hurry to reach him. Kowalski was found dead of a heart attack. Seamus was found by him at the foot of the stairs. His neck was broken."

Danny looked down for a long moment. Moira saw that he had gripped the back of the chair her father had just vacated. His knuckles were as white as her own.

"When did it happen?" he queried.

"Sometime early this morning."

Danny still wasn't looking at her. She couldn't see his eyes, but when he looked up at last, she couldn't even begin to read his expression. Suddenly he pushed the chair away and started striding toward the door.

"Where are you going, Dan?" Jeff asked.

"You just told my father you'd be the host here to-night," Moira called after him.

He paused, his back to her for a minute. Then he turned. "I will be. I'll be back within the hour."

He started out once again, then swung around, returning to the table.

Andrew McGahey had been sitting there, awkward and silent, through it all. Now Danny stopped dead right in front of him. "Who the hell are you?" he demanded.

"Danny!" Moira said, horrified.

"Andrew McGahey, Irish Educational Charities," McGahey said flatly. He didn't offer Danny his hand.

"Oh," Danny said. He stared at the man a moment longer, then exited the pub with long strides.

Moira found herself taking the part of the stranger she had so mistrusted. "I'm really sorry, Mr. McGahey," she said. "This isn't Danny's place. He had no right to be so rude."

"He loved old Seamus," Jeff said quietly.

"It's quite all right, and please, just call me Andrew," McGahey said. "Look, I'm going to get out from underfoot right now. Please extend my deepest sympathies to your father and the rest of your family, and tell Patrick we'll talk at a better time." He reached for Moira's hand. She allowed it to be taken. He shook it briefly, nodded to the others, then departed the pub.

Moira felt Michael's hands on her shoulders. Strong, supportive. Guilt didn't even kick in. She was still feeling too stunned.

She offered him a weak smile but moved away, walking to the pub door. Above the etched Kelly's in the cut glass of the upper part of the door, she could see the street.

Danny hadn't gone that far. He was across the street, looking from the pub door down the street to the corner where a turn would lead to Seamus's house.

As Moira watched, Andrew McGahey walked over to him. Danny watched him come. Then McGahey blocked her view of Danny. She could only assume the two men talked. Then they walked off in opposite directions, McGahey to the right, Danny toward the corner. Moira couldn't see exactly where he went without opening the door, but she didn't need to. She knew he was walking toward Seamus's house.

She felt Michael behind her once again. "Tell me what I can do," he said softly. He turned her around to face him. She started to cry. The tears she'd been blinking back streamed down her face. Michael took her in his arms very gently. "It's all right, it's all right," he said softly. "Sounds as if he departed the world in a very noble way. He led a good life."

"He's gone," she said simply, against his chest. Michael, rock solid, there with her. She felt in her heart then the way she had betrayed him. He was here with her, while Danny was running off somewhere, half-cocked. And Seamus...

Seamus with his strange mutterings. Jeff telling her that people needed to keep their mouths shut. Blackbird. Politicians. Talk of assassination. Seamus, Seamus, Seamus...

Seamus had been afraid. Talking. Unnerved. And now Seamus was dead. He had gone to the aid of a friend. A friend dead from a heart attack. He had tripped, fallen.

Or had he?

Seamus, if…

If what?

Seamus, if something was going on, if the picture we see is a lie, I swear, we won't just let it go, we'll find the truth.

"He's gone, and you should cry," Michael soothed. "You lost an old friend. Oh, honey, I am so sorry. Hey, I'm not worth much in a pub, but it's slow as a snail in here right now. Go into the office, or upstairs with your folks."

Moira pulled back, looking at him. She covered his cheek with her palm, shaking her head. Michael. He didn't deserve… But that would have to wait. Seamus was gone. Tears blurred her eyes again. Michael was right. She needed some time to pull herself together, but she could see behind him now. Chrissie was at the bar, talking to Jeff, her head bowed, her crying audible. And Moira's tears were drying. Suspicion was setting in far more deeply and, with it, a sense of indignation and a longing for the truth.

Whatever it might be.

"No, Michael," she said. "Thank you for the thought. But I told my dad we'd manage."

"You know, you could just put a Closed Due to Death in the Family sign on the door," Michael suggested.

She shook her head, drawing away from him with a slight smile. "I can't. It wouldn't be my dad's way. It wouldn't be the Irish way. Seamus's friends, bar cronies, will arrive tonight. They'll need their drafts. They'll need to talk about him. I'm all right. Honestly. And thank you. Would you check on that couple in the back for me? I'm going to tell Chrissie to take a few minutes. The band will be coming in, so Jeff won't be able to help. We're not busy this minute, which is good."

Michael nodded as if understanding that her way to cope was to start moving. "I'll be here," he promised.

"You really are incredible," she told him.

"Thanks." He started to walk away, then came back to her. "This isn't the time," he said. "But remind me, I need to talk to you later."

"Sure."

He left. She walked to the bar, hugged Chrissie, cried with her for a minute. Then she sent Chrissie to the office, offering her the night off. Chrissie wouldn't take it. There would be a wake at Flannery's Wednesday night, but this would be the night when everyone learned of Seamus's passing, and Chrissie needed to be a part of it, too.

It seemed that as soon as she sent Chrissie back, people began slipping in. A group from the business offices down the street, the dinner crowd.

Just when she was beginning to think she couldn't handle the bar and the floor, and that Michael didn't know enough about what he was doing, she saw her brother come down with Colleen. Behind the bar, Colleen took a moment to hug her tightly, no words needed. Then she joined Patrick, working on the floor. When the pub was really filling up, Danny finally returned. He had a green ribbon with him, and he roped off Seamus's stool, then set a rosary on top of the ribbon. Liam arrived just as he finished. Danny put an arm around Liam and began talking to him.

Old Liam began to cry, tears running down his wrinkled cheeks. He took his stool, next to Seamus's empty place. Other regulars were there, as well, Sal, the Englishman Roald and his wife. Danny spoke briefly to Jeff, then went up to the small stage, where the other musicians had gathered. He took the mike from Jeff and asked to make a statement. He addressed those who had just stopped by as well as those who considered Kelly's a home away from home. He told them that Seamus wasn't with them anymore and described his hurry to help a fellow man and his quick death for his pains. He spoke about Seamus as a man and a friend, then said that a round would be served on the house in his honor. He hoped that every man and woman there would offer up a prayer and a toast to Seamus, who had heard the banshee's wail and gone to meet the God in whom he had so deeply believed.

He stepped down from the dais, and the band played "Amazing Grace" while Moira and the others quickly served drafts for the prayer and the toast.

As she stood behind the bar busily pouring ale, Moira noted that Kyle Browne, in a mauve sweater tonight, was at the corner table he'd occupied the first time she'd seen him.

She decided to serve him his draft.

She called to Chrissie that she would be on the floor for a minute. Chrissie nodded in acknowledgment.

Moira walked over to Kyle Browne. "Did you know Seamus?" she asked, setting the draft down.

"No, but I'm very sorry to hear of his death."

"Thank you. So what have you seen?"

"As yet? Well, as I've said, I'm watching."

"I've been told this isn't a good place to talk," she said.

"Oh?"

"I think that Seamus might have kissed the Blarney Stone in his youth. He got carried away talking, sometimes."

"Oh? And what was he saying?" Browne asked her, leaning forward, pretending to accept the draft.

"I was actually thinking of wandering down to the police station," Moira said. "Asking about my friend Seamus myself."

"Good," Browne said. He leaned back in his seat, watching her. "I'll be there."

Moira nodded and walked away from him, wondering if she was losing her mind. Had she just hinted to a police officer that someone in her father's pub was a killer? No, she had done more than hint.

Behind the bar again, she found herself shaking. Patrick had walked Seamus home. That meant that Patrick had been the last one to see him alive. Except—if her suspicions were correct—for the killer, and maybe Kowalski. Though most likely he'd heard the noise of Seamus's fall, come out to see and had his heart attack on finding the body. If she went to the police, would it be tantamount to suggesting that her brother had somehow caused what happened? Managed to give Mr. Kowalski a heart attack and bring Seamus crashing down the stairs? After all, her brother was right here, while the killer might be only a figment of her imagination. Unless Patrick...? No. She wouldn't go there.

Arms slipped around her from behind. Michael. "Are you doing all right?" he asked gently.

"Fine. And you've been great on the floor," she told him.

"I'm not so sure. I think I'm wearing a great deal of corned beef and cabbage. Didn't actually have a meal, but the mashed potatoes and gravy I had to lick off my wrist were really great."

"Glad to hear it," she told him, then noted that a woman at a table was waving a credit card in her hand and looking at Michael.

"I think you're being summoned."

"Yeah, looks likes it. Maybe she's a big tipper."

"Hey, go for it."

He lifted his chin. "I'm an associate producer. I don't keep the tips, I put them in Chrissie's jar."

Moira smiled, taking his hand, brushing a brief kiss on the back of it. There was so much she was going to have to deal with once they got through all this. "I'm sure you're making her a bundle. And I'm sure she appreciates it."

"I'd better go take care of that."

"Right. You don't want another customer walking out on you."

"What?"

"Remember when the folks walked out on you? You don't want it to happen again. The pub can probably stand the loss, but your ego was severely injured, remember?"

"I'm on it."

"Good man."

"You bet."

Michael walked off. Moira saw Liam sitting, staring at his empty glass.

She walked down the bar, took his glass and refilled it. Liam was a slow drinker. He still liked his beer warm.

"You okay?" she asked him.

He nodded. "Who will I argue with now?" he asked her mournfully.

"Dad. He's always good for an argument," Moira assured him. She touched his face. "You be careful with yourself, you hear? We really need you now."

Liam nodded. He lifted his glass. "To Seamus."

"To Seamus," she agreed.

When she turned, Josh was behind the bar waiting for her. He didn't ask her how she was doing. He gave her a hug. "You coherent?" he asked.

"Yup, I'm doing fine."

"This is a note from your mum. And I have a question for you. Who is Sally Adair?"

"Oh!" Moira exclaimed, clapping a hand over her mouth. "She's a friend. A wiccan."

"She practices witchcraft, you mean?"

"Yes, she lives in Salem. We went to Catholic school together."

"And now she's a witch?"

"She's a Universalist and a wiccan. I sent her an e-mail about what I was doing, and she suggested we do some taping in Salem. You know, it's a great city for getting into holidays. I take it she called?''

"Yes, she just wanted to know your schedule.''

"I'll have to call her.''

"Call her in the morning. I told her that a friend of the family had died, and that you'd call her in the morning.''

"She knew Seamus. She'd understand.''

"Moira, I don't want to put pressure on you, but what do you want to do? Call off any more taping? We can put together a program with what we've got.''

"No, no...I think there's a lot more we can do. I want to help my dad in the morning, though, make sure everything is set. They'll have a wake on Wednesday night...and bury him Thursday morning. That is, if the autopsy is done and the body is released. And I still need to talk to Brolin's people about that interview.''

"All right, Moira. You need tomorrow morning for your dad, then we'll worry about the show. Take it easy tonight—wow, that's a dumb statement. Tonight's in full swing, and it doesn't look as if you're taking it easy at all.''

She smiled. "You know, it's been the best thing for me. I almost feel guilty about sending my dad upstairs.''

"Don't feel badly. He's been with your mom.''

"I've forgotten about the kids and everything.''

"Everyone's fine. I took Gina back to the hotel a while ago. Patrick and Siobhan's three are in bed a while, all curled up with their mum. The pub is running smoothly. What I was saying is that you can take all the time you need tomorrow with your dad, then figure out what else you want to do about taping. Just let me know.''

"This is your show, too, Josh.''

"The show is mine, but not this episode. This one is all yours, and it's going to be great. I'm going to take off now. But you know, if you need me, I'm just a call away.''

"You know, Josh, you really are the best man in my life. Thank God we never got intimate."

He smiled and kissed her cheek. "Good night."

When Josh left, she realized she was still holding the note her mother had sent down. She opened it quickly.

"Brolin's people called. Instead of calling, you should stop by for a personal chat tomorrow afternoon and set up what you want to do. Love, Mum."

"What's up?"

Jeff Dolan had come to the bar. The band was on break.

Moira wasn't sure why, but she quickly crumpled the note in her hand and despite her father's warnings of clogged plumbing throughout the years, inconspicuously washed it down the drain in the sink next to the taps.

"Nothing. How are you doing?"

"Good. And you?"

"Fine."

"Jeff."

"What?"

"Do you think Seamus talked too much?"

Jeff paled. "He fell down the stairs trying to help a friend. We'll never know. Can I have a draft? It's been a hell of a hard night."

"Of course."

She poured him a beer.

Michael walked over to her, setting down a bar rag. He offered her a rueful smile. "It's all under control now. The place is thinning out. You should go up to bed."

"Soon," she said.

He sighed. "Moira, I wish there was something I could do for you. I'm an outsider here."

"No, Michael, it's not that."

"I *am* an outsider. And I guess you need your family. And friends," he added with a strange note. "I'm going to head back to the hotel. Unless you want me to stay."

"Michael, you've done so much."

"I'm going to do more. I'd like to hold you and comfort you, but it seems you really want to be alone."

"I'm just fine. Really. Working is good."

"I understand. I *will* hold you and comfort you, though, you know."

"A pub is a different kind of place, Michael. I'm good here. Picking up glasses, scrubbing them will be good."

"Josh said he talked to you. You know how to reach me. I'll wait to hear from you."

"Thank you," she said softly.

"Want to walk me to the door?"

"Sure."

She came out from behind the bar and allowed him to slip an arm around her shoulders as they walked to the door. There, he paused and kissed her lightly on the lips. She frowned suddenly. "What did you want to tell me?"

"Tomorrow," he said.

"Now. You can tell me now."

He paused, looking around the pub.

"I'm not sure..."

"I'll get my coat. We'll step outside."

She slipped her coat from the hook by the door and stepped out with him. It was warmer than it had been. The walk was clear of ice. Maybe spring really was on the way.

"What is it?"

"I still don't think I should be telling you this now," he said.

She shook her head. "Why? What is it?"

"Maybe something you already know. But...I ran a check on your friend Danny."

"What?"

"I'm sorry, I couldn't help myself."

"A check?"

"I have some sources. Anyway, I'm ashamed to admit it, but I was jealous and worried. He seems...a little dangerous. And...well, I wasn't sure if you really knew him."

"In what way?" she asked.

"Well, he's from Belfast—"

"I know that."

"But did you know why he grew up with the uncle who brought him here all the time?"

"His parents died."

"They didn't just die. His father was shot and killed by an off-duty member of a British army unit. He had a baby sister who was shot and killed at the same time. His mother died a year later, in the middle of a rock-throwing war between rival factions."

Moira stared at him. No, she hadn't known any of those things about Danny. She hadn't known about her own mother and father, and she sure as hell had never known that Danny's past had been so bitter and violent.

"My God," she breathed.

"Moira, I'm telling you because what happened to him was certainly horrible, but he also...well, my sources say that he has been involved with some really radical groups in Northern Ireland. I just want you to be careful. Keep your distance from him as much as you can."

"You went out with him all day," she murmured.

"Well," he said ruefully, "if I can't be with you, I intend to keep an eye on him."

She moistened her lips and nodded. The entire day had been strange. And sad. Suddenly she wanted a tea with whiskey and a full night's sleep, so she could have a few hours in which to forget everything.

"Moira, I'm sorry to do or say anything to upset you. I just want you to be careful. The door to the top floor of the house locks, right?"

"Right," she murmured. She didn't tell Michael that Danny had keys to every lock the Kellys had.

"Your friend could be nothing more than a great guy with a spotty past," Michael said. "But lock yourself in at night. Protect yourself. You're very precious, especially to me," he told her.

She nodded again. She tried not to think about the fact that he was doing everything so decently, while she had betrayed him with the very man from whom he wanted to protect her.

"Get back into the pub before I leave," he said.

She nodded and went in. As she walked to the bar, she wondered if he had noticed that she had been too stunned, tired or simply shell-shocked to offer him so much as another hug good-night.

When she walked behind the bar, she was stunned to see Granny Jon sitting on the bar stool to the left side of Seamus's empty seat. "I came for a nightcap, child. I needed one this evening," she said, lifting a brandy snifter to Moira. "A blackbird," she said. "Join me?"

"Of course. Give me a second."

Moira made herself a drink, then went to stand before her grandmother. They clicked glasses. "To Seamus," Granny Jon said. Moira was startled by the volume of her voice. Rich and deep. It reached every ear in the pub. "To Seamus. And to all men of peace. And may all who would kill innocent men, women and children for their cause, no matter what it might be, be damned."

She downed her drink. The pub was silent, watching her.

Then Jeff Dolan cried, "To Seamus and the Irish. To the golden age of learning, and a future of peace."

"Salute!" someone called.

Glasses throughout the pub were raised.

Granny Jon set her snifter on the bar. "Good night," she said softly to Moira, and walked around the bar, heading for the stairs.

Patrick came to stand next to his sister. "What was that all about?" he murmured worriedly. "You don't think that this has...unhinged her a little?"

"She's in pain," Moira replied.

"Yeah," Patrick said. "Do you want to go up? Colleen, Danny and I can close down. You've really been working tonight. It must have been a long day."

She was ready to demur, determined to stick it out strongly to the end, then she changed her mind. "All right. Thanks, Patrick."

She turned and left him, following her grandmother's footsteps up the stairs. When she reached the landing, she hesitated, wanting to lock the door then, with her brother and sister still downstairs. They both had keys. Probably not on them. And then again, whom would she be locking the door against? Her brother—or Danny?

She walked down the hallway, passing her room to listen at her grandmother's door. She could hear water running in the bathroom.

She went to her room, washed her face and brushed her teeth by rote and started to climb into bed. Her mind seemed to be running at a million miles an hour. She was exhausted, but she was never going to sleep.

Lie down, just lie down....

She crawled in. Seamus was dead. Her mother knew Jacob Brolin from way back. Danny's entire family had died tragic deaths. She had slept with him. Jeff had told her that something might be going on in the pub. Seamus was dead. He had talked. Granny Jon had come downstairs and made a strange speech....

She jumped out of bed and walked to her grandmother's door. She tapped on it lightly.

"Yes?"

"It's me, Granny, Moira."

"Come in."

Granny Jon was awake, lying in her bed, watching a television that had no sound coming from it.

Moira walked over and sat on the edge of her bed. Granny Jon arched a brow, then stretched out her fingers, curling them around Moira's.

"That was quite a toast you gave downstairs," Moira said.

Granny shrugged. "I may be old, but I like to let my mind be known now and then."

"Are you worried about something?" Moira asked her. "Something going on?"

"I'm sad. We've lost an old friend. And maybe I am a little worried. There's a lot going on these days."

Moira stared at her, then changed the subject. "You know, I take it, that Mum was once acquainted with Jacob Brolin?"

Granny Jon nodded. "Naturally."

"What do you think is going on?"

Granny Jon shook her head. "Just a feeling in these old bones, my girl. And, I suppose, a history filled with a violence I never want to see repeated. It makes me angry, because Ireland is such a wonderful country. Ah, Moira, you've been there. Is there anything like a summer's day in Connemara? The wind blowing over the grass...all of the island. In the North, the Giant's Causeway, those ancient rocks rising like bizarre steps cast down on the earth from heaven above. You can almost believe the legend of Finn MacCool."

Moira smiled and began musing. "Finn MacCool, warrior, leader of the Fianna, who defended Ireland from foreign invaders. He was strong and had the gift of second sight. He could suck his thumb and gain wisdom by doing so." She smiled. "I remember that Mom and Dad couldn't get Colleen to stop sucking her thumb when she was a little girl. She would argue with them that sucking her thumb was going to make her smart like Finn MacCool."

Granny Jon smiled. "Well, now, very good. But it wasn't just Colleen who used Finn as an excuse to suck her thumb. I believe she got the idea from you. I need a trip home. I want to go to Armagh again and see the great cathedral rising out of the land, and the fields rolling and green and so lovely. It's a magical place. I need to see it again.''

''You've been back many times.''

''I know, but I get homesick. I love the States, and I'm proud to be a citizen. But I want to drive around and see the beauties of my youth.''

''We need to plan a trip, then,'' Moira said lightly.

''We'll see. Let's get through the next few days, eh?''

Moira nodded. She hugged her grandmother. ''I love you very much.''

''I know, Moira. And I love you, too. Dearly. We're all very, very proud of you, you know. And of Patrick, and Colleen, too, of course.''

''May I ask you something?''

''My girl, in life, we can ask anything we like. Getting an answer is an altogether different thing.''

Moira smiled. ''Will you tell me the truth about Danny?''

''What truth is that?''

''I never knew before that his father and sister were murdered.''

Granny Jon was silent for a minute. ''Where did you hear that?''

''I'd rather not say. Is it true?''

''Yes, they were killed before his eyes.''

''Why didn't anyone ever tell me?''

''Danny never talks about it. I imagine it's a painful subject for him. Even after all these years.''

''But it's important. It's something that could...''

''Could what?''

''Well, it could definitely make someone...''

''Crazy? Is that what you're trying to say?''

''No, no, not crazy. Just...radical.''

''Some people, maybe.'' Granny Jon shrugged. ''As it happened, he was raised around the world. He puts his feelings into his writing.''

Moira realized that her grandmother was not going to speak ill of Daniel O'Hara. Even so, she had learned what she needed to know. Michael had told the truth.

"Granny Jon...maybe it's not a good time to be making speeches. Even if you're only making a toast to an old friend."

"I'm an old woman, girl, and I can speak my mind when I choose. That's a gift that comes with age."

"You're not all that old."

"Oh, yes, my dear, I am."

"Seamus was old, but there was no reason we should have lost him."

"Ah, Moira, you feel his death deeply, I know. We all do."

"It's more than that," she murmured.

"You're feeling something in your young bones, eh? Well, then, I promise I'll behave and keep my feelings to myself, if you'll be doing the same."

"Discretion is my middle name," Moira promised.

"Give me a kiss, then, and let me get some sleep."

Moira kissed her grandmother, then rose reluctantly. She was tempted to ask her to move over and let her share the bed.

She walked to the door, wondering why she felt such a strange and deep-seated fear. She decided she wasn't going to frighten her grandmother.

But she wasn't going to leave.

She was going to take a seat right outside her door for the time being.

She opened and closed the door silently and nearly screamed aloud when she almost tripped over something in the hallway. A body, a man. Kneeling, sitting, crouching? It didn't matter. Even as a scream formed in her throat, the man moved. He was instantly up. Before the terrified sound could rip from her lungs, a hand was clamped hard over her mouth.

14

"Shh."

She was shaking in his hold but didn't really need the voice, even in so hushed a monosyllable, to know it was Danny. She had felt him. Been close enough to breathe in his scent.

"Moira, it's me. Dan. Shh."

She choked back sound but continued to stand there, shaking. Danny. The man she had known so well and never really known at all.

He released her. She forced herself not to run screaming down the hall. "What are you doing here?" she whispered furiously.

"Watching over your grandmother."

He was watching over someone?

"Why?" she asked.

"I don't know," he said flatly. "Not exactly. What are you doing here?"

"I live here."

"In your grandmother's room?"

"She *is* my grandmother."

"Right. But what are you doing here *now?*" he asked.

She was unnerved but also determined to stand her ground. "Watching over my grandmother."

He was silent. In the shadowy hallway, she couldn't begin to read his expression.

"You can go to bed," he told her. "I intend to stay here awhile."

Moira bit her lip, wondering if this wasn't like the wolf offering to guard the lamb. They were in her home. Her father and brother were both asleep down the hall. The house was full of people.

He couldn't possibly be planning on doing anything.

So what was he worried about? And what was *she* worried about?

"I intend to stay here. You can go to bed," she told him.

She felt Danny's eyes in the shadows. He took her hand suddenly. "Fine. That's my place against the wall, there. That's yours."

He stubbornly sat down. She sat next to him stiffly. They were still close enough to touch. She didn't know whether to be afraid or not.

To just start screaming or not…

"Really, you can go—" she began.

"I'm not moving."

"Neither am I."

"Then we'll just have to sit here together, won't we?" he said.

And so they sat.

Time ticked by. At some point she must have fallen asleep. She woke suddenly, with a sense of alarm, not knowing why, or even where she was or what was going on for a moment. Then she knew. Her neck hurt. She had fallen asleep with her head on his shoulder. And he was suddenly sitting up, alert, tense, listening in the shadows.

Moira straightened without letting out a sound. As tense as he, but she didn't hear a thing.

He leaned very close to her. "Your family is all home for the night?" he mouthed.

She nodded. Then she realized she didn't really know. Patrick, Colleen and Danny had all still been downstairs when she had come up. She had gotten ready for bed and gone straight into her grandmother's room. She really had no clue as to whether they had come up and gone to bed or not.

Danny rose, silent as a wraith. She stood beside him. To her horror, her knee cracked. He paid her no attention but started moving down the hallway to the entry. On bare feet, Moira tiptoed behind him. He came to a sudden halt, turning around, frowning severely and motioning that she should turn back. She glared at him indignantly.

He turned again, tense. Then she saw his body suddenly ease. He turned to her. "It doesn't matter now. They're gone."

"Who's gone?" she inquired.

"I don't know. I wish I did."

"I didn't hear anything."

"You were sleeping."

"Well, what did you hear?"

"Something...at the main door."

"Like what?"

"Like...a key in a lock."

"Oh," she said. He was lying. Her family had keys to the front door, and he had a key. No one else. She looked at her watch. It was just after five.

"Mum could be getting up soon," she said, staring at him flatly.

He looked at her, jaw at a slight angle and locked.

"What is suddenly the matter with you?" he asked.

"Nothing is the matter with me," she said, hoping she didn't sound nervous. "My mother wakes up very early. The household stirs. You can leave now, and I'll be very careful to lock up in your wake."

"You don't want me in your house?" he said. It was more of a statement than a question.

"Danny, this was a hard day. You're right. I don't want you up here."

"All right. It is almost morning. And the threat is gone."

"What threat? Maybe you're the only threat around here."

She realized that she was at the head of the hallway and he was in front of her. She was rather like a dachshund trying to pretend it was a Doberman, with her family safely behind her. But she had begun this. She needed to bluff it out.

"I'm a threat?"

"Yes. I think you are."

She thought he would argue. She was even afraid he would get angry and go after her. This time she was ready to scream before he could come anywhere near her.

But he didn't approach her. He turned and headed for the stairway to the pub, leaving the house without ever looking back.

Moira remained in the hallway, shivering, for long moments.

Had he really heard something? *Was* her grandmother in some kind of danger, just for speaking her mind?

And damn it, was Danny not just a loose cannon but one primed and ready to strike?

She started to walk to her room, then hesitated. She paused at Colleen's door, then quietly twisted the knob.

Her sister was sound asleep.

At the door to the master bedroom, where Patrick slept with his family, she paused longer. To Colleen, she could easily explain her presence. She couldn't sleep. She wondered if Colleen, too, was awake and in need of company. Patrick was sleeping with his wife. If Siobhan awakened, what explanation could she give? *Sorry, Siobhan, excuse me, I was just checking up on my brother.*

Still, she had to be sure. She tried the knob, hoping that they hadn't locked the door. Of course, if the door *was* locked, that had to mean Patrick was in bed. Siobhan wouldn't lock the door if her husband wasn't in.

Seconds ticked by. Moira twisted the knob as silently as she could, thanking God that her father kept everything in good working order, all hinges oiled.

She looked in. Stared against the darkness. A night-light burned from the bathroom, but the bed was in shadow. The light was left on for the kids in the adjoining room.

After a moment, however, she could make out the bed. There was only one body in it.

She stood there, feeling icy cold and frozen in place. Then she closed the door quickly, realizing that Siobhan could awaken with her standing there. She walked down the hallway to the kitchen and was about to turn on the light when she heard a key turning in the lock to the door that led to the pub.

She froze against the refrigerator. The pounding of her heart seemed so heavy and hard that she was sure the sound would give her away.

If Danny had returned, she was going to scream. She was going to waken the whole house and tell her father that they had to get Daniel O'Hara out of their home.

But it wasn't Danny. As she watched in silence, her brother entered the house, his shoes off and in his hand. He closed the door very quietly. Locked it. On his stocking feet, he started through the entry to the hallway.

"Took you a while to close up, eh?" Moira said softly from the shadows.

Patrick spun around, pale as a sheet, and stared at her. "Damn it, Moira, what is the matter with you lately? Are you trying to wake the whole house?"

"Where have you been?"

"Are you my newly elected parent?"

"Where have you been?"

"Why don't you talk a little louder so my wife can ask me that question and she and I can have a real fight?"

"Patrick, I asked you—"

Her brother strode to her in the shadows. "Out, Moira, with friends."

"On the night Seamus died?"

"Yeah, on the night Seamus died. It's kind of an Irish thing, you know? I was with some other friends of Seamus's, as a matter of fact. Now, if you have any more questions, why don't you put them down on paper? I'm going to try to sleep for a few hours."

He left her standing in the kitchen and started down the hallway. She was both furious, and afraid. She loved her brother.

But where the hell had he been?

Had he come back to the house before, sensed that there was someone there and waited? No, that didn't make any sense. He could have come in at any time and had a reasonable explanation. He lived there.

She was suddenly really tired. And it was after five.

Maybe a few hours' sleep would make things a little better.

She walked to the main door and studied it. She wondered if the top bolt still slid. It hadn't been used since they'd gotten out of high school.

She tried it. It groaned and at first wouldn't budge. Then it slid home. She walked through the house to the door that led to the curving stairway. Once upon a time there had been a chain bolt on it. The chain was missing now. It didn't matter, or shouldn't have mattered. There was an alarm system on the pub.

She turned from the door and walked down the hall. She headed for her own room but didn't go in. She went to Granny Jon's room, slipped in, locked the door and carefully settled next to her grandmother. She put her head down, thinking she still wouldn't be able to sleep.

She'd locked the doors. And still, she had to wonder if

she was locking out the danger that might threaten her household or locking herself in with it.

Amazingly, she was so tired that she slept.

She woke to the sound of her mother's panicked voice.

"Eamon! Moira's not in the house!"

She'd slept with her head at the foot of the bed. She bolted up, turned to see her grandmother rising and staring at her with surprise. She offered a rueful smile and leaped up. She was so tired she was dizzy. She raced out the door to the hallway where her mother was standing, tears starting to flood her eyes.

"I'm here, Mum. I'm here."

"Oh, Moira, dear," Katy said, taking her into her arms. "I'm so sorry. I was going to awaken you to go with Dad to Flannery's, I didn't mean to pry, and then I saw that you weren't there...and there's just so much going on lately that..."

"I'm here, I was just...I, uh, I just decided to crawl in with Granny Jon."

Katy pulled away and nodded as if she understood.

"I do want to go with Dad, though. I'll hop in the shower, then be right out."

When Moira emerged, her father and sister were dressed and waiting.

"Do you want some breakfast, Moira?" Katy asked.

"No, Mum, I'm fine."

"Have a quick cup of tea."

She would have refused, but her mother was already pouring it. She looked at her father, her eyes offering an apology for keeping him waiting.

"Is Patrick coming with us?" she asked, taking the tea from her mother and sipping it.

"Patrick is going to stay with his wife and children," Eamon said. "Whenever you're ready, Moira."

She gulped the tea, kissed her mother on the cheek and

followed her father and sister out the door. Flannery's was only about five blocks away, so they decided to walk.

She and Colleen sat on either side of Eamon as they went through the arrangements. Seamus had already picked out his coffin, they discovered. It was a simple one, but with a carved claddagh on the lid above a large cross. The mortuary attendant told them that it was a stock piece for them, so many of their clientele were Irish. The attendant had spoken with the medical examiner's office, and they expected to be able to pick up the remains that afternoon. The wake could be on Wednesday night, as Eamon wanted, and the funeral could be held Thursday morning. Father Mulligan was already aware of the death and would read the service.

As they walked home, Eamon told them, "There were two things he always said he wanted. He told me he wanted to look down from heaven and see you girls doing 'Amazing Grace' in the church. And he wanted me to do a eulogy with every word polite and full of flattery, whether I choked on the words or not."

"We'll sing, don't worry," Colleen said. Then she hesitated. "But what if...what if we break down, Dad?"

"You won't. But if you did, that would be fine with Seamus."

When they returned, the household was up. Siobhan was putting coats on the kids. "We're going down to pick out some flowers for Seamus. Brian thinks that we should choose a very special wreath for him."

Shannon walked to Moira, who bent down and hugged her. "Molly thinks that we should put a few chocolates in the box with Seamus, so he can look down from his place with Jesus and think of us and remember that we loved him. Do you think it would be okay for us to put a few chocolates in with him?"

"I think it would be lovely," Moira said, squeezing her niece.

"Brian says they'll melt and get yucky," Molly said, coming up.

Moira looked at Brian, who looked very mature and serious in his winter coat. "Brian, I don't think that it will matter too much. I had a friend who buried a few cigars with her dad. Since it's your granddad who has the final say in everything, I'm pretty sure it's going to be okay to bury Seamus with a few chocolates. I think it will make you feel good. That's what matters."

Siobhan gave her a grateful smile, taking the little girls by the hands. "We're off."

"Where's Patrick?" Moira asked.

"Still in the shower. He can catch up with us—if he chooses to," Siobhan said briefly.

"Hey, I'll come with you," Moira said. Siobhan frowned at her but made no protest. When they had gotten down to the street, her sister-in-law stared at her. "Were you just trying to get out of the house without your father swearing that you might need an armed escort?"

"No," Moira protested. But Siobhan was still staring at her. "All right, maybe. But not really on purpose...okay, I guess it was Freudian or something. I'll really come to the flower shop. Then I do have a few errands."

As they walked, Siobhan allowed the kids to move a few feet ahead. "It's got to be hard for you right now. Even before this accident with Seamus, your dad was all worried about the murders. Frankly, I don't see the danger. Not that I'm saying anyone deserves to be murdered, but if there is a new serial killer out there, he's targeting prostitutes."

"I know. And I'm sure Dad knows. Have you tried to leave the house alone at night?"

"Yeah, the night you came in. I was only going to a dinner my folks were giving. Your father drove me. My parents aren't a mile from here. But don't feel bad—it's not just your father. My father drove me back."

"I guess we should be thankful we have them," Moira said.

"Yes, I know. Something like this happening to Seamus makes you realize how delicate life can be."

"It does," Moira murmured.

Siobhan was watching her curiously. "Have you met Andrew McGahey?"

"Yes. Just yesterday."

"And...?"

"And what?"

Siobhan shrugged. "I find him...smarmy."

"Smarmy?"

"I don't trust him."

"Really?"

"Oh, he gave us a tape about the kids in Ireland...but he's rich himself, grew up in the Hamptons, and I haven't heard about any of his own contributions. He's been in Ireland often enough. But I haven't figured out what he does for a living, except spend his parents' money."

"I really didn't see him long enough to make a judgment," Moira said.

Siobhan shrugged. "Maybe I'm wrong. But I think smarmy fits him perfectly. I don't know, maybe if I actually see him do something I'll change my mind. So far, it seems he's at his most passionate when he talks about fishing. He likes Patrick's boat."

"I agree about one thing—we'll have to see what the man does," Moira murmured. Siobhan's words disturbed her. Siobhan and Patrick were definitely having their differences. She loved her sister-in-law, and she was very sorry to see it.

And she was mistrusting her brother herself.

"Maybe we're just getting older and more like our dads than we want to be—paranoid about everything," Moira murmured.

They reached the flower shop. Siobhan was a great

mother, keeping patiently sane and quiet while the children all explained just what they wanted for Seamus. Moira picked out a bouquet for the funeral. Seamus was the kind of fellow who would want donations to a good charity given in his memory rather than too many flowers. But they were his family, as her father had said, and some flowers were necessary.

When they finished, Moira glanced at her watch. Nearly noon.

"Where are you off to?" Siobhan asked.

"I—" She hesitated briefly. *The police station, because I don't trust people living in our own home.*

She couldn't say that. And she sure as hell didn't mean to implicate her brother in anything. She just wanted to voice her concerns.

"I have a few things to check on for the show," she lied.

"Well, I'm glad I got you out of the house without a lot of grief," Siobhan said. "I won't be back for a while myself. There's a subway station right up the street. I'm going to take the kids to see my folks."

"Great. Tell them hello and best wishes for me," Moira said.

"Will do."

They parted and went in opposite directions. As Moira walked, she wondered if she was doing the right thing. She was going to the police with rumors they'd already heard about. And what was she going to tell them? That Seamus might have had a few things to tell them, but Seamus was dead? She loved her brother, but he couldn't really be doing anything wrong. She simply couldn't believe it. Then there was the fact that they had a guest staying with them who had real cause to be a gun-toting radical....

She wasn't at all sure. And ridiculously, she found herself looking over her shoulder as she approached the station. What did she think? That there were eyes following her everywhere?

She saw a man outside the station, leaning against the wall, smoking a cigarette. When he saw her, he tossed the cigarette away and walked toward her. He was in a very basic suit and overcoat this time. It was Kyle Browne. He made his way to her as she approached the door.

"You probably don't want to go in there," he told her.

"Why?"

"I think we should walk, maybe get some coffee, talk. But you don't want to be seen in the police station."

She hesitated, then stepped around him. "I think I should go in."

"Suit yourself."

She kept walking; he didn't stop her. She got all the way to the door, and he still made no move to stop her. She turned and headed toward him.

"I'm not sure what good this does. As if people don't know you're a cop."

"I'm not exactly a cop."

"What exactly are you, then?"

"Different agency," he said. He let out an impatient sound. "This is an international situation, surely you realize that."

"Are you FBI?" she inquired.

He was already moving ahead of her. "You go into that station," he told her, "and the name badges you'll read will be O'Leary, Shaunnessy, O'Casey, and maybe you'll find a Lorenzo, a Giovanni or an Astrella. Sure, the local cops are on guard duty."

"I had wanted to see somebody about Seamus," she murmured.

"The autopsy report just came in. Broken neck. Kowalski died of a heart attack. Just like the cops read it at the scene."

"So it was...natural?"

"If you want to call a broken neck natural."

"I'm telling you, my father—"

"Your father is probably pure as the driven snow," Kyle said impatiently.

"Then what—"

"There's a coffee shop right up here. Let's slip in." They did so. The place was narrow, with tables stretching far back. Kyle headed for the farthest corner. They sat and ordered two coffees from a disinterested waitress.

He didn't talk again until their coffee had been served. "So, what do you know?" he demanded.

"I'm sure I know a lot less than you do. I wanted to go in and talk to someone to make sure that what happened to Seamus really was an accident."

"Why? What was Seamus doing?"

"Doing? Nothing. But he was talking."

"Saying?"

"That there were whispers in the pub. Rumors about a conspiracy or something. A plan to attack Brolin when he was in the city. And apparently the code word *was* supposed to be blackbird. You ordered a blackbird."

"I thought I'd see what feathers rustled when the word came up."

"It is a drink and also the name of the house band."

"Yes, of course. And not a bad code name. Innocent enough. All you have to do is use it in conversation and see what response you get. So who's in on it?"

"You're acting as if I know."

"You must know something. Your brother has been involved in a lot of anti-Union politics lately."

"He wants to educate orphans. That's hardly anti anything," she murmured protectively. "And actually, isn't the whole thing absurd? Any nut could pull out a gun at a parade—"

"But any nut would have to get close enough. And I'm

assuming the trigger man doesn't want to get the death penalty.''

''There is no death penalty in Massachusetts—''

''There can still be a death penalty for a federal crime,'' Kyle said impatiently. ''But I'm assuming our man wants to get away with murder.''

''Get away with murder as in make it appear like an accident? Like someone breaking his neck falling downstairs?''

Kyle shrugged.

''Then why would you need a 'piece'?''

''A piece? Who was talking about a piece?''

''I...I don't know. It was just something I overheard.''

''You've got to think. Who?''

''I don't know. It was outside the pub. People whispering. I never saw their faces. They were in shadow.''

''Think. What about the voices?''

''Just whispers.''

''Come on, now, you must have recognized something.''

''I didn't.''

''Did they see you?''

''I...yes, I guess so. I think one of them brushed past me, pushing me down on the ice.''

''And you didn't see anything, think anything, feel anything, hear anything more?''

''Yeah—I felt pain when I landed on the ice.''

''Then what?''

''Then a friend was picking me up.''

''A friend? What friend?''

''Dan O'Hara.''

''And you saw him come out from the pub to help you?''

''No, I...'' She'd had no idea where Danny had come from that night.

Browne kept studying her. "You know, your friend has a shady past."

"I know that...."

"You know his father was shot and killed?"

"Are you after my brother or Danny? Or someone else in the pub?"

"Your band man deserves a lot of watching, as well."

"Well, that's what you've been doing, right? Watching."

"Miss Kelly, you don't seem to understand. You may be in personal danger. It's important that you come to me with anything you learn, anything at all."

Kyle was staring at the door. She felt at a disadvantage; she couldn't see what he did. She twisted. Two uniformed officers had come into the coffee shop. As she turned to face Kyle, he lifted a hand as if waving to them.

She lowered her head, feeling her stomach turn. There was too much that she hadn't known about Danny.

And she'd slept with him. Fallen into her pattern of physical and mental familiarity and longing.

"You've got to protect yourself," Kyle said. "Stay near those you know from other walks of life. Your partner, your New York lover."

"What about my family?" she asked dully.

"Your family will be occupied with the death of your friend."

"They are, but...the pub is open. After the wake tomorrow night, it will be crawling with people."

"I'll be there. You'll be safe."

"The way Seamus was safe?"

"Look, this is all you have to do. Keep your mouth shut. Pretend you don't know a damned thing. For God's sake, don't snoop. Keep out of it completely. But if you hear anything, anything at all, come to me. Don't let people see you looking for the police. You'd be waving a red flag, just like a matador teasing a bull."

"What do you suggest I do? Lock myself in my room?"

"Live your life normally. Keep out of it. And tell me everything."

"I've told you what I know."

"No, you haven't."

"I haven't?"

"You didn't mention the fact that it was your brother who last saw Seamus alive."

"He walked him home. Seamus went inside alone."

"So he says."

"How did you know that?"

"It's my job to know. I'm good at my job. Now, go about your normal life. And keep your mouth shut, unless you're talking to me."

"I'm supposed to be filming in the area."

"Don't film in or around the pub right now."

He rose, finished with her. "Want me to walk you back?"

"No, thanks, it's broad daylight, I'm not far, and I've got a few errands to run."

They exited the shop together. Kyle lifted a hand to the cops at the front. They waved in turn.

Kyle watched her as she started down the street. She walked to the first corner, then turned, not sure where she was going. She didn't really have errands; she just wasn't ready to go home. She felt dull and afraid, sick at heart.

Then she knew. No matter how tough Kyle Browne might be, Seamus had died. And though it certainly appeared to be an accident, that didn't make it so.

She ducked into a drugstore and pretended to read cold remedy boxes. She purchased one, looking around all the while. Her next stop was a shoe shop, then a clothing store. She bought a blouse, watching all the while.

Finally, she headed in the direction she had determined to go.

* * *

"Where's Moira?" Dan asked Eamon, who was behind the bar checking his inventory again. Dan had thought she was safe enough that morning, at Flannery's with her father and sister.

"She went out with Siobhan and the kids."

"Where'd they go?"

"Buying flowers. Of course," Eamon said with a frown, "that was some time ago. Then I think Siobhan was taking the kids to spend some time with her folks."

"You think Moira went with her?"

"Maybe."

"You know, maybe I'll call them and find out," Dan said.

Moira wasn't with her sister-in-law.

"Do you need her?" Eamon asked.

"No, not really. I just wanted to see if I could give her a hand."

Eamon shook his head. "Well, she might be with that fellow of hers."

"True," Dan said, feeling something knot in his stomach. "What do you think of him, Eamon?"

"Good-looking fellow."

"Yeah."

"Very bright."

"Yeah."

"Seems willing to bend over backward for her."

"Yeah."

"And..."

"And?"

"He's an American. Doesn't fly in and fly out every time he gets her heart going."

"Eamon, you know I love her. But I wasn't settled in my heart and mind."

"Ah, well, that's life, eh?"

"You think I've lost her?"

"Well, now, you know, she's a fine daughter, but she's

not quite shared her feelings with me. Looks like a good thing for her, though. The fellow is part of her business. Works for her, with her. Dotes on her. Takes her places. Like they say, what's not to like?"

"Yeah, Eamon, I guess you're right," Dan said, turning away. He needed to get out.

"Danny?"

"Yeah?"

"There's still something in her eyes when she looks at you. Something sparks when I see you arguing with one another."

"Thanks, Eamon."

Dan walked out the door.

Moira took a circuitous route to the T station to catch the subway. Once there, she bought her ticket, wondering if she had become completely paranoid. She tried very hard to survey the crowd around her, but it was impossible. She had seldom seen the subway system this busy during the day.

When she emerged from the subway, she was certain that she hadn't been followed. She hurried along with brisk steps.

When she reached the hotel, she slipped into the ladies' room and waited a few minutes, then found a house phone. She was afraid she might have difficulty getting through to Jacob Brolin's room, but the operator connected her right away, and she was answered by a deep, very businesslike male voice with a rich brogue.

"My name is Moira Kelly," she told the man. "Mr. Brolin said that I might stop by today."

The man asked her to wait just a minute, then asked if she was in the hotel and if she could come right up. Brolin had an appointment with city officials soon, but he would love to see her.

Moira headed for the elevator.

* * *

He sat in a chair in the lobby, watching her. She didn't see him, of course, because he kept his newspaper high, blocking his face.

When she was gone, he let the newspaper fall.

It was perfect. Everything was going according to plan.

One of the huge men who had been with Brolin downstairs at the restaurant opened the door to the suite. "Hello, Miss Kelly, welcome. Mr. Brolin will see you in the den. Can I get you some coffee or tea?"

"Oh, no, thank you."

"Nonsense, you must have some tea," Brolin called from the doorway to the room. "A meeting of the Irish, from the old country and the new, we must have tea."

Moira smiled and shrugged. "I guess I'll have tea."

She approached Brolin, smiling and offering a hand. He took her hand, then kissed both her cheeks. "Actually, I'm a coffee man myself, but everyone seems to want the Irish to drink tea. Wherever I go, they serve tea in my honor."

"We can have coffee," Moira said politely.

"Which do you prefer?"

"Either. I've had a bit of coffee already today."

"So have I. We'll stick with the tea."

He ushered her into the den, indicating a comfortable armchair. "So, now, shall we discuss what you'd like me to do on your show?"

"I'd like you to say and do whatever you want," Moira told him. "What I do is a travel show about the wonders of America, sometimes big events—which I think we can consider Saint Patrick's Day in Boston to be—and sometimes small events, like a quilting bee in Nebraska. I love to do shows on what makes us special in America, which includes all our different ethnic backgrounds. Of course, Irish emigration to America has been huge over the years.

The Irish have certainly put their stamp on this country.''
She paused as the large man came in with the tea.

"Thank you, Peter," Brolin said.

"Yes, sir, my pleasure."

Peter left them.

Moira leaned forward. "Actually, Mr. Brolin, I didn't
come to see you about the show."

"Oh?" He arched a brow, offering her a deep smile. "I
never met your father, but I know many people who have.
By all accounts, he's a truly fine man. I never had an affair
with your mother, if that's what you've come to discover."

Moira stared at him for a moment. "Oh, no! I didn't
come to quiz you about my mother, Mr. Brolin."

"Ah. Well, that wasn't much of a fine moment for a
politician, eh? Offering information where none was requested."

"Mr. Brolin—"

"If you'll be good enough to call me Jacob, I'd be delighted to call you Moira."

Moira nodded, taking a breath. "Jacob, I want you to
know you're in danger."

A slight smile curled his lips. "I've been in danger, you
know, from the day I was born."

He wasn't being patronizing. He was reminding her
gently that he knew his business and his life very well. He
saw the distress on her face and knew that she was gen-
uinely concerned. "Strange, but peace is a dangerous way
to some. But I'm grateful, truly grateful, that you would
come here to say this to me."

"Mr. Brolin—Jacob—I'm afraid that something may be
going on in my father's pub. There's a rumor going about
that it was to be…a meeting place, I guess, for people
arranging to assassinate you while you were here in Boston."

He set down his tea and leaned forward, hands together,
listening intently. "What have you heard?"

"I can tell you what I've pieced together—which I'm afraid seems totally vague. We have a house band, a very good band, which plays Irish music. Pop, as well, but a lot of Irish music. They're called Blackbird. We also have a drink called a blackbird. My dad invented it years ago, though I hadn't heard an order for that drink in a very long time. Apparently, the word was to be used between people when they came into the bar to connect with other people. If someone made a mistake in looking for a contact, it could be easily solved, since the word also signified the drink and the band. My father had a very good friend who died the night before last. He fell down a flight of steps, trying to help the man who lived beneath him, or so the police assume, since they found both men dead."

"I'm assuming autopsies were done?"

"Yes," Moira said, a little frustrated. "And Mr. Kowalski, the man living downstairs, died of a heart attack. Seamus died of a broken neck."

Brolin was silent.

"But you see, Seamus had been muttering about hearing strange whisperings in the bar, about the name blackbird the night before he died."

"I see."

"I really believe that someone, and I'm afraid it might be someone I know, might be part of a plot to kill you. And, it isn't just me. There's a government man who has been coming into the pub, watching people."

"A government man, you say."

She nodded. "I've spoken with him."

"And what has he told you?"

"To be careful, really careful. To stay around friends who aren't Irish."

"Ah, that's difficult, when your father owns the pub."

"Yes."

"So this man told you to be careful, and you came straight to me?"

"I thought you had to be told. Of course, I don't really know anything solid at all, it's just that...that I felt you had to be warned. Maybe you shouldn't ride in the parade."

Brolin's smile deepened. "There may be many people walking around Boston right now who would like to kill me."

"I know."

He leaned back in the sofa, still watching her with a half smile.

"You're a very brave young woman."

"Not at all."

"You're here."

"Yes, but everyone knows that I want to interview you for the show."

"True."

He leaned forward again. "Moira, I agree with what the government man told you. You must be very careful. Stay close to good friends and family, preferably in groups. And keep quiet about your suspicions regarding the death of your father's friend. And..." He hesitated, but only for a moment. "We'd had word about the rumors. Actually, there are several possible danger zones in the city. Comes with the territory. We Irish like to be dramatic. What more noticeable than an Irishman killed on Saint Patrick's Day? I'm afraid that the situation is prime for people who still believe that terrorism is the only way. Naturally we've looked into many rumors regarding trouble here. We're watching your father's pub, as well, and though a man such as myself is always vulnerable, I have some strong support behind me. We have computer technology to trace people and the friendship of the government to help us. This is a free country, and no one can make your dad's place into an inquisition chamber. Again, I thank you sincerely for coming to me. Now, I want you to pretend that you know nothing, and watch out for your personal safety.

You must behave as if everything is completely normal. Go about your business, but be wary. Most important, watch out for yourself. For me, will you take care to do that?''

She nodded, not really feeling assured, just colder. Brolin had heard that there might be a conspiracy.

Stemming from Kelly's.

"When is your father's friend's funeral?''

"Thursday morning.''

"What time?''

"The church service is at nine. We'll be at the graveyard around ten.''

"Ah. The parade starts at eleven," Brolin mused. "Will it work for you if I give you that interview you want right after the parade? I believe that I get off the float at about one in the afternoon.''

"I would love the interview whenever you have time to give it.''

"You're frowning, Moira. You're afraid that I'm not going to live long enough on Saint Patrick's Day to spend time with you.''

"Oh, no! You've got to live.''

"I will," he promised her. "I will.'' He rose. "Come, we're going to give you an escort downstairs and pretend that all we've talked about is the interview. We'll do it at Kelly's. As soon as I'm free from official duty, I'll come to the pub.''

"It will be crowded to the gills," she said worriedly.

"And I'll be delighted to be the center of attention in an authentic Irish-American pub," he told her. "Trust me, we will survive it. And we'll drink to Ireland, and to America.''

Moira rose to join him. He reached for her hand.

The tall blond man was just outside in the parlor area of the suite, glasses low on his nose as he read from a file folder.

"Peter, we're going to escort Miss Kelly down," Brolin said.

"With pleasure," Peter assured him, setting aside his file and rising.

As he did so, Moira noted that his tailored suit covered a shoulder holster and gun. Brolin was certainly being protected, but she wondered if any amount of strength and firepower could stop someone who was really intent on murder, especially if—as she feared—they were willing to die to achieve it.

Peter opened the door for them, stepping into the hallway first. Brolin spoke casually about the weather. Strange, it had been so cold, so much snow that winter, ice on the walks, and now, suddenly, the days were warming, almost as if the heavens were bringing spring a few days early, just for Saint Patrick's Day.

"We're expecting a high in the sixties tomorrow," Brolin said as they stepped into the elevator and pushed the button.

"That will be nice," Moira replied casually. "It was a rough winter. Even in Manhattan, we had snow piled on the sidewalks."

They reached the lobby and walked together into the center. Brolin made a point of kissing her cheeks.

"It will be wonderful to chat on camera with such a lovely young lady," he said, his voice carrying to the registration desk and beyond. "I look forward to it. I have a few old tales I can tell on camera for you. And a few new ones, too, of course."

"Thank you so much for your time, and thank you so much for agreeing to the interview," Moira responded.

She thanked Peter and said goodbye, then headed for the large main doors. She knew without looking that they stood in the lobby and watched her until she was headed down the street.

As she went down the steps to catch the T to the pub,

she was deep in thought regarding her conversation with Brolin. *So they knew.* There were several possible danger zones, but Kelly's Pub was one of them, and they had known.

There was nothing for her to do. Everyone was warned. The Irish were watching; the American government and the police were watching. She had done all she could. Now all she had to do was watch out for herself.

And pray that her brother wasn't a terrorist.

And Danny...

She had to go about normally. Work, stay with groups of people, act as if she knew nothing, suspected nothing.

The wake was tomorrow night; the pub would be very busy. It would be busy tonight, as well. She had to help her father; that would be normal.

Tonight...tomorrow night.

Saint Patrick's Day.

She remained deep in thought.

And never noticed the man following her down into the bowels of the T station.

15

As she hurried down the steps to her train, Moira wondered again at the number of people. She had been on the South Side, a busy enough place and often filled with tourists, but it still seemed like a lot of commuters. She found a spot just behind the worn line on the pavement in front of the tracks, anxious to make sure she got on the train. As she stood waiting, she noticed movement on the tracks. A few rats running feverishly here and there. She wondered how many of them died, run over or electrocuted. She couldn't help feeling sorry for the creatures, even if their species tended to be disease-ridden and had carried the fleas that spread bubonic plague to Europe.

From the distance, she heard the arrival of the train. The crowd started to surge forward.

Suddenly it didn't seem like the natural surge of a crowd. She was being pushed.

"Whoa, excuse me," a heavyset man behind her apologized, as he was pushed against her.

"Hey!" a woman at her side cried with alarm.

Moira tried to slide between them, realizing she was dangerously close to the edge.

"Who the hell is pushing?" another man cried angrily.

But as he spoke, there came another massive crush as someone at the rear tried to get closer, shoving everyone forward.

"Stop!" the woman screamed.

Another hard push nearly sent Moira flying. Grabbing at the coat of the man to her right, she kept from soaring over the edge of the platform, but the impetus at her back sent her sprawling.

Her lower body was on the platform.

Her upper body hung over it.

She lay breathless and stunned. She noticed the rats again. Scampering around at a maddened speed.

Of course. The train was coming. Trying to rise and looking the tracks, she saw the nose of the vehicle bearing down on her with the speed of lightning.

"Back off!" someone from the rear shouted with furious authority.

She desperately tried to gain her balance.

"Jesus!" breathed the woman at her side.

The fat man was down, reaching to get hold of her legs and help her as she struggled to get on the platform.

"Back off!" she heard again, and then there were more hands, grabbing her, angling for a good grip. She was lifted off the platform.

The train whizzed by her, groaning and screeching as it came to a halt, the nose a hundred feet beyond her. She felt the wind it created on her face, so close that it was like facing a twister. Her hair tangled before her eyes. She swept it back, blinking, balancing, turning into the hands that still held her so strongly.

"Danny!" she gasped with shock.

His hair was as windswept as hers. The look on his face was dark and strained. His teeth were clenched.

"Are you all right?" the heavyset man asked, catching her arm. Despite her brush with death, people were still pushing around them to get on the train.

"Fine, fine."

"You shouldn't be allowed on the streets," Danny muttered.

"Don't get mad at her because other people are so rude," the woman gasped.

Danny didn't seem to notice the people around them, either those brushing by to get on the train or the two who had risen to her aid and now her defense.

"You could have been killed," he said.

"You could have killed her," the big man said.

Danny turned and stared at him. Whatever the man saw, he didn't like. He hurried past them to get on the train.

"You tell him where to go, honey," the woman said, stepping on the train, as well.

Moira was shaking too badly to move, to do anything other than stare at Danny. What the hell was he doing there?

She'd fallen on the ice. And he had been there.

She'd tripped—or been pushed—in the pub, and he'd been there.

And here...now...

How could one man orchestrate such a mob scene? How could he zero in on her? Any one of the people close to the edge of the platform might have been killed.

"Moira, are you all right?" The question didn't seem to be voiced with concern. He was still angry. Maybe she wasn't supposed to be all right.

She pulled away from him. "Yes, thank you. I'm fine. I'd just as soon get off this platform, though."

"Let's go out and get a cab."

They exited the T station. She tried to keep from shaking, from giving away any of her thoughts or feelings. He had taken her arm again. She wanted to scream and wrench away from him. But that wouldn't be acting normally. Since he was holding her, he could surely feel her shaking. That was all right. She might have been decapitated. Or sliced cleanly in half.

It would only be normal to be shaking.

They came to the street. The sun was blazing. Danny

still held her arm as he shook his head with disgust. "Jesus, Mary and Joseph," he breathed. "Where were the T attendants? There should have been someone down there, stopping that kind of mob crunch."

She looked at him. "It all happened in a matter of seconds," she said.

"There should have been someone there. In fact, a report should have been filed. And people should have been arrested."

"Which people?" she asked, staring at him. "There's no way to tell who started pushing and no one to arrest."

He didn't answer but took her elbow, hurrying her along the main street. "I guess the best place to get a cab is over by the aquarium," he said.

"Danny?"

"What?"

"How the hell did you happen to be in that T station?"

"I was looking for you."

"Why?"

"I was worried about you."

"Why?"

"That should be obvious."

"Because you think I'm in danger? Not just 'Shut up and don't speak Gaelic' danger but real danger?"

"You seem to be having a lot of strange difficulties these days."

"All explainable, of course. A slide on the ice, tripping over my own purse, which I had somehow lost and not seen by the bar. And now...a crowd in a subway."

"You could have been killed."

"Yes, this time. But you were there to save me. Pretty incredible."

He cast her a sideways glance. "You think I would push you under a train?"

"I didn't say that. I just said it's incredible that you

were there. How in God's name would you think to look
for me at that T station?''

''Well, let's see. No one knew where you were, but your
mother was talking earlier this morning about Brolin wanting to talk about an interview with you. That's his hotel.''
He pointed.

''How did you know that?'' she inquired.

''I read the newspaper. The entire city knows where he's
staying. I didn't need to be Sherlock Holmes. Neither did
you.''

''Your timing was convenient.''

''My timing was heaven-sent. That fat man would have
had you both in the gulley in his gallant efforts.''

''Hey, he was a stranger who was trying to save me.''

''Right. A good man. But also an incompetent one.''

They were nearing the aquarium, and as Danny had suggested, there were plenty of cabs. He started to hail one,
then hesitated. ''Do you want to go back? Do you want to
get a drink somewhere first?''

''No,'' she said quickly. ''I have to get back. I have
work to do.''

''Ah, yes, of course. Work must go on.''

He lifted his hand, flagged down a cab. Moira slipped
into it; Danny followed. ''So what's your plan?''

''My plan?''

''You said you had work to do.''

''Yes.''

''So...what's on your taping schedule for what's left of
today?''

She didn't have a schedule, but as she stared at him
blankly, she came up with one. ''I'm going to be out of
the city.''

''I thought your show was on how Boston celebrates
Saint Patrick's Day?''

''Actually, my plans have changed. But it's great that
you're here, Danny. In Boston. I'll be able to leave for the

rest of the day and know that you'll be here with Dad. He's going to need a lot of help today. The morning was hard for him, making the arrangements for Seamus."

Danny fell silent. She felt his presence so close to her in the cab. He still looked just like the man she had known for so many years. Tall, straight, striking in his long leather coat, hair smoothed back, face somewhat taut, eyes enigmatic as he trained them out the window on the scenery they passed. She saw his hand where it lay on the seat between them. The long fingers, neatly clipped nails. He had powerful hands. Watching his hand where it lay, she was tempted to reach out and touch it. She bit her lip. She knew him far too well in that regard. His shoulders appeared broad in the coat. He had an exceptional build, lean, wiry, not an ounce of fat on his frame. He possessed a very strong jawline and striking features. Those eyes, hazel, not hazel, amber, gold. In the cab, she could breathe in the scent of his cologne. She knew what lay beneath the clothing; the problem was she hadn't really known the inner man. It chilled her to think what he must still feel in the lonely dark of night. He had watched his father and sister shot down. That would surely create a wealth of bitterness in a man's heart. He had to want revenge. How far was he willing to go to take it?

He turned and stared at her suddenly, as if reading her mind. "I wish you would trust me," he said quietly.

"I do."

"You're a poor liar, Moira. You always were."

"There's something going on, Danny, and we both know it."

"Isn't it a pity we don't know more?"

"I think you *do* know more."

"And I think there's a lot you're not telling me."

"There's nothing I could possibly tell you, Danny."

He turned his gaze to the window again. In another few

minutes they were outside the pub. Danny paid the driver, and they exited the cab.

"Thanks," Moira said briefly, heading for the door.

"For the cab ride, or for rescuing you from dismemberment?" he asked dryly.

"Both," she murmured, and escaped through the doorway to the pub.

The dining area was still half-filled with the end of the lunch crowd. Liam was on his stool, with Eamon leaning on the bar from the opposite side. They smiled and waved as she walked in; she still thought that her father looked terribly sad, and older today. He was going to miss Seamus so much.

"Hi, Dad."

"Hi, daughter. Everything all right?"

She nodded, coming to him, hugging him. "And you? How are you holding up?"

"Well. Very well. You know, it's best to talk to people. And talk about people. And keep moving, keep going."

"You're sure you're all right?"

"I'm where I should be. Working. And with friends. My friends, Seamus's friends."

"Moira Kathleen," Liam said, "don't y'know? That's the way of the old Irish wakes. Sitting with the one passed on, right by the coffin, lifting pints as we gathered round, just talking. The waking and the funeral have never really been for the dead but for those left behind."

"Of course, Liam."

"We should have had two nights of waking, Eamon," Liam said.

"Seamus told me what he wanted, and wrote it down, as well. I'm following the man's wishes, Liam, nothing more." Eamon turned his attention back to her. "If you have work to do, Moira, you go ahead and do it."

"Dad, I'll be here with you tonight when it gets busy," Moira said. "But may I borrow the car? I'm thinking of taking a camera up the coast a bit, to Salem. Tomorrow I've got to edit and get the main tape out, then coordinate with Michael and Josh regarding the live feed we're going to do of the parade.''

"He's called twice,'' Eamon said.

"Who?''

"Michael. Best give him a call.''

"Can I use your desk?''

"Of course.''

Moira went into her father's office and sat behind his desk. She wasn't sure that what she was doing was right—perhaps she should remain at the pub during the afternoon, as well. But she really needed to get away. Danny would be at the pub.

And Patrick...

Well, it didn't seem that anyone ever really knew where Patrick would be.

She put a call through to Sally Adair at the Magik Maiden, her friend's shop in Salem. Sally answered, delighted to hear from Moira and glad that she was coming up.

"But are you sure? I read in the paper today about your old friend Seamus. This must be a hard time for you.''

Harder than you can imagine, Moira thought.

"That's partly why I'd really like to come up today. I need to get away. I'm not bringing a crew, just a handheld camera. If it's all right with you—and you're willing to sign a waiver, of course—I'll film a bit in the shop, and then you can escort me around to see the town's Saint Patrick's Day decorations.''

"I'd love it.''

Sally extended her sympathy to Moira's dad and family, and they chatted a minute longer, then Moira hung up and tried Michael in his hotel room. He wasn't there, but she hadn't really expected him to sit around all day waiting. She called his cell phone and found him.

"Hey, beautiful, I've been looking for you."

"You knew I was going with Dad, and then I had a few errands. And I went to see Jacob Brolin. He's going to come to the pub after the parade and let me interview him here."

"Fantastic! I knew you could get him."

"I'm delighted, but we won't have him for the original airing, since we need to get the tape we have in tomorrow if we want to show it with the live feed. They'll have to edit him in for the repeat of the broadcast at night."

"I'm sure that will be fine. So...were you planning on staying around to help your dad today?"

"Actually, no. How soon can you meet me here?"

"Ten minutes, why?"

"I want to take a trip up to Salem."

"Oh?"

"I'd like some tape from Salem to compare to Boston's festivities. Nothing major, just the handheld camera."

"Moira, whatever you want. I've been reviewing what we've got and made arrangements to get the tape out tomorrow once we've finished up. Plus I made the last of the arrangements for the live setup."

"Great. Thanks, Michael."

"Hey, it's my job, remember? Besides, in all honesty, Josh has done a lot of the work."

"It's his job, too," she reminded him. "Is he at the hotel?"

"I believe he is. Editing the pub door thing."

"I'll give him a call."

"I've got the camera. If you can't reach him, we can just take off and leave him a message."

"Great."

She hung up and went to the bar. She looked around, but Danny hadn't followed her in.

"Do you know where Danny is?" she asked her father.

"Haven't seen him," Eamon replied.

"How about Patrick?"

"Your brother went out a while ago, said he was going to meet Siobhan at her folks' place."

"You're sure you haven't seen Danny?"

"He took off a few hours back. Haven't seen him since."

Moira wished that he had come in, that she could see him and know he was here. It was making her uneasy not to know where he was.

"Think he's in his room?"

"No, I don't think he's there, but give a knock on his door if you're worried."

Moira nodded, then walked toward the back of the pub. At Danny's door, she hesitated, listened, then knocked. He didn't answer. She tried the door and found it open. Walking into the room, she found that he kept it impeccably neat, bed made, clothing put away, only a jacket over a chair. A notebook computer was running on the desk, and next to it were several maps of Boston. She hesitated, then curiosity got the best of her. The file that was running was something Sara's Night. She began to read.

"There was only one thing to do when taken in by the Royal Ulster Constabulary under the Special Powers Act. Lie. And Sara lied."

Moira kept reading.

The soldiers were none too gentle when they broke into the house. Naturally, they came in the dead of night, when the fog lay heavy over the streets. She had always thought there would be a warning, but she was wrong. She had barely lifted her head from the bed when they dragged her from it. The nightgown she'd worn was torn off her, just as the sheets were stripped from the bed. They were taking no chances that she might have a weapon hidden somewhere on her body or in her bed.

When they finished with their search, she was shaking and humiliated, and wondering what weapon could be so minute that she might have hidden it in the orifices they violated.

Clothes were thrown at her. She dressed.

They took her to the "Infamous Place," Long Kesh, with barbed wire and towers that sported machine guns. She was taken alone, which frightened her more than anything. This wasn't a general sweep of all suspected terrorists. This was aimed at *her*.

When she arrived, she was escorted to the man in charge. She knew his name. And his reputation.

"Miss O'Malley, is it?" he asked, reading from a folder. She had been seated in a chair before his desk, and he was speaking politely. She had heard about prisoners being tortured, terrorized. This man was being courteous. Courtesy, she had learned, was deadly.

"Yes. Sara O'Malley. And I've done nothing."

"You were recognized, Miss O'Malley, as the woman who pretended to be distressed, who lured Sergeant Hudson from his car while your friends set a bomb beneath it. Hudson and three soldiers were killed when that bomb went off."

She had been willing to give her life, or so she had believed. But she had never imagined what it would be like when a bomb went off, when an explosion ripped through the air, the fire, the screams, the smell of human flesh burning...

"I don't know who thought they saw me. I was nowhere near the scene."

He leaned forward. "Poor silly girl. I don't really want to see you go to prison...or die. You're a young thing, with your whole life ahead of you. You could escape, run to America. What I want from you are the names of the men who are doing the bombing. It's very easy. You give me the names. I help you escape."

"I can't give you names. I wasn't there."

He nodded, as if accepting her word. "Fine, we'll give

you some time to think about it. Maybe you will come up with something.''

She'd had no idea that a man had been standing behind her until she was blindfolded. A hood fell over her head. Arms reached for her. "Call the lady's escort, please."

Her escort.

She never knew exactly where she was taken. Or how many soldiers "escorted" her.

She had been willing to give her life....

In the end, they left her on the concrete, still blindfolded.

The hours passed in a nightmare. She imagined the smell of the burning bodies once again. She shivered with the cold. Names. She couldn't give names....

They brought her into the office again the next day.

"Miss O'Malley, have you thought of anything to tell me?" he asked her.

She shook her head. "No."

"I'm sure in time you will. Meanwhile, let me have you escorted back to your cell."

She tried not to let him see the way she was shaking. Her lip trembled.

"I'm sorry—did you think of something to say?"

She shook her head, trying to steel herself for what was to come. The "escort" arrived. She tried very hard not to think or feel. One of the soldiers, bending over her, whispered, "Hudson was my cousin." When he finished with her, silent tears fell down her cheeks in such a flood, she nearly choked on them.

"Enjoying the story?"

Moira slammed down the screen of the laptop, stepping back in horror. Danny had come into his room. He was leaning against the doorway, staring at her with narrowed amber eyes.

"Danny..."

He moved toward her. "I asked you if you're enjoying the story."

"What do you care what I think? I'm sure you have plenty of fans."

"Do *you* ever buy my books?" he asked politely.

"Of course. Sometimes. I will now, of course."

"Of course. You want to see how it ends."

"I've got to go."

"Right. You have work to do today."

"Yes."

She tried to brush past him, but he caught her arm. He didn't hurt her, just brought her too close against him.

"What did you want?"

"What?"

His body seemed as hot as a furnace. His hold on her flesh reminded her of the lean power in his arms and chest. The anger in his eyes seemed to shoot through her.

"You're in my room. What did you want?"

"Nothing."

"Just nosy?"

"No...I was...looking for you. To make sure you'd help my father if he needed it until I got back. I'll only be gone four or five hours."

"You're a fool, Moira."

"The computer was there—"

He shook his head with impatience. "Do you think I give a damn if you read what I write?"

"I've got to go," she insisted.

"Moira, damn it, you need to talk to me."

"Why, Danny, when you've never really talked to me?" she asked.

"You're shaking."

"I've got to go."

"Moira?" She heard her father's voice as he called from the bar.

"Let me go. My father is calling me."

His eyes pinned her for another moment, and he pulled her slightly closer. "Moira, I...damn," he muttered, then released her, almost pushing her away.

He watched as Moira fled past him.

16

"Michael is here," Eamon said as she rushed to the bar. "Let me get the car keys."

"Thanks, Dad. I'll be back for the post-dinner rush."

"Thanks, but you go do your own work. I can manage the pub."

"I'll be back," she said firmly, catching the keys as he tossed them to her.

Michael was standing at the door, waiting, a backpack with camera equipment thrown over his shoulder. He slipped an arm around her shoulders as she joined him at the door.

"You're shaking."

"Am I? Just a little chill. Let's go."

The attendant at the garage brought the car around. When it arrived, Michael set a hand on her shoulder. "I think I should drive."

She was about to protest, but he was right.

They pulled onto the road.

"Are you sure you want to do this today?" he asked her, sliding a hand over hers. "This is a rough time for your family. Even I could see that Seamus was much more than a customer."

"Yes, I'm fine. I'm happy to be getting out of the city. And I've given so little attention to what I've been doing, I'll be amazed if we have a show left."

"You're not supposed to worry about the technical aspect of the operation, Moira. You're the talent."

"I'm also a producer."

"Josh is on top of everything. You don't need to worry. And," he reminded her lightly, "you do have me."

"I've used and abused you both."

"I love it when you use me, you know."

He was teasing. His fingers tightened around hers, and she smiled again, but she was sure it was a sick smile. He didn't know that she had betrayed him. With a man who might be planning murder. Who might already have tried to murder *her*.

Then again, Danny had been there, picking her up each time. Of course, if he'd failed in his attempts to cause her harm, what better way to disarm her suspicions than by being the man to rescue her?

What about the night she had come downstairs? They had been alone together for a very long time. He could have done something then. What? Slit her throat in a bed in her father's house?

"Moira, what's wrong? I'm here, you know."

She looked at Michael. What was wrong, indeed? Here was a man most women would kill to be with. He had done nothing wrong; she had. But she wasn't ready to come clean with him—not while all this was going on. And she knew she couldn't resume their relationship until she had done so.

"I don't know. I suppose I'm just upset, worried about a lot of things."

"You know, we don't need this segment. We could just take the day off. Find a charming New England inn and...forget about everything."

"Oh, Michael, I'm so sorry, I've been horrible, and—"

"It's all right. We'll go to Salem."

He kept driving, then said, "I'm sorry—I think I upset you more, telling you what I found out about O'Hara."

"It looked like you two were getting along fine on your pub door excursion."

"Yeah, well..." Michael murmured ruefully. "I think I'm sorry about what I told you. I should have kept my mouth shut."

"Why?"

"Because we did have a decent day. You know, it's a little intimidating when the family friend turns out to be a man who looks like real competition."

"He isn't competition," Moira murmured. Lord, she was lying. Or maybe she wasn't. Some things didn't change easily. Maybe Danny would always have a physical power that beckoned to something in her senses. And maybe the sheer logic of everything she knew about him would be enough to convince her that even if he wasn't contemplating murder, he wasn't what she was looking for in life.

"No, I guess not. He told me that if I made you happy, no one could ever wish me greater blessings in life. Sounded a lot like your brother. We had an interesting day." He fell silent for a moment, then said in a serious tone, "You think there's something going on in your dad's bar, don't you?"

"Pub," she corrected automatically, giving him a rueful shrug. "There is a difference. And there could be something going on anywhere," she murmured.

"I think you should stay close to me for the next few days. Will you?"

She turned and looked at him. "I'm with you now, and we're on our way out of town."

"So let's have a good day."

"Michael," she murmured. "I—"

"No more talk about the pub or Seamus. You have your

interview with Brolin, and everything is going to be all right.''

"How can it be all right? Seamus is dead.''

He was quiet for a minute, then said, ''Moira, I talked with your dad. I know what happened, and I know you're disturbed. But it was an accident. A man trying to help a friend. Now let's just try to enjoy the day, okay?''

She smiled and agreed, but inside she was still cold and worried.

"Josh, where did she go?''

Dan had barely waited until Moira left his room to call her business partner, hoping he would be in his room at the hotel.

"Hang on,'' Josh said. ''I just got in, but I've got a message here. They went to tape in Salem, with Moira's friend Sally Adair. I never met her. Do you know her?''

"Yes, I met her years ago. She used to live around here, then moved up the coast. Are you going to join them?''

"I wasn't planning to. I'm assuming Moira planned on using just the handheld camera, and since Michael is with her, he can handle it.''

Dan hadn't closed the door to his room; he was startled to see Patrick Kelly standing in the doorway.

He lifted a hand in acknowledgment of Patrick's presence.

Patrick smiled and nodded, waiting for him to finish his conversation.

"I think I'll take a drive up,'' Dan said. ''Just in case they need a hand.''

Josh was silent for a minute. ''Dan, I'm sure they're going to be fine. And...you know, this is none of my business, but...she's been seeing Michael steadily ever since they met.''

"I know. Look, if it turns out that he's what she really wants to be happy, I swear, I'll back off so far you'll never know I was around. Moira has been really upset though, lately, with Seamus and all.... Why don't you drive up with me?''

"All right. But if we don't move—"

"We'll move now. Right now. We can catch them. They just went out the door.''

"All right. I'm on my way.''

"Where are you moving to?'' Patrick asked from the doorway.

"Salem.''

"Dad said Moira had taken off with Michael to see Sally.'' Patrick studied Dan. "You don't think you should leave the two of them alone?''

"Maybe I should. But I'm not going to, not now, in the midst of everything here...with Seamus's loss and all. Hell, did you need me for something?''

Patrick shrugged and laughed. "Actually, I came to see if you wanted to take a drive up to Salem.''

"*You* were planning on following them?''

"Yup.''

"Why?''

"I guess I'm a little worried about her. And Michael...well, maybe she's madly in love with him, but he hasn't really known her that long. I'm her brother. I've known her forever, and if she needs support right now, I think I'm better qualified to offer it. And I had a feeling you might be willing to join me.''

"Yeah, I'm willing. And Josh is on the way.''

"Good. That makes it okay for us to go up and you to get into the middle of her relationship, right?'' Patrick asked. "Never mind, don't answer. I'll drive.''

"Hey, do me a favor. Make sure your dad is going to be okay, then keep a lookout for Josh. Give me a minute here. I'll be right out.''

"Sure.''

Patrick left. Dan dialed the phone again. He never called Liz on the house phone. This time, however, he did.

"Liz, tell me you've got something new for me."

"All right. This charity fellow that Patrick Kelly is working with...Andrew McGahey. There's a man walking a really fine line. Want to hear about him?"

"Shoot."

"You're on the house line," she accused him suddenly.

"Just tell me quickly what you've got."

"He was in Belfast several times in the last few years. Each time he went, he had a number of meetings with Jacob Brolin—and members of the Real IRA. You need to keep your eye on him—and Patrick Kelly. Although I will say this, McGahey has been doing all the right things legally for that charity. His papers have all been filed correctly."

"Well, of course. Patrick Kelly is a good attorney," Danny said dryly.

"There's been another man in the pub, as I'm sure you know."

"I'm aware of Browne."

"Good. Watch yourself. He's not working alone."

"I know the main prize, Liz. I've been watching out for Browne. Jesus, there should be something else by now. Have you gotten anything else on Michael McLean?"

"Why? Are you itching to take the fellow down? Don't go getting obsessive."

"Just keep at it," he said. Obsessive? Well, yes, he could be obsessive. And he wasn't even sure why. He'd managed to spend the afternoon with Moira's new beloved and discovered that if there was something behind the facade, it was damned well hidden. The guy had been decent all day, humorous, intelligent. It appeared that he really loved Moira, which should have made Dan feel some guilt, but didn't. Maybe he was wrong, and the guy was simply perfect, and he himself had blown everything over the years.

"I told you," Liz said wearily, "every record we have squeaks. Don't go getting tunnel vision. There's too much at stake."

"I don't have tunnel vision." Maybe he did. Liz was right; there was too much at stake.

"You know that Moira Kelly went to see Brolin today."

"Yes, of course, I know that."

"Good. You've been on that line too long."

"I was on it too long the second I called you," he said impatiently. "Listen, I want to see what you have."

"On what?"

"McGahey, Patrick, the charity. And on McLean."

"Dan..." she said warningly.

"I want to see what you've got. It's my ass on the line here, big-time. Now I'll get off the phone." He hung up, grabbed his coat, patted the inner lining to make sure he had everything and went out. He spoke quickly with Eamon, praying the man would tell him that he was fine and had plenty of help. Eamon said exactly that.

Dan hurried outside to join Patrick. They waited on the street for Josh to arrive.

As they passed the sign telling them that they were entering Salem, Michael asked Moira where she wanted him to park.

"There's nothing much by the shop. I usually park in a space around the common when I come here. It's only a few blocks to her shop, and the town is really charming."

Michael drove past pretty houses to park in the first space he could find around the common. He took the camera from the trunk, and they walked along the street, past the Hawthorne Inn toward the waterfront.

She grinned at him. Getting away from Boston had been good. She felt as if she had cast aside a burden, if only for a short time. She could almost forget that tomorrow would bring a wake, that Seamus was dead.

"One more block to Sally's shop."

The camera was over his shoulder. He took her hand as they walked. She didn't protest.

"Ah, there you are."

Sally was standing outside her shop, as if supernaturally aware of just when they would arrive.

"See, she is a witch, she's expecting us," Moira told Michael seriously. She moved ahead, hugging her friend. Sally had ink-dark hair that went well with the slinky black caftan she was wearing. The V neck of her garment displayed the silver pentagram she wore. Silver orbs dangled from her ears and highlighted her almost powder blue eyes.

"You must be Michael," Sally said, stepping forward and extending a hand.

"I must be. Sally, great to meet you. I admit, you're my first witch."

"Sally. I love the window," Moira said, looking into the display window, where her friend had created an Irish tableau with fairies and leprechauns and a charming statue of Saint Patrick.

"Thanks. You don't think it's overkill? I had such a good time." She grinned at Michael. "The Irish may be very Catholic in general, but they do love their fairies, leprechauns, banshees and the rest."

"Michael comes from an Irish family, too."

Sally laughed. "Probably not quite as Irish as yours. Is anyone—even in Ireland—as Irish as your dad? Hey, come on in," Sally said, slipping her arm through Moira's, leading her into the shop and whispering a mile a minute, as she tended to do. "He's a hunk. Of course, I'd already heard he was good-looking. The others are already in the shop."

"The others?" Moira asked, frowning, pulling back. But they were inside, and she came to a standstill, frozen as if she'd suddenly been sheathed in ice. Patrick, Josh and Danny were all there. Josh had a camera and was already filming, Patrick was studying a display case, while Danny seemed to be perusing the sachets of herbs that offered to heal or bring money, love or peace of mind.

"Hey, what took you so long?" Josh asked cheerfully.

"What the hell are you doing here?" Moira exploded without thinking.

Josh frowned. "Sorry. I thought I was part of this."

Moira quickly gathered her wits. "No, Josh, I'm sorry, I—"

"I don't think she meant you in particular, Josh," Patrick said.

"Or you," Danny murmured, so softly Moira wasn't sure she really heard him.

"You didn't know they were coming? How nice that they've surprised you," Sally said cheerfully, apparently missing Moira's tone. "Anyway, the window is special for Saint Patrick's Day. I have some books on Ireland over there. Oh! And there's my banshee. Isn't she great?"

The banshee *was* great. She was swathed in black and seemed to float in the air in the archway between the front of the shop and the rear. She had a strangely beautiful porcelain face, with dark eyes and a mournful expression.

"She's very impressive," Moira heard herself murmur.

"She's beautiful," Michael said.

"Well, originally, banshees must have been beautiful," Sally said. "You see—"

"Wait, wait," Josh protested. "Moira, sit down with Sally. You can interview her about the banshee."

A few minutes later she was seated in a chair alongside Sally, the banshee swaying to Sally's right. Moira introduced the piece and filming began.

Sally's discussion of the banshee made a nice complement to Granny Jon's tales. When she was done, Moira smiled and looked at Josh. "I think it's perfect."

"Really? I did well? You're going to use the tape?" Sally asked.

"It was great."

"And I won't end up on the editing room floor?" Sally queried.

"No way," Danny said. Moira looked at him, irritated that he would answer such a question in her stead. "Well, she was definitely more interesting than the pub doors we taped," he said with a shrug. He spoke lightly, but the way he stared at her disturbed her. He was still angry, she thought, that she had been on his computer, reading what he had been writing.

"Well, then, I have to take you to lunch to celebrate," Sally said.

"No, we'll take you to lunch, for your wonderful speech," Moira said.

"I insist," Sally said.

"We're going to make big bucks on you, Sally. Let the production team of Whalen and Kelly take you out," Josh insisted.

"All right," Sally agreed. "Randall and Meg will be here in just a minute. They do palm reading," she explained to the others. "They're wonderful, if anyone is game for a palm reading."

"I'm afraid I'm more game for lunch," Josh said. "It's nearly three. I'm going to embarrass myself with abdominal rumblings soon."

"Why don't you guys go ahead? I'll call my friend Martin McMurphy, so he'll be expecting us all. Just introduce yourselves—he'll have a table."

Michael, near Moira, leaned to her and whispered softly, "Martin McMurphy? Is that name for real?"

A smile twitched her lips. So what if Danny, her brother and Josh were here? She was in a crowd; she was safe. She just needed to steer clear of Danny. She was going to make the day a pleasant one.

"All right, we'll head on out."

"The restaurant is completely decorated. Leprechauns—and the usual stuffed wiccans, ladies in black, none on broomsticks—are decorated with green bows. Marty also owns House of Haunts. It's a year-round spook house, but he's added some extra banshees, evil leprechauns and green-glowing skeletons for Saint Paddy's Day. He says you're welcome to run tape there, as well."

"I'm for it. But lunch first. So how do we get to this place?" Josh asked.

"Straight down the mall. The restaurant is across the street in a quaint little eighteenth-century house. The horror house is right next door."

"Well, since we're all still standing here, I'll do the heading on out," Patrick offered. As he started out the door, the Pelhams—Randall and Meg, Sally's palm readers—came slipping through the door. They were both at least sixty and could have passed for thirty. Randall's head was shaved, and he had a Yul Brenner look. Meg had apparently been born with the kind of platinum blond hair that turned to shimmering silver with age. She had an abundance of it, streaming down her back and over the long black cloak she wore. Sally explained that she was off to lunch and they headed for the door.

"Moira," Meg called just at the last moment.

She stopped, looking back.

"Have a nice lunch. But be careful. There's a darkness around you."

"A darkness?" Moira murmured.

Meg looked worried. "Just avoid darkness. Scoot, go, go. I'm sorry I stopped you."

Moira gave Meg a quick kiss on the cheek and hurried out. The others followed. As they headed down the street, she realized Danny was right behind her. It was that aftershave. She knew it so well.

"Hey," she accused him suddenly and angrily as he came up beside her. "I asked you to help my father."

"Your father is fine. He's with Liam, Chrissie is there, Colleen was on her way down, and Jeff and the band were coming in early, in case they needed to help out."

"Really? You talked to my dad?"

"I did, and so did your brother."

"Why are you here?"

"I'm worried about you."

"Why? I seem safe enough when you're not around."

He caught her shoulders, swinging her around to face him. "You really think I'd push you under a subway?"

She stared at him stubbornly, her chin in the air. The others were ahead of them and kept walking, unaware of the drama playing out behind them.

"Moira, I'm a writer. I put things on paper. Is Stephen King a mass murderer? Is Dean Koontz a psychotic killer?"

"Let's just have a nice lunch, Danny."

"Yeah, right. And when we get back, why don't you search my room, see what else you can find?"

She ignored him, pulling away and hurrying to catch up with the others.

A few minutes later they arrived at Martin McMurphy's restaurant. He greeted them with pleasure. He was tall, sandy-haired, freckled and immensely charming. As they walked to the table, Moira nudged Sally. "There's an adorable guy for you."

"He's a great friend, but I'm afraid his boyfriend likes him, too."

"Oh. Sorry."

"Don't be sorry, they're both two of the best friends I've ever had." Sally laughed. "You'll meet Dirk later. He works in the haunted house."

They sat at a table done up with a green tablecloth, green napkins and leprechaun salt and pepper shakers. The

place was usually a theme café, with model monsters, gar-
goyles, fake spider webs in the corners and little plastic
rats to hold the menus. Now the witches and goblins were
all decked out in green.

Martin waited on them himself. As they waited for the
meal, Michael produced a release form, and then Josh followed Martin and Moira around the room, filming. When
the food arrived, they all took their places at the table
again. The food was delicious, and the green beer was
crisp and cold. Coffee was served with McMurphy's Finest
Shortbread, and no one was able to pick up the check
because McMurphy refused to give them one.

"But we're a crowd," Sally protested.

"And this is the best kind of business expense," Martin
retorted.

"This has been wonderful, but we've got to be getting
back, I'm afraid," Moira said.

"You've got to do the haunted house first," Sally told
her. "It only takes a few minutes."

"Dirk will be waiting for you," Martin insisted.

"Do you mind if we tape in the haunted house?" Moira
asked him.

"I want you to go in and become delightfully spooked,"
he said. "No taping—I can't give away my trade secrets.
Besides, scary things aren't so scary in the light."

They thanked him for his hospitality and headed for the
spook house next door. There they were met by Dirk. He
was tall and striking, with dark eyes and hair, fine cheek-
bones and a quick smile. He kissed Sally's cheek and
smiled broadly as everyone was introduced. "All right,
then, I guess I should give my usual spiel. Being a little
bit scared is fun, being really frightened is not. This
doesn't look like a crowd to be really frightened. Or even
scared," he said with a sigh. "But if anyone is upset at
all, just yell, and we'll get you right out into the open air,
okay?

"And now..." He swept his arm dramatically through the air, gave a low bow and opened another door, ushering them in.

The place was well done, with black lights and realistic effects. Moira walked in with Sally, and they paused together in the first room, the den of Bram Stoker, who was writing while horrid visions of vampires danced on the walls. The next room highlighted the contrast between the witch of legend and the true wiccan, who honored the earth as the mother and respected all things within the universe. Next came a room filled with werewolves, vampires, demons, mummies and, special for the upcoming holiday, crazed leprechauns and evil banshees. A vampire was bent over a bed where a beautiful young woman slept in a silk gown. As Moira went to study the tableau, both the victim and the vampire suddenly turned, the woman dripping fake blood, the vampire snarling. Moira let out a startled scream, and her brother, Michael, Josh and Danny were instantly at her side.

"Moira?" Patrick said.

"I was startled." She laughed. The vampire and victim had resumed their deadly pose, as if they had never moved.

"There are live performers throughout," Sally told them. "Those two should get a raise."

Danny was right behind Moira. She rushed ahead, not wanting to be close to him. Michael had asked Sally something, and the two were walking together, deep in conversation, while Josh told Patrick that they really should do a separate show on Salem.

They entered a room with psychedelic lighting and a floor that rotated. Moira moved quickly, wanting to shake Danny. She found herself spinning, then emerged into a pretend graveyard. Mist rolled across tombstones. Banshees swept through the air, letting out mournful cries. A figure dressed as the grim reaper suddenly leaped out from behind one of the tombstones. Moira jumped, startled again, but she smiled rather than screamed as the figure circled her, not touching her but tapping his scythe on the floor. "You guys are good," she told him softly, moving on. The grim reaper didn't say a word, just walked among the tombstones, ready to startle the next guest. Moira hurried on, hearing the revolving floor rotate, bringing the rest of her party from beyond.

She passed through a doorway hung with fluttering gray silk.

Here was a church scene, with mourners standing by an open grave. Above the dead man floated another of the black-draped banshees.

She walked through another doorway and found herself in a hall. Eerily lit signs pointed in either direction. She moved to the right and found a door warning of the dangers of the countryside. In this scene, there was misted light and a rainbow. A leprechaun sat on a pot of gold at the foot of the rainbow. But as she approached, something triggered the leprechaun. He spun around, offering a face of pure evil. There was something so eerie about his expression that she suddenly found herself uncomfortable. She quickly exited the room and returned to the hallway, only to find herself completely turned around, and going back the way she had come.

She found herself in the graveyard again. Music played, low and macabre. "Sally? Guys?" she called softly. It seemed they had come and gone. "Hello?" she murmured, hoping the black-clad grim reaper would reappear to show her the way out.

Nothing. The banshees floated by, singing in a high-pitched wail that made her flesh crawl.

"Damn it!" she muttered, and started for a doorway. A sixth sense warned her that she was being followed. She spun. The grim reaper. "There you are. I don't believe it, but I'm lost. Can you show me the way out?"

He walked past her and stopped, blocking the doorway.

Suddenly he drew his black-clad arm from beneath his cloak. The light caught on something in his hand. A knife. A big knife, glittering in the dim light.

"No need for that, I'm already scared," she told him.

She gasped, stunned, as he reached out and grabbed her, twisting her into his arms. She felt the blade of the knife at her throat. A ragged whisper touched her ear as he pulled her close against him.

"Iss binn beal 'na thost!"

Despite the blade at her throat, Moira screamed.

17

The creature shoved her forward. Moira raced through the door and down the hallway, took the wrong turn and burst into the rainbow room again.

The leprechaun turned, grinning evilly.

The right, the right, she had to go to the right to get out. But somehow she found herself in the graveyard again, colliding in the dim light with a man. She screamed.

"Moira, it's me."

Danny. He gripped her shoulders, shaking her slightly. "Why did you walk off like that? We've all been going in circles, looking for you."

Lights suddenly came on. The grim reaper—revealed as a tousle-haired college kid with his hood and mask removed—came rushing into the graveyard scene, followed by Dirk. "Moira, I'm so sorry. Are you all right? You rushed on ahead. What on earth frightened you so badly?"

Glaring lights betrayed the fact that the gravestones were nothing more than foam and the flying banshees black-clad figures on strings as the others came rushing in. Michael and Sally came from the revolving floor behind her, Patrick and Josh from the forward doorway.

She stared at the grim reaper. "He threatened me with a knife!"

"Adam?" Dirk said with bewilderment and anger, staring at the kid.

"I didn't threaten anyone with a knife," the boy protested, and looked at Moira earnestly. "Honestly, I only carry the scythe. And it's rubber—look." He proceeded to show her how the blade of his weapon moved, bending at his slightest touch.

"Someone threatened me," she murmured. "With a real knife. And he—"

Sally came over to her, wrapping her arms around her. "Moira, I'm so sorry. We should have all stayed together. But none of the employees ever carry real weapons. Ever."

Moira realized that they were all staring at her. She was never going to convince them that she hadn't managed to let her imagination get out of control.

Michael came up to her then, putting his arms around her. "Maybe a haunted house wasn't such a great idea right after the death of a friend," he murmured, smoothing her hair.

She allowed him to hold her and turned in his arms, looking at Sally and the three men before her, Danny, her brother and Josh. She was suddenly certain that none of Dirk's employees had threatened her. And someone here knew she wasn't lying.

Whichever one of them had threatened her.

"*Iss binn beal 'na thost,*" she said softly, repeating the Gaelic words the attacker had whispered. "A silent mouth is melodious."

"A silent mouth is melodious?" Michael asked, frowning as he tightened his arms around her securely. His tone, however, suggested that, despite his longing to have faith in her, he was losing it. "Moira, honey, what is that?"

"An Irish proverb," Patrick said, watching his sister and looking puzzled. "My grandmother used it often enough when we were kids."

"When my folks said it, it meant shut the hell up," Sally said lightly.

"Sweetheart, that's not really a threat," Michael said softly. "It's rather pretty. An Irish proverb. I like it."

"Dirk," Sally said, "I guess we should get out of here."

"Yes, of course. Adam, it's all right. Take a few minutes. We won't let any more groups through for a while."

"Thanks," Adam said, but he still hesitated, approaching Moira but maintaining a safe distance from her. "I'm real sorry if I frightened you."

"You didn't," she told him.

He frowned, nodded and passed by. She could just imagine what he would have to say if he was with friends and happened to flick a television to the Leisure Channel and catch her show. "Man, I met that lady once, and let me tell you, she is one pathetic wacko!"

"Come this way," Dirk said. "I'll get you all out of here."

They followed him. With the lights on, Moira saw how small the place really was, and how unbelievably *un*realistic. He led them into a gift shop that led to the front porch of the house.

"Look, I'm really sorry. I should have kept you together and stayed right with you," Dirk said.

Sally put a hand on his arm. "It's all right. Moira doesn't usually overreact like this. She's been under a lot of stress."

"I haven't been under stress," she insisted, knowing it was a lie.

"Moira, going home after being away is always stressful. Especially when you're Irish," Sally murmured. "And then Seamus... Anyway, Dirk, thanks."

"You're welcome, but I am so, so sorry," he said again.

Moira walked up to him. "Please, you and Martin have been wonderful. The restaurant is great, and this place is the best in Salem. Really. I look forward to coming back."

"Thanks."

"But we've got to get home. My dad will need help tonight, I'm certain," Moira said.

"Yes, we've got to get back," Patrick said.

Everyone began saying goodbyes. Moira escaped to the sidewalk with Sally and hugged her friend.

"Honestly, Moira, I'm so—"

"Please, don't you dare tell me you're sorry again. You've been wonderful. Listen, as soon as this Saint Patrick's thing is over, we'll make real plans to get together." Sally nodded, and Moira glanced at her watch. "It really is getting late."

"I'll go find the others."

Moira knew when Danny came up behind her a moment later.

"I thought you didn't speak Gaelic?" he said.

She spun around. "You know, Danny, I can also tell you how to say kiss my ass in Gaelic but that doesn't mean that I speak the language. Yes, I know a few words. I've heard it my whole life. Why? Was that you in there, testing me?"

"What?"

"Did you steal one of the costumes and threaten me, just so you could come out and call me a liar?"

He crossed his arms over his chest. "Moira, now you're being absurd."

"Am I?"

The others were coming out behind him. Moira walked past him, linking arms with Sally again. "Walk with me so I can have a few minutes with you before we take off. You know, it's true, since we've both moved away, we hardly see one another anymore."

"Moira…"

"I'm all right, really. Let's move on ahead."

When they had gotten out of earshot, she asked Sally, "Where were you all when I went ahead? Still together?"

"Um…wow, I'm not really certain. No, we weren't actually all together. I was talking to Dirk in the Bram Stoker room. He was out of there like a bat out of hell when he heard you scream. Most of the walls in there are false. You can travel the whole place in a matter of minutes if you use the pathways behind the walls. I tried to follow him, and I think I came in by the other door. I don't even remember right now. Why?''

''I just wondered,'' Moira said, frustrated, but trying not to let Sally see it.

''Moira, it couldn't have been a real knife. There aren't any in the place.''

''Well, I was definitely fooled.''

''And why would someone threaten you with a knife, then come out with an old saying our grandparents used? I know there's no one saner than you in this universe, but maybe you…maybe you have been working too hard.''

''Maybe,'' Moira agreed. She looked back, making sure the others were still a distance away. It was almost five o'clock; the streets were dark. Maybe they were even too far away. She didn't like the darkness anymore. She wasn't sure if she wanted to be with people or if she felt safer alone. She could see Josh and Michael carrying the cameras, with Danny and Patrick behind them. She looked at Sally again. ''Please, don't be worried about me. I'm fine. You're sure you weren't with anyone else?''

''Well, yes, I told you, I was with Dirk.''

Sally was perplexed. Moira decided that she wasn't going to say any more—her questions weren't getting her anywhere.

As they crossed the street, Michael caught up with them. ''We're parked at the common, so I guess we should split up here.''

''I guess,'' Sally said. ''Michael, it was so nice to get to meet you. And, Moira, please take it easy, and send your parents my love and sympathy.''

As she spoke, Danny reached them.

"Where are you parked?" he asked Michael.

"At the common."

"Wait for us to drive around and we'll follow you home."

"That isn't necessary," Michael told him.

"I'd like to be behind my sister," Patrick said, coming up.

"We're all going back to the same place," Josh said, joining them. He took Sally's hand, thanking her and telling her that it had been great to meet her.

Moira kissed her friend on the cheek one last time. "See you soon," she promised, and started walking. Michael caught up with her, slipping an arm around her shoulders.

"Hey, are you all right?"

"I'm fine," she lied.

He didn't try to talk again as they walked to the car. She was grateful. When she slid into the passenger seat, she leaned back, exhausted. She had been afraid. Terrified. It had happened in split seconds. Or had it happened at all? The ghouls in the horror house weren't supposed to touch the customers, but she had been touched. Or was she losing it? The evil leprechaun had made her uneasy. Maybe...

No. Someone had purposely scared her.

But she hadn't been hurt. She'd been frightened, then released. Naturally. The place was small, filled with people. Someone was bound to come quickly once she screamed. Of course, if the blade had crossed her throat...

And here she was, alone with Michael. What if it had been him? What if, for some bizarre reason, he wanted to kill her? She was alone in a car with him. Night had come. He was driving. He could drive anywhere....

Except that he hadn't started the car.

He was looking in the rearview mirror.

"There they are, behind us," he murmured

"If you lose them on the road, don't worry about it."

"I won't lose them."

They drove down the street, turned and headed out of town. Moira looked out the window. They passed the restaurant and the haunted house. She noticed a group of kids on the next street, in front of a gingerbread Victorian. One boy was sitting on a parked car, something in his hand. It glinted in the streetlight. A knife.

She sat up straight, staring at the kid as they passed. He was out of makeup, but she still recognized him as the boy who had played the vampire.

"Stop the car!" she told Michael.

"What?"

"Stop the car. Pull to the curb and stop the car."

"Moira, are you sick?" he asked, doing as she asked.

She jumped out of the car, ignoring the question. She might have been insane at that moment; she almost hoped so. She wanted to look insane and scary. She strode across the street, dodging traffic heedlessly, aware that Michael was hurrying behind her and not caring. She was dimly aware that Patrick had pulled over, as well.

She reached the group of kids ahead of everyone else and walked up to the car, eyes narrowed, teeth gritted. The kid looked at her with real alarm in his eyes, trying to jump off the car and get away, but she caught him by the lapels of his jacket before he could do so.

"You!"

She *was* insane. He was still holding the knife, and it was real.

"You little two-bit jerk," she breathed furiously.

He was surrounded by his friends, but his face was white and the other kids were dead silent. "Why did you do that to me? And don't even think about lying, because I know it was you."

"I didn't hurt you. I was just supposed to scare you!"

He was probably sixteen. And though he might have

been a big man at his high school, he suddenly looked like just a sixteen-year-old kid.

"Who told you to scare me?"

"A man...I needed the money. He came by maybe an hour before you did. Lady, he gave me a hundred bucks, and I really needed it."

"*What* man?"

By then Michael had reached her. He had her by the shoulders. "Moira—"

"Let me go, Michael." She returned her attention to the boy. "Tell me, *what man?*"

The others had reached them. Danny took the kid by the shoulders, spinning him around. "She asked you a question."

"I'm going to call my mother."

"Good. She can come down to the police station with us."

"Hey, it isn't even a real knife. Okay, it's a knife, but it's a magician's prop. It's steel, but it retracts. Please, man, you can't call the cops on me! Please."

"Then answer the lady's question!" Danny roared. The kid might have been frightened of Moira, but he was terrified of Danny.

"What man?" Moira repeated more calmly.

The kid shook his head. "He didn't give me a name. And it was dark.... He talked to me in the haunted house. He was tall, I think. A little taller than me. He..." He looked around at all of them, staring from Josh to Patrick, Danny to Michael. He swallowed hard. "He...he, oh, man, I don't know. He was tall...like all your friends. I think his hair was brown. He was a nice guy. Said he just wanted to pull a prank on a friend. Scare her, whisper a few Irish words. I don't even know what I said. Honest. He made me memorize the words. You gotta understand—he gave me a hundred bucks. I had a fender bender in my dad's car, and my mom covered me, and I've got to pay her back. If my dad found out, he'd have made me quit the football team. You don't know my dad. He'll kill me. Honest, I am so sorry, lady, so sorry. I'll do anything. I'll give you the hundred bucks, just please don't call the police. I swear to God I'll never do anything like it again."

"Let him go," Moira told Danny softly.

"Let him go?" Danny asked indignantly.

"We should call the police," Patrick said firmly.

"I think he's right," Josh murmured.

"No, just let him go."

Danny slowly released his hold on the boy. "Remember," he said softly, "we can come back and get you any time."

"I swear, I'll give you the money—" the kid began, but Moira was already walking across the street to the car. She had all she needed. She hadn't been threatened by anyone who had been with her.

She thought Michael was behind her at first, but knew before she turned that it was Danny. That aftershave again. "I think an apology would be nice."

"I'm sorry," she said stiffly.

"And I'm not so sure that walking away is a good thing."

"Why?"

"You don't know who paid the kid."

She stopped and turned. "And you know damn well that there's no way to find out. If I call the cops, they'll drag the kid down to the station, where he'll cry and try to remember more about the man, but he won't be able to. He talked to him in the dark. The kid is scared out of his wits now, and it will only get worse if we do drag him down there. Let's just go. I think I've proved my point. I'm not crazy."

"I never suggested that you were crazy," he said softly.

Danny sighed. Michael had caught up to them. Patrick and Josh were still dodging cars. "Hey, Moira, you should really call the cops. Who the hell would want to scare you like that?" Michael said now.

She couldn't tell him that as long as it hadn't been one of them, it didn't really matter.

"Who knows, maybe someone who hates travel shows," she said lightly. "Please, guys, let's just go home."

They both stared at her unhappily as the other two caught up.

"Please," she repeated.

Michael sighed, walking around to open the passenger door so Moira could slide into the car. As he went to the driver's side, she saw, in the rearview mirror, that the others were getting into their car, as well.

As they drove, she felt the anger drain from her. Despite the fact that someone had paid that kid a hundred dollars to frighten her, she was relieved.

It hadn't been one of them.

Exhausted, she leaned back.

"My shoulder is here," Michael said softly.

"Thanks. I'll take it."

She was amazed to find herself able to doze against him as he drove. When she awoke, they had reached her father's garage. Michael was prodding her gently, fingers brushing her hair from her face. "We're here."

She climbed out of the car just as Patrick drove up behind them. When they had been joined on the sidewalk by the others, Moira smoothed her hair and said, "Not a word about any of this to Mom and Dad, you understand?"

"You should have called the police," Danny said irritably.

"Would you listen to me for once? My father is dealing with enough right now. Not a word. I mean it."

They all stared at her, jaws locked. She felt a sudden surge of wisdom regarding men. None of them liked being told what to do.

She turned and headed toward the pub, the rest of them following her.

The place was a zoo. Word of Seamus's death had been in the paper, and more old friends had turned up to drink to his memory.

Moira wasn't sure what the men behind her decided to do. The minute she came in, she stowed her purse and coat and hopped behind the bar. Seamus's old friends from his days at the shipyards had heard the news and forsaken their local pubs to come here. They talked about the difficulties of their work, of the times Seamus had done something funny, of the times he had stood up for other men when conditions had been bad.

She was serving a Guinness when she heard a man say, "The obituary was really beautiful. Eamon told us you wrote it up. That was nice, Dan. A real tribute to the man."

She swung around. Danny was behind the bar, filling a tray of wineglasses with Chablis.

"Thanks, Richie."

"You're a talented man with a pen."

"It's not difficult to write about a man like Seamus," Danny said.

"Yeah, the pen is something," the man named Richie said. "Mightier than the sword. A weapon like no other, so they say."

"The written word can cut like a knife," Danny agreed. He picked up the tray. Moira hadn't realized that she was blocking his way out of the bar area until he looked at her and said, "Excuse me."

"I could have gotten those for you. You didn't have to come back here."

He said nothing as he walked past her. A few minutes later, her father was behind her. "You're needed on the floor," he told her softly. She turned and looked at him with surprise.

"For Seamus. The dock fellows have asked for you and Colleen to do 'Amazing Grace.' And 'Danny Boy.'"

She nodded, wondering if she was too unnerved to get through the songs. She walked out, met her sister on the floor. Colleen squeezed her hand. They walked up to the band. Jeff made the announcement that the next two songs would be in honor of Seamus and anyone was welcome to join in.

From the time they'd been little, they'd been singing "Amazing Grace." Eamon Kelly had always been proud of his daughters' natural ability to harmonize together. They fell into it instantly now, the pipes adding a mournful tone. They went straight from "Amazing Grace" into "Danny Boy," Moira nearly cutting her palms with her nails, her hands clenched so tightly as she sang the words.

They finished to applause and Liam's teary-eyed statement that, "Sure, but old Seamus is looking down now, happy in heaven that he had the love of women such as yourselves."

Moira smiled stiffly. Colleen had little trails of tears trickling down her cheeks. Moira hugged her sister tightly and slipped behind the bar.

Danny was there again, making a drink.

"What's that?" she asked sharply.

"A blackbird. For the fellow in the corner."

She looked. Kyle Browne was back. She should bring the drink, take the chance to talk to him, tell him what had happened that day.

"I'll take it to him."

"No, Moira, I'll be taking this."

She watched Danny leave the bar, watched as he delivered the drink. She couldn't hear anything over the music and the crowd. She could see, though, that they were talking. Both men were tense.

"Moira, another Guinness this way, darlin', please," Liam called to her.

She served the drink to Liam, squeezed his hand affectionately and started along the length of the bar, making sure everyone was all right, still trying to keep an eye on Kyle Browne and Danny.

"Miss...hey! You're Moira Kelly, right? Wow, that's smart, you're...Kelly's Pub."

Moira looked at the young woman who had spoken. She was probably about Moira's age, but she had a slightly haggard appearance, as if she had put in a lot of miles over the years.

"I am Moira Kelly. And welcome to Kelly's. Can I get you anything? Would you like to see a menu?"

"No, this is fine for me. One beer. I have to get home. But I've seen this doorway forever. I grew up in a pub, too. Well, not a pub. A bar. Nothing so nice as this." She flashed Moira a smile that made her look younger. "I've always wanted to come in here. Tonight I did. There's a good feeling here, not like...not like a few of the places I go."

Looking at her, Moira suddenly thought she knew why the other woman had such a sad, hardened appearance. She continued speaking, her words seeming to verify Moira's thoughts. "I've been so nervous lately...two girls dead. Those prostitutes. Strangled. It makes a woman nervous to step into a bar."

"Do they know that the killer has been finding the women in bars?" Moira asked. She felt sorry for her and was glad that she had come in—as long as it wasn't for the purpose of solicitation. This was her father's very reputable place of business.

The woman, with huge dark eyes, circles under them, looked at her as if she had read her mind. "I'm just here for a drink," she said, sounding a little bit desperate.

"Of course," Moira said instantly.

The woman lowered her voice. "I think he must be meeting them in bars. In fact...I was at my dad's place the other night, doing some stocking, down below the bar. And I'm not certain...but I thought I saw the girl who was killed in there. With a man. A nice-looking man, and of course, she was a beautiful girl...once. I've been watching the papers. I saw her face...I think.''

"Did you go to the police?"

"Are you kidding?"

"Someone is murdering people," Moira said very softly. "The police won't—"

"You don't understand. You don't go to the cops from my father's place." She hesitated. "More drugs go through his bar than come out of Colombia. Someone would kill me for sure if I went anywhere near the police."

"More people could die—"

"But I'm not certain what I saw. Maybe it wasn't her. And the guy... It was dark. I don't know that I'd recognize him."

"But—"

"I shouldn't have talked to you, but I'm scared. I shouldn't have come in here. I don't belong in a place like this."

"You're welcome in here. Come in any time—for a beer."

"Of course," the girl said, and laughed.

Then, suddenly, the strangest expression came over her face. She was staring at a point beyond Moira.

Moira turned. The young woman was looking into the antique mirror above the bar that advertised Guinness. Moira stared into the mirror. She couldn't see anything but heads moving and people sitting. There was a watery reflection of the band, Danny picking up empty glasses from the table next to Kyle Browne's, her brother and Michael, in the center of the floor, serving plates of food.

Moira turned to look at the young woman.

She was gone.

Moira swore.

"What's up?" Chrissie came up and asked her, worried.

"There was a girl in here, a frightened girl. I think she was a prostitute, and she said something about maybe having seen one of the murdered girls in her father's bar, but she refused to go to the police...and then she disappeared."

Chrissie looked at her. "Moira, every prostitute and 'escort' in the city is probably nervous right now. She probably went home. And if she does know anything, I bet she will wind up speaking to the police sooner or later."

"She's afraid. Her father has a bar where a lot of drug deals go down."

"Well, she's gone. There's nothing you can do now."

"I'm worried about her."

"Moira, I know you always want to help everyone, but there's nothing you can do, so just forget it. We've got our own problems here, these days."

Moira was afraid that Chrissie was going to start crying over Seamus again.

"The girl sounds smart enough to watch what she's doing, Moira," Chrissie said.

"I guess you're right."

"Don't say anything to your father if you ever want to take ten steps on your own again," Chrissie warned.

"You're right about that," Moira murmured. She went behind the bar, got busy and decided that Chrissie was right. There was nothing she could do, and she did have her own problems. Big problems. Kyle Browne was still in the corner. Alone.

Moira decided this was her chance. She quickly put together another blackbird. Before she could take it to the man in the corner, though, she was interrupted.

"Miss Kelly, your song was beautiful."

She stopped, staring at the young man who had spoken to her. He had dark hair, hazel eyes and looked familiar.

"You don't remember me."

"Yes..."

"I'm Tom Gambetti. Your taxi driver. Remember? I dropped you off here the night you arrived."

"Oh, yes, of course. I'm sorry: it's just been really crazy here."

"I see that. I gather that this is a tough time for your family. But you and your sister really did just do a great tribute."

"Thanks. We've done those songs forever. Put us in a karaoke bar, though, and we're just awful, I promise." He was pleasant, but she still needed to escape. "Tom—"

"I know, you're busy. I'm not trying to be a pest. I'm just reminding you that I'm around if you should need transportation." He grinned. "Besides, I *am* half Irish. Your dad's pub is great."

"Thanks. And I have your card. I promise, I will call you if I need a taxi."

She slipped past him and took the drink she had made to Kyle Browne.

"Miss Kelly, how nice to see you."

"You, too."

"Did you need to talk to me?"

"I was nearly pushed onto the subway tracks this morning."

"Oh?"

"And someone paid a kid in a haunted house to frighten me with a trick knife. *Iss binn beal 'na thost.*"

"What?"

"It's Gaelic," she said. "It means, 'A silent mouth is melodious.'"

"Did you call the police?"

"No. What could they have done? The kid couldn't describe the man who had paid him."

He looked at her thoughtfully. "Sounds something like, take care, or you'll be sleeping with the fishes. You should heed the warning. Do like I told you. Stay away from everyone who could possibly be involved."

"Well, it's a little late for that, and I don't know who the hell is involved, anyway."

"Maybe you should be keeping as far away from your 'friend' O'Hara as you can."

She stared at him. "Danny was with me when I questioned the kid, and he didn't identify Danny as the man who had paid him to scare me."

"Maybe the kid took one look at your friend and decided he'd rather face the police. Or maybe I'm wrong. Maybe your brother is up to no good. Or your pal Jeff over there. Hell, maybe your dad is still fighting a war."

"If you say another word about my father—"

"Can you get into O'Hara's room?" he interrupted. "I bet you can. In fact, I believe you've been in there before. You might find something very interesting in there, if you chose to look."

"What are you insinuating?"

"Me? I don't insinuate."

He was right, though. She did have a way into the room.

"Don't stand here any longer," he told her. "And think about what I said."

She turned and left him, retracing her steps to the bar. Danny was onstage with the band. He and Jeff were singing together, an old Irish drinking song that Seamus had loved.

Josh approached her. "Things are winding down here, so I'm going to go. I won't see you in the morning. I'm going to the studio to finish editing and get the tape out. You stay here, get some rest. Take care of your folks."

"I should be helping you."

"I have Michael if I need help. I know you'd like to see the tape yourself, but you know you can trust me. We're partners, remember?"

She kissed his cheek. "Thanks, Josh."

"Stay home, stay with family, you got it?"

"I got it. Give Gina and the twins hugs and kisses for me."

Josh walked to the door, then stood there, waiting. Michael came over to her. "Maybe you should come back to the hotel with us."

She shook her head slowly. Was she being a total idiot? He would forgive an indiscretion. And she would be safe at a hotel. Away.

All right, she was a total idiot. She was going to stay here.

"Thank you, Michael. But tonight my place is here."

"I understand."

No, you don't, she wanted to insist, but she didn't. He cupped her face gently, gave her a soft kiss and reminded her that he and Josh would be at the studio most of the day.

The crowd thinned further. Moira noticed that Kyle Browne was gone. Andrew McGahey had arrived and was at a table in conversation with her father and brother. Colleen came over to the register and rang up a check. "I'm giving last call," she told Moira.

"Good idea."

"You look tired as hell," she said.

"Hey, we're working hard here. It's a good thing it's your face that's getting so famous—you're getting some major dishpan hands."

"It's worth it. I'm glad we're here. For Dad. For Seamus."

The bar began clearing out in earnest. Moira saw that Andrew McGahey was gone. So was her brother.

Had he left with McGahey or gone upstairs with his wife?

At the tail end of the night, Patrick came back from wherever he had been. Colleen, Moira, Patrick, Danny helped Eamon and Jeff clean up. Then Eamon told Jeff to go on home, he'd been going above and beyond. Colleen and Moira suggested that their father go upstairs; Patrick firmly insisted that he do so. When they were down to the last few glasses, Moira told her sister and brother to go on up.

"Hey, kid, you worked today," Colleen told her. "I can finish."

"And I can help her," Patrick said, staring at Moira sternly. He and the others had kept their word, not saying anything about the scare in Salem. But Patrick was giving her his older-brother stare, trying to be fierce.

"Please," she said, "I've got some extra energy to burn. You two go up."

She knew that Danny was staring at her, more than baffled by her obvious intention to be alone with him. He was all-out suspicious. She didn't look up, just kept cleaning glasses.

"All right. But don't get carried away here. A cleaning crew will be here in the morning."

Moira nodded, and her brother and sister left. She kept washing the glass. What the hell was she doing?

Why did she just want, with her whole heart, to prove that Danny was innocent? Or did she just want that one last chance to sleep with him before...

...before admitting he was a cold-blooded assassin who just might be willing to kill even her?

She swallowed hard.

"That glass must be very, very clean," he said.

She looked up. His amber eyes were on her intently. His features, taut and tired, were compelling and hard. The glass slipped from her fingers to land in the sudsy water without breaking.

"Well, thank God you've got such energy. I'm beat. I'll let you finish up."

To her amazement, he turned and walked to his room, closing the door behind himself.

She set down the glass, turned off the water and dried her hands. She walked to his door, contemplated knocking, but didn't.

She reached for the door, hoping he hadn't locked it. He hadn't. He was stretched out on the bed, leaning against the headboard, arms folded over his chest, watching the door. He'd known she was coming.

"All right, just what the fuck are you up to?" he demanded.

"I didn't want to be alone."

"I see. You accused me of trying to throw you onto the subway tracks. You thought for sure I'd tried to knife you in that haunted house, threatening you. So sure, come spend some time with me."

"All right. Never mind," she murmured, deciding to leave. She was no good at this.

He moved with the speed of lightning, ending up in front of her, his hands on her, drawing her in. He locked the door.

"Hell, I don't care why you're here. I only care that you are."

There was nothing subtle or seductive about him. He put both hands on her waist, pulling her close, then found the hem of her sweater and pulled it over her head. Danny knew how to remove clothing quickly. He didn't fumble at all but found the clasp of her bra, and in seconds it landed on the floor. He lowered his head, his lips closing over her breast. Despite herself, the magic of his mouth, the heat of his laving tongue, sent currents of fire sweeping through her.

She tugged at his hair. "Danny…"

"What?" He mouthed the word against her flesh.

"I need a shower."

He didn't release her. One hand remained on her hip, while the other slid lower, roamed over her jeans between her thighs.

"Danny..."

He groaned and looked at her. "Great. I feel like Vesuvius, and all you want is a shower."

"It's been a long day." She slipped past him, heading for the bathroom. She shed the rest of her clothing along the way, aware that he was watching her. She turned on the shower quickly and stepped beneath the hot spray, lathering with the speed of light. She knew that he would follow her.

He did. A moment later, he was behind her. The steam billowed around them as he took the soap from her. His hands, filled with the suds, moved over her back. Curled over her buttocks, came around to the front. She bit her lip, feeling the steam, feeling what he could do to her. She closed her eyes. He was an extremely talented and imaginative man with soap. Hands curving over her breasts, fingers splayed, erotically moving over her nipples. Down her torso, moving with light pressure over her hips, at an angle over her abdomen, down, between her thighs. The soap fell to the floor. His fingers pressed, entered, explored. Her breath was coming quickly; she leaned against him. Felt the steam of the shower enter her with the rotation of his touch. She let a soft groan escape her as she turned to face him, the lather on her body covering his. He found her mouth, kissed her deeply, wetly. Her fingers fell from his chest, swiftly downward, found the hardened length of him. His arms tightened around her. *She had been in love with him so much of her life. No one could do what he did. No one felt like him, laughed like him, talked like him, touched like him, made love like him.*

She broke off the kiss, gasping uneasily. "This...is too slippery."

"Slippery?"

"Yes, I'm getting out."

"You wanted to get in."

"I know...but...I want to make love, not break a leg."

She stepped from the tub, grabbed a towel, wrapped it around herself and exited the bathroom, closing the door behind her.

She had seconds, just seconds. She dropped to her knees by the bed, looking beneath it. The door from the bathroom opened. Danny hadn't bothered with a towel. Sleek, wet, naked and still hard as timber, he stared at her. She jumped to her feet, looking at him.

"What the hell are you doing?"

"I dropped my ring."

"It's on your finger."

"I know. I just put it back on."

He strode over to her, lifting her chin. "Curiosity killed the cat," he said.

She stared at him. "Are you going to kill me, Danny?"

He ran his fingers through his hair, frowning. "Jesus Christ! It's an expression, Moira. Look, do you want to stay—or go?"

She didn't answer him.

He unwrapped the towel from her body. "Stay, or go?"

Her silence must have been the answer he wanted. He cupped her chin, kissed her lips. His mouth ran gently along the left side of her throat. Down between the valley of her breasts. He dropped to his knees. Hands cupped her buttocks. His tongue moved.

She stood shaking. She couldn't do this.

Warmth, fire, staggering sweetness, filled her.

Oh, yes, she could, quite easily.

She gripped his shoulders, her fingers locked into his hair as she surged against him. Shivered, burned, knees giving, body rigid, going weak. She feared she would collapse. She forgot her self-imposed mission. He rose, supporting her when he felt her give, letting her fall against him. Within seconds they were on the bed, locked together, Danny aggressive, inside her like steel, so hard and forceful he seemed to have become a part of her. She melded against him, forgetting everything then but the sensations that rocked and overwhelmed her, the hunger, the need...the volatile, breathless peak, the eruption of climax.

Later, she lay beside him, staring into the darkness. This was so wrong. But she had to—*had to*—know.

"And to think," he murmured, "my pride nearly forced me to make you stay away."

"I need to go," she whispered, a little desperately.

He rolled her over, staring at her. "Listen to me, and for the love of God, believe me. I am not trying to kill you."

"We're still in my dad's house," she whispered.

"I don't give a damn where we are. I would have wound up sleeping in the hallway tonight if you hadn't come here."

"Why?"

"I think that someone did try to get into the house the other night."

"Why?"

"I'm not sure."

"There was no sign of a break-in. My father would have noticed if there had been. Only the family and you have keys."

"Ah, there we are. Me again. Go to sleep, Moira, I'll wake you in plenty of time to get upstairs before your family wakes up."

She could stay, she thought. And when he fell asleep...

"You'll be fine," he said, as if reading her mind. "I wake up at the drop of a pin."

Tomorrow night, then. She would have to get back here while he was still at the wake. It was her only chance.

"I should go up."

"You should sleep."

"I'm still...restless."

"Too much energy to burn," he murmured. "Hmm...let me help you out with that."

She felt his hands, the subtle caress of the tip of his tongue.

Soon she wasn't restless at all. Just exhausted. She fell into a deep sleep. Dreamless. She might as well have been...

Dead.

She didn't want to waken when she felt his touch on her shoulder.

"It's morning, Moira. Time for you to get upstairs. And by the way, when are you going to quit pretending that you're still with Michael? I think the next time I see his arm around you, or watch you go up on your toes for a delicate little kiss, I'm going to haul off and deck the guy."

18

Moira spent the day with her family, watching Brian, Shannon and Molly for a while in the morning, then helping her dad make phone calls so everything would be perfect for Seamus's wake and funeral. She made sure that the substitute band was coming in, since Blackbird had been given the night off. The group would probably be in with the rest of the mourners after the wake, and they would probably wind up playing. But they had all known Seamus, and they were all to be given the time.

The wake would end at ten. At that time, everyone would be invited back to Kelly's. There would be food and drink, and no one would be charged.

When Michael called from the studio, she tried to explain it to him. "The wake will run from seven to ten. Colleen, Patrick and I will take turns being here during that time for an hour each."

"Why?" Michael asked her.

"It's...it's just the way we do things."

"So your dad is going to allow anyone in? Why doesn't he just put up a notice that he's having a private party?"

"Because...well, I think it's a way to really honor Seamus. In the old days, Ireland was known for her hospitality. Strangers were never turned away. Seamus was...part of that spirit of Ireland. There were no strangers to him, just people he hadn't met yet. I rather like it. I think it's part of what can be so beautiful about the nature of the Irish.''

''Your dad's going to go broke feeding people.'' He sighed. ''I guess I'm not Irish enough to really understand, but hey, I'm here to weasel my way in. Where you go, my love, I will be. And what you do, I will support.''

Tremendous guilt swept through her. But it would be good if Michael came back to Kelly's with her when it was her turn to host the bar during the wake.

That would keep Danny from thinking that he had to be with her.

''By the way, the editing is going great, and the live feed will run from twelve till twelve-thirty. And you've got a great place on the dais to watch the parade.''

''Thanks, Michael,'' she said softly.

''It's my job, ma'am. Just my job,'' he teased.

She hung up after telling him she would see him at Flannery's that night. She was due there with her family at six.

The afternoon went quickly. Patrick and Danny were both in attendance all day as they readied everything for the family's departure. Moira served in the bar for a while, then helped her mother, Granny Jon, Colleen and Siobhan upstairs; Katy Kelly was preparing a lot of food for that evening.

When she was alone with her sister, chopping vegetables, Colleen spoke to Moira softly. ''You're looking haggard, kid. You were downstairs again last night.''

Moira stared at her sister, startled.

''You've got to make a decision, you know.''

''Decision?''

''Regarding Michael. I saw him watching you last night.''

''Colleen, I just want to get through tomorrow—''

''I know. I understand. It's just that…well, I think he's starting to suspect something's going on between you and

Danny. He doesn't say a word, but the way he was watching last night...well, you know, he is a man, and he has his pride as well as his feelings."

"I just have to get through tonight and tomorrow. Things will be better after tomorrow, although..."

"Although what?" Siobhan asked, coming into the kitchen and joining the conversation.

"I don't know. Everything seems very...strange, lately."

"Why?" Colleen asked. "What else has happened?"

"Happened?" She felt guilty, looking at her sister, wondering if Colleen, too, knew that something was going on in the bar, if she knew that Kyle Browne was a Fed looking for a would-be assassin.

"What's strange?"

She thought of the one thing she could say. "There was a girl in the bar last night. I'm certain she was a prostitute—pretty, well dressed."

"A hooker? In Kelly's?" Colleen said. "Dad would be furious."

"She wasn't soliciting. She was just having a drink because she was afraid to be out alone with a killer on the loose."

"What was so strange?" Colleen persisted.

"Well, she was talking to me, saying maybe she had seen one of the victims, maybe even the killer. But she wouldn't go to the police. I think her father deals drugs."

"Then what?" Siobhan asked.

"She looked into the mirror over my head and turned white. When I looked into the mirror to find out what she was staring at, she disappeared."

"Obviously she saw something that scared her," Siobhan said.

"Yeah, like the cop who sits in the corner every night ordering blackbirds," Colleen said.

"You know he's a cop? How?" Moira asked.

"Jeff told me he's almost sure of it."

"You know, once we get through all this...if you're still worried," Siobhan said, "I'll take a walk to the police station with you, and you can tell them about the girl and what you heard. Maybe you'll feel better then."

"It probably won't do much good," Colleen said. "First, they'd have to find her, and this is a big city. Then they'd have to get her to talk. And maybe she didn't really see anything at all."

"You're right," Moira told her sister. "But Siobhan is right, too. It might make me feel better."

Later on, when Siobhan was helping her arrange cookies on a plate, her sister-in-law looked at her and said, "There's more bothering you than a conversation you had with a girl at the bar. It's Danny, isn't it? His being here is getting to you."

"No," Moira lied.

Siobhan shrugged. "I think you're lying. You'd like to believe he's come to stay. You don't want to face the truth. Well, take it from me, the truth is always better than doubt. I'd give my eyeteeth to know the truth now."

"Patrick adores you," Moira said, defending her brother.

"I'd like to believe that. I might, if he were with me more. I think he's even forgotten that he has kids. He keeps talking to Michael about taking the boat out and bringing Andrew McGahey along, so they can all talk about Ireland. Guess what? He hasn't mentioned bringing me or his kids on this exciting first trip of the season."

Siobhan walked away.

Finally it was time to get dressed and ready, and then they were on the way to Flannery's. Molly and Shannon had their chocolates to go into the coffin. Siobhan had wondered whether or not to let Molly see Seamus in his coffin, but the undertaker had done such a fine job that her worries had been laid to rest.

"I still don't understand, Auntie Mo," Molly said to Moira when they were standing beside the coffin. "Mommy says it's like he's sleeping. Why does he want to sleep in a box?"

"Well, Molly, Seamus is really in heaven, with God. His body is resting in the box, and we'll bury him, and that way, when we want to say a prayer for him or think about him a lot, we can go to the cemetery, to his grave, maybe bring him a flower."

"Or a pint," Danny suggested wryly from behind her.

"Bring him a little something," Moira continued, "and feel close to him. But Seamus himself, his soul, the real Seamus, is with God." She picked up her niece. "Here, I'll lift you, Molly. You can set your chocolates right in his hand. Next to the rosary Auntie Mo just put in."

Molly put her chocolates in the coffin. Shannon did the same. Even Brian, the doubter, had brought a Snickers bar.

Soon it was time for the doors to open to the public. Eamon Kelly, Katy by his side, still knelt at the coffin. A moment later he rose and took a seat in the first row of pews. The first hour had begun.

Patrick had returned to the pub, to tell any lost mourners the way to Flannery's, and to let them know they would be welcome at the pub later.

Michael, Josh and Gina arrived, without the twins. Gina whispered to Moira that they'd managed to get a baby-sitter. Josh told Moira that he and Gina would head to the pub with her when it was her turn to go; she told him that Michael was coming with her, and that she would appreciate it if they would stay at the funeral home so they could bring Colleen back for the last shift.

From then on, it was wild. Seamus had never married, but he'd acquired his share of lady friends. The room was so crowded that Moira took to the halls. She heard the keening from within as friends from the old country cried over the loss. When she went back inside, she sat with her father, as people kept coming up. Friends from the bar. Friends with whom Seamus had worked. All shook her hand and told her how wonderful a man Seamus had been. Finally Moira rose again, needing some breathing room. As she walked from the viewing room, she was startled to run into Tom Gambetti.

"I just came to pay my respects," he told her, as if he was embarrassed to be there.

"That's very nice of you. Please, go on in."

"If I'm being too pushy...?"

"No, no, you're fine. I'll see you at the pub later— you're more than welcome, if you'd care to come by."

He nodded his thanks.

Moira went into the broad windowed hallway that ran along the front of the building. She could see Danny outside on the porch, lighting a cigarette. Many people approached him. He listened, shook hands and apparently accepted condolences on behalf of the family. She narrowed her eyes when one woman, middle-aged, with silver gray hair, approached him carrying a brown parcel. He leaned low, kissing her cheek, apparently thanking her for coming.

When she walked away, the woman no longer had the parcel.

"You doing okay?" Michael came up to her, slipping an arm around her shoulders. His hand moved to her nape, and he massaged her neck.

"I'm fine."

"It's almost time for us to go back to the pub."

She saw Danny come back into the funeral parlor. To her surprise, he walked into one of the viewing rooms that wasn't in use.

"Moira?"

"Oh, yes, we have to go. In just a few minutes. Excuse me, Michael, I'm going to try to find my father."

She slipped through the crowd, not sure why, but knowing that she didn't want Michael to know her destination. She walked up to Siobhan and asked her if she'd seen Danny.

"No, not in a while."

"I think I saw him slip into a room over there. Can you find him while I speak to Dad? Tell him that we need him to...carry something. Heavy."

Siobhan left. When Danny came out with her, he didn't have the bundle. Moira avoided them and raced into the room. No bundle, but there was a drapery over a coffin stand. She rushed to it. The brown bundle was there. She felt it. Not a gun. She sighed in relief, realized it was a group of folders.

She could hear people talking just outside the room.

"What did she want?" It was Danny.

"I don't know, Danny. Moira just said that you were needed," Siobhan responded.

"Well, where the hell is she?"

"Probably with Eamon, by the coffin."

They moved off.

On an impulse, Moira grabbed a few of the folders and shoved the bundle back where it had been. She slipped the folders beneath her jacket and hurried out. Michael was in the hallway.

"Moira, everyone is looking for you. You needed something moved?"

"Never mind, the funeral parlor people took care of it. It was a flower arrangement," she babbled quickly. "Hey, let's go."

"Don't you want to tell your dad we're leaving?"

"He'll know. Let's go, Michael. Now."

Patrick had taken his own car; Moira and Michael took her father's. She was silent as they drove. Michael slid a hand over hers. "I love you."

She smiled at him weakly.

"You're so distant."

"This is almost all over."

"Yes."

They reached the pub. Things were quiet. The substitute group was setting up, and Patrick was behind the bar, serving the lone man in a business suit who was sitting there. The tables were empty.

"We're here, Patrick. You can head back. I don't think Siobhan wants to stay much longer with the kids. I was thinking she could come home with Colleen when she leaves. Josh and Gina will be with her, too. Then you can stay with Mum and Dad until I get back."

"Sounds good," Patrick said, rubbing his neck. "Guess I'm on my way back, then." He paused, looking at his sister. "You all right? Michael is here with you, anyway."

"I'll break the bottle over the head of any asshole who comes in here and scares her," Michael said.

Patrick nodded. "Good deal." Then he grabbed his coat and was gone.

"Michael, that guy is just drinking beer. Can you step behind the bar for a few minutes? I think I'll use Danny's bath to freshen up," Moira said, seeing her chance.

"Sure."

He stepped behind the bar, and she hurried into Danny's room. She tore through the closet, heedless of the mess she made.

Nothing.

He had stopped her when she'd looked under the bed. She crawled beneath it and caught her breath.

There was the gun. She didn't know a damned thing about firearms, but this had to be a sniper's rifle. A really good, high-tech one. There was a scope on it. The gun was taped to the underside of the bed. She crawled out, tears in her eyes. It was time to call the police.

When she stood, she was dizzy, so she sat at the foot of the bed for a minute. She felt the file folders she had stuffed under her black suit jacket poke against her flesh.

She pulled them out, tears still stinging her eyes. There were names on the folders. Her brother's name was on the first. She flipped through it. There were pictures, records. Her vision blurred.

The next one bore the name Michael Anthony McLean. She opened it idly, wiping her eyes. Michael's picture leaped out at her. Or was it Michael's picture?

Blurred. It was the tears in her eyes. No...it was Michael. Yes, surely. Dark hair, blue eyes, same face...

"So you know. I was afraid you'd seen the way that whore stared at me the other night in the bar."

The door was open. Why hadn't she heard it open? She stared across the room. Michael was standing there. He entered the room and closed the door.

The band started playing just outside, the closed door doing little to muffle the sound.

So you know...the whore...

The picture of Michael. Close...so close...but not Michael.

Denial, disbelief, made her talk desperately. "Michael," she said, "Danny's planning on assassinating Jacob Brolin—"

"Yes, of course, good try," he said coldly. "That was the plan, of course. To get you going on Danny, discover the rifle...who the hell knew that you would find a picture of the real Michael McLean?"

The sudden clarity of the truth that had been around her all along was staggering. It was too horrible to believe. And yet...

God, there it was, staring her in the face!

She stood, her eyes glued to his. She didn't even think to scream, she was still so stunned, though part of her mind knew it wouldn't have mattered even if she had screamed; the music was way too loud.

"I don't understand, Michael," she murmured, bluffing.

"We have to call the police. Danny has a rifle taped under his bed—"

"And you have the dossier right in front of you that proves I'm not who I say I am," he said coldly. Leaning against the door, he stared at her. His eyes were like chips of blue ice. When he spoke, it wasn't with the level voice and even accent she had known. His tone was harsh—and his brogue was heavy. "You know, Moira, I had planned to be with you, right from the beginning. That's one of the reasons I've always been so adept at my chosen vocation. I'm good with women. But, though you really won't believe this, I never lied when I said that I loved you. I've been trying to figure if it might be possible to really become Michael McLean—who is, of course, dead, you must realize. Do this one last job, a triumph for freedom, and then live a normal life. Marry you. But you were supposed to help me set up your old friend for a fall, not sleep with him. You did sleep with him, right?"

"Look, Michael, I don't know what you're talking about."

"Of course you do. Blackbird. You knew something was going on in the pub. An attempt to assassinate Brolin. This was to be the meeting place. And it was. Dan O'Hara was to be the perfect fall guy—arrested for the crime. You were to help with that, though you didn't know it, and you were moving along in just the right direction. But now...you know. You betrayed me, Moira. You pretended to love me, and you fucked him."

The horror, the magnitude of what had being going on struck her full force. From the time he had taken the job with her, he had been planning this. No, from before that time. He had found a man with the right look and the right credentials, and he had killed that man, then applied for and won the job in his stead. He had taken the time to court and seduce her. He had studied her family, the pub.

He had been so thorough, so careful. And when he hadn't been with her...

He had been strangling prostitutes.

"I—I love you, Michael," she lied. He was between her and the door.

He shook his head. "No. We were apart too much. And you didn't mind. I minded. And I needed company. Actually, you're a lot like those whores, Moira. You couldn't keep your mind on me, you lie and cheat, and you're nosy as hell. I didn't think I'd have to kill you—I was spending a lot of time on that fantasy where I married you in the family church and was welcomed like a son into the bosom of the family. A pretty fantasy. I should be grateful you cheated. Because Michael McLean is going to have to disappear now. After tomorrow, of course. But...well, I'm going to have to deal with you first. And Danny boy...I'll have to deal with him later."

"Michael, my family is going to be home any minute. And...you're wrong about all this. I love you, we can—"

"Oh, Moira, please! I don't think you're stupid, and you know damn well I'm not. You really have complicated matters, but...let's go."

"Go? I'm not stupid. Where do you think I'm going with you?"

He started walking toward her. She jumped up, but there was no way out of the room except through the door he was blocking. Still, she was desperate to preserve her life at all costs. She screamed, praying someone would hear her over the band. He reached the bed, and she crossed to the other side. It was hopeless. She tried to race past him, but he caught her viciously by the hair. She screamed again, trying to wrestle away.

That was when she saw his hands.

He wore gloves. And carried a cloth with a strange, sickly-sweet odor.

Fighting wildly, she tried to avoid his hand. She kicked,

screamed, bit. The hand, and the cloth, came over her mouth.

She tried not to breathe.

Eventually she had to.

He caught her before she could sink to the floor. He lifted her up and met her eyes with his own, the cold, ice-blue eyes of a killer, before the light began to fade.

Fade out...

The world became black and existed no more.

Moira wasn't there. Dan was irritated, cursing the fact that she had been looking for him immediately after he received the files. He'd flipped through them all quickly, then focused on the one about Michael. He'd immediately realized that something wasn't quite right. He had been studying the file when Siobhan called.

He went all over the funeral home looking for Moira. He even waited in front of the ladies' room. When a gray-haired dowager in a pillbox hat came out, he apologized and headed into the room where Seamus's remains lay. He checked with her family. She hadn't told anyone she was leaving, but Eamon told him that she had probably headed to the pub with Michael, as planned.

As soon as Eamon said the words, something clicked in Dan's mind. He excused himself and left, hurrying to the empty viewing room where he had stashed the files. Heedless of who might be watching him, he dug through the stack.

A few were missing. Moira must have them. He didn't know why or how he was so sure of that, only that he was.

Suddenly his mind processed what he had seen.

Dropping the files, which scattered all over the floor, he strode through the outer room, deciding that it would probably be just as quick to walk the distance as to try to flag down a cab. But as he walked out, someone called to him, "Hey, heading for the pub?"

It was a young man, brown-haired, hazel-eyed. Maybe twenty-six or twenty-seven.

"Who the hell are you?" Dan demanded.

"Tom Gambetti."

Dan stared at him blankly, grudging every second that passed.

"I'm a cabdriver. I drove Moira home when she got off her plane."

"You're a cabdriver?"

"Yes."

"Your cab is here?"

"Yeah, right there."

"Great. I *am* headed for the pub, and I need you to get me there as quickly as you can."

When they pulled up in front of the pub, Dan told Tom to wait right there, then strode inside. There was no one at the bar except a man complaining of no service. One of the band members came up at that point, offering to help him. "Hey, buddy, cool it. I'll find you a beer. There's been a death in the family. Bad time, you know."

Dan ignored the customer and addressed the band members. "Where's Moira Kelly?" he asked.

"She came in here just a few minutes ago with some man. Took off to freshen up or lie down or something like that. She must be really broken up about that guy's death. Her friend went to look for her, and when he came out with her, he said she was in really bad shape. Could hardly stand. He was supporting her. Said he was going to take her back to the family, that she was in no condition to hold down the fort."

Dan's insides seemed to congeal. He raced to his room, throwing open the door. The spread was askew, nearly on the floor. The closet door was open, clothing everywhere.

Whatever had happened, it had happened quickly. He closed the door. The musician was still behind the bar.

"How long ago did they leave?" he asked tensely.

"A couple minutes ago. Literally. They walked out just before you walked in."

"Thanks."

Dan burst out to the street. As he stared up and down the sidewalk, the cabdriver stuck his head out the window. "Hey, if you're looking for Moira, they just left. Looked like she was sleeping. I waved, but the guy driving wasn't paying any attention."

Dan was instantly in the cab. "Turn around. Follow them."

"Follow them? I don't know where the hell they were going."

"They're only seconds ahead. You can find them."

"Wait a minute! Who are you and what—"

"Damn it, turn around, follow them. Her life is at stake."

Tom Gambetti apparently believed him. He spun the cab around and began to take the streets of Boston like a madman.

"Careful, we don't want a cop on us—not unless we find them first. Hey, there they are. They're in her father's car. Turn here."

"This is a one-way street—"

"Turn anyway."

Gambetti did. Dan had to admit the guy could drive. They missed a tan Suburban by inches. Moments later they were in traffic, just three cars behind Eamon Kelly's.

"What now?" Gambetti asked.

"Keep on him," Dan said, keeping his eyes steadily on the vehicle ahead. They were at a light, wedged between a Corsica and delivery van, when Eamon's car made a sudden turn.

"Shit, I'm going to lose him," Tom Gambetti swore.

"Never mind, we know what direction he's going. Turn as soon as you can."

Gambetti did as he was told.

"Pull over to the curb," Dan said when they reached the wharf. "Just let me out. And listen." Dan was scratching a number on a scrap of paper as he spoke. "Call this number. Tell them you're calling for Dan O'Hara. Tell them to get to the wharf, to the *Siobhan,* as quickly as they can. Tell them lives are at stake. Understand?"

"Yeah, of course." He was fumbling in his pocket. "I've got a cell phone right here. Hey, you sure you don't want to call yourself?"

Dan was already gone, sprinting down to the docks.

She wasn't dead. Yet. Her head pounded; her stomach churned. She felt as if she were being tossed around by a cruel hand.

She opened her eyes very slowly. Colors dimmed by pale light floated in her vision. She could hear voices. Men...talking. She fought to clear her vision. She blinked, thinking she was seeing things. She was on a narrow sofa, looking at a compact dining booth in front of her. There were flowers on the table. Suddenly she recognized her surroundings. She was in her brother's boat; he always arranged to have flowers on the table, for Siobhan, for their first sail of the season.

The men...arguing. Who were they? What were they saying? She closed her eyes again, listening, trying to ignore the pain in her head, still her stomach and discern what was going on and how to survive.

"One damned day. We needed one more damned day. This was asinine."

"Don't you get it, man? She had a fucking file. She knew the picture wasn't me."

"Great. So now she's got to disappear tonight. That screws tomorrow."

"We can come up with a different plan. We've got the

best weapon in the world, we just need a point to fire from. I'll need another new identity, though.''

''This has to be done. It would have been perfect if you could have been near Moira. So close, and yet you still could have disappeared into the crowd.''

''It would have been great, but now we need a new plan.''

''It was that O'Hara bastard,'' Michael—for she didn't know how else to think of him—said.

''We should have fixed him to begin with.''

''He was to take the fall.''

''Fucker wasn't who he said he was, either. Obviously he's on the inside somehow. How the hell else did he get that kind of dossier on you?''

''Damned if I know. Hurry up—we need to get this boat out of here, drown the girl and sink it.''

''Why didn't you just strangle her? Seems like you were getting pretty adept at that.''

''Get the boat moving. I'm going to make sure she's still out.''

Moira heard footsteps. Despite the pounding in her head, she leaped up. Patrick kept a loaded gun in the safe in the master cabin. She wasn't a great shot, but point-blank, she couldn't miss.

She made it to the master cabin just as the hatch opened. She heard Michael swearing. Terror filled her, but she slammed the door and locked it. Her fingers were frozen and shaking as she jerked open the latticed closet door and started twirling the numbers on the safe.

They clicked home.

''Moira, come out. I'm still trying to make this painless.''

The safe opened just as the flimsy door to the cabin burst inward.

She reached into the safe for the gun. It was gone.

She stared into the empty safe, then into the eyes of the

man she had known as Michael McLean. He watched her dispassionately from the doorway.

"Your brother is as easy as you are, Moira," he said. "I guess he never mentioned that he and his buddy Andrew McGahey brought me down to the boat on one of those mornings when you were being the family girl. Good old Patrick, expecting no evil. He never knew I spotted the safe. And a safe like that...well, it's no problem to a man such as meself."

There was another weapon in the cabin. Maybe one he didn't know about.

She made a dive across the small room, flinging open the top drawer of the bedside table. Her fingers curled around the knife.

She knelt on the bed, the hilt of the knife in both hands. "Come near me and I'll kill you, I swear it."

He smiled slowly. "Moira Kelly, you're no killer, and you know it. Give me the knife."

She raised it as he came near, then slashed at him when he leaped at her, cutting his arm severely. He didn't seem to notice the pain. He caught the knife with his right hand, her throat with his left. The knife was wrested from her. He pressed her downward on the bed, straddling her, his fingers around her throat in a death grip.

"It's going to be a while before we reach the open sea. You know, I wasn't lying to you, Moira. I really fell in love with you. Enjoyed you wholeheartedly. Why don't you try to make it up to me?"

She was nearly choking.

"Can't answer? Sorry."

He eased his hold.

She still couldn't move, but she looked into his eyes as she spoke. "When I'm gone, they'll search for me. They'll find you."

"Who is ever going to think that I've taken you out on your brother's boat?" he asked, smiling. "Oh, babe, I'm sorry that it has to end this way. Want to draw it out a little longer? Entertain me? Live? Hope that some miracle will occur, and you won't have to die?''

He reached out to touch her face.

A sound like a growl suddenly erupted from the doorway.

''Touch her, you pile of shit, and I'll shoot you in the balls so you can bleed to death in agony!''

Michael was startled enough to roll halfway off Moira.

They both froze for a minute. There was Danny, hair tousled as always, standing in the doorway. He had a gun in his hand. Not a big rifle with a scope, but a small weapon that, in the tiny room, looked just as lethal.

Danny. The man she had condemned...

''Move, Moira,'' he commanded.

She tried to flee, but Michael still had the knife. She felt the point in her back when she would have leaped up. She froze

''Trust me, I learned a trick or two in my youth,'' Danny said softly. ''I can shoot you before you can do more than scratch her. But I think she's been hurt enough, don't you?''

Danny took aim. Michael eased away with the knife.

''You fucking traitor,'' he told Danny. ''You bastard. You should have been the one killing Brolin. God knows, you stupid bastard, you should be at the forefront of the fight.''

''Oh, I believe in the fight. A fight of words and negotiation and persistence. Not a fight of killing children and innocents.''

Footsteps. She heard footsteps coming up behind Danny.

He heard them, too, and turned, but Moira cried out, ''Danny, it's all right. He's a cop.''

Danny hesitated at her words.

Kyle's gun exploded. The bullet seemed to burst directly into Danny's chest. Into his heart.

19

Moira screamed. A shriek of horror that went beyond fear for her own life. She raced toward Danny, who had fallen facedown on the floor, but Michael caught her around the waist before she could crouch to see if he was still alive.

"You shouldn't have shot him," Michael told Kyle.

Caught in Michael's arm, Moira was beyond hysterical. She clawed at his arm, kicked, spat, tears blinding her eyes. "You!" she raged at Kyle. "A cop!"

"I never said I was a cop."

"FBI—"

"I never said I was anything, Miss Kelly. I let you believe what you wanted. I did spend an entire day sitting in front of the police station, waiting to catch you. Ah, Miss Kelly, you were so mistrustful of those you knew. You helped us right along."

She kicked out at him, the man who had killed Danny. She caught him right in the belly, and he doubled over, stunned and groaning in agony.

She lashed out again, kicking backward. She managed to catch Michael's shin, but though he might have been in pain, he didn't release his hold on her. Instead he slammed her against the wall, and her head began to spin again.

"Want to hear a good Irish expression, Miss Kelly?" she heard Kyle Browne grate the words out. "The back of my hand to the front of your face."

The blow was stunning. She melted against the cabin wall like a water balloon thrown against concrete. Stars burst in her vision.

"Jesus, don't leave bruises all over her," Michael swore.

"It needs to look convincing, like he beat her up, and then she shot him. Now let's move. We don't have forever."

She felt Michael dragging her up from the floor. He was strong, but she was deadweight. She saw Danny's body stretched out on the floor. She wanted to cry out in sheer agony once again, yet her lips refused to open.

Danny had fallen on top of his gun.

But the knife had wound up just inches from her hand....

As Michael fumbled with her weight, she shifted and fell again. Intentionally, this time.

On top of the knife.

She managed to curl her fingers around it. She let him lift her then, prodding her before him. The hallway was narrow. As he shoved her along, Kyle Browne followed, but he was caught in the passageway behind Michael. Halfway along, before reaching the area where the hallway broadened into the salon area, Moira decided to make her move. Fury and pain aided and abetted her effort. She twisted and struck, using all her strength to force the blade through Michael's flesh and muscle.

Shock stopped him as much as the injury. He stared at Moira, who looked at him with tears of loathing and defiance. His face had drained of color.

"Move it, Michael," Kyle commanded.

Michael had no breath to reply.

Moira took that moment to run. She raced down the hallway and up the three steps that led topside. She leaped out on deck and slammed down the hatch, locking it.

A bullet tore through the hatch just seconds after she moved away.

The hatch would not stay locked long.

Another bullet ripped through it....

And another.

She ran to the stern, where the dinghy was tied. They'd left the dock, and the tiny boat was her only way back. She dropped to her knees and struggled against the rocking waves to untie the ropes that held the small rowboat in place. Perhaps, she thought, she should just jump in the water.

She wouldn't last long, she knew. This time of year, the ocean was lethally cold. She would have only a few minutes' grace if she threw herself into its inky depths.

Just as she untied the dinghy, she was grasped from behind, dragged to the deck and thrown flat.

She looked up. Michael was standing over her. He didn't have a gun or a knife, but that didn't stop him. He reached for her, his hands winding around her throat.

She fought him, her will to survive strong enough to drive her to struggle even when all hope was lost. She slammed against his wrists, bucked against him, clawed his arms. She couldn't loosen his grasp against her throat. Her breath was going....

Somewhere, distantly, she heard an explosion. She thought at first that it was the sound of dying.

Then, miraculously, Michael was gone and she could breathe.

She gasped, choked, tried to inhale, tried to see past the patches of darkness that had formed before her eyes. At first she heard only the water lapping against the hull of the boat. Then she became dimly aware of the sounds of a struggle. She sat up, then blinked furiously. A man was down, sprawled over the hatch, his legs trailing along the deck. Further to the fore, near the helm, two men were struggling.

She stumbled forward. Kyle Browne was the man lying over the hatch. His eyes were open, but he saw nothing. He was dead.

She carefully tried to sidle around him, but the waves rocked the boat, throwing her against the dead man. She steadied herself and reached the helm just in time to see Danny and Michael go over the side of the boat together. A pool of blood stretched along the deck and over the hull.

Danny had been shot. In the chest. It was amazing that he had even gotten up. He was bleeding to death. And he was in the water....

"Danny." She meant to cry out his name, but she merely croaked.

She rushed to the side and leaned over. A hand rose from the water, and she reached for it, desperate with fear.

A head rose to join the hand. Her heart sank. Michael. His face no longer seemed human, it was knotted into such a snarl of hatred and malice.

He jerked on her hand, and the motion sent her tumbling into the water.

It was cold, so cold it stole the breath she had just regained. She was barely aware at first that her hand had been jerked free by the impetus of her fall. For long moments she seemed to speed downward into the freezing stygian depths. She realized that she would die if she didn't force herself to act. She kicked hard and began to surface. She broke through the waves, but the boat seemed impossibly far away. Her muscles didn't want to work; her arms didn't want to move. Her teeth chattered hard, and it seemed ridiculously difficult to breathe. She forced herself to head for the boat. She reached it, but couldn't reach high enough to grasp the rail and pull herself up.

Suddenly she was propelled upward. Her midriff met the rail, and she crawled over, fell, gasped for breath. Danny! Danny had to be alive. Shaking violently, she crawled over to look into the water again. He was rising, using long strokes against the icy waves to reach the boat. He made it to the hull, and she reached out with both hands to pull him to safety.

"Danny." It was a whisper as she saw the golden glint of his eyes. As she spoke, he was suddenly jerked under again.

"No!" It was a scream, but nearly silent. Michael must still be there, still alive, still attacking Danny. She rushed to the dead man and shoved him aside searching for his gun. She found it and half walked, half crawled to the side where Danny had last surfaced. She desperately searched the dark water, holding the gun in both hands.

A ripple...

A hand...and then a head appeared. Someone was swimming toward her again. Fingers curled over the hull.

"Moira, help me up."

Danny!

She set the gun down and reached for him, using all her strength. Somehow she succeeded in pulling him high enough, and they fell together onto the bloody decking.

They lay there for several seconds, both shivering violently, gasping for breath. Then Moira jerked into motion, going for the gun again.

He rose, stretching out his arm, gently taking the gun from her.

"He might come after you again."

"No."

"But—"

"He won't be coming back up to the surface again, Moira."

She let him have the gun, but she kept staring at the water, barely aware of how frozen she was until she felt Danny behind her again, covering her shoulders with a blanket. Still she stared at the waves lapping against the boat. So black.

He pulled her against his chest. "Moira, he won't be coming back up," he repeated softly.

She heard a whirring sound; it was a helicopter above them. Danny began to wave wildly, and they heard a male voice over a loudspeaker.

"The Coast Guard is on its way. The Coast Guard is on its way."

The helicopter remained above them as Danny held her. Knowing it was over, Moira began to shake more violently.

"You're alive," she said through chattering teeth. "But he...he shot you in the chest. Point-blank. I saw him...."

"I'd been getting a little wary lately. Bulletproof vest."

She turned to look at him, barely aware anymore that she felt like a Popsicle. "Are you a cop? And you didn't tell me—"

"No, Moira, I'm not a cop."

"Then what are you?"

"An Irishman," he said with a rueful smile. He opened his mouth to offer a further explanation, then didn't. He took her into his arms suddenly, kissed her lips with a warming fervor, then held her against him. She could hear the motor of the Coast Guard vessel as it came near.

From then on, the rest of the night became a blur.

20

There had been so many surprises that night. As she had guessed, Michael McLean wasn't really Michael McLean. The real Michael McLean, a quiet man long estranged from his family, a solitary man with film as his only love, had been murdered shortly after his arrival in New York City the previous December, shortly after meeting up in a bar with the terrorist Robert McMally, who had been on the lookout for just such a man. Kyle Browne was not a cop, nor was Kyle Browne his name. There was a real Kyle Browne who was an FBI agent, and the name had been chosen with the expectation that someone would verify his identity with the government agency.

Moira gained a greater understanding of the intricacies of what had been going on in her own home through one of the greatest surprises of the evening—the fact that Jacob Brolin was aboard the Coast Guard cutter that came to rescue them from the *Siobhan*. That he hugged her warmly was certainly pleasant and rewarding, but the way he greeted Danny was astonishing. Danny might have been his long-lost son. With a cup of steaming cocoa in her hand and more warm blankets around her, Moira stared at the two men.

"All right, what is going on?" she demanded. "If you're not a cop," she accused Danny, "you must be something with the...Irish government? Northern Ireland government?"

Moira found herself shivering again, looking at Danny. "From things he said...I think that Michael...Robert McMalley was the one murdering prostitutes."

Danny's eyes met hers. He knew what she was feeling. She had trusted a man, slept with a man, who had come to take human life so lightly that no one mattered if they threatened his goals in any way.

His eyes held hers. "We'll probably never know exactly what happened."

"Almost back to shore," Jacob said lightly, pointing ahead.

There was an emergency vehicle waiting. Moira didn't want to go to the hospital and said that she was fine, but Jacob Brolin insisted. Her neck was a definite shade of blue, he said, and Danny had most likely a few broken ribs.

She stared at Danny, dumbfounded. He shrugged. "Yeah, I think he's right. I would be dead if Jacob hadn't warned me it was time to start being careful. Thing is, the vest saves your life, but being shot that close..."

At the hospital, Moira didn't want to leave Danny's side, but she was gently, politely forced into another room for medical care. She was in a cubicle alone, waiting for word about Danny's X rays, when she heard Brolin, who had been doing the talking with the police thus far, suddenly begin talking to someone else.

She heard her father's voice, deep and concerned. Then her brother and her mother.

"I am perfectly calm," Katy Kelly announced, sounding only a shade shrill. "And I want to see my daughter."

A moment later Katy came bursting into the cubicle. She stopped at the curtain and looked at Moira in her hospital gown, stretched out on the gurney.

"Eamon!" she cried to her husband, who had come in right behind her. "Look what they've done to me baby."

Katy promptly passed out.

Luckily Eamon was there to catch her.

Eamon looked at his daughter. "Ah, lass, she's the strongest woman I've ever known—you just don't threaten her children."

He couldn't drop his wife, so his enveloping hug for his daughter came only after an orderly had appeared, an ammonia vial had been broken, Katy had come to and the hug could be a family affair.

Soon after, Patrick, Colleen and Granny Jon were with her in the small space, as well, and the way she was kissed, hugged and enveloped by her family made her realize that she had to be one of the luckiest people in the world. When Patrick held her in his arms, she was able to whisper, "Patrick, oh, my God, I am so, so sorry. There were times..."

"When you were suspicious of me," he whispered back. "It's okay. I understand. I love you, and I'm so sorry I didn't see what was going on in time."

Then the police insisted on speaking to Moira. They ushered her family out, except for her parents, who refused to go.

Katy Kelly gave the police only so much time, then put her foot down and forced them out. Moira would give them any information they needed once she was declared fit and well and had had some rest, Katy informed them in no uncertain terms.

When they were gone, Moira told her mother, "I don't want to rest. I just want to see Danny."

"We'll see to it," Eamon said firmly, and she was taken to the cubicle where Danny's ribs had just been wrapped. He was sliding into the clean shirt the Kellys had brought from the house. Moira rushed to him, suddenly bursting into tears.

Danny held her. "Ah, Moira, my love. It's all right now. Truly. Oh, hug me, darlin', just not quite so tightly, please."

"He should be staying in the hospital," the stern-looking doctor on duty said.

"For observation," Danny told him. "Believe me, sir, these good people will observe me." He looked into Moira's eyes. "No one can watch me better than she," he added softly.

She didn't leave his side. It would have done little good to attempt to go to bed or sleep that night, anyway. None of the Kelly household slept, except for the children. Siobhan would explain things the best she could to them when they awakened in the morning. As for the rest of the family, they hadn't been able to return to the house until nearly four a.m. Seamus's funeral was still planned for nine.

Eamon gave the eulogy, a fine speech. Moira was to have performed another rendition of "Amazing Grace" with Colleen, but since her voice remained a throaty croak, Colleen was on her own. She, too, did beautifully.

Seamus was duly laid to rest. Jacob Brolin had quietly attended the funeral service at the church; at the graveyard, he gave a short speech, honoring Seamus as both a fine Irishman and a fine American.

Moira had spent a few minutes closeted with Josh. Colleen was going to take over her sister's announcing duties for the live feed, because not only was Moira's voice gone, she had been invited to ride with Jacob Brolin on his float.

Moira did, however, do her own interview with Jacob Brolin at the pub that afternoon, surrounded by a full house, with a real Saint Patrick's Day bash in full swing. Jacob was wonderful, talking reasonably about both sides of the conflict. Many people in the North had legitimate complaints, he said, and he meant to see to them. They needed more Catholics on the police force, more good faith among men, and yes, they had a long way to go, but they had also made immense strides in the direction of peace. "Northern Ireland is beautiful," he said, "and there is one thing that draws all of us together, and that is the desire to let the world know just how beautiful, and to welcome travelers with the hospitality of old. Our future lies in our ability to lay out a level playing field for all men. Oscar Wilde once said, 'If one could only teach the English how to talk, and the Irish how to listen, society would be quite civilized.' We all need to learn how to talk—and how to listen.''

The pub had been open to the public throughout, and Brolin's speech was heartily applauded by all. Many of the customers were amazed that Eamon had gone ahead with the opening of the pub that afternoon, after everything his family had faced.

Eamon had said, ''Why not? Close the pub? I've never had more reason to celebrate in my life. My child was in danger, but she is here with me, and I am a blessed man, with all my family and my friends. Saint Pat was looking out for us from up above, and I'll be thanking God for the rest of my days.''

There had been no way to keep what had happened from the newspapers and the networks, and Kelly's Pub became famous across America that day.

Josh ably handled the media, arranging for questions from four to five, then the absence of cameras in the pub thereafter.

It was busy, and Moira insisted on remaining behind the bar, washing glasses as she listened when it was time for Danny to be quizzed by the reporters.

Being Danny, he managed to explain the truth, tell a story and speak lightly all the while. At the end of the session, a seasoned reporter asked him, ''What's next for you, Mr. O'Hara? Will you be going home to enter Irish politics?''

''Oh, no,'' Danny replied. ''I'm staying in America. I'm getting married, you see.''

Moira was so startled she dropped a glass in the water. Still in shock, she met Danny's eyes.

''If she'll have me,'' he said softly.

Epilogue

Belfast, Northern Ireland
The Present

The street had changed. There were handsome shops all along it now.

Danny stood on the sidewalk, taking a moment, as he always did in Belfast, to go back in time. Not to dwell on the misery of loss. Just to remember the family that had once been his.

He did love Belfast and all the North. They had been to Armagh just the other day, visited Tara, walked along endless hills of rolling green, felt the expanse, the wildness, the beauty and the magic of ancient times. Then they had returned to Belfast, and joined the hustle and shove of the busy city.

Today it seemed especially important for him to stand here. The last year had been the best of his life.

He would never forget his youth. In a corner of his heart, there would always be the pain of his loss. Yet even though that pain would never go away—*should* never go away—it had changed. The pen really *was* worse than the sword. He had done a great deal to change the world, or, at least, his world. His parents, he thought, would be proud. And Moira…Moira had allowed him to find his own peace, and a man could truly bring it to others only when he had found it in himself.

"Danny!"

He saw her coming down the street. She was in green. Kelly green, at that. A neat little suit that displayed the length of her legs and the indentation of her waist. Her hair, shining in the sunlight, bounced and waved over her shoulders. There was a slight touch of concern in her blue-green eyes as she reached him, taking his hand, placing a light kiss on his lips before studying his eyes again.

"Are you all right?"

He smiled. "Absolutely."

"I was worried. I didn't know where you had gone."

Okay, so he had ducked out on the luncheon. Andrew McGahey was being honored in the grand ballroom of the hotel for his efforts on behalf of the children of Ireland. And Andrew wasn't alone. He and Sally Adair had been introduced at the wedding, and they had been together ever since. Of course, Andrew remained a dedicated Catholic. Sally was still a wiccan. Maybe they would make it anyway. Anything was possible in America.

Danny had listened to most of the speeches, had watched his brother-in-law be merciful to the crowd and accept his plaque with a few words only, thanking his family and the Irish in America. Then a rather longwinded professor had taken the dais, and Danny had given in to the overwhelming urge to take a walk. It was important for him to come here. He always did, wherever he came back to this city of his birth.

"This is where it happened?"

"Yes."

She squeezed his hand. "Danny?"

He arched one brow. It still amazed him that they were man and wife. He had always loved her, but he had known when they were very young that he hadn't been right for her. That he had a few demons to battle himself. And then...

There had been times when she had lain beside him

shivering, and he had known that she was still haunted by her memories. A man who had said he loved her while needing other women…and disposing of them as easily as if they were laboratory rats who had fulfilled their purpose and needed to be destroyed.

All in all, though, they had come through quite well. The wedding had been spectacular. Mass at the family church in Boston, Moira in a shimmering long dress and veil, not quite traditionally white, but a combination of white and silver and mauve that seemed to spread magic with every move she made. Naturally the reception had been at Kelly's.

They'd taken two weeks on a remote private island in the Caribbean. There had been times when they had spent hours just talking. Times when they had just made love, a little desperately on some occasions, gently on others. Either way, it had only mattered that they'd had one another, that they were together, a bastion against the past, a team to forge through the future.

Life was good. He had Moira. It was impossible to love anyone more. Humbling to be so loved in return.

Incredible to have such understanding.

His book, written about the events that had formed Jacob Brolin's life and political perspective, was due out in a month. It was sure to cause some controversy.

That was fine. He still liked a certain amount of controversy. There was nothing like a good, hard-fought argument to be waged—and won. And of course, Moira was opinionated, so they had lots of heated discussions, and lots of wonderful moments of passionate apology. He had become a resident alien in New York City; Moira had already, in the single year of their marriage, taken six trips to Ireland with him. Their first trip, they had come alone, here, to Belfast, then traveled beyond, into the North.

Their second trip, they had taken Granny Jon and the family to Dublin. Everyone had come, including Siobhan and the children. They had made a day out of traveling down to Blarney to show the kids the castle and, of course, kiss the Blarney Stone. Katy Kelly had remarked that it seemed rather unnecessary, since most of the time they were all full of it to begin with.

It had been a great trip. Showing Ireland to children for the first time, showing them the source of so many of the tales they had heard, had been wonderful. Seeing Molly's eyes widen for a ride on a chubby Irish pony through fields of emerald, Brian's fascination with the tales of knights in shining armor, and Shannon's pleasure in the quaint charm of the small towns.

Moira had brought her own brilliance to their travels. She had expanded her show, and they now did segments on American vacationers returning to their roots in foreign countries. Colleen's was still the face on hundreds of magazine covers, but she had also taken to hosting more shows for her sister. That allowed Moira more travel time. For himself, it was easy. Writing was an exercise of the mind. Of course, it helped to see all the places that stirred his imagination and brought back the trials and triumphs of history, near and far.

Life was good. He couldn't imagine that anything could be better.

"Danny," Moira said again.

He looked at his wife. *Wife.* He smiled. "Sorry, love, I was wandering."

She shook her head. "I worry about you when I know...you've come here. I think about my family. Patrick, Colleen...my folks. When I see Molly, Brian and Shannon, and I think about what happened...I know I couldn't have come through...as you did."

"I only come here because I loved them so much. It's a way of saying hello, telling them they'll always be with me."

She smiled. "You feel that they're here, with you, a little bit?"

"Maybe. But I'm okay, Moira. I have been for years. Never as good, though, as since I've been with you."

Shoppers passed them by. A pretty woman walking a dog smiled and said hello. A man in a tweed cap tipped it to them.

"Hmm..."

"What?"

"I was actually waiting for us to be alone somewhere incredibly beautiful and romantic...."

"Excuse me, but my city *is* incredibly beautiful and romantic."

"Oh, I know, I know. I meant like our bedroom in the hotel, the lights all muted, music playing, roses in a vase...."

"Champagne in a bucket? A tub full of suds? You wearing nothing but bubbles here and there, at strategic spots?"

"Something like that."

"I like it—let's go."

"Wait, Danny, the point was that I want to tell you something. And I've just decided to tell you here."

"Great. Get me all hot and bothered, then make me stand on the sidewalk where I can't do a damn thing about it."

"Danny, we're going to have a baby."

He couldn't have imagined that anything could be better, but he'd just been proven wrong.

"We're...pregnant?"

"No. *I'm* pregnant, but *we're* having a baby."

He folded his wife into his arms. Kissed her. Tenderly. On her lips, both cheeks, her forehead, her lips again. "A little Irishman," he whispered.

"Or an American woman," she reminded him.

He cradled her face in his hands. Studied her eyes, kissed her lips again. "Whichever, I'm thrilled. I'm...God,

I'm thrilled.'' He smiled and looked up. ''Hear that, Mum? A grandchild.'' Suddenly he got a questioning look in his eyes.

''You're certain?''

''Absolutely.''

''Maybe we should test again.''

''Why?''

''Because then you can tell me again, in the romantic room, with the music, the champagne....''

''Danny, I won't be drinking champagne any time soon,'' she told him.

''I didn't intend for you to drink it. I think it would be better for you to, oh, wear it,'' he told her.

''Oh.'' She smiled. ''Shall we go?''

He put his arm around her, and they started down the street.

''My God, I'm shaking,'' he said. ''I'm going to be a dad. To a wee bit of an Irishman.''

''Or an American girl.''

''Maybe it will be a lass,'' he agreed. ''A little Irish lass.''

''Or an American boy.''

''Fine. Have it your way—the first time,'' he teased. Then he stopped again in the street, cradled her face once more, kissed her and drew her to him.

''The best of Ireland, and of America, will be in our son or daughter,'' he said softly.

''Oh, Danny, that's lovely.''

''You think so?''

''Yes.''

''Good, then let's move on. I'm definitely in the mood for champagne.''